When Love

Finds You

Also by Virginia Wise

Where the Heart Takes You

"An Heirloom Christmas"
in *An Amish Second Christmas*

Published by Kensington Publishing Corporation

When Love Finds You

Virginia Wise

ZEBRA BOOKS
KENSINGTON PUBLISHING CORP.
www.kensingtonbooks.com

ZEBRA BOOKS are published by

Kensington Publishing Corp.
119 West 40th Street
New York, NY 10018

All Kensington titles, imprints, and distributed lines are available at special quantity discounts for bulk purchases for sales promotion, premiums, fund-raising, educational, or institutional use.

Special book excerpts or customized printings can also be created to fit specific needs. For details, write or phone the office of the Kensington Sales Manager: Attn.: Sales Department. Kensington Publishing Corp., 119 West 40th Street, New York, NY 10018. Phone: 1-800-221-2647.

Zebra and the Z logo Reg. U.S. Pat. & TM Off.
BOUQUET Reg. U.S. Pat. & TM Off.

First Printing: January 2020
ISBN-13: 978-1-4201-4780-3
ISBN-10: 1-4201-4780-3

ISBN-13: 978-1-4201-4783-4 (eBook)
ISBN-10: 1-4201-4783-8 (eBook)

10 9 8 7 6 5 4 3 2 1

Printed in the United States of America

To Aunt Louise,
whose love will stay with me always

Chapter One

Pennsylvania Backcountry, 1738

Catrina Witmer stood alone in a field of blue. The wildflowers swayed in a breeze that carried the scent of warm grass, damp earth, and new possibilities. She knew she had made the right decision to join the Amish. She had finally found her home.

But that didn't stop her from feeling alone. From *being* alone. She closed her eyes and lowered her head. The wind rippled through the sea of blue petals and whipped a tendril of black hair from her prayer *kappe*. Would she always feel like an outsider, even in the midst of a close-knit settlement?

Catrina heard a sharp thump and a shout. Her head shot up. Another shout carried on the wind. Catrina frowned, lifted her long skirts, and hurried across the clearing. The earth felt soft and familiar beneath her leather shoes. She had memorized the predictable rhythms of life here, the names and faces of each neighbor. So who could be here, behind her grandparents' cabin at this time of day? This was not a time for visitors to come calling. In fact, she should be getting back to her chores. There were chickens to feed and dinner to get and water to draw.

She heard another thump as she reached the path that wound past the clearing. She slipped through a stand of pine trees and saw a wooden handcart blocking the path. Catrina gasped. Newcomers to the isolated settlement! She started to shout a greeting when a mallet flew up from behind the cart. Catrina gasped again and hopped backward. The mallet whizzed past her face and landed with a thud in the dirt behind her.

She heard a bang from beneath the cart and the rickety-looking planks shuddered. A deep male voice grunted. Catrina glanced behind her, then back at the cart. Who *was* this new arrival?

The cart shifted and a man's legs scooted out from underneath. A long torso and strong upper arms followed. Finally, a freckled, kind-looking face topped with tousled red hair appeared. The blue eyes widened when they saw Catrina.

"Oh!" The man rubbed his head and scrambled to his feet. "Oh dear!" He stared for a moment and kept rubbing his head. His body was tall and lanky, with lean muscle and a casual, unassuming air. Catrina laughed and the man's face broke into a sheepish smile. "I, uh, I didn't know you were there."

"No," Catrina said. "I should think not."

"Oh. Oh dear." The man frowned. "I've hit my head, you see. I'm sorry to disturb you."

"No harm done."

"No?" The man's frown deepened and he swallowed. "That mallet I threw . . . It didn't . . ."

Catrina laughed again. She nodded. "It did."

"It didn't hurt you, though?"

"No. I dodged it. But just barely."

"Well thank heaven for small mercies." He rubbed his head again. "Having a little trouble."

"With the cart?"

"I'm afraid so. Can't fix the wheel." The man shrugged and grinned. "Not cut out for all this, I suppose."

Catrina smiled. "Nor was I."

"Ah." The man stared at her for a moment. He cleared his throat. "I'm Eli Webber."

"Catrina Witmer."

"A pleasure to make your acquaintance Mrs. . . . Miss? . . . Witmer."

"Miss."

"Ah! Miss." Eli broke into a boyish grin, then reined his expression back in. He cleared his throat again. "Mmmm. Well. Best be getting back to it. I really haven't any idea how to get that wheel . . ." He glanced around the clearing. "Are we near the settlement by any chance? You must live close by."

"Yes. You've made it. If you're trying to reach the Amish settlement, that is. We've taken to calling it New Canaan, if you haven't heard."

Eli grinned again. "New Canaan." Catrina liked his grin. It held a childlike joy and contagious warmth that made her feel giddy inside. How unlikely that a smile should have such an effect. And those eyes. She had never seen such a friendly spark behind a man's eyes before. It made her feel as if they had known each other for ages, even though they had just met. And how sweet and bashful he seemed! Catrina smiled. His awkward manner really was quite endearing. *How strange. I am not myself at all today.* She had always been drawn to the strong, silent type. Her idea of a good match was a confident, self-assured man who proved stronger and tougher than the rest. Catrina frowned. Eli Webber was the opposite of everything she'd ever looked for in a man. *I really must regain my self-control.*

But that boyish laugh!

Eli hesitated. "Are you all right? You look as if you've just had an unpleasant thought. Or a bad surprise. Well, there was that flying mallet . . ." Eli looked sheepish but concerned.

Catrina shook her head and forced a careless smile. "Oh, I am perfectly fine. I was just thinking . . ." *That I should not be drawn to you!* "Well, it is nothing, really." Her eyes skimmed the cart. "Is that a loom?" Catrina's forced smile transformed into a genuine grin. She stared at the bulky, wooden beams crammed into the cart.

Eli returned the grin. "Why, yes it is. I'm surprised that you recognized it as such, dismantled as it is."

"I know a loom when I see one, even if it is in pieces."

"You weave?"

"Yes. And how I have missed it." She walked to the cart and ran her hand over a stout, wooden beam. The smooth surface whispered beneath her fingertips. She remembered the clack of the shuttle, the gentle swish of wool against wool as she weaved in the small, sunny room above her parents' shop in Philadelphia. It was a skill every woman should know in order to clothe her family. But here, in the wilderness, a loom was a luxury. When fully assembled, the heavy crossbeams would fill an entire cabin. And what a trial to transport a loom through narrow footpaths! "Will you settle here? We don't have a weaver."

"Ah." Eli ran his hand down one of the loom's

smooth wooden crossbeams. "That's what I hoped to hear. We'd like to live among the faithful."

"We?"

"My widowed sister, Gertrud, and I." He frowned and glanced down the path. "I cannot imagine where she has gone." He took off his black beaver-felt hat, wiped his forehead, and pushed his hat back onto his head.

"She's here?" Catrina's attention snapped back to Eli. "Another newcomer? Is she my age? How delightful!" She clapped her hands together and grinned.

Eli cleared his throat. He looked up and down the path again. "She's older than you I'd reckon. But only by five years or so."

"Wonderful good!"

Eli rubbed the back of his neck. "Mmmm, yes. Wonderful good, I'm sure." His voice lacked enthusiasm, but Catrina didn't notice. She was too busy standing on her tiptoes and peering into the pine grove that lined the path. "Wherever can she be? Do you think that she is all right? There are bears in these woods. And mountain lions."

"Oh, I am sure she is."

"But how can you be sure?"

Eli smiled. "We would have heard her by now if she had met a bear. And, quite honestly, I doubt a bear would dare."

Catrina laughed. "Eli, you cannot be serious."

Eli raised his eyebrows. "Mmmm."

A sharp cry echoed from the pine grove.

"Ah." Eli nodded, then sighed. "Right on cue."

A woman pushed through a thick swath of branches and stumbled onto the path. She brushed off her white apron and adjusted her prayer *kappe*. "There is nothing here, Eli. Absolutely nothing." She frowned and brushed her apron more forcefully. "Nothing but wild things, that is."

"That is why they call it the wilderness, dear. It is quite wild, I am afraid."

"Humph. Why I agreed to come along on this harebrained scheme, I have no idea. This is not at all like the other places we've been. There is nothing here. Nothing at all! I told you when we had to trade down from a wagon to a handcart that it was a bad idea. Roads too rough for a wagon to traverse! Why, the very idea! You'll work yourself to death, pushing that thing by hand. You may be stubborn, Eli, but you're no mule! The very idea. If I've told you once, I've told you—" Gertrud stopped in midsentence and snapped her head around to stare at Catrina. She narrowed her eyes for a long, tense moment and Catrina had a strange feeling that the woman recognized her.

So many strangers passed through her father's shop in Philadelphia that it was not an unlikely prospect. Catrina had grown up wandering aisles stocked with luxury goods and cajoling her father into giving her a stick of peppermint, the latest and most fashionable hat, or the shiniest pair of leather shoes. This was before Catrina had converted to the Amish faith with her grandparents, taken on the Plain way of living, and made the arduous trek to America's first Amish settlement.

How much she had changed since those days in Philadelphia! And, oh, what a terrible, terrible thought that someone from those days might come here and recognize her. Someone who couldn't possibly know how very much she had changed. Catrina felt her stomach constrict. *This cannot be happening. Please, der Herr, do not let this be happening! Do not tell me I came this far and escaped so much to be recognized now.* A dark shadow of shame gurgled upward from Catrina's belly. She pushed the sensation down and forced a polite smile. "I am Catrina Witmer."

Gertrud sighed. "Gertrud Schulp." She did not smile. "We have arrived, then?"

"*Ja.*"

Gertrud sighed again. "Well."

Catrina waited for Gertrud to say more, but the woman just tightened her lips into a thin line and stared back. Catrina could not tell if Gertrud's expression meant that she recognized Catrina—and remembered the rumors—or if Gertrud always looked as if she had swallowed a lemon. Catrina turned back to Eli. His blue eyes sparkled and Catrina thought that they held a hint of an apology.

Catrina waited for Eli to speak, but he looked hesitant. He took off his black beaver-felt hat and raked his fingers through his red hair until it stood straight up from his scalp. Catrina laughed.

Eli looked confused for a moment, then winced. "Oh. I've done it again, then." He smoothed his hair back down and replaced his hat. "Nervous habit of mine, you see." He cleared his throat and looked away. "Not that I'm nervous. There's nothing to be nervous about. Nothing at all." He looked down at his feet.

Catrina felt unexpectedly pleased. Her looks had always had this effect on men, but something felt different this time. She felt that Eli's reaction to her actually mattered. Oh, sure, men tended to shuffle and stammer in the presence of her raven-black hair, vibrant blue eyes, and perfectly proportioned features, but Catrina had become immune to the admiration. She had learned that men rarely—if ever—saw past her skin to the person inside.

And yet, she felt strangely moved by Eli's flustered response to her. She sensed that there was something more to his admiration than a shallow attraction to a lovely face. She wondered if he could see past her looks to the woman inside. *What foolishness! We've only just met. I really must regain my good sense. Eli can't possibly see anything but my looks.*

Catrina looked from Eli to the loom crammed into the cart, then back to Eli again. "We can fit the loom into my grandparents' cabin." She gazed into Eli's eyes with that disarming stare of hers.

"Oh!" He rubbed the back of his neck with his hand.

Gertrud narrowed her eyes.

"*Ja.*" Eli swallowed and Catrina watched his Adam's apple bob. "That would be most appreciated."

"But it will not be necessary," Gertrud added. She turned her thin, pinched face away. Her eyes roved over the tree line. "We'll build our own cabin here. Isn't that right, Eli dear?"

Eli cleared his throat again. "Quite right. Quite right." He took off his hat and turned it around in his hands. "Although . . ."

"Although what?" Gertrud narrowed her eyes another fraction.

Eli swallowed again. "Although it does make sense to get the loom up and running right away. It will take some time to build our cabin."

"The Witmers would not welcome the inconvenience of a loom inside their home, I am sure."

"I would welcome it," Catrina said. "If you would allow me to use it, that is."

"Ah, of course." Eli nodded. "You would like to strike a deal. If you house our loom then you get to weave on it."

Catrina frowned. Was that what she had meant? Or had she been motivated by the thought of seeing more of Eli Webber? "I didn't mean it to sound quite so businesslike, but I suppose so. I do want to weave again. And our cabin is larger than most. We've tried to make our home as comfortable as possible. We lived quite comfortably in Philadelphia, you see. We never fancied ourselves as settlers before."

Eli laughed. "No, I can see that."

"Can you?" Catrina hesitated. "Why is that?"

"It's just that you seem so . . ." He shook his head. "I mean . . ."

"Oh for heaven's sake, Eli." Gertrud closed her eyes and pinched the bridge of her nose.

Eli cleared his throat. "You just seem so perfect. Nothing is out of place. Why, there's not even a wrinkle on your apron. That's not the mark of a woman who roughs it in the backcountry."

Catrina laughed. "I'm not sure if you've just complimented me or insulted me."

"Oh." Eli looked down. He shifted his weight from one foot to the other. "A compliment, of course. Not that I would take the liberty of complimenting you when we've only just met. But not that I would insult you either. What I mean to say is—"

"What he means to say is that it has been a long day and we really must set up camp," Gertrud said.

Eli frowned. "Quite right, dear. But, I do believe that Catrina has made a sensible offer."

Gertrud sighed sharply. "Yes. I am sure she has."

Eli's face lifted into a happy grin as his blue eyes met Catrina's. "We would love to take you up on your offer."

Catrina's stomach jumped. She felt disarmingly satisfied at the arrangement. *What has gotten into me? Eli Webber is nothing different or special! Don't let your emotions sweep you away! Sure, he seems charming and genuine, but you know better than to fall for that.* Memories of Philadelphia swept through her in a cold, hard wave. Oh yes, that she knew all too well.

Chapter Two

Eli stared at Catrina and tried to form the right words. His mouth filled with sand and his thoughts bumped around in his head like a man fumbling in a dark room without a lantern. He knew that she was far too pretty for the likes of him. Women like that didn't fall for men like him. He had learned that the hard way. But he wasn't sorry that he had taken her up on her offer to house the loom. No, sir, he was not sorry at all. He refused to be sorry.

Maybe, just maybe, she would let him be her friend. He would be willing to take that, such as it were. And, he had a distinct feeling that she would make a lovely friend. Eli watched Catrina as she led him and Gertrud to her grandparents' house. Her expression remained so placid, so calm. And her hands danced like birds when she spoke. She moved with grace and control. Oh yes, she would make a wonderful friend.

Eli realized he liked something intangible about Catrina that went beyond her looks. That was the moment he knew that he had fallen too far to recover himself. Oh, sure, she was beautiful. But the world held plenty of beautiful women. Far more rare was a woman of grace and confidence. A woman with an air of mystery she wore like a shimmering cloak. Eli quickened his pace. Oh yes, he was hooked. And there was nothing he could do about it.

"We really can't tarry," Gertrud said as she followed Catrina on stout, sturdy legs. Gertrud's small, compact figure looked out of place beside Catrina's tall, willowy form. Eli's sister carried an air of practical sensibility, while Catrina showed nothing of the sort.

"But you must stay for dinner," Catrina said. "My grandparents would like to welcome you to New Canaan. *We* would like to welcome you to New Canaan."

We*! She said* we*!* Eli felt his chest jump. He reminded himself that a pronoun did not necessarily carry a secret sign or promise. She was simply being friendly. *And didn't I just decide that I would settle for friendship?* He frowned. That wasn't really what he wanted. Not when the promise of the word *we* hung in the air.

"Thank you, but we really shouldn't—" Gertrud began to say.

"Yes, of course!" Eli interrupted. "Thank you so very much for the invitation! We would absolutely love to stay! In fact, I was just thinking—" Eli stopped himself. His face turned undeniably red. He heard Gertrud's familiar, frustrated sigh beside his ear. Eli cleared his throat. He forced his words out slowly and politely. "What I mean to say is, yes, thank you. Very kind of you to ask." *There, much better. Quite the gentleman, really.* Eli rubbed the back of his neck. *Oh, who am I kidding! It's hopeless. Completely hopeless!*

Catrina laughed, but the emotion behind it seemed pleased and amused, not irritated or embarrassed for him. "Well, it's settled then. I'm glad you're pleased."

"*Ja.* I am." Eli nodded enthusiastically before he remembered to rein himself in again.

"We must eat in haste, I fear," Gertrud said. "Night will fall soon and we have a camp to make."

"Yes, of course, dear. Quite right, dear."

"I can help, you know," Catrina said.

She wants to help!

"Thank you, but no." Gertrud shook her head and continued to stride forcefully across the field. "Eli and I have made camp every night for weeks. It has been a long, arduous journey and I have learned my way around a campsite, I can tell you."

Catrina lowered her head. "Yes, of course."

Eli did not like the expression on her face. It looked remarkably close to rejection. But that was impossible. Women like Catrina Witmer didn't know the first thing about rejection.

They passed through a sea of wildflowers and Eli watched the delicate blue petals tremble in the wind. The movement rippled the blooms in a wave that reminded Eli of the ocean that had carried him and Gertrud to the New World seven years earlier. That was before the *Charming Nancy* sailed and most of the other Amish immigrants began to pour into Pennsylvania. That was before . . . Eli cut off the thought. He didn't want to think about what had happened before. This was a new chance, a new life. He smiled and bent to pluck a wildflower from the earth. The stem broke free with a satisfying snap. He studied the brilliant blue petals for a moment and then handed the flower to Catrina on a whim. "Same color as your eyes," he said, and then looked away. He swallowed and tried to push the embarrassment down. *What a foolish thing to say!*

But Catrina's face lit up as she took the flower from his hand. Her soft, delicate skin brushed his and he felt a happy jolt. She liked the flower. She liked that he had done something foolish. Eli grinned. But Gertrud's expression stole the look from his face. He felt the victory seep out of him. Gertrud was not amused. Not at all.

"You said that you're from Philadelphia?" Gertrud asked.

Eli thought that Catrina winced, just for an instant, before her expression smoothed. "*Ja*," she said, then nodded toward a log cabin at the edge of the clearing. "Here we are." A wall of pine trees rose behind the rough, wooden home. A trail of smoke rose from the stone chimney and whispered into the woods. Eli felt cozy and optimistic to see a safe, stout house in the shadow of that foreboding wilderness. "My grandparents will be so happy to meet you. We'll have chicken for supper. You'll like that, won't you?"

Eli nodded. A hot chicken dinner sounded like heaven after weeks of salt pork and corn cakes fried over a campfire.

"Oh, and pie! I've just made a pie."

Eli's head shot up. "Did you say pie?"

Catrina smiled. "Rhubarb."

Eli gave a happy sigh. "Gertrud, we came to the right place."

"Mmmmm." Gertrud did not return the smile. "And what did your father do in Philadelphia, dear?" She stared at Catrina and studied the young woman's reaction. "Did he own a shop, perhaps?" Gertrud's expression looked like she already knew the answer.

"*Ja*. A shop." Catrina picked up her long skirts and quickened her pace. "I'll just hurry along and let them know we have company." And with that, she raced out of earshot. Eli watched Catrina race across the dirt yard and past a chicken coop. A haughty-looking rooster glared as she stepped around him. He flapped his wings and then settled back down to peck at the bare earth.

"She certainly is in a hurry to avoid that question," Gertrud said in a low voice.

Eli patted her on the shoulder. "Now, Gertrud. Let's enjoy a nice meal with a nice family. No need to look for trouble where there isn't any."

Gertrud frowned. "My dear brother, I never look for trouble where there isn't any."

"Ah." Eli took off his hat and ran his fingers through his tangle of red hair. "Of course."

"I just thank *der Herr* that you have someone sensible in your life to look out for you."

Eli started to respond, but the cabin door swung open and an elderly couple stepped out to meet them with waves and smiles and a hearty round of well-wishing. Eli suddenly felt brighter, warmer. He believed that he could make a home here, among these people. He had finally found a place to start his life anew. He would worry about Gertrud's comments later. There were no problems here as far as he was concerned. There couldn't be! He would not allow it.

Catrina's eyes sparkled as she introduced Georg and Frena Witmer. The couple looked comfortable amongst the austere farmyard. Eli sensed a determination in the elderly couple that he admired. They must be committed to a Plain lifestyle to have ventured to this isolated settlement at their age.

Eli noticed that Catrina's eyes held a mischievous

mirth as she looked at him. She was trying not to laugh. *Now, why on earth* . . . Eli looked down and realized that his hat was in his hands. Oh bother! He had succumbed to that nervous habit of his again. He had removed his hat, raked his fingers through his hair, and left each strand standing straight up into the air. *I must look like that rooster in the yard with the red comb jiggling atop his head.* Eli cleared his throat and smoothed his palm over his scalp in a quick, hectic gesture, then replaced his hat. "Um, lovely to meet you both. Wonderful good. *Ja.*"

Catrina giggled, but her expression remained kind. He didn't think that she was making fun of him. No, her expression almost seemed . . . *intrigued.* But that was preposterous. Positively preposterous.

Dinner was better than Eli could have imagined. A fire crackled merrily and the warm, musky scent of wood smoke mingled with the rich smell of roast chicken and root vegetables. He shoveled bite after bite down his throat until Catrina laughed out loud. "Wherever will it all go, Eli?"

He grinned back, took another generous bite, and chewed enthusiastically. "I'm just getting started."

"You must save room for dessert."

"Catrina, there is always room for dessert. That is the first rule of life. There is always, always room for dessert."

Catrina laughed. "But really, Eli, how ever do you have the room?"

Eli smiled and patted his lean, muscular stomach. "Gertrud has been warning me for years that it will all catch up with me one day. But until that day . . ." He leaned forward and took another helping of chicken. Steam curled up from the golden skin as he dropped the meat onto his wooden trencher.

"I've been warning him about more important things as well," Gertrud said in a flat voice as she cut her eyes to Eli. He shrugged and pretended that her comment didn't sound so uncharitable. He didn't want to call her out in front of their new friends.

Georg frowned and Frena looked uncomfortable. Gertrud maintained her steady gaze, completely undeterred.

"You'll never believe what Eli has brought," Catrina said in a cheerful voice.

Eli smiled. She had saved him from an awkward moment.

"What?" Frena asked.

"A loom!" Catrina clasped her hands together. "A real, full-sized loom!"

"Has he really?" Frena looked surprised but pleased.

Eli nodded. His mouth was too full to answer.

"I've asked if we can keep it here. Can we, Grandfather? We can, can't we? We must. We really must!"

Georg smiled indulgently. "*Ja*. If it makes you happy." His eyes darted from one end of the cabin to the other. "It will be a tight fit, but, *ja*, we will manage." He nodded at Catrina.

"It does make me happy! Eli has already promised I can use it as often as I please. He has to make a living, of course, but whenever he's not here."

"We won't keep it here long," Gertrud said.

Eli glanced up at his sister. "The cabin will take some time to build."

"Even so. We won't be a burden for long."

"No burden at all," Frena said. "The settlement has

Virginia Wise

been in need of new cloth for some time. It is a blessing that you've come. We didn't think anyone would make the trek with a loom this soon. The roads are—well, they aren't roads at all. Just footpaths, really. I don't know how you got it through."

Eli grinned. "I don't either. But here we are."

"*Ja.*" Gertrud sighed. "Here we are."

Catrina waited by the cabin door and listened to her heart skip against her chest. She told herself that her excitement was merely because of the loom. It would arrive at any moment. But as she smoothed her white prayer *kappe* and straightened her apron, Catrina knew there was another reason. That reason stood six foot three, flashed a warm, open smile, and gazed at her with attentive, sparkling eyes. She told herself that she was being ridiculous. After all, Eli Webber was not her type at all! She looked for strength and boldness. She wanted to be swept off her feet. She couldn't possibly be interested in a stammering, bashful young man. And yet, here she was, peering across the clearing, waiting for that unpretentious, endearing smile of his to appear. She wondered if he would smile as soon as he saw her. Would his face light up as it had yesterday, when she invited him to dinner?

Catrina frowned and turned away from the doorway. She shouldn't let herself get carried away. If Eli's face lit up to see her, then it could only be for one reason—her looks. Men had always fought for her attention. And, somewhere along the way, she had realized that she was little more than a status symbol to them. Her face was a prize that men wanted to win.

They wanted the world to see that they could have the most beautiful bride around. But Catrina refused to be seen as a prize. She'd had enough of that in Philadelphia. Here, in New Canaan, she wanted things to be different.

But Eli didn't seem like other men. Maybe that was what had captivated her. Eli seemed so genuine, so sincere. . . . Catrina turned back to the doorway and grinned. There he was, struggling to push the hand-cart across the clearing. She laughed out loud when the cart hit a stone, jolted to a stop, and slapped into him. Eli tumbled backward, into the dirt, then jumped back up with remarkable enthusiasm. Mud coated his woolen hosen and breeches, but he just shrugged and went right back to pushing the cart. *He isn't the strongest or toughest man in these parts. But he's the friendliest man I've ever met. And the sweetest.* Catrina laughed again. *That dear, ridiculous man. How will he ever get the mud out of those breeches!*

"You certainly are staring at something. And I'm not sure that it is the loom."

Catrina jumped and clapped her hand to her chest. "Grandmother! I didn't know that you were there!"

Frena laughed. "No, I'm sure not." The old woman's gray eyes danced. Settling into the backcountry had not been easy, but the hard work had not stolen her spirit.

Catrina smiled and looked down. "Silly of me, isn't it?" She felt her cheeks blush red.

"Silly?" Frena shook her head and stared at Catrina with a knowing expression. "I've only met him once, but I'd say he's just right for you."

Catrina glanced back through the open door. Eli continued to trudge across the clearing. He saw her and took one hand off the cart to wave. The cart slipped backward and he slapped his hand back down to catch it. He looked up at Catrina again, shook his head, and grinned. She grinned back. "Do you really think so?" Catrina asked her grandmother while keeping her eyes on Eli. "He's so . . ."

"Clumsy?"

"*Ja.*"

"And shy?"

"*Ja.*"

"And unsure of himself?"

"*Ja.*" Catrina sighed. "As I said. How silly of me."

Frena laughed. "I've not finished. He's also thoughtful, and cheerful, and hardworking."

"*Ja,*" Catrina said. "He seems to be all of those things."

"He's nothing like—" Frena caught herself and cleared her throat. "Well, he's not like any of the suitors you had in Philadelphia."

Catrina felt that familiar stab of shame and regret. "No," she whispered. "Not at all."

"I think that's a good thing, Catrina. We came here for a new beginning. You don't start new by repeating your past mistakes."

Catrina dropped her gaze and studied her leather shoes. "No." She didn't want to talk about it. She didn't want to be reminded. Catrina closed the door. She had watched Eli long enough.

Frena pushed a strand of silver hair beneath her prayer *kappe* in a nervous gesture. "I've said more than I meant." When Catrina looked up again, Frena had left her side. She had hurried across the room to begin some meaningless task to distract her from memories that were better left unremembered.

While Catrina waited for Eli to reach the cabin, she swept the earthen floor with a broom made of twigs tied together with twine. Soon, the hard-packed dirt looked smooth and clean—or clean for dirt, anyway. *How I miss hardwood floors and throw rugs!* But those were luxuries for the city, not for far-flung settlements at the very edge of the colonies.

Catrina heard a knock on the door. Her head shot up. Sunlight poured through the cracks in the hand-hewn door and lit the dust motes that her broom had thrown into the air.

Frena gave a knowing smile and stirred the fire in the hearth. "I will let you answer that."

Catrina tossed the broom aside, dusted her hands against her crisp, white apron, and bounded for the door. She skidded to a stop just before she ran into the rough, wooden slats, and pulled the door open. Catrina's grin dropped into a look of surprise.

Gertrud stood at the threshold with a pinched expression. They stared at each other for a long, strained moment. "Expecting my brother, were you?" Gertrud said at last. Catrina could hear her grandmother bustling about the hearth. An iron cauldron banged against stone. Gertrud waited for an answer.

"What? Oh. No. Well, yes. He's bringing the loom. So I suppose you could say that I was expecting him."

"Hmmm." Gertrud's gaze did not soften. Catrina felt as if the woman could peel away the present and see into her past.

"It's the loom, don't you see. I am so looking forward to weaving again. It's all so very exciting."

"Ah. Of course. The loom. I am sure that explains the entirety of your excitement."

Catrina swallowed and stared. She wasn't quite sure

what to say. There was something about Gertrud's no-nonsense demeanor that tied Catrina's tongue.

"Are you planning to invite me in?" Gertrud asked in a flat tone.

"*Ja. Ja*, of course." Catrina pulled the door open so fast that it bumped against her shoe. She frowned and forced herself to slow her movements, to regain her signature calm. What was it about Gertrud that left her so flustered? *It's because she knows. . . .* Catrina forced away the thought. *No! She doesn't! She can't! I did not escape to the ends of the earth for nothing.*

"I think that we can assemble it there," Gertrud said as she swept past Catrina. "We'll have to push the table aside." Gertrud looked prim and proper in her white prayer *kappe*, fitted gray bodice, and long gray skirts. The stiff fabric swirled about her ankles as she surveyed the one-room cabin. Catrina's modest outfit looked similar, but on Gertrud the Plain attire had a dreary, severe effect. Catrina, on the other hand, looked as fresh and bright as a winter field covered in new snow.

"Hello, there!"

Catrina heard Eli's friendly shout and spun around. She tried to transform her big smile into something soft and sweet. She failed. But Eli returned her enthusiastic grin and she wasn't sorry. Instead, she felt positively *eager*. Until she remembered that Gertrud stood behind her, watching. She glanced back and saw the crossed arms and serious expression as Gertrud stared at Eli. Eli's grin fell away and he cleared his throat, then gave a more distant nod. "Well, then. I suppose we best get to work."

"*Ja.* Of course." Catrina felt an odd sense of embarrassment, as if she had done something wrong. *There's nothing wrong with smiling.* Catrina looked away. *Except when there is. How foolish of me to be so obvious. How embarrassing and downright forward. I must regain my dignity. I will* not *be seen as forward. Anything but that.* The familiar, icy grip clamped around her chest. Her throat burned. *I must remember myself. I must remember how quickly everything can fall apart.*

Catrina raised her chin a fraction and smoothed the expression on her face. "I believe that Gertrud has chosen a place for the loom."

"Wonderful good." Eli looked at Catrina and she could feel the warmth of his gaze fill her. "You'll help me? I could use another expert."

Gertrud sighed and headed outside, to the handcart. Catrina felt her mouth twitch. She could feel Gertrud's disapproval. Catrina wanted to smile. Oh, how she wanted to smile. "That would be fine," she said in a distant tone, without smiling. She knew it was the right attitude to take. But, how wrong it felt.

Chapter Three

Catrina watched Eli and Gertrud assemble the loom as if it were a giant puzzle. Eli whistled as he fitted notches into grooves and strained to pop heavy shaft frames into place. Catrina hovered beside him and handed him a mallet now and then or helped steady a crossbeam. Gertrud fluttered over the project with nervous fingers, barking orders and nodding approvingly as the loom took shape.

"Thank you," Gertrud said as Catrina stood with her hands clasped, ready to spring forward and help. "But I don't think there's anything more that you can do."

"She can hand me that warp beam," Eli said as he nodded his chin toward the component.

"This one?"

"*Ja.*" Eli smiled as he took the heavy beam from her. "And then the ratchet wheel."

"I've taken care of that," Gertrud said. She had gathered the remaining parts in front of her.

Eli kept the smile on his face, but Catrina thought she noticed a shift in his eyes. "Ah. Well, then."

Catrina studied Gertrud's expression. The woman looked focused and purposeful. *Perhaps it isn't personal. Perhaps she just wants to do it herself. I am a stranger after all, and this is their livelihood.* Catrina moved her gaze to Eli. She watched his strong, steady hands. She could sense a quiet peace within him, a sense that he belonged and knew who he was. She wondered what it must feel like, to know who one was. Sometimes she felt so unsure of herself that it seemed her body might float away, across the fields and into the empty sky.

"I'll make some refreshments," Catrina said. *That's one thing that I can do right.* "We have a good store of white sugar."

"Dessert?" Eli's attention shot to Catrina. "Well, doesn't that sound perfect."

Catrina gave a satisfied smile. "Apple pudding? It should only take a few hours." *The way to a man's heart is through his stomach, after all. Oh no. There I go again. I am not aiming for his heart. He is a friend only. No, not even that. An acquaintance. An acquaintance with a warm smile and a kind face and . . .* Catrina turned away in a swirl of skirts. She brushed off her hands and rummaged through her food stores. She had memorized the recipe years ago and ran through the ingredients in her head:

> *Three apples, chopped*
> *Three spoonfuls white sugar*
> *Pinch of cinnamon*
> *Grating of nutmeg*
> *Pinch of cloves*
> *Butter*

No cloves or nutmeg. No cinnamon, either. Well, it couldn't be helped. Thankfully, she had some butter stored in the springhouse. She had churned it from cream that came from Greta Miller's milk cow. There were apples stored in a barrel. And there was the precious store of white sugar. Catrina peered into the burlap sack and sighed. Nothing was so beautiful as those sparkling crystals of pure, refined sugar. She glanced behind her to make sure no one was looking, then scooped out a pinch of sugar and dropped it in her mouth. The granules crunched beneath her teeth and exploded with sweetness. Oh yes, she could manage just fine without the spices. When one has enough sugar, anything is possible.

Catrina listened to Eli's happy whistling as she diced the apples on the wooden, hand-hewn table. Gertrud said nothing as she worked alongside her brother, but Catrina could feel the woman's silent, guarded presence.

"I'll fetch the butter," Frena said as she stepped around the assortment of loom components that littered the dirt floor.

"Thank you. It is rather muddy today and—oh never mind." Catrina laughed, then shrugged. "But you can't expect me to change everything about myself just because we live in the middle of the wilderness. I've always hated wet feet and dirty hosen and I always will."

Frena shook her head and slipped outside. She had learned to accept her granddaughter's ways years ago.

"I can see that," Eli said.

Catrina didn't realize that he had been listening. She frowned. She had the distinct feeling that her clean apron and shiny shoes irritated other people in the settlement. It made her look as if she didn't work as hard as they did. "Oh, you've noticed. It's not that

I . . . well . . . I just like things to be neat and tidy." Catrina scooped up the diced apples and dropped them into a worn wooden trencher.

"Not cut out for farming, then," Eli said.

Catrina's frown deepened. "No. I suppose not." She kept her eyes on her work and felt inadequate.

"Nor am I."

Catrina's stomach jumped. *Did he—a man on the frontier—just admit he is not cut out for farming?* She glanced up and met his eyes. They looked genuine and sheepishly honest. "No?" Catrina gave a shy smile. "And yet you came here?"

Eli laughed and locked a crossbeam into place. "Why do you think I've brought this?" He slapped the loom affectionately, the way one might pat the warm, solid side of a favorite horse.

Catrina had never heard a better answer. She had never met a man who openly admitted he didn't want to do the dirty, exhausting work that men were supposed to do. And she understood. Oh, how she understood! She didn't want to do the dirty, exhausting work that women were supposed to do. She didn't want to boil the laundry in lye soap that burned the skin from her fingertips, or clear ash from the fireplace, or muck out the chicken coop, or slog through muddy fields to catch the pigs that roamed free until autumn.

Catrina stared at Eli for a long moment, then sprinkled a handful of sugar over the apples in the trencher. She sighed. "Aren't you the lucky one, then."

Eli shrugged. "*Ach.* You don't have to stay with farming, you know. Not if there are other things that you're meant to do."

Catrina's hands stopped. They hovered over the

wooden bowl. *Could there be another path for me?* When she left Philadelphia for the backcountry, Catrina had given up on any other way of life. She would live on a farm in the wilderness until she married a farmer and went to live on another farm in the same wilderness. She would sweep dirt floors, and sweat beneath the sun during the harvest, and scrub mud from her skirts and her menfolk's hosen until she died. *Better not to get your hopes up.* She knew what happened when you pinned your dreams on something that wasn't yours to have. "You're a dreamer, aren't you?" Catrina shook her head and reached for the burlap sack of wheat flour.

Eli laughed that clear, open laugh of his. "I'm a realist."

"Are you?" Catrina poured flour into a smooth wooden bowl until it formed a cream-colored mountain, like the snowy peaks of Switzerland where some of New Canaan's Amish settlers had been born. Others had been born in Germany's rich Rhine Valley and fled to Philadelphia when roving soldiers threatened the peace.

"I make a living doing what I want, don't I?" His face became serious and he gazed up at Catrina as she stood over the table. "And I'm happy, more or less." He hesitated and ran his hand over his mouth. "Although, I'd like to find—"

"If wishes were horses then beggars would ride," Gertrud interrupted. "My brother is a dreamer, no matter what he says. He doesn't know what's good for him." Her eyes narrowed as they moved to Catrina. "That's his problem."

"Oh, Gertie. You and your sharp tongue." The sentence might have sounded like a rebuke on anyone else's lips, but Eli made the words sound playful and loving, although his face looked wistful. "Gertrud keeps us on the straight and narrow, you know. We balance each other, I suppose."

Catrina recognized the appreciation that Eli had for his sister and admired his devotion to the widow. But, she could not help but wonder how he managed that calm, patient demeanor with her. *She looks as if she's choking on sour lemons every time I look at her!* Catrina realized that there might be a reason why and suddenly regretted judging the woman. *Who knows what she's been through? Who knows what lies trapped inside her heart, crying to be heard?*

Catrina wondered what Eli had been about to say when Gertrud cut him off. What would he like to find? A wife? She turned to the hearth to hide the red that flared in her cheeks at the thought. *Well, that certainly is a bold thought! You've gone from friendly acquaintance to husband quicker than you can make an apple pudding. Won't you ever learn your lessons, Catrina?* She plucked two eggs from a basket on the dirt floor and cracked them on the edge of the wooden bowl. Frena breezed in with a slab of butter wrapped in a linen cloth.

"Perfect timing." Catrina grinned and pushed thoughts of her future aside. Now was the time for pudding—not for silly dreams that could crumble as quickly as a poorly made pastry. Although her pastries were never poorly made. That was one thing that she did well, even in the middle of the wilderness. And Eli seemed just the sort of man to appreciate her talents in the kitchen. *Oh, no you don't! You just promised yourself to put those thoughts aside.*

Catrina poured a jar of cool water into the bowl,

then kneaded a pound or so of butter into the flour. She worked the sticky dough in silence. The click and thump of wood against wood filled the one-room cabin as Eli continued to piece together the loom. Smoke and embers billowed from the fireplace as Frena fed a fresh log to the flames.

Catrina glanced out the open window to check the position of the sun. Her grandfather would be back from the fields soon and she wanted the pudding ready before he returned. She scooped the ball of dough from the bowl and dropped it on the wooden tabletop in a soft thump. Her hands flew as she rolled out the dough with a wooden rolling pin, added knobs of butter to the surface, and then folded the sheet of dough into thirds. She repeated the process three times, wiped her hands on her crisp, white apron, and stretched her back.

"Finished?" Frena asked.

"*Ja.*" Catrina slid the diced apples onto the pastry dough and brought the edges together to form a pouch.

"Here." Frena handed Catrina a square of white linen and a length of twine.

"*Danke.*" Catrina drew the cloth around the pastry and tied it closed, then dropped it into the big black cauldron that hung above the fire from an iron chain. The settlers kept water boiling in their cauldrons all day long, so there was always hot water on hand. Catrina watched the linen bag bob beneath the roiling bubbles. In an hour or two she would have a good, hot pudding sealed inside a moist, flaky crust.

"Doesn't that smell delicious," Eli said as he slid the loom's warp roller into place. He turned the round piece of wood with his fingers and nodded with satisfaction. "I think that I'm going to like this arrangement."

Catrina smiled and nearly said that she agreed. But that would have seemed much too forward. Even though she had to admit that it was true. She felt a warm sense of anticipation inside her chest as her mouth slipped into a smile. She could almost ignore the strained expression on Gertrud's face in response to Eli's announcement. Almost.

Eli patted his stomach and gave a long, contented sigh. "A man could get fat on her cooking. That's for certain." He remembered the warm, happy steam that billowed up from the apple pudding when Catrina pulled the linen bag from the cauldron, dropped it in cold water to set, and then—finally—cracked open the crust with a pewter serving spoon. Nothing had ever smelled so good as those hot, sugared apples and rich, buttered pastry.

Gertrud didn't answer. She cut across the field alongside her brother, toward their camp. The sun had dipped behind the tree line and purple shadow-fingers crept across the tilled earth. Dark, dense woods ringed the cabin and clearing, as solid and sturdy as a wall.

"I could eat like that every day."

"Oh, Eli, I do worry about you." Gertrud's voice sounded strained.

Eli laughed. "I'm not planning on getting too fat. I'll make sure that I can still fit through a cabin door."

"That's not what I meant and you know it."

Eli sighed and his expression sobered. "I think it's all right."

"I've seen how you look at her, you know."

Eli shrugged. "It's all right, I said."

"Eli, you've no one left to take care of you. And I've no one left but you. It's my place—*my duty*—to keep you from harm. You do understand that."

Eli sighed again. "You're a good sister, Gertrud. But you worry too much."

Gertrud grabbed Eli's arm. Her fingers felt hard and frantic in the dim light. "There are two kinds of women, Eli. The ones who make good wives and the ones who don't."

"You've told me that before. And, if you haven't noticed, I'm not married yet." He rubbed his eyes in a tired gesture. "I'm not even courting anyone. I've *never* courted anyone!"

"But you've never had a woman like *that* look at you like *that*."

"Wait." Eli stopped walking and turned to stare at Gertrud. "You said she looks at me like *that*." His lips curled into a slow half smile. "Does she? Does she really?"

"Don't look so cocky, brother mine. She's no prize."

"Ha! She does look at me like that! She really does."

"Eli, you're not hearing me."

"Oh, I'm hearing you all right!" He beamed. "You're worked up because you think that she's interested in me. In *me*!" Eli shook his head and grinned. "Imagine, a woman like *that* interested in a man like *me*."

"Eli, I'm trying to help you. I do wish you'd listen."

"What on earth does she see in me? I'm not exactly—"

"Eli. You said it yourself. A woman like *that*."

"By *that*, do you mean beautiful, angelic, and the most talented baker in the colonies?"

"Eli." Gertrud's face looked rigid.

"I do know my name."

"That isn't what I meant."

"Oh, Gertie. Can't you just be happy for me? What if something comes of it? What if a woman like that really could see something in a man like me?"

"Please listen to yourself. A woman like that does not make a good wife."

"I've a happy, full stomach right now that disagrees mightily."

"Use your brains and not your belly, Eli!"

"Oh, Gertie." Eli smiled indulgently, leaned down, and kissed the top of her head. "You've nothing to worry about. A woman that beautiful is not going to want a suitor such as myself. She'll find a stout farmer who could wrestle a bear with his bare hands, shoot a deer from a thousand paces, and plant a hundred acres without breaking a sweat. Isn't that the kind of man a woman like that wants?"

Gertrud nodded and her face softened. "Let's hope so."

Eli frowned. "Let's not."

"You'll meet other women soon. You'll see. There's sure to be someone sensible here." Gertrud made a noise in her throat. "I mean, really, Eli, of all the women you could find in the backcountry why on earth would you look twice at one who doesn't want to dirty her hands with hard work? She won't survive the year, I tell you. She'll be back to Philadelphia before the snow flies again."

"You don't know that."

"Have you seen her shoes? They've never touched

mud. And her apron hasn't a single stain. You noticed yourself. You even said so."

Eli sighed. "Is that why you've set yourself against her? Because you think she hasn't got what it takes to survive out here? You think she won't do what it takes?"

Gertrud opened her mouth, then closed it again. She picked a fleck of mud from the front of her gray homespun bodice. "That seems evident."

Eli cut his eyes at her. He had the feeling that Gertrud was not telling him everything she was thinking. But what could his sister possibly have against Catrina?

Chapter Four

Catrina's fingers flew over the loom. She slid the shuttle between the rows of yarn and caught it when it reached the other side. She pulled the heavy beater bar toward her, then pushed it back again. The wood creaked and thumped back into place. She pressed the treadles with her feet to bring up one shaft—a wooden bar that held strands of unwoven yarn—and bring down another shaft. Now, she could pass the shuttle back through, between the strands of yarn, to add another layer to the cloth. The process was simple and repetitive and she loved it. The steady, hypnotic rhythm sang through her hands and reminded her that all was well, all was familiar and safe.

"You'll have enough cloth to sew a new waistcoat for Georg in no time at all," Frena said as she laid a warm hand on Catrina's shoulder. "It is wonderful good to see you weave again."

The loom clicked and shuddered as Catrina's fingers flashed across it. "*Ja.*" Catrina tried to make the word sound cheerful, but she knew her tone was flat and dull.

Frena sighed. Her hand stayed on Catrina's shoulder

for a long, still moment. "I've wondered if we did the right thing," she said finally.

Catrina's hands and feet stopped and the loom shuddered to abrupt silence. The cabin felt too quiet, too static after the loud, steady movement. "No. Don't say that. Don't ever say that."

Frena nodded. "You've done well, Catrina. Others don't realize it, they don't know what you've—"

"No. Don't speak of such things."

"What you've overcome, Catrina. What you've overcome. That's all I was going to say."

Catrina shook her head. "Even so." She passed the shuttle through the rows of yarn, but slower this time. She couldn't find her rhythm again. Her foot pressed the treadle. "You wish I hadn't come with you?"

Frena's breath caught in her throat. "For heaven's sake, no. That is not what I meant. Not at all."

Catrina shifted on the bench as the loom shuddered back to life. "I never meant to—"

"No. Of course not. And we're not speaking of that, remember?"

"No. Of course not."

"All I meant was . . ." Frena hesitated. She watched the blur of yarn and shafts and shuttle. ". . . Perhaps it is too much for you. Perhaps *der Herr* did not make you to work a backcountry farm."

"*Ach*, well. Here I am. So it doesn't matter now, anyway."

"But it does. It most certainly does."

"No. It doesn't, because there is nothing to do about it now."

Frena smiled. "I think there is."

The loom stopped again. Catrina spun around on the bench and looked up at her grandmother. "What?"

"You should work with Eli and Gertrud."

"But there's only one loom and Eli will soon be here to claim it for the day. And besides, you need my help."

"No. I'm tired of seeing you restless and unhappy. You'll never be content sloughing through the mud to weed or plant or harvest. But you can make yourself useful in plenty of other ways if you set your mind to it."

"I've tried so hard to find contentment here. And I am content . . . it's just . . ."

"If *der Herr* wants you here, don't you think he'll use the talents he gave you instead of wasting you on work you despise?"

Catrina swallowed. She felt a tiny bubble of hope rise from her chest.

"You could dye the yarn. You know the plants to use. And you can work the loom when Eli's not here. And there's the spinning as well. You know how much time it takes to spin enough for a single bolt of cloth. Gertrud could never spin enough on her own. They'll pay you, either in coin or trade goods, it matters little which."

"Do you really think so?"

"Those two have more work than they can manage. Everyone in New Canaan is threadbare and in want of cloth. And don't forget that Gertrud will be busy running their home. They mean to settle here, remember."

"*Ja*. That's true." Catrina's face brightened. "It would be almost as if we ran our own little shop. And I do love to spin and weave and create something from nothing." Her words came quickly as she imagined a life closer to what she knew in Philadelphia—

but with the simple, honest ways that she had learned among the Amish. Catrina bolted up and stood to face her grandmother. Her expression looked earnest and excited, as if Frena had just unraveled a great and wonderful secret. "*Ja.* That is what I will do. What I *must* do."

Frena nodded, patted her granddaughter on the arm, and bustled out of the cabin to fetch water from the spring. Catrina settled into the rhythm of the loom and let the *click clack swoosh* fill the small, silent cabin. The treadles squeaked beneath her feet and the beater bar felt solid and familiar beneath her palms. She kept the shuttle flying between the rows of yarn until she felt a prickly feeling on the back of her neck. Someone stood behind her, watching.

Catrina's hands stopped and the loom shuddered to an abrupt halt. She heard boots shuffle against the earth, the low cough of a man clearing his throat. Catrina recognized that nervous, self-conscious sound. She felt her stomach tighten. How long had he been hovering behind her? She felt tense and exposed. Had Eli been watching her? It did not seem like him to be so forward . . . and yet, he had been standing behind her for some time. . . . She did not want Eli to be like other men. She hoped he had not been watching her. But she could not shake her concern.

Catrina spun around on the bench and stared up at Eli. His tall, lean frame filled the doorway as he stood in the threshold. Sunlight poured around his silhouette and cast long yellow shapes on the dirt floor. His face looked sheepish and Catrina knew that she had caught him off guard. She reminded herself that Eli always had that sheepish, shy expression, but thoughts of the past—of another man whom she had trusted—pushed into her mind. Catrina adjusted the white neckcloth that a modest woman wore to cover the skin above the low neckline of her bodice. She felt confused. She had thought Eli was different. No, she had *wanted* Eli to be different.

"Oh. Hello there."

Catrina's brows knitted together. "How long have you been standing there?"

"A little while. A little while too long, I suppose. I was just . . ."

"You were just what?"

Eli cleared his throat again. He took off his black beaver-felt hat and ran his fingers through his red hair. "I didn't want to come in, seeing that you're alone. Didn't seem proper."

"No," Catrina said in a crisp, tense voice. "I should think not."

"So I was just . . ."

"Staring?"

"No."

Catrina raised an eyebrow.

"Well, yes. Strictly speaking. But . . ."

Catrina's eyebrow remained raised. Her face had become a calm, distant mask.

"What I mean to say is, you certainly can keep pace on a loom. You're very fast, you know."

"Yes. I know."

Eli swallowed. "I'm sorry. I wasn't . . . I just . . ." He turned his hat around in his hands. "*Ach.* Sorry. I'll call again later. When your grandmother's home."

Catrina nodded and turned back to face the loom. "Yes. Do that." Everything in her wanted to turn around and tell that warm, friendly, embarrassed face that it was all right, that she knew he had done nothing wrong. It was perfectly normal for a friend to linger in a doorway without announcing his presence . . . wasn't it? Was she overreacting? She did not know anymore. She was afraid to believe Eli could be as kind and good as he seemed. She had believed in kindness and goodness before. And she had promised herself she never would again.

Eli's throat had caught when he ducked through the open door, paused just beyond the cabin's low threshold, and saw Catrina. Her smooth, pale skin flashed as her arms moved against the loom. The back of her neck curved in a delicate arch and he could see a whisper of silky black hair at her nape, beneath the edge of her white prayer *kappe*. He had stood and watched for a moment longer than he should have. The *click clack swoosh, click clack swoosh* of the loom mesmerized him and he couldn't pull his eyes off the soft lines of her silhouette, the graceful pull of her fingers, the impossible straightness of her spine.

And then she had stopped and spun around. Their eyes had locked and he saw the disappointment and surprise in her face. She thought that he had been staring! Well, he had been staring, but not for the reason that she thought. Sure, he had been taken in by her beauty—any man with eyes would be—but that was not why he was staring. There was something more to her than physical beauty, and that something came to life as her hands glided over the loom in a graceful dance. She glowed with confidence and poise. Was that even possible? Could a woman *glow*?

Eli realized that he should have said something right away. He should have explained himself. But instead he had stood there with his hat in his hands thinking about how she had glowed. *Oh what a fool I am!* He wanted to sink into the ground as he slunk back across the field and retreated to his campsite. *What must she think of me now? Well, she thinks that I hover in doorways and stare. That's what she thinks!* And the worst part of it was that it was true. He *did* hover in doorways and stare.

Wet, spring mud sucked at his boots and woolen hosen as he slogged across the tilled earth. But Eli didn't notice. He was too busy agonizing over the fact that Catrina Witmer must think that he was just like every other man. And there was nothing that he could do to convince her otherwise. It didn't matter that he wasn't staring in *that* way. It didn't matter one bit!

"You're in a fine state," Gertrud said as he stormed into their camp.

Eli kept his head down and growled as he stomped past. *Wait right there, did I just* growl? *I am not a man who* growls. *What in the heavens has happened to me? First I stare? Now I* growl? *Whatever is next? Will I march into Catrina's cabin, scoop her into my arms, and carry her off, straight to the altar?* He realized he rather liked that idea, actually. He could imagine her laughing and her eyes shining as he set her down in front of the bishop. Her soft, warm hand wrapped in his hand . . . *Now, just hold on. That's quite enough. That's more than enough!*

"Getting to know Miss Witmer better, are we?" Gertrud looked up from the campfire and gave a smug little half smile.

Eli shook his head and began to scrape his muddy boots on a fallen log. "Well, I was trying to."

"Ah."

Eli pushed his boot against the log so hard that the rotten bark cracked. His foot slipped through the jagged wood, up to his ankle. He yelped and threw his hands out for balance as he struggled to stay upright on one foot. "Oh, for goodness' sakes!"

Gertrud laughed and flicked water onto the cast-iron spider that sat atop a bed of coals raked from the campfire. The water sputtered and danced across the surface until it evaporated. "The skillet's hot. Sit down and have a corn cake. Food always improves your mood."

Eli pulled his foot out of the rotten log, stomped on the ground to shake off bits of bark, and slumped onto a three-legged stool by the fire. "Oh, I'm too far gone for food. I'm not even sure I'm hungry."

Gertrud laughed again. "So dramatic! Whatever has she done to you?"

"*Ach.*"

Gertrud poured batter onto the cast-iron spider, then looked over at Eli with a mischievous glint in her eye. "Will I get to tell you that I told you so?"

"No, you will not." Eli listened to the sizzle of corn-cake batter as he watched a billow of steam whisk into the evening air. He sighed, took off his hat, and threw it onto his bedroll. "It wasn't her. It was me."

"Now, Eli . . ."

"Don't 'now Eli' me. It's the same as always. Beautiful woman meets incompetent, ridiculous man. Incompetent, ridiculous man slinks away in shame. End of story."

Gertrud's voice tightened. Her face became somber. "You are not incompetent and you are not ridiculous."

"*Ach.*" Eli set his elbows on his knees, slouched forward, and rested his chin in his hands. "Tell that to Catrina."

"Mmmmmm." Gertrud frowned and eased a spatula beneath the corn cake. "Do try to stop pouting like a child."

"I am not pouting." Eli scowled. "I don't pout."

"Of course not, dear."

"Pouting! The very idea."

"*Ja.* The very idea." Gertrud flipped the corn cake and it landed back in the skillet with a satisfying splat. She leaned back on her heels and sighed. "Now, what were we . . . Oh, right. I was just about to tell you that, once you stop pouting, you can go to the worship service tomorrow, meet another woman, and move on. I'm sure that there's more than one eligible woman in New Canaan."

"What if I don't want to meet another woman?"

"Oh, Eli. Of course you do."

"No, I don't."

Gertrud set the spatula down with a clang. She turned her head to face her brother. "Really, Eli. You do."

"No. I. Don't."

Gertrud narrowed her eyes. "Well, you would if you would stop pouting over that woman!"

Eli's face darkened. "I won't tell you again, Gertie. I am *not* pouting. I am a grown man and I *don't* pout."

Gertrud stared at him. "Well, you told me, didn't you." But the expression on her face said otherwise.

"*Ja.* I most certainly did!"

"Of course, if you weren't pouting, you wouldn't be here, brooding by the fire. You would be with Catrina right now, having a conversation with her instead of running away. Did you even try to explain yourself?"

Eli's expression shifted. He opened his mouth, closed it again, and scowled. "All right, then. Let's see who's pouting now." Eli leapt up from the three-legged stool so fast that it tumbled backward. He grabbed his black beaver-felt hat and punched it down over his brow.

Gertrud's mouth fell open. "Wait! I didn't mean . . ." But it was too late. Eli had already stormed out of the campsite. She made a face and slapped her forehead with the heel of her hand.

Eli thought he heard his sister call after him, but he wasn't listening. She might have said something about being sorry and that she hadn't meant to send him back to *her*, but he didn't care. He wouldn't let this nonsense go on any longer. He would make it right. He would make Catrina understand that he wasn't a man like *that*. He would never stare like *that*. He was Eli Webber—shy and awkward and gangly and . . . *Oh dash it all! What on earth will I say to her? What on earth would she ever see in me? The shyness and the awkwardness, that's what.* Eli stopped and stood in the middle of the empty field. Darkness crept in from the woods and bruised the sky. Night would be here soon. *I should give up. There's nothing for me in the cabin ahead. It doesn't matter if I explain myself. It doesn't matter if I convince her that I'm a gentleman. She would never, never look at me with any affection. How could she? She's the most beautiful woman I've ever met and I'm . . . well, I'm me!*

Eli hesitated in the dusk as he stared at the silhouette of the cabin. He had a strange feeling that this was a decision that could change the course of his life. He could storm up to the cabin and boldly defend himself—declare his true feelings even!—or he could slink back to the campsite and accept that he would never be a man who took control of his life or swept a woman off her feet.

Eli sighed. He swallowed hard. Gertrud had told him to march back there and tell Catrina the truth. Maybe he should take her advice, for once. But what would he say? How could he ever make Catrina understand?

Chapter Five

Eli knew who he was and he knew who he *wasn't*. *I'll bet Catrina has had a host of suitors and I'll bet none of them stopped to think how she felt about anything. I'll bet that they never saw past her beauty. Well, I'm not one of them. And, dash it all, I'm going to make sure that she knows it!*

Eli nodded with resolve, straightened his hat, and marched across the field toward Catrina's cabin. It occurred to him that he wasn't even one of her suitors yet. And he certainly wasn't like any suitor that Catrina would have had before. Women like that attracted the strongest, boldest, most dashing of men. *Perhaps I've been a little hasty to put myself in the same category. Perhaps I'm on a fool's errand about to make a fool of myself. Again. If there's one thing that I know how to do, it's how to dig a deeper hole once I've already fallen in. . . .*

"*Ach!*" Eli set his jaw and marched onward. *Sometimes you just have to do what you have to do. It's as simple as that.* Eli *told* himself that it was as simple as that, but when he saw Catrina's slender figure outlined against the purple sky as she scattered grain for the chickens, his stomach clenched. He took a good, deep breath and quickened his pace. If his courage faltered now, he would never get the words out. And that wouldn't be fair to Catrina and it wouldn't be fair to him.

Catrina straightened her back and stood still for a moment. Eli knew that she had seen him and that she was watching him, but he couldn't see her face. The evening shadows covered her features. He swallowed and lifted a hand in greeting. Her hands stayed by her sides. He thought she raised her chin slightly, defiantly. He hoped the movement had been a trick of the fading light. He swept off his beaver-felt hat and ran his fingers through his hair. His heart beat against his throat. *Dash it all! Why did I have to fall for a woman who is so completely out of my reach?*

Catrina stared for another long, uncomfortable moment, then turned away, toward the cabin. A chicken pecked at the earth by her foot and she side-stepped it gracefully.

"Catrina! Wait!"

She froze. Eli saw her shoulders rise and fall in a long, heavy sigh. She didn't turn back around, but she didn't walk away, either.

"Catrina." He broke into a jog. She waited.

When Eli reached her she didn't turn to look at him. He had to walk around her to see her face.

"What do you want? It's too late to use the loom. Grandfather is already abed."

Eli swallowed. "I didn't come to use the loom."

"No?" Catrina stood as still as a statue. She stared into his eyes with quiet dignity. But something flickered behind her careful expression. He could sense that she felt conflicted and confused. "I thought you were different. But when I saw you looking at me like that . . ." She turned away. "It's all you see. It's all any of you see." The words came out in a low whisper.

"No, Catrina." Eli's voice sounded warm and comforting. He softened his deep voice to match her whisper. "That isn't all that I see."

"I am not a fool, Eli Webber. That is the one thing that I'm not."

"Catrina. I came to say that I'm sorry. Yes, I was staring. But . . . it wasn't what it looked like. Something about you captured me . . . something deeper and more real than how you looked. Something . . . well, I can't explain it exactly, but it's your strength and dignity, your graceful calm, your kind, courageous spirit . . . Dash it all, I'm sorry but I'm not good with words. I guess that's all I have to say." He ran his fingers through his hair and looked down. "I guess I've said too much. It sounds rather foolish, I'm sure. But, well, it's what I felt."

Catrina stared at Eli. For a long, terrible moment he was sure that she was going to slap his face, or storm away. Or much, much worse, he was afraid that she would laugh at him. But she did none of those things. She just stood and stared at him. And finally, when he didn't think that he could stand it another moment, she spoke. "No one has ever said anything like that to me before."

Eli's face jerked. "No?"

Catrina smiled a soft, distant smile. "No."

"I can't believe that."

She sighed. "And yet, it's true."

"What fools."

"You shouldn't talk like that."

"No. I'm sorry. I just can't bear to think that . . ." He shook his head and looked away. He didn't understand why he felt such a sudden, fierce anger. "You deserve better than that."

"Why? Why do you say that?" She looked at him with an earnest intensity that made Eli want to cry. He didn't, of course. He was trying to sweep her off her feet, after all.

"Because you're you."

"What?" Catrina laughed. "Whatever does that mean?"

Eli smiled. "There's something special about you. Something different. And it's more than your beauty. It's your quiet strength, your commitment to the faith. It's the way you make me feel like I'm not alone anymore. That's all that I am trying to say."

"Then you've said quite a lot, Eli Webber."

"Yes. I think that I have."

Catrina could not sleep that night. She stared into the rafters and heard Eli's words over and over again. *Did he mean what he said? Could he really mean that she was special for more than her looks?* Catrina shifted onto her side and punched the feather pillow to make a hollow for her head. She listened to the steady whistle of her grandparents' breath across the cabin. *I've heard words like that before. And I was foolish enough to believe them.* Catrina remembered the smile of another man who had stood over her and whispered sweet, desperate words. Was Eli the same? They were both men after all.

The other man—she would not say his name, not even in her mind—had flashed his teeth when he smiled, same as Eli. But the other man had not smiled with his eyes. No, his eyes had been calculating. They were not eyes that crinkled at the corners and danced as Eli's eyes did. Eli smiled with his eyes—no, with his whole face, his whole *body*. Catrina's lips curled upward and she realized that she was smiling at the thought of his smile.

She jerked her mouth back to a frown. *Oh no you don't. Oh. No. You. Don't.* Catrina tugged the quilt off her legs. She felt too hot and stuffy. The room was closing in on her. *I won't fall for another man again. I won't risk it.* Oh sure, she had run after Jacob Miller when she first came to New Canaan. But that was different. *She* pursued *him.* She had been in control. She had reeled him in like a silvery, slippery fish on a hook.

Of course, it had been a disaster. A complete and total disaster. But she had never relinquished control. She had never let him run after her or whisper sweet nothings into her ear or tell her how much he loved her. In fact, he had never loved her at all. She had always known that, deep down. And it had felt safe, in a way. Or familiar at least. No man had ever loved her for her. No man had ever looked at her and seen beneath the surface to the woman inside. She laughed out loud, then remembered that her grandparents slept nearby. *Oh, the irony!* Of all her childhood friends she was the only one unmarried. She, the one who had always been considered the greatest catch, was the only one who slept alone in the dark, listening to the emptiness clang inside her heart with every beat.

Well, Eli was no Jacob Miller. Eli was interested in her. Eli looked at her in a way that Jacob Miller never had. And that was the problem. Because, when he looked at her with affection, she could only think of *him*—the man in Philadelphia whose name she wanted to forget.

But she would never forget that man, would she? And the memory would follow her like a dark stain that she could never hide or wash away. The shame of it. The shame! And the worst part was that she had been fooled. Oh yes, she had been completely and utterly fooled by him. *And I will not be fooled again. Never, never again.*

Catrina threw back the quilt and let the cool night air rush over her skin. She shivered in her thin linen shift and rolled off the narrow straw pallet. The cabin felt too small, too confining. She had to get outside. She fumbled in the dark for her skirt and pulled it over her shift, then shrugged into her bodice and fastened the ties. She didn't bother to pull on her woolen hosen or pin the removable sleeves onto her bodice. There was no one to see her. New Canaan stood at the edge of the colonies, surrounded by dense and endless woodlands.

Catrina slid her bare feet into her leather shoes and wrapped a wool cloak around her, then slipped out the door. The stillness of the night hit her like a slap. The wilderness felt so empty. And yet, she knew it was full of life. Somewhere, beyond the clearing, bears and bobcats roamed the hillsides. Owls swooped through the dark air. Possums waddled on tiny feet, snuffling for food. But those night creatures would never reveal themselves to her. She wrapped the cloak more tightly around her and listened to the silence. Somewhere, far, far away, a wolf howled. Another wolf answered and the cry echoed against the Blue Mountain and disappeared into the cold white stars. She was alone, completely alone.

No, that wasn't quite true. Her grandparents were on the other side of the log wall and they loved her. So did her friends in the settlement. But there was still that emptiness, that ache inside that told her she was alone among a group of people. A cool wind swept across the field and brought the smell of fresh, damp earth to her. Her thick black hair rippled and fluttered away from her face. *I should have put on my prayer kappe.* She pulled the hood of her cloak over her head and held it in place with her hand. Another wolf howled. The first two wolves joined in and their cries rose together in a strange, mournful song that cut through the darkness. *Not even the wolves are alone. Only me. Always me.*

A light caught Catrina's eye. She squinted and took a few steps forward. *There, behind the tree line, just beyond the field.* She recognized the flicker of orange and yellow. A campfire. Eli's campfire. He must be sitting there now, staring into the flames. Was he thinking of her? Did he feel alone in the night too?

But she knew that wasn't the question to ask. She knew that he was thinking about her. Men always did. *What* was he thinking about her? *That* was the question.

Eli woke up feeling like a new man. He whistled as he shrugged into his waistcoat and fastened his leather shoes. He whistled as he chopped a log for kindling. When he set down the ax, Gertrud narrowed her eyes at him. He grinned and slapped his sister on the back. "Beautiful morning, *ja?*"

"*Ja.* Beautiful." She followed him with suspicious eyes as he walked to the campfire, still whistling.

"Ah. Fried salt pork. My favorite."

"You hate fried salt pork. Why, just last week you said that you would scream if you saw another piece of fried salt pork. You said that you are sick to death of it."

"Did I?" Eli grinned. "Funny thing, that."

"*Ja.* Hilarious." Gertrud stooped down and pulled the cast-iron spider off the coals. "Whatever has gotten into you, Eli Webber?"

Eli shrugged. "A man can't be in a good mood?"

"No."

Eli laughed. "Just happy that I took your advice, I guess."

Gertrud froze. She dropped the cast-iron spider onto the dirt. The salt pork slid in the grease and almost slipped over the side of the skillet.

"Hey! Watch out for my breakfast!"

Gertrud ignored Eli. Her eyes narrowed. "What advice?"

Eli tried to pick out a slice of salt pork with his fingers, but he jerked his hand back and shook it. "Use a spatula," Gertrud said.

Eli popped his finger in his mouth. "Burned myself."

"*Ja.* What advice?"

"Oh, that." Eli took the spatula out of Gertrud's hand and slid a fat slice of salt pork onto a pewter plate. "You know, that advice you gave me last night." He waved his hand distractedly. "To tell Catrina how I really felt about her."

Gertrud stared at him. "I said no such thing."

Eli shrugged and bit into the pork. He had to tug

hard with his teeth to work off a bite-sized piece of the tough, dried meat. "Mfu mfed fu fell fer—"

"I can't understand you."

Eli shrugged again and kept chewing. Gertrud stared at him with narrowed eyes until he swallowed. "Man's got to eat," he said.

"What exactly do you think that I told you?" Gertrud asked.

"Oh, you know. To march right over there and set things straight. And tell her that I care about her for who she is, not how she looks."

"I most certainly did not."

"No?" Eli cocked his head. "I guess not. That was more me."

"It was all you."

"But I never would have said anything if you hadn't told me to go set things straight."

"Are you telling me that you declared your feelings to Catrina *and* that I'm the one who encouraged you to do it?"

"That's exactly what I'm saying, sister mine. And I do want to thank you for it. I have no regrets. No regrets at all."

"No regrets?! NO REGRETS?!"

Eli flinched. "Really, Gertie. That face does not become you. Let's lower our voice, shall we? Shouting is bad for the digestion, you know."

"Eli Webber, I have spent the last two days warning you about Catrina. And now you tell me that *I* encouraged you to declare your . . . your . . . your *feelings* for her?"

"Mmmm." Eli was still smiling. "That's exactly what I'm saying."

"I did no such thing and you know it!"

Eli shrugged and gave a wide, satisfied grin. "Well, I guess you shouldn't have told me to stop pouting and go back up there."

Gertrud began to shake, actually *shake* with frustration.

"You've got no one to blame but yourself, sister mine." He picked up another slice of salt pork. "You've become quite the matchmaker, as a matter of fact. Quite the matchmaker indeed."

Chapter Six

Catrina did not know if she was eager to go to the worship service or if she dreaded it. Not the service itself, but seeing Eli again. She knew that he would be there and there would be no way to avoid him. Part of her wanted to run to him and grin and tell him that she understood him and believed him and that everything was wonderful. But of course, that was foolishness. Pure foolishness. *And I promised myself to never, ever be foolish again.*

Catrina felt her stomach contract as she crested the hill above the Miller cabin and saw the clumps of people in the clearing. The settlers took turns hosting the worship service and this week fell on her friends Greta and Jacob. Yes, she now considered Jacob her friend, even though she had run after him shamelessly before she admitted that he and Greta were perfect together. Catrina supposed that she should be embarrassed, but after what had happened in Philadelphia, her forwardness with Jacob seemed inconsequential. She couldn't be bothered to obsess over that mistake—not when there were *real* mistakes to obsess over. And what a mistake she had made in Philadelphia!

"Are you all right?"

Catrina flinched. She had almost forgotten that her grandparents strolled beside her. A bird trilled high in a pine tree and another one zipped across the path with a flash of blue wings. "Of course." Catrina forced a smile.

Frena put her hand on Catrina's elbow. "You look pale."

"*Ach*, let her be, Frena," Georg said. "She's thinking about that young man and hoping that he's thinking of her too."

Catrina's mouth dropped. Her head swiveled to her grandfather. She didn't know what to say.

Georg winked at her. "It's about time, you know."

"Oh." Catrina turned paler, if that were possible.

"Georg." Frena laughed. "You've gone and embarrassed her."

Georg shrugged. "I'd like to see her with a nice young man."

"You are being mighty hasty, Grandfather."

"He seemed nice enough when he came to dinner. Not like some of those other boys. You know the ones who run around trying to impress everyone, but have the character of a toad. Smooth-talking boys like—"

"Georg!" Frena elbowed Georg in the ribs.

Georg cleared his throat. "*Ach*. Well. Never mind then."

Catrina sighed. "It's all right."

"Of course it is," Georg said. "It'll turn out all right. Just you watch and see."

"We don't know Eli," Catrina said. "Not really. He might not be so nice, you know."

Frena frowned and looked down the hill, to the people gathered in the Millers' clearing. "A wise thought, to be sure. Best to be cautious. But he certainly does seem to be a nice young man. . . ."

Georg shrugged. "Leave it in *der Herr*'s hands. But just remember that running away doesn't ever really get you anywhere."

The color leached from Frena's face when Georg said the words *running away*. She coughed. Georg frowned and tugged at his long gray beard. "She knows what I mean, Frena."

Catrina looked down. She was tired of hearing them talk around the truth. They all pretended that *it* had never happened, and yet they all knew it did. That knowledge felt like a fourth person living alongside them—a silent, brooding fourth person. Would she ever be free from the past? Would she ever be allowed to truly move on?

"I'm going ahead to see if I can help Greta," Catrina said.

Georg looked frustrated and Frena looked concerned. Catrina forced a smile. "It's all right." She patted her grandfather's arm. "Really." And then she hurried down the hillside before they could say anything more. Was her grandfather right? Was Eli a nice young man? Her heart said yes. But it was her heart that had betrayed her in Philadelphia!

Eli came out of the open cabin door just as Catrina rounded the corner of the threshold to go inside. He thumped into her and she jolted backward. He looked contrite as he threw up a hand, grabbed her shoulder, and balanced her. His hand felt warm and gentle and she knew that she wouldn't fall. She laughed when she realized that he had been the reason that she almost fell—and the reason that she didn't.

"Steady there." He frowned. "Sorry about that. I was just . . ." He cleared his throat and returned her grin. "*Ja*. Funny, I suppose." His face dropped back into a serious expression and he looked at her carefully. "You're all right? Nothing hurts?"

"No, of course not. It was nothing."

He nodded. "You're sure?"

"Eli, it's fine. Really." Catrina realized that she was glad that he had bumped into her. His reaction made her feel that he cared. His expression seemed so apologetic and concerned. He was getting to her. Really getting to her. Well, she wouldn't be taken in. Not this time. She felt a protective shield snap down over her emotions.

But the words that he spoke the night before flashed through her mind. *There's something special about you. Something different. And it's more than your beauty. It's your quiet strength, your commitment to the faith. It's the way you make me feel like I'm not alone anymore.* He had seemed so genuine as they stood in the field at dusk, the last smudges of sunlight lingering in the sky behind his tall, lean body. She pushed the memory away. *They* all *seem so genuine.*

"I need to get on," Catrina said in a clipped voice. Her heart told her to soften her tone, to linger with him for a moment, laugh at their little accident, enjoy the moment. But she slammed her heart shut and turned briskly on her heels. She could feel Eli watching her as she strode away. She glanced back and his face crumpled. He rubbed his hand against the back of his neck in a confused, contrite gesture. Catrina turned away and did not look at him again.

* * *

Eli's chest felt tight throughout the service. He knew that he should appreciate the moment—here he was in a new settlement created just for the Amish!—and yet, his heart felt as heavy and sharp as an iron blade. The congregation sat on rows of backless benches in front of the Millers' cabin, men on one side, women on the other, and sang the slow, familiar a cappella songs from the *Ausbund.* Eli tried to steal a glance at the women's side of the congregation, but Gertrud's stern brown eyes met his instead of Catrina's. Gertrud raised an eyebrow as if she knew exactly what he was thinking and he snapped his gaze back to the men's side. *This isn't going well. This isn't going well at all.*

Is it because I bumped into her? Was that such a terrible thing? He frowned. *Well, it wasn't exactly debonair.* It wasn't the way you sweep a woman off her feet. Or, to be completely accurate, it was. But not in the way that he wanted to!

Eli replayed last night's conversation with Catrina. She had looked up at him with soft, vulnerable blue eyes. And those eyes had widened, ever so slightly, when he told her how he felt about her. She had seemed so moved by his declaration. But today . . .

Everyone had stopped singing. Someone beside him cleared his throat and Eli realized that he was the only person still standing. He felt his face burn red as he dropped to his seat. Had she seen that? Of course she had!

It was hopeless. Truly and completely hopeless.

An elderly man in a somber waistcoat, dark jacket, and sensible leather boots walked to the front of the congregation, took off his beaver-felt hat, and began to speak. Eli tried to listen to the man, but his mind stayed fixated on Catrina Witmer. He analyzed each word that he had spoken to her the night before. His face fell when he realized that her response to his declaration had been meaningless. *You've said quite a lot, Eli Webber.* That was all she had given him. She had not actually given him any reason to believe that she had been moved by his words.

He had thought that they had connected. He had thought that they had felt a shared revelation. But why on earth had he thought that? She had given him no sign. Perhaps he had just hoped for it so badly that he had misread her. *Of course I misread her. How foolish of me to think that a woman like her could be interested in a man like me.*

After the service, everyone stayed to share a meal. Eli felt overwhelmed by the parade of strangers who hurried to welcome him and wish him well. He found himself looking for Catrina in the crowd and thinking how soft and familiar her presence would be. But Catrina was nowhere to be found. Had she left early? Was she so eager to run away from him? Well, of course she was. *She wants to send a clear message without having to come right out and say it.* Eli frowned. *She's too considerate to come right out and tell me that I don't deserve her.*

"Isn't that so?"

"What?" Eli's attention jerked back to the two elderly men standing in front of him. Abraham and Amos, those were their names, right? He did remember that the taller fellow had just been elected bishop. He had no idea what the two men had just said. "Yes. Indeed."

Abraham nodded and ran his fingers through his

long beard in a thoughtful motion. "And Friday will work for you and Gertrud?"

"Uh, *ja*. Friday." Eli hoped that he wasn't agreeing to something irreparable. He forced himself to pay attention to the conversation and not let his thoughts drift back to Catrina.

"You've chosen the tract of land?"

Eli stared for a moment. "Ah. *Ja*. A tract of land. We have. Camped there now. Adjacent to the Witmer place."

Amos grinned and slapped Eli on the back. Eli flinched. He really was terribly distracted. How soon could he slip away and look for Catrina? "We'll have you a stout cabin up in no time," Amos said. "I'll let everyone know to be there."

"*Wunderbar.*" Eli gave a genuine smile as he caught up to the conversation. At the week's end the entire settlement would come together and help him build his cabin. This is what he loved about being Amish. No one was ever alone.

A solitary figure caught his eye and drew his attention beyond the silver-haired men, to the edge of the clearing. Catrina stood by herself, eyes distant, her hands holding a wooden trencher piled high with food. She wasn't eating. Eli frowned. She looked alone, even among the smiling, chatting crowd. Her posture looked regal, her spine straight, her chin slightly raised. Did she want to be alone? He couldn't read her. She was unreachable, untouchable. She was too good for him.

"Eli."

"Huh?"

Gertrud stood beside Abraham and Amos, staring at him. He had not noticed that she had joined them.

"The loom," she said. Her expression looked tired and impatient.

"Yes. The loom."

Amos nodded as if he expected a more elaborate response. Eli just nodded in return.

"So it will be how long?"

"Until . . ." Eli cleared his throat and tried to look engaged in the conversation.

"You have the cloth for a new pair of breeches." Amos tapped his knee where the linsey-woolsey fabric had worn thin. "Can't keep going like this."

"Right. No. Of course not." Eli cleared his throat again. "Let's see, it depends on how long . . . Working alone it will be some time before . . . Gertrud will have her hands full keeping house I imagine, and well . . ."

Frena Witmer strode over and wedged herself between Amos and Abraham. "I couldn't help but overhear. And, as a matter of fact, I've been thinking the same thing. Catrina too. We were discussing you— that is we were discussing your work and . . ."

Catrina was discussing me! Eli felt his heart thump into his mouth. He swallowed.

"You should speak to her, I suppose," Frena continued.

"Ah. Is that so?" Eli wanted to ask exactly what Catrina had said about him, but he cut the thought short when he saw Gertrud's expression. She had bitten into a lemon again.

"Eli, there's someone I'd like you to meet," Gertrud said.

"All right. I'll just speak to Catrina first."

Eli nodded to Abraham and Amos and smiled at Frena, and then headed across the clearing to where

Catrina stood alone. Eli felt his stomach flutter with expectation. He had a reason to talk to her! A genuine reason—not some contrived excuse that would make him look foolish.

"Eli, dear, I do want you to meet someone." Gertrud pulled on his arm. "She and her sister are right here. Do come along. You can speak to Catrina later." Gertrud's face said that she had no intention of letting him speak to Catrina later.

Eli looked toward Catrina and frowned. The sun caught a tendril of midnight black hair that had fallen from her prayer *kappe* and made it glimmer. Eli sighed. "I'm sure whoever it is can wait."

"Humph." She tugged his arm harder. "I'm sure they can't."

"*Ach*, Gertie. Why are you set on keeping me from speaking to Catrina?"

Gertrud's face tightened. "It's not that I am keeping you from speaking with her. It's that there are other women who I am sure you would rather speak to."

Eli kept his eyes on Catrina's solitary figure across the clearing. He wasn't really paying attention to his sister. She always said the same thing in different ways.

Gertrud steered Eli toward two women in line at the long wooden table set up in the yard. They hovered over the trenchers of roasted turkey, corn cakes, and rough, brown bread.

"My brother, as promised," Gertrud said as they neared. She elbowed Eli to capture his attention. "This is Christina." The younger of the two women turned and smiled. She looked eighteen years old or so, and was pretty in a fresh, innocent way. Her blue eyes seemed wide and trusting and her cheeks held the red flush of youth.

"Gertrud told us about you. We're so glad that you're here. We have sheep. Did she tell you that?"

"No." Eli looked down at the open, friendly face and the hint of blond hair that peeked from beneath the white starched prayer *kappe.* He wondered why he didn't feel anything for the girl. She was certainly pretty enough to grab a man's attention, but he felt no pull, no connection. He glanced over her head and saw Catrina watching him in the distance. Her expression clamped shut and she quickly turned her face away. *Was she watching me? Now, wouldn't that be an interesting turn of events. . . .*

"It's almost time for the shearing," Christina continued. She did not notice that Eli's attention was elsewhere.

The second woman set her trencher down on the wooden table and nodded at Eli. Her features looked similar to the younger woman's but they seemed harder and more serious. Eli guessed that she was a decade or more older than the first woman. But it wasn't her age that made her less attractive than her sister; it was the subtle strain that she wore on her face like a mask. Eli thought that she and Gertrud would get along just fine. Two peas in a pod, those two.

"My sister gets ahead of herself," the older woman said. "I'm Hilda. Nice to meet you. And yes, we've wool to trade."

"Ah." Eli smiled. "Splendid." Eli glanced behind him to make sure that Catrina was still standing alone, across the clearing. He looked back to the women. "Lovely to meet you both." Then he nodded, turned away, and strode across the yard. He heard Gertrud's heavy footsteps hit the dirt behind him. He sighed. "Yes, dear?"

"Eli, what is wrong with you?"

"Not a thing, sister mine."

"Christina is a very nice young woman. She's pretty and cheerful and wholesome. She does seem quite wholesome, doesn't she?"

"Mmmm. Yes. I'm sure she does." Eli yawned and did not slow his pace.

Gertrud grasped his arm. "So you will call on Christina this evening? I'll chaperone, of course." Gertrud's expression looked smug and self-assured. Eli knew that face. It was her *I-have-a-foolproof-plan-and-my-brother-will-fall-right-into-it* face.

Eli pushed down the irritation. *Patience, man! Patience. Remember what you owe your sister.* He patted the work-hardened hand that gripped his elbow. "Oh, what poor timing. A shame, really." He shook his head and tried to look contrite even though his eyes sparkled with mirth.

"What is?" Gertrud's eyes narrowed.

"I already have plans to call on someone else."

Gertrud's face whitened. "And who might that be?"

"Catrina."

Gertrud's lips narrowed. Her jaw clenched. "And how long have you had these plans?"

Eli shrugged. "Since I looked up a moment ago and saw that Catrina isn't standing over there any-more." She had slipped away while Gertrud slowed him down to talk about Christina. Eli smiled a rather wicked smile. "You really should have let me speak to Catrina first. But since you insisted I meet Christina first, well, looks like I will have to make a special trip over to the Witmer cabin. And then I'll have to sit a spell and visit. Can't be rude, you know."

Oh, what a sour lemon Gertrud had bitten now! Her face puckered with frustration. She made a sound between a huff and a grunt as her eyes bored into Eli's. He just grinned.

Chapter Seven

Catrina heard a knock at the cabin door as she scrubbed the last supper dish in a wooden bucket beside the hearth. She rose from her knees and wiped her forehead with her sleeve. Her grandfather sat on a backless, handmade bench alongside the wall, oiling the leather harnesses for the mule team. Her grandmother swept the dirt floor with the twig broom. "I'll answer," Catrina said as she smoothed her white apron and straightened the neck cloth tucked into the top of her bodice. She felt a catch of expectation in her stomach—and clamped the feeling down when she recognized it.

It could be anyone at the door, she told herself. And yet, that creeping desire whispered to her that she hoped it was Eli Webber. She frowned and straightened her spine. Emotions are such silly things. Such silly, silly things. And they lead to such devastating traps.

Catrina opened the door and there he was, his tall, lean body leaning casually against the doorframe, his black, beaver-felt hat in his hands. Eli snapped to attention when he saw her. He could not pretend to be calm and casual. His mouth opened, then closed again and he stared at her for a moment, his spine straight and self-conscious. His red hair stood up atop his head. He had been running his hands through his hair again. She had noticed that he did that when he was nervous. *Good. Let him be.* She wanted to push him away. She wanted to shake her head and shut the door and tell him that she knew all about what men had to offer and she was not interested. Not interested at all!

And yet.

Catrina swallowed. How could she think those things about *this* man? This man who turned his hat in his hands and looked down at her with that sincere expression. Oh, for goodness' sakes! She wanted to invite him in and stare into those honest blue eyes. She wanted to see that shy smile and hear what he wanted to say. She wanted to let him prove that he was not any other man. That he was different.

Catrina hesitated. For two years she had thought that her hardness and cynicism were her strength. But as she stared into those clear, open blue eyes she suddenly wondered if her hardness and cynicism were her weakness. Perhaps opening her heart . . . being vulnerable . . . being *human* was true strength. She slammed the thought away and raised her chin a fraction.

"Good evening, Eli. It is too late to use the loom tonight. Come back on the morrow."

Eli looked down, then up again. He shifted his weight from one foot to the other. "*Ja.*" He cleared his throat. "I came for another reason."

"Did you?" Catrina raised an eyebrow. *Of course you did.* She maintained a cold, distant expression.

Eli cleared his throat again. He looked as if he

might pass out from the tremendous effort of standing his ground in front of her. "I wanted to speak with you, if I may." Eli ran his fingers through his hair and the wild red strands stood up even higher from his scalp. "But first, if I could just say how . . ."

He paused and Catrina knew what he would say. He would tell her how beautiful she looked. She was still afraid that was all he saw in her, even after his declaration the other day. It was all any man had ever seen in her before.

Eli took a deep breath and steeled himself. "How bold and statuesque you look. I believe you could keep a pack of wolves from the door if you looked down at them like that."

"How *what?*" Catrina's placid expression cracked. Her eyebrows drew together. She had not expected that.

Eli's face flushed red. He looked like he wanted to sink into the earth. But he swallowed and repeated, "Bold. You look bold, Catrina. Like a . . ." A muscle in his neck twitched from the strain. "A queen."

Heaven help him, I think he really might pass out. Indeed, Eli's face had emptied of color. The blush of embarrassment had disappeared as the blood drained from his cheeks. But he held his ground and stared directly into her eyes. You *are the bold one, Eli Webber, for saying that to me and meeting my eyes.* Catrina hesitated. She liked what he had said. Oh, she liked it very much! She felt the words sink into her chest and melt a tiny corner of her icy heart. No one else had ever complimented her character before. Only her face, her tiny waist, the smooth, porcelain perfection of her skin. *How to respond? How to parry* that?

"A queen?" she said after a moment, and smiled a

smile that gave nothing away. "Of a backcountry cabin?"

Eli laughed. "*Ach*. You make any home a castle." His eyes crinkled at the corners. A genuine smile.

Catrina paused again and let the words settle into her. "You are good with words, Eli. But words are only words. They mean little." She felt her stomach contract as the glimmer faded from his eyes and his expression slackened. He nodded. "I apologize. I haven't much experience with women, truth be told. And I speak before I think. I didn't mean . . ." He sighed and looked away. He couldn't meet her eyes anymore. "I should not have said what I was thinking." Eli looked as if he had been punched in the gut. His entire body sagged.

The heaviness in Catrina's stomach thickened. She had hurt him. And if she had hurt him . . . Well, sweet-talking men whose words meant nothing—they didn't get hurt when a woman rebuffed them. They just flashed a lazy smile, winked, and shrugged. They had nothing invested beyond . . .

Catrina felt her spine stiffen. Could it really be true? He had told her straight out, beneath the stars the night before. He had said that he liked her for *her*. For more than her looks. And as she stared at his contrite expression, his slumped shoulders, she could not help but believe him. At least a little bit. No, more than a little bit. But she could only admit to herself so much. She could only risk so much.

"No need to apologize."

Eli's head shot up. His posture straightened. "Oh. All right. Thank you. I mean. For understanding. I mean . . ." He kicked the doorjamb. "*Ach*. I'm just glad you aren't sore about it." He shrugged. "Look,

Catrina. I'm not a man who is good with words. I just say what I think and hope for the best. I don't know the first thing about how to c—" He cut the sentence short and clamped his mouth shut. His jaw flexed.

What was he going to say? That he does not know the first thing about how to court a woman? Catrina felt a surge of expectation flash through her. Giddiness, almost. *Giddiness?! Oh, for heaven's sake. Calm yourself.* But as much as she tried to clamp down on her emotions, Catrina could not deny that somewhere, deep down, she liked the idea.

She gave a calm, kind smile. "You ought to come in."

"Oh? Really? That would be *wunderbar*. Thank you."

Eli had wanted to die. Well, maybe not die. But cease to exist. Or at least disappear. For a long, long time. He had wanted to sink into the ground as he stood before Catrina and said those ridiculous words. Whatever had possessed him?

But then, a miracle! She had smiled. Smiled! And then she invited him in. Oh yes, she was too good for him. Too statuesque, too confident, too graceful, too *perfect*. And yet, she had invited him in. . . .

Eli tried to tell himself that it meant nothing. But he had seen a spark in her eyes when she smiled at him and asked him inside. Other women shook their heads and dismissed him. Some had even laughed in his face. But Catrina had seen something in him that made her come to life, just a little bit. He had seen her expression shift. She had liked what he had said, even if she did not want to admit it.

Frena and Georg did not look surprised to see him. They both nodded and insisted that he take the three-legged stool by the fire, since there was a chill in the air. Catrina clattered about the hearth behind him. He felt awkward and exposed sitting so close to her. He wanted to turn his head and catch a glimpse of her but he didn't dare. Not after the last time he had been caught staring at her.

Georg made small talk about the weather and the likelihood of a good crop as he rubbed oil into the mule harness with an old rag. Frena set the twig broom aside, picked up her mending basket, and settled onto the bench beside her husband. Eli liked the calm quiet of the cabin. He liked the casual conversation and long stretches of friendly silence. He felt comfortable and welcome.

He heard a swish of skirts, sensed Catrina hovering beside him, and jerked his face upward. She lowered a pewter plate into his hand. "Dried apple pie. I didn't think that I needed to ask."

Eli grinned and balanced the plate on his thighs. The three-legged stool was too short for his legs so he stretched them out and crossed his boots at the ankles. He sighed with contentment. "You are a wonder, Catrina. Dried apple is my favorite."

Catrina found something to do behind his back and he couldn't see her expression. Metal clanged against metal. Kindling scraped against stone and he heard the fire hiss and crackle. Eli bit into the pie and savored the buttery goodness of that crumbly, flaky crust and sweetened, dried fruit. He sighed again. "Best I ever had. I mean it," he said as he dug his fork in for another bite.

Catrina didn't answer and Eli wondered what she was thinking. He wondered what he could say to her that wouldn't sound completely ridiculous. *You look like a queen.* Had he said that? Had he really? Eli frowned and kept eating. Then he remembered the reason—the excuse, really—that had brought him to Catrina's door. He had been so distracted that he had almost forgotten.

Eli set his fork down. The metal clanged too loudly in the quiet room. "Today, after the service, Frena mentioned that—well, I mentioned that I had a lot of work to do, and she said that you had been talking about me—no, not about me. That's not what I meant." Eli cleared his throat. Frena shifted in her seat and kept her eyes on the woolen hose she was mending. "You were discussing my work. And . . ." Catrina did not respond, so he twisted on the stool to catch a glimpse of her behind him at the hearth. She crouched over the fire, staring into the flames with empty eyes. He wondered if she had been listening. She looked deep in thought. Or completely disinterested in anything he had to say. Eli cleared his throat again. He tried to concentrate as he watched the firelight sparkle inside her blue eyes. "I've got too much work on my hands, you understand. You do understand, don't you? That's what—"

"*Ja,*" she said in a clipped, low voice. "I will help."

"Oh!" *That was quick.* "Wonderful good! I knew you hoped to use the loom for yourself some, but to work with me every day—that will be a tremendous help. The orders are already piling up. I met five people today who wanted a good length of wool, or linsey-woolsey, or linen—" Eli cut himself off. He was rambling. He always rambled when he was nervous. Or excited. And he was both right now.

Eli hopped up so fast that he tipped over the stool. "I'll be getting on home then. We'll get an early start." He reached down to right the stool and his fork slid off his plate and clattered to the ground. He bent to pick the fork up at the same time as Catrina and bumped her shoulder. Hard. "*Ach*. Sorry." He grimaced and started to reach for her, then thought better of it and dropped his hand.

Can it get any worse? Eli retreated a step and glanced over at Frena and Georg. They both looked as if they were stifling laughter. Frena coughed and looked back down at the woolen hose she was mending. Georg kept staring.

Oh yes. It could get worse.

Eli refused to meet Catrina's eyes. He had accomplished his mission and now it was time to retreat. Fast. He stumbled to the door, mumbled a quick good-bye, and fled. He made it ten steps before he noticed the night air whipping across his bare head. He groaned, turned on his heels, stalked back to the door, and knocked. He thought he heard laughter cut short, the word *hush* whispered, and then Catrina's clear, soft voice beckoned him to come in. He pushed open the door, grabbed his hat from the hook by the door, and escaped into the safety of darkness, where no one could see him blush from humiliation. He had forgotten to say anything. Should he knock again and explain that he had left his hat? No, they knew that already. They had seen him take it. But should he knock again and say good-bye? No, that would seem ridiculous. Blast it all. This was no way to woo a woman.

The Witmers waited until Eli was sure to be gone—and not reappear again—before they broke into a second round of laughter.

"I like that young man," Georg said, and wiped a tear from his eye. He couldn't stop laughing.

"He isn't like—" Frena cut herself off, then cleared her throat. "He isn't like the others."

"That's for sure," Georg said. He shook his head and set down his oil rag. "He even made our serious Catrina laugh."

"So clumsy," Frena said, and clucked her tongue. "But so genuine. He's not out to impress."

"Not with that performance," Georg said.

"Be nice." Frena cut Georg a look. Georg shrugged and winked at Catrina.

Catrina's face fell back into a somber expression again. She sighed. He had made her laugh, yes. But it had been more than that. It was his earnestness, his eagerness to please. He didn't seem puffed up with himself. He didn't seem sure that he could snag her and show off his catch to his friends. Catrina felt another sliver of her heart begin to melt. Any man who knocked over a stool, dropped a fork, and bumped into her could not be working too hard to impress her. He must be telling the truth about his feelings for her. Either that, or he was the worst seducer in the Americas!

Chapter Eight

Eli knocked on the Witmers' door before the sun rose above the tree line. Georg gave Frena a knowing look as he wolfed down the last bite of his corn cake and headed to the fields for the day. Frena returned the look. Catrina pretended not to notice. But she could not pretend away the stab of anticipation that jolted through her stomach. She smoothed her expression along with her apron and opened the door.

Eli bounded in, all smiles and big hand gestures. He spent the morning making her laugh as they sorted through his supplies, determined what else they needed, and what orders should take priority.

"Abram Ziegler put in a good crop of flax this year," Catrina said when they realized they did not have enough to weave a bolt of linen.

"Did he, now?" Eli's eyes sparkled. "Everything is falling together, isn't it?" Something in his voice caught Catrina's attention. She suspected that he alluded to more than the weaving. His hand brushed over hers as she opened a burlap sack filled with raw wool. Catrina hesitated, then let herself smile. "*Ja.* It's true." Her face heated and she looked away. Catrina knew that she meant more than the weaving too.

A knock at the door startled Catrina and she pulled away from Eli's side. She felt embarrassed and exposed for some reason, even though she had not said anything out of the ordinary. But she knew her heart had meant more. So much more. Catrina straightened her posture and her prayer *kappe* as Frena opened the door. A very sour Gertrud squeezed past Frena without a smile. "Good morning," she announced briskly, and headed straight for her brother. "I've come to take over."

"Oh. Well. Hello. We have it all in hand. But thank you. No need to stay . . ." Eli stumbled over his words, then let them die away as Gertrud maintained that steady stare.

"Even so," Gertrud said. "I've come."

Catrina waited for Eli to argue, but he just sighed a little and shrugged. Gertrud stood over Catrina and waited. Her foot began to tap.

"Oh," Catrina said as she looked up into Gertrud's steady gaze. "You want me to move?"

"*Ja.* That's the idea."

Eli flinched but said nothing and Catrina wondered why he didn't insist that she, Catrina, stay at his side. *No reason to stir up trouble, I suppose.* Catrina nodded and stood. "I need to start on the baking, anyway."

"You understand," Gertrud said without looking at Catrina. "Eli and I have so much to get settled."

Catrina could feel Eli's eyes watching her as she crossed the room. She glanced back at him and noticed the slump in his shoulders. *There's something about Gertrud that he can't stand up to.* Catrina listened to the low murmur of conversation between the siblings as she stoked the fire. Red sparks flared upward. Gertrud kept her voice low and Catrina got the feeling that Gertrud was intentionally trying to shut her out from the conversation. Catrina frowned. *I'll just have to wedge myself back in, then.*

A few moments later, Catrina stood over Eli and Gertrud with three pewter cups of steeped redroot. The steam whispered upward from the hot water and moistened her face as she smiled. "Refreshments."

"Ah!" Eli looked up from his seat and grinned. "*Wunderbar.*"

Gertrud hesitated, then gave a stern nod. "*Danke.*" She continued to rifle through a burlap sack with one hand. "We haven't enough yarn to weave the cloth for Bishop Amos's knee breeches. That's our first order."

Eli blew across the surface of the redroot tea. "It's a good thing that we have a second spinning wheel, then. It will take two spinners, for certain." He jerked his chin toward the spinning wheel in the corner of the cabin. "Catrina can spin a fine thread, I'm sure."

"*Ja.* Catrina is a fine spinner," Frena said from where she sat at the table, snapping peas from the kitchen garden.

"So that settles it," Eli said, and grinned. "Gertrud goes back to our camp and uses our spinning wheel, while Catrina uses this one." He looked at Catrina, then at Frena. "Do you know if anyone else has brought a spinning wheel? It will take a lot of spinning to meet the need here."

Frena shook her head. "Only drop spindles. No one else was willing to haul a spinning wheel through the wilderness."

"Hmmm. Drop spinning is slow going." Eli shrugged. "Well, we will make do the best we can. Anything is better than nothing, I always say." He glanced at Gertrud as she stared into a burlap sack with narrowed eyes. "Best get going, sister mine. I'll be home after supper."

Gertrud's eyes snapped to his face. "Oh, I think not, brother mine."

Eli frowned.

"You can bring my spinning wheel here."

"There is barely room for the loom. How can we squeeze in another spinning wheel? We'll be elbow to elbow."

Gertrud hesitated, as if thinking. Then she smiled. "I am sure that Catrina would like company. And I would get terribly lonely by myself in that camp. Anyway, would you have me work outside in the rain? I think not."

Eli looked disappointed. "Ah. Well. We can't have that, can we?" He rubbed the back of his neck and looked to Georg and Frena. "Can we fit another spinning wheel in? I hate to ask but . . ."

"We haven't a choice," Georg said, and laughed. "The women have spoken."

Gertrud opened her mouth, but a knock on the door stopped her from speaking. She snapped her mouth back into a tight line and continued to ruffle through a burlap sack. Catrina wondered what Gertrud had been about to say, then decided it was better not to know. She rose from the bench and padded across the dirt floor. The room felt too quiet. Gertrud had a way of sucking the comfort from the room and leaving everyone on edge. *She means well. Doesn't she?* Catrina frowned. *Even so . . .*

A bear of a man stood at the threshold when Catrina opened the door. "Why the serious face, darling girl?" he boomed as he grinned widely. His blue eyes crinkled at the corners.

"Abram!" Catrina returned the grin. "We were just talking about you."

"Ah. All good I hope." He raised one eyebrow, then shouted loud enough for the folks inside to hear, "Been gossiping about me, have you, Frena?"

"*Ach!*" Frena shouted back.

"Get in here, man. They've been talking of weaving for two days straight. Give me something—the latest hunt, where the wolf pack last roamed, the health of Jacob Miller's new foal. Anything but this confounded talk about linen and looms!"

The middle-aged man bounded into the cabin. His big-boned frame and bulging stomach made the cabin feel even smaller than it was. Or perhaps it was his energy that filled the air and made the room crackle. "What have you got for me, Catrina, darling? I'm near starved to death." Abram patted his ample midsection.

"Ha! After your last visit, there's nothing left in the larder."

Abram laughed and his tangled, bushy beard shook. "Right you are." He wiped his mouth and dropped onto the three-legged stool in front of the hearth. His massive legs folded up to his chin and made the stool look miniature in size. "I suppose I'll just sit here and wither away then. Can't blame you for denying me a decent meal." He sighed dramatically. "But, a man hates to go hungry."

"Oh, Abram. You are incorrigible!" Catrina shook her head and began to rummage around the hearth. "I've a few cold corn cakes left from breakfast."

"That'll do just fine."

"Indeed it will."

"Don't act so happy to see me."

"Abram. What will we do with you?"

"Set me out to pasture, I reckon. I've one foot in the grave, already. Did I tell you I'm near to fifty years old?"

Catrina laughed. "About fifty times already."

"Don't listen to him," Frena said. She snapped a pea and tossed the husk aside. "He's not a day older than forty-five."

"Which is almost fifty," Abram added.

"*Ach.*" Frena shook her head but her eyes looked merry.

"Now," Abram said, and shifted on the too-small stool. "I am going to have to disappoint you, Georg. There will be more talk of weaving."

Georg shook his head. "Came to discuss your flax, did you?"

"Hmmmm." Abram clapped his hands together and rubbed them. "Let's get down to business, shall we?"

"I saw you at the service yesterday, but didn't get a chance to speak," Eli said. "Eli Webber. And I heard you have flax."

"Indeed I do."

"And we are in need."

"That is what I like to hear."

"The price is—"

"Now, just hold on, young man." Abram jerked his chin toward Gertrud. "Who's this fine young miss?"

"My sister, Gertrud."

Gertrud's face snapped up. Her eyes looked as if a fire had been kindled within them. "Fine young miss?" she asked with an irritated expression.

Abram laughed. "Would you rather I call you a poor old miss?"

Gertrud's nostrils flared. "I would prefer that you do not speak of me at all."

Abram raised an eyebrow. "Not kind to strangers?"

She opened her mouth, closed it, then opened it again, rather like a fish caught out of water. Catrina wondered if anyone had ever stood up to her before.

"Ah, well." Abram turned back to Eli. "Sadly, your sister is not taken by me." He shrugged, but his eyes twinkled. "Just as well, I suppose. Being so popular with the ladies can become tiresome, truth be told."

Eli stared at Abram. He clearly did not know what to say.

Catrina rolled her eyes. "He's joking, Eli. This old bachelor has never had any luck with 'the ladies.'"

"Catrina, you wound me." He looked up at her with a broad, smiling face and rosy cheeks. "Now, where is that corn cake you promised me?"

She passed a wooden trencher to him and a pewter cup of redroot tea.

Abram grinned. "Catrina, you are good to me." He looked over at Frena and Georg. "What will we do when she marries away?"

"I suppose you'll make a nuisance of yourself wherever I live," Catrina answered.

Abram nodded. He did not try to defend himself. His mouth was too full of corn cake. His black, bushy beard shifted up and down as he chewed. Gertrud refused to look at him. She acted as though the contents in the burlap sacks in front of her were intensely fascinating. Abram finished off his food in two big bites, wiped the grease from his beard with his sleeve, and set down the pewter plate with a satisfied sigh. He leaned forward and rested his elbows on his thick knees. "You may not like me, Gertrud. But you will like my flax. Best flax in the backcountry."

"It is the only flax in the backcountry," Catrina said, and laughed.

Abram winked at her. "Even better. No competition." Gertrud did not turn around while Eli and Abram discussed terms. She refused to look at them. But every once in a while Abram glanced at her straight, steely back and his eyes twinkled.

After Eli and Abram shook hands on their business arrangement, Abram tipped his hat, winked at Gertrud, and lumbered out of the cabin. She continued to ignore him. Eli chuckled to himself—not loud enough for Gertrud to hear, of course. He wondered if she had met her match with the jovial frontiersman.

Georg headed to the fields, Frena to tend the kitchen garden, and Eli went to fetch the spinning wheel from their campsite. When he returned, sweating and muttering as he wrestled with the bulky, unwieldy contraption, Catrina met him at the door with a cool cup of water. Eli felt his knees weaken. He forgot that he was frustrated and hot. All he saw were shining blue eyes and that cup of cold, clear water. Nothing ever tasted so good.

Soon, Eli, Gertrud, and Catrina fell into a gentle, familiar rhythm. The loom clacked and whooshed beneath his nimble, calloused fingers while the spinning wheels clattered and whirred. They worked without speaking, but the silence did not feel awkward. Rather, it felt comfortable and friendly, as if they did not need to speak to feel companionship.

That was how Eli and Gertrud often worked—lost in their own thoughts—and Eli liked to see that Catrina fit right into their way of doing things. Already, she almost felt like one of them.

Eli stopped for a moment to study the pattern of the weave. He cracked his knuckles, stood, and stretched. Gertrud rose from her spinning wheel and walked to the loom to see the progress herself. "*Ach.*" She shook her head. "You need to watch your work." She ran a finger over a section of fabric. "See that?"

Eli squinted his eyes and leaned forward. "See what?"

"Should we switch jobs, Eli dear? Perhaps you are overly tired."

Eli frowned. He jammed his hands into his pockets and glared at the cloth, but did not respond. He hoped that Catrina had not heard, but of course she had. Weaving was the one thing he did not mess up on. For goodness' sakes, he could not even walk a straight line without tripping over his own feet. But this—this was where he excelled. He would have liked for Catrina to see that he could do something right. He might not be big and burly and fit for the backcountry. But at least he could make a good living with his hands. At least he was skilled at something!

For just a moment, Eli wondered if Gertrud had *claimed* there was a mistake simply to tear him down in front of Catrina. He pushed the thought away. *Bah. What foolishness. Gertrud is stern and set in her ways, but she would never do that . . . would she?* Oh well, the damage had been done, no matter what the motive. He had been knocked down a peg in front of the lovely Catrina Witmer. *And just when I thought I had regained my dignity after bumping into her twice yesterday.*

The pedal on Catrina's spinning wheel stopped pumping. The soft whir of the wheel died away. Eli turned around as Catrina strode across the room with graceful steps. She offered him a soft smile. Eli rubbed the back of his neck and looked away. He did not want to face her. Catrina leaned over the woven cloth and ran her pale, smooth fingers over it. "Hmmmm. This weave looks perfect to me." She turned to Gertrud and frowned. "Gertrud, dear, perhaps you are in need of spectacles. Eli is a fine weaver. I would say more to compliment his work, but I would not want to tempt him to the sin of pride."

Eli grinned and then turned away when Gertrud glared at him. He coughed to cover up a chuckle. Catrina had defended him. Defended him! Oh, it was too good to be true. He could taste the victory—and it tasted sweet! But then, Eli remembered himself. He looked down at the floor and tried to rein in his emotions. *Be careful. It's easy to forget that you owe Gertie everything. You should not hurt her by siding with Catrina.*

But even his guilt could not steal the sweetness of the moment, or the glimmer in Catrina's eye when he looked back up and their gaze locked.

Catrina clenched her hands into fists to keep herself from saying more. She tried to squeeze all of her emotions into her hands as she tightened them. She forced a placid expression on her face. Sure, it was a small thing. Gertrud had only criticized Eli's work. The siblings were business partners. Perhaps that was the way they did things—inspecting and criticizing the other's efforts. But Catrina had never heard Eli criticize Gertrud. No, Catrina had only heard him speak to his sister softly and patiently. Too patiently, to be honest. She wondered why Eli did not stand up, shake his head, and tell his sister enough was enough.

So Catrina had done it for him. Oh, not too boldly. Just enough to make a stand. Catrina made it sound like a neutral observation, not a challenge. And she had kept that placid expression and soft smile on her face the whole time. She refused to stir up a confrontation. But, at the same time, she would not allow Eli to be torn down in front of her.

Catrina walked back to her spinning wheel with slow, purposeful steps, chin held high. She kept her fists clenched as she struggled not to say anything more. Oh, how she wanted to spit out a clever retort to Gertrud! But she would not. She would maintain her dignity. *She* would be the better person. Even if it killed her!

The spinning wheel began to whir beneath Catrina's hands again. She pumped the pedal in a steady, focused rhythm. The soft, raw wool twisted and formed between her fingers. The smoothness of the material felt calm and familiar against her skin. As her frustration eased and the wool threaded through her fingertips, she began to realize how good it felt to defend Eli.

Catrina stole a glance at him. He sat at the loom with his back to her. She studied the lean, muscular outline of his torso and the gentle sweep of his hands as they flew across the loom. She had never defended a man before. She had never wanted to—never needed to. The men she had known walked with a swagger and spoke in loud, staccato bursts. They were bold, defensive, quick to prove their strength and masculinity.

Not Eli. Eli did not try to prove anything. Catrina

had never heard him raise his voice or square his shoulders as a show of strength. No, he just smiled a knowing smile and looked adorably sheepish.

It was in that moment that Catrina knew for certain that Eli was not like any other man she had known—and certainly not like *him*, the man from Philadelphia she could not bring herself to name. Eli was not trying to impress her, woo her, lead her on until she was his and he could drop her as he wished.

Catrina's spinning wheel stopped clacking and spinning as the certainty hit her. Her hands froze and the wool stopped whirring through her fingers. Eli had proved himself to her. And in the strangest of ways! He had taken his sister's insults like a real man—calmly, with dignity. He did not allow Gertrud to engage him—even in front of the woman he wanted to impress.

And Catrina knew that Eli wanted to impress her. It was written all over him, in the trembling of his hands, the shakiness of his breath, the adoration in his eyes when he stared down into hers. *Well, he did it. He has impressed me.* Her lips curled into a surprised smile as her foot began to pump the pedal again. *Let's see what he does to impress me next.*

Chapter Nine

Eli had a lot to think about. Catrina had stood up for him. What a strange, uncomfortable moment, that had been. And yet . . . Eli had liked knowing that she cared. And she *had* cared. She had marched over and put Gertrud in her place. Well, not *marched*. *Glided* was more like it. She had slid across the room with that regal grace and impossible calm. And then she had spoken in such a respectful, careful manner that no one could accuse her of stirring up strife.

A treasure. She was a treasure.

But what to do about it. Did he dare to hope? Dare to dream? She had defended him, after all.

Eli stoked the campfire and stared into the orange sparks.

"Going to gaze into the fire all day, brother mine?"

Eli sighed and scraped his corn cake crumbs into the flames. "Good morning to you too, Gertie."

Gertrud frowned, then dropped onto the log that Eli had rolled beside the fire as a makeshift bench. "I'm sorry." Her stout, tanned fingers picked at an invisible spot on her apron. "You have to understand."

Eli did not move his gaze from the fire. "Understand what?"

"My concern for you."

"That is what this is?"

"*Ja.* Of course. What else could it be?"

Eli raised an eyebrow, but did not turn to look at his sister. "I don't know . . ." He rubbed his neck with the back of his hand. ". . . Jealousy."

Gertrud's eyes widened into fiery saucers. "Jealous! Ha! You have no idea, baby brother. *No* idea."

Eli wondered if he should ask. He hesitated, poked at the fire again with a stick. A burnt log turned over and released an explosion of sparks into the morning air. "No idea of what?"

"That you are playing with fire."

"I am a grown man, Gertie. I think I can stoke a campfire."

"*Ach.* You know what I mean."

Eli did not want to engage her. He wanted to settle back into his cozy, dreamy thoughts of Catrina, then head across the field and see her smiling face as she opened her cabin door. Today would be a good day. They would work side by side and—

"Well, don't you?"

"What?"

"Know what I mean."

"Oh, that." Eli waved his hand. "It will be all right, Gertie. I won't leave you, if that's what's worrying you." His face hardened into an expression of kind resolve. He turned to look at her straight in the eye. "I have promised you that. And I will keep that promise. I won't leave you."

Gertrud nodded. "Even so . . . you do see that she is all wrong for you, don't you? Surely you do."

Eli turned back to stare into the fire.

"That Christina girl. The one that you met after

the worship service with the sheep. Wasn't she a dear? Much more your type."

"No." He rubbed his eyes. "I mean, I am sure that she is fine—lovely and charming and kind and all of that. But, no. She's not for me."

Gertrud sighed through her nose. "What am I going to do? How can I protect you from yourself?"

"Oh, Gertie. Enough." He spoke gently, softly, but he meant the words. "I can look out for myself."

"You don't know how I would blame myself. I know her—" Gertrud cut herself off and lowered her voice. "I know her type." She glanced behind them, as if *her type* might be lurking in the woods, listening, ready to pounce on the virtuous and upright.

"I don't think you do." Eli's voice was so quiet that Gertrud could barely hear him. But there was unmistakable power in his tone. He was not going to back down.

"I didn't think that anything would come of it. Not until yesterday, when she walked over to the loom and tried to come between us. As if you need defending from me. Your own sister! I have never been so frustrated. She doesn't . . . she doesn't understand how much I care for you." Gertrud swallowed and looked away. She dropped her voice to a whisper. "Sometimes I don't think that you do, either."

"Come here, Gertie." She looked away and did not move. Eli scooted down the log until he reached his sister's small, compact body, which sat rigid and still as a statue. He threw a long arm around her shoulder and pulled her against him. She softened and let him press her into his warm rib cage, but she did not speak. "I told you, it will be all right." He squeezed her and rested his chin atop her prayer *kappe*. "I love you, Gertie. You know that. And I know how much you care. We'll always take care of each other. I promise."

"Then you won't pursue her."

Eli let out a long, hard breath. "That's not fair, Gertie."

Gertrud didn't answer and Eli stood up from the log. "I've got a lot of weaving to do. I need to go."

"Don't make me gossip, Eli. I don't want to. But maybe I should. Just this once."

"Gertie, what are you talking about?"

Gertrud's mouth drew into a tight, colorless line. She hesitated. "I do not want to accuse an Amish sister."

"You've either said too much or too little."

Gertrud shook her head. "I would not have to say *anything* if you would just listen to me. If you would *believe* me."

Eli bent over and put his hand on his sister's shoulder. "I do believe you."

Gertrud's face shot up to his and her expression shifted to surprise and relief.

"But I also believe my feelings," Eli added, his eyes still on hers, hard and unyielding.

Gertrud shrunk back from Eli and shook his hand off her shoulder. Her body slouched and she looked away. "Feelings. What do you know of feelings? Feelings are not real, Eli. They are just that—feelings."

Eli gazed at her profile with a solemn, thoughtful expression. "Even so, Gertie. Even so." And then he turned on his heels and strode away.

He would do something nice for Catrina. He would do something to show her how much he cared. Eli stopped in the middle of the field and took in the blue flowers and wild grasses that swayed in the warm spring breeze. Every time the settlers cleared land, hardy weeds shot up to reclaim the earth. Eli sent up a prayer of thanks to *der Herr* that he did not have to farm the land. He was fortunate to have been apprenticed as a child in Germany to a master weaver. True, it had been a bleak, tiresome childhood, but whose hadn't been? Life had not been easy in the Rhine River Valley.

But here, in the new world—in New Canaan—life was whatever one made it. There were no roaming soldiers, no corrupt tax collectors, no rules to keep his people under anyone's thumb. And, because of his sacrifices as a child, he could make a living without toiling beneath an unforgiving sun. He said a prayer for his mother's soul, grateful that she had had the foresight to send him away, even though the separation had been almost unbearable for them both.

He had returned home a man, ready to make a good, honest living for himself. But, times were troubled and uncertain, especially for the Amish. Wars and rumors of wars . . . their corner of Germany was no place for an outcast religious sect to thrive, not when everyone around them wanted a scapegoat. Amish lands were seized, Amish sons pressed into military service, despite their pacifist beliefs. It was no way to live, uncertain and insecure, wondering when the next battle would spill over into their green valley.

And so, Eli and Gertrud had left their home forever to take their chances in the New World, where it was said a man could live free if he worked hard enough for it. They had arrived six years before most Amish began to arrive. And now, Eli knew that he had come to the right place at the right time. Catrina had confirmed that to him. She was everything he had ever dreamed of. If only she felt the same way about him . . .

Eli remembered the blue of her eyes and that they matched the blue flowers surrounding him. He would take her a bouquet and tell her. He would tell her everything. But, once the bundle of wildflowers filled his arms, the gesture felt contrived and shallow. He sighed. Many, many men must have made silly, shallow attempts to woo Catrina. Flowers were the first thing those men would have thought to give. She would not be impressed. She would see him as one more in a long line of silly, shallow men.

Eli opened his arms and let the flowers drop to the ground. He took off his black beaver-felt hat, ran his fingers through his red hair, and replaced his hat. The flowers looked sad and crumpled in the dirt. *What does Catrina love? What matters to her?*

A thought snapped through him and he smiled. Sugar. Catrina loved sweets. He remembered when she made the apple pudding she had snuck a taste of sugar and her face had glowed as she bit into the soft white crystals. She had not known that he was watching her. But he had seen. And he could not forget the joy in her eyes in that moment.

He had white sugar. Well, he and Gertrud did. He wouldn't take it all. He would leave half for his sister and take half for Catrina. That was a gift worth far more than the wildflowers that grew just outside her door. Anyone could pick weeds from a field. But sugar! Sugar was a rare and glorious commodity.

Eli doubled back to his campsite. Gertrud squatted over the iron spider, scrubbing the surface with pebbles to clean the baked-on grime.

"Hello, there," Eli said.

Gertrud gasped and jumped. Eli laughed.

"You startled me!" Gertrud said as she sat back on her heels. "You did that on purpose!"

"I said hello."

"Exactly."

Eli laughed again and their eyes met. Gertrud shook her head, then laughed. "All right. You got me." She went back to scrubbing, then wiped her hands on her apron and sighed. "Can't get it clean. I wish we had some sand."

Eli looked at his sister's cracked red hands and frowned. "Try the creek bed," he said.

She nodded, wiped her hands again, and stood. "I need to fetch water anyway."

"Here." Eli lifted the heavy yoke and settled it on his sister's shoulders. A wooden bucket dangled from each end. "I wish you would let me."

"I might be half your size, but I can certainly manage to haul a few buckets of water." She shrugged to settle the yoke into a more comfortable position.

"I don't like to see you work so hard."

Gertrud waved her hand. "*Ach.* I'm not an invalid." She started to walk away, then stopped and turned. "What are you doing back here, anyway?"

"I forgot something."

"Oh."

Eli waited a few beats, wondering if Gertrud would ask what he had forgotten. He would tell her if she asked, of course. But if she didn't ask . . . well, there was no sense stirring up trouble that did not need to be stirred up. Half the sugar was his to do with as he liked. And if he wanted to go for the next six months drinking redroot tea without sweetener, that was his choice.

Gertrud only shrugged and turned back toward the woods. "I will be at the Witmers' later," she said as she walked away. "There is much to do here first."

Catrina opened the door and smiled. "Good morning. I've already spun—"

Eli nodded solemnly and cut her off. "Good. Very good. Thank you. I . . ." The words trailed away and he paused.

Catrina cocked her head to the side. "Eli, whatever is the matter?"

He forced a wobbly smile. "Nothing. I . . ." He reached out his hand and tried to pass her a burlap pouch tied with a length of twine. "Here."

She reached for the pouch and Eli let go of it a moment too soon. The package tumbled to the ground, bounced off his brown leather boot, and lay still. Eli laughed nervously. "*Ach.* Sorry." He took a step toward the pouch and accidently kicked it farther away. "Oh. Well. That's not what I meant to do."

Catrina laughed. Eli did not meet her eyes when he straightened back up to his full height and pushed the pouch into her hands. This time he held it there for a moment too long, just to make sure her soft, smooth fingers gripped it tightly. He nodded and took a step back. "There you go."

"What is this?" She felt a jolt of excitement. The weight, the size, the way the contents gave way beneath her fingers . . . could it be? She glanced up at Eli and he allowed his eyes to meet hers.

"I hope you like it."

Her eyes sparkled as she fumbled at the string until the knot gave way.

"Careful," Eli said. "Not that I have any authority to warn someone else to be careful, but it is—"

"Oh, Eli!" Catrina shouted, and threw her arms around his neck. She had to jump to reach him, but she felt so excited that she leaped high enough. It was sugar. Sugar! Enough to bake three cakes, or five puddings, or to sweeten their tea for months to come. "How did you know?" His shoulders felt warm and hard beneath the soft flesh of her arms. She could feel his breath run down the back of her neck. He stood without moving, frozen in place as she squeezed her arms around him and held on tight. Her feet dangled above the ground like a child. And suddenly, she realized how very foolish she was being.

"Sorry. I didn't mean . . ." She let go of his neck and slid back to the ground. Her feet landed on the dirt with a quiet thud. She looked down and straightened her prayer *kappe*, then smoothed the front of her gray bodice. "It's just that I do love sugar."

"I know you do." His voice sounded kind and warm, and edged with hope.

Catrina let her eyes rise to his. "You noticed?"

He gave a crooked little smile as he jammed his hands into his pockets. He was having trouble meeting her eyes. "Of course I did." He swallowed. "I notice things about you. What you like, what you don't like." He hesitated and rubbed the back of his neck with his hand. "How special you are."

Catrina felt as if she could hug him again. She

wouldn't, of course. She had been friendly enough for one day. Scandalously so. But, she wanted to. Oh, how she wanted to feel the warmth of his smile and his safe, strong arms again! He had noticed *her*! Not how she looked, but her personality. And he liked her for who she was. Some people thought that she spent too much time baking and not enough time doing practical, down-to-earth work, like weeding the kitchen garden, or cleaning the oil lamps, or making lye soap from ashes. But those jobs were so tedious, so meaningless. She was good at baking. She enjoyed baking. And most of all, she enjoyed eating what she baked!

Eli enjoyed the rest of the day. He savored every moment that he sat near Catrina, listening to the clack and whir of her spinning wheel behind him. Occasionally, he found an excuse to turn around and speak to her, or walk past her and meet her eye. Her smile gave him a bolt of energy that kept his hands flying over the loom until evening.

Gertrud came to the cabin and spun for part of the day, then headed home early to cook supper over the campfire. At the end of his workday, Eli swung his arms as he strode across the field toward the fire that glowed in the evening shadows. He took off his hat and let the wind whip through his hair. It had been a good day. A very good day.

He could not stop grinning as he wandered into their campsite and dropped onto the log by the fire. Gertrud stood facing the fire as she wiped her hands on her white apron. Eli leaned back on his hands and let out a long, contented sigh. "How are you, Gertie?"

Her back stiffened.

Uh-oh.

"How am I?" Gertrud turned around slowly. "How *am* I?"

Eli's grin evaporated. "That's what I asked."

"How do you think I am? I went to fetch a measure of sugar for stewed apples, and what did I find?" Her eyes narrowed. "What did I find, Eli?"

"My half is gone."

"Why? Why on earth?" She pointed a stubby finger at him. "I know you have a sweet tooth, but this is absurd! I needed your half to cook for us both!"

"I didn't think about that. I just figured I'd go without."

Gertrud's face jerked. "You figured . . . you mean you didn't . . ." Her mouth and eyes opened wide, then slammed shut. "Oh no. No, no, no. Please tell me you didn't, Eli."

"I did."

"You didn't eat it. You gave it away."

"*Ja.*"

"To *her.*"

"I am sorry, Gertie." He looked away from her and into the orange flames. "I just figured it was mine to do with as I liked."

"*Ja.* I suppose it was. I just thought . . ." She shook her head. "I can't cook the things you like anymore. We are going to run out twice as fast now."

"It's all right, Gert."

"Don't call me that. You know I hate that name."

"*Ach.* It's cute."

"No, it is not."

"All right, Gertie. It'll be fine."

"But why, Eli? Why would you do such a thing? Don't you know how much sugar is worth out here, in the middle of nowhere, where there is none to be had?"

"*Ja.*" Eli sighed. Despite Gertie's ruffled feathers, he still felt like smiling inside. "That's why I did it."

And then, Gertrud did something that Eli had never seen her do before. She burst into tears. Eli jumped up from the log. He reached for her, then let his hands drop. What had he done? He had not meant to make his sister cry. Not after all he owed her. Not after . . .

He felt miserable. As miserable as he had been happy just moments before. What kind of man was he, making his own sister cry? He took off his hat, tossed it aside, and ran his fingers through his hair. He took a step toward her, then stopped. He did not know what to do. The last time she had cried was that terrible, terrible day four years ago when she had lost what was dearest to her. She had not cried since then. Not one time. She had become hard and distant and careful with her emotions. And he couldn't blame her. He could only blame himself. It had all been his fault.

"Oh, Gertie." His voice lowered and softened, as if he were talking to a child. "I am so sorry. I didn't mean to hurt you. I didn't mean . . ." He did not know what to say. He was not even sure why she was crying. Because he had taken his half of the sugar? That did not make sense. She had always been stoic. She had often gone without luxuries before.

Gertie squeezed her eyes shut and pulled up the

bottom of her apron to cover her face. She pressed the white linen cloth against her skin, hiding the tears.

"Gertie. I am so sorry."

Her head shook from behind the apron. She looked comical, like a child playing beneath a bedsheet, and if the circumstances had been different, he would have laughed. He did not.

"You don't understand."

Eli swallowed and stared at the outline of her nose and chin beneath the damp apron. "You think I am upset about the sugar. I don't care about the sugar!" Her voice rose to a wail.

"Oh. All right then. It's not the sugar. What is it, Gertie?" Had something happened that he did not know about? Had someone died? Had something terrible happened?

"It's because you have fallen for her. I have been so afraid of this. And now . . . giving her all that sugar. You love sugar! You love sweets!" Her head shook beneath the apron. "You would not have done such a thing if you were not completely taken by her."

Eli stared at her. What could he say to that? Why should he deny it? He flexed his jaw, torn between protecting his sister to whom he owed everything, and living the life he wanted to live. "I am so sorry that it hurts you, Gertie. But you are right. I have fallen for her. And I think . . . I think she might feel the same about me. At least I hope she does."

"No!" She tore the apron from her face. "Don't you see, Eli! Please, please tell me that you see!"

He shook his head, lost.

"She is not who you think she is." Her red, swollen

eyes bored into his. "She isn't the . . . girl that you imagine her to be. I know, Eli. I *know!*"

Eli swallowed. He felt a cold pain sweep through his body and settle in his chest. His words came out slow and steady and purposeful. "I do not want to hear what you think you know, Gertrud." His teeth clenched as he fought to maintain a calm, even tone. "I do not want you to say another word. Not unless you want to damage our relationship—yours and mine—forever."

"I love you, Eli. I'm your older sister. It's my duty to protect you."

"It is your duty not to succumb to gossip. I don't know what you think you know. But it can't be true and I won't listen to it. And you won't tell me, Gertrud. If you love me then you will never tell me because I never want to hear lies about the woman I love."

The woman I love. Had he said that out loud? Yes, he had. And it felt good. It felt right.

Gertrud raised her chin. Her lips quivered. A single tear slipped from her eye and slid down the hard plane of her cheekbone. She swallowed and kept a steady gaze on her brother. She said nothing.

Eli did not know what to do. His heart sang with the realization that he loved Catrina. He did not just like her, it was not just affection that he felt for her. He loved her. Truly and fully, as he had never loved another woman.

But, at the same time, he had torn apart his sister's heart. The one person to whom he owed his complete loyalty. After what had happened . . . After what he had done four years ago. He took a deep breath and let it out slowly. Gertrud still did not speak. She just kept staring at him, her face crumpled with hurt. Eli lowered his eyes first. He bent to pick up his beaver-felt hat, jammed it onto his head, and stalked into the dark woods. He needed to be alone.

He had no idea what he was going to do.

Chapter Ten

Catrina flitted around the table, humming tunes from the *Ausbund*.

"I have never seen anyone so taken by a bag of sugar before," Frena said with a wry smile.

"I told you that I liked that young man," Georg said as he pulled on his black leather boots. "How about making another apple pudding today? I think that would be just about perfect."

"You only like Eli because he gave us more sugar, right when we were about to run out."

Georg raised an eyebrow. "Should I *not* like him for that?"

"*Ach*. Grandfather!" Catrina smiled and pressed her hand into the dough that lay on the rough wooden table. She had to finish kneading the week's bread before she could begin the day's spinning. Eli had several new orders and the spinning wheel would need to turn day and night to keep up with demand.

"Don't forget your scoop," Catrina shouted to Frena as the woman headed out to help Georg with the spring planting.

"Right. Thank you, dear. I never remember these things." Frena plucked the straw hat from its hook on the wall, pushed it onto her head, and tied the ribbons beneath her chin. The straw bill scooped downward where the ribbons pulled it, giving the hat its distinctive name.

"That's why Catrina has perfect skin," Georg said. "She never forgets to wear a hat over her prayer *kappe* to keep out the sun."

"Are you saying that I don't have perfect skin, Georg Witmer?" Frena asked with a stern face.

"Ah. Well. It goes without saying that you have perfect skin, of course."

Frena winked at Catrina and Catrina laughed. "Are you sure you don't need me to help?" Catrina worried that her grandparents were getting too old for the heavy labor the backcountry required. "No," Frena said. "Take care of the baking, then spend the day spinning. That's the best way to help us all. You'll do more good for the family working with Eli then you would in the fields with us."

"All right. If you're sure."

"Of course we are sure."

"Just make certain I get a new waistcoat," Georg said as he loped through the threshold. "And new knee breeches," he added. "And a new dress jacket and woolen hosen."

"Georg!" Frena swatted him as he passed her. She turned back to Catrina and smiled wistfully. "It is what we love, you know. Being outside, working our own land. Being free."

Catrina nodded.

"But it isn't for everyone. It isn't for you. We know that. You were meant for other things."

"I worry that you work too hard," Catrina said. When they had first arrived, she had not realized how hard her grandparents worked. She had been so overwhelmed by her new life that she could barely function. But now . . . she could see and appreciate their sacrifices. And she wished that she were more like them, more able to cope with the rigors of the frontier. They seemed truly happy to work the land.

"Don't worry, Catrina. And don't ever feel bad about the way *der Herr* made you." It was as if Frena knew her granddaughter's thoughts. "You were not made for the farm. You could never take to it. Georg and I, we love it. It is all we've ever known. We could never settle down in the city the way your mother did when she married your father." She shrugged. "One day we will be too old to work the land. But that day has not come yet. And when it does . . . well, when it does you will do well enough with your weaving to support us all. I am sure of it. So do not doubt yourself. Get the baking done, get to your spinning, and know that you are doing the right thing. For all of us."

Eli seemed more distracted than usual when he and Gertrud arrived to do the day's weaving and spinning. When he smiled and nodded at Catrina, his eyes held the same twinkle, the same adoration, but his jaw was set in a most determined manner and his face dropped into seriousness too soon. He and Gertrud barely spoke. Of course, Gertrud was not one for amicable small talk, but today they did not even talk about their work. They just sat elbow to elbow without turning to look at each other. It was almost as if they were pretending not to notice each other. Which was ridiculous in a one-room cabin crammed full with Georg and Frena's bedstead, Catrina's pallet, a wooden table, two benches, a three-legged stool, a loom, and two spinning wheels. Not to mention the cauldron, iron spider, and sacks of food-stuffs that filled the hearth, or the dried herbs that hung from the rafters. No, it was preposterous to pretend that one could not see someone else in that crowded, dirt-floored room.

They worked with the door and shutters open so that sunlight and fresh air filled the cramped space. The weather was warm enough that Catrina had already taken down the oilcloth that covered the windows during the winter. In warm weather, the oil would soften and drip until it left greasy streaks down the log wall. Worse, oilcloth only let a soft glow of light inside the cabin and turned the outside world into a mysterious blob of color. Finally, after the long, dreary winter, she could see outside again!

Yellow light danced across the white wool as Catrina threaded it through the spindle and listened to the steady *clickety clack* of the spinning wheels and the *click thump whoosh, click thump whoosh* of the loom. The air felt fresh and new as she breathed in the smells of damp earth and wild grass that drifted inside. She almost felt content. *Almost.* There was that troubling furrow in Eli's brow today and that trou-bling, stifling silence.

After Eli's gift, Catrina had thought that he would have bounded into the cabin today, all smiles and boyish exuberance. She *had* let him know how much she had appreciated the sugar, hadn't she? He did know that she had been taken in by it—by him, if she were completely honest. Didn't he? There had been that scandalous hug . . . she had been giddy in his arms, positively giddy! She had felt so right, so at home in his arms . . . well, it did not deserve further thought. She must maintain *some* dignity.

She had thanked him, hadn't she? She had let him know that she appreciated the thoughtfulness of the gift, and not just the gift itself. Or had she? Catrina ran through the encounter in her mind as the wool sped through her fingers and her foot pumped the treadle. She could not remember the details, only the joy she had felt when she realized that he had noticed something about her beyond her looks. And of course, she remembered the feeling of security that his strong arms had given her . . . but she had already determined not to dwell on that.

What if he was worried that she did not appreciate his thoughtfulness? What if he was worried that she did not care?

The wool twisted in her fingers and she stopped pumping the treadle. Bother, she would have to unwind that—her mind was elsewhere. *Do I care about him? Do I really, truly care?* She replayed her interactions with Eli as she fumbled to unwind the length of botched yarn. She remembered the way he looked at her—as if he had never seen anyone quite like her before. She was not just another woman to him. His eyes spoke the truth about that. She remembered the way he fumbled and tripped over himself whenever he felt nervous—which was every time he spoke to her. She remembered the way his face had become soft and serious when he stood outside beneath the purple evening sky and announced that he saw more to her than her beauty.

Her breath caught in her throat and she started to pump the treadle again to hide the sound of her surprise. She *did* care. She really, truly did. But it was more than that. She felt something deeper. Something real and lasting that she had never felt before. She was not drawn to Eli for looks, or rugged toughness, or sly, dark charm. He was good-looking—in his own boyish way—but he had no rugged toughness. And he certainly had no sly, dark charm. There was no slyness in him. No darkness. And his charm came from an honest heart, not practiced flirtations and calculated words. It was an unintentional charm—the charm of a man simply being himself. And when a man is caring, and thoughtful, and honest, there is no greater charm.

Catrina felt a stab shoot through her chest and zip all the way down to her toes. She leapt up from the spinning wheel and nearly toppled the stool. She did not just care about Eli; she loved him. She *loved* him! She had found him. She had finally found the man who would love her for who she was, who would never pretend to be someone other than he was, who would always appreciate her for who she was in return.

The loom shuttered to a sudden stop and Eli spun around in his seat. He looked startled and concerned. "Catrina, are you all right?"

Catrina swallowed. She stared at him and blinked. Was she all right? *Was she all right?* Oh, she was more than all right. She was wonderful. She had found him. And he was right here, in front of her, concerned that she was unwell. If only he knew. If only . . . well, she would have to tell him. But not now. Not in front of Gertrud . . .

"Catrina?" Eli's brow furrowed more deeply than it had all morning. He stood up. "Are you unwell?"

Catrina realized that she was standing and staring

in a most unbecoming manner. She forced herself to close her open mouth—had she really allowed it to hang open so foolishly?—and adjusted her prayer *kappe*. "*Ja.* I am fine. I . . . just realized something."

Eli's face remained serious and concerned, but he hesitated, unsure. After a moment, he nodded and slipped back into his place at the loom.

He does not know if he should approach me. He is not sure of how I feel about him. But he will. Oh, he most certainly will!

Eli watched Catrina as she stumbled out of the cabin and into the bright afternoon sun. He sat at the loom without moving, studying her as she stood just outside the door. The light set her crisp white prayer *kappe* and white apron aglow. She leaned her shoulder against the doorframe and inhaled deeply, then exhaled. She closed her eyes to the sun. Was that a faint smile on her lips?

What on earth had come over her? He had been sure that she would faint. Her face had looked shocked, as if she had had a terrible, unsettling thought. Or perhaps she had taken ill. He rubbed the back of his neck with a calloused palm. Would she be all right? His mind sped ahead to a dreadful conclusion— Catrina wasted away on her sickbed, until the life ebbed out of her. There was not a doctor closer than a three-days' journey in any direction. And even if there were, what would he do? Bleed the poor girl until she weakened even more? Doctors were ghastly, really.

Eli frowned. *Oh, for heaven's sakes.* He was not accustomed to entertaining such dramatic thinking.

Catrina would be fine, of course. Why wouldn't she be? He was the one whom he should be worried about. What on earth had come over *him* to make him worry so?

An overwhelming need to keep Catrina Witmer in his life, that's what.

Eli's frown deepened. Catrina would be fine. But he wouldn't be. He was pining away for her—thinking about her every moment, obsessing over what he would say for hours before he spoke to her, eaten up with the need to know *exactly* how she felt about him.

Eli watched as Catrina drifted away from the doorway and disappeared beyond his view. The problem, if he was willing to face it, had become far more complicated than whether or not she had developed affection for him. The greater problem was that Gertrud could not be persuaded to open her heart to Catrina. She would not even entertain the *idea* of Catrina in his life.

He wondered if other brothers suffered at the hands of demanding sisters. No, probably not. Other brothers had not made such terrible, terrible mistakes that they now owed their sisters everything—which then forced the brother to sacrifice his own happiness.

"She's fine, Eli," Gertrud muttered. Her spinning wheel had not stopped turning. "Just a touch of the vapors." The wheel clacked. "Brought on by a need for attention, if I dare to say it."

"You don't know that."

Gertrud raised an eyebrow. Her hands did not slow. She did not seem distracted in the least. "That is why I introduced you to Christina. She would not succumb to a distracting episode of the vapors in

hopes that you would go running to rescue her."
Gertrud sighed through her nose. "How very vexing.
That wool will not spin itself." She nodded her chin
to Catrina's spinning wheel while her hands and foot
maintained their steady rhythm.

"You think she wants me to go after her? You think
that she set that up for me? For attention?" A stab of
hope speared through Eli's chest. His face must have
shown his feelings because Gertrud's mouth turned
downward and she shook her head. He jumped up
from the loom. *She* wanted attention from *him*!

"That is not what I meant."

Eli grinned. "But it is what you said."

Gertrud did not speak for a few beats. Her lips
stayed in a tight line. "Do as you like, Eli. But remember that I have asked you—no, pleaded with you to
be cautious. If you go barreling after her right now,
I . . ." For the first time that day, Gertrud's spinning
wheel slowed. The steady rhythm faltered. "I won't be
able to bear the worry. Knowing what I know."

Eli ran his fingers through his hair. His heart
pounded against his throat. Everything in him
shouted that he must follow Catrina. He wanted to
rush after her, scoop her into his arms, and tell her
he loved her. Yes. Loved. He knew that his feelings
for her had grown deeper than mere affection, and
far, far deeper than a passing fancy. He had never,
ever felt this way about a woman before. He would go
after her. He had to.

And yet, he sat back down. Not because he wanted
to. Everything in him still shouted, pleaded with
him to storm outside and gallantly sweep her off
her feet—he could lift her off the ground and twirl
her around, her face outlined by the bright blue sky,

her skirts swishing around him like the feathers of a bird—he cut off the thought. He could not rush after her. Not with Gertrud sitting beside him, pleading the opposite.

And he owed his sister a debt that he could never repay. Even sacrificing the woman he loved would not be enough to make up for what he had done. So he sat on the bench in front of the loom and made no move to leave. He stared at the threads. He swallowed. He felt as if his heart would tear from his body. His hands trembled and he laid them flat against the loom's wooden crossbeam.

Gertrud let out a heavy breath of air. "Thank you, Eli."

He did not answer. He just kept staring at the threads in front of him.

"You are a good brother."

"No," he said in a voice almost too low for his sister to hear. "You know that I am not."

The room felt stifling. The air crackled with unspoken words. Still, Eli did not move. The spinning wheel kept turning, but more slowly, the rhythm broken and uncertain. "Today you have shown me that you are."

Eli's eyes shut. He wanted it to go away. All of it. The guilt, the weight of the past, the memory of Gertrud's face the day he had told her what had happened. What he had done. He clenched his eyes harder, but it did not go away. It never did.

He wanted to tell his sister that she didn't know anything about Catrina. No matter what she claimed to have heard. But he did not. He would not argue with her about that again. He would not make Gertie cry twice in as many days. Not when she had not shed a single tear in four long years. What was wrong with him? What kind of man makes his grieving sister cry?

And yet. In that moment he could barely manage to maintain his duty to her. In his mind, in his heart, he was outside, running toward Catrina, his arms outstretched, ready to pull her to him and tell her that he loved her.

He sighed and pushed away the dream. His hand closed around the shuttle and slid it between the threads. He pulled down the beater and pushed the treadle with his foot. He would do what Gertrud wanted. He would do his duty.

Eli told himself that it was for the best. He told himself that Catrina might not even care for him, anyway. How could she? He slid the shuttle back through the threads and pulled down the beater a little too hard. He was not a man who deserved to be loved. Especially by a woman like Catrina. She was probably just humoring a silly, clumsy, heart-struck man who dared to hope for something out of his reach. That made him love her even more. She was kind. She was thoughtful, even to him. She could not possibly feel any affection for him.

He almost believed that. Almost.

Chapter Eleven

Eli had made a decision. It was the only decision he could make. He would have to forget all about Catrina. What else could he do?

Oh, sure, he could break his sister's heart again. He had been the one to break it four years ago. She had crumbled because of what he had done. She had lost her husband and her son. She had never been the same again.

No, there was no choice. He would do his duty. He would give up his feelings for hers. He did wonder, briefly, if this choice might hurt Catrina. What if she *had* begun to fall for him? She had seemed so enamored of that gift of sugar. Her eyes had sparkled and she had leapt into his arms—no, he mustn't entertain dangerous, painful thoughts.

What were the chances that she had fallen for him, anyway? He was not the type of man that women—much less *Catrina Witmer*—fell for. Telling himself this helped take the edge off the longing. She would find someone better suited to her. Someone who was free to love her. Someone who deserved her. Whoever it was, that man would be strong and tough and unyielding. He would be able to wrestle down a wolf pack with his bare hands and build a stout log cabin without any help—just the sweat of his brow and the power of his own biceps. Eli was not that man.

Would that man be kind, though? Would he consider Catrina's feelings? Her needs, her fears, her dreams and hopes? Eli frowned and jammed his hands into his pockets. He slouched as he stalked back to his campsite. Why was he imagining Catrina's future husband? What foolishness. What nonsense. She would find the right man for her. And of course he would be handsome and dashing and rugged. And if he was not thoughtful, well, that could not be helped. That was not Eli's problem. It couldn't be. He had Gertrud to consider.

He always had Gertrud to consider. What he would give to be free. He pushed away the desire. It was his fault that he was in this situation. His fault. If he had not made that terrible mistake then, Gertrud would have a four-year-old child by now, maybe a new baby as well. She would have a devoted husband, her own home and hearth. Yes, he had made his bed and now he must lie in it.

Gertrud was already at the campsite when Eli arrived. She usually left her spinning an hour before Eli quit weaving so that she could get supper for them both. He did not know how to react when he saw her. She looked peaceful and satisfied. Relieved. He had made her happy.

He just wished that making Gertrud happy did not make him so unhappy.

"You've put in a good day today," Gertrud said as Eli approached.

"*Ja.*"

"I . . ." Gertrud frowned and stirred the cauldron

that hung above the fire. Eli wondered what was inside. Some sort of watery stew. "I know that you did the right thing today," she said after a moment's hesitation. "And I know you did it for me." She looked at him. "Thank you."

Eli nodded. His chest felt heavy. Was this what it felt like to do the right thing?

Gertrud took a step toward him and stared into his eyes. She put a hand on his sleeve in a pleading, hopeful gesture. "But you did not just do it for me. You did it for yourself. Because this is what is best for *you*. I promise."

Eli just stared back at her. He knew if he said anything it would only start another quarrel.

Gertrud's hand tightened on the sleeve of his black coat. "You *have* decided not to pursue her, haven't you? When you refused to go after her—that meant something, didn't it?"

Eli swallowed. But the lump in his throat did not go away. "*Ja*. I won't pursue her. Not when it hurts you so much."

Gertrud closed her eyes and exhaled. "It hurts me because it would hurt you, Eli. I promise you. It would have hurt you to pursue her."

He nodded again, but his lips stayed in a tight line. He wished that he believed her. It would be so much easier if he could. "I think I'll take a walk."

Gertrud's expression quivered. She did not let go of his sleeve. "You'll be thankful one day, Eli. Trust me. You have saved yourself a bitter future."

Eli released a long, slow breath. He gently extracted his sleeve from her clenched fist.

"Your supper's ready. It isn't much, but I tried to make what you like."

Eli nodded. He tried to smile, but it came out as more of a grimace. "It'll keep."

Gertrud watched as he stalked away and disappeared into the woods. She did not call after him.

Many men were afraid of the woods. And with good reason. They hid all manner of hungry, creeping beasts well armed with teeth and claws. Or, even without the beasts to worry about, one could get lost in the vast, old growth wilderness. Trees as wide as four men standing abreast towered into a distant sky, covered by a silent canopy of leaves and needles.

But, Eli was not one of those men. He had never been afraid of the vast silence or the animals that stalked the damp shadows of the forest floor. Eli savored the solitude and beauty. Even so, he should have brought his musket. Ah, well. If he met a bear, so be it. He was feeling rather too fatalistic this evening. But it wasn't every day that one decides to put a clamp on one's heart for the sake of duty.

He briefly wondered if there could be any truth to Gertrud's warnings. Bah. Not *his* Catrina. Or rather, not Catrina. He had already determined that she could not be *his* Catrina. She was pure and perfect and beautiful, inside and out. Like the purple evening sky that he could just make out through the dark silhouette of the leaves above him. *Oh, for heaven's sake. What foolishness.* He had to stop thinking of her.

That was impossible, of course.

Eli jammed his hands in his pockets and stalked deeper into the forest. There was no path, but the canopy was thick enough that very little could grow beneath its shadow, so the forest floor stayed clear. A wolf howled in the distance. The eerie, otherworldly shriek made the hair stand up along the back of his neck, even though Eli knew there was little to fear. Wolves did not hunt humans, not unless they were rabid or starving. The Old World tales of bloodthirsty wolf packs were quite unfair, really. Still, he should have brought his musket.

Eli sighed and had started to turn for home when he heard the shout. No, it was a scream. A woman's scream. He jumped a good foot into the air at the sound. Everything in his body tensed. His stomach constricted into a cold, hard knot. Someone was in danger. There was not time to go for his musket. He began to run.

Catrina had tried to concentrate after her realization that she loved Eli. But how could one concentrate with such thoughts on one's mind? Even worse, Eli made no move to speak to her—or even look at her—for the rest of the day. How very vexing.

Well. She would find a way to get his attention. That was the least of her problems. The real problem lay with Gertrud. It was clear the woman did not care for Catrina. No. It was worse than that. Far worse. Gertrud did not *approve* of Catrina.

Did Gertrud know?

Catrina had tried to keep that question from her mind all day. It was a terrible, pointless question. If Gertrud did know, there was nothing that Catrina could do about it. Which, of course, made it even worse. The powerlessness that Catrina felt was altogether unbearable. She could not change what she had done in Philadelphia. And she certainly could not change who knew about it. Many people had heard. But, how hopeful she had been that no one here, in this isolated wilderness, would have caught wind of it. Oh, the scandal. The humiliation!

Once Eli left for the day—after barely nodding a hasty good-bye to her—Catrina had decided to call on a friend. She needed a distraction. She wished that she could tell Greta or Christina everything. But that, of course, could not happen. She would keep her secret a secret, as one must. But, at least she could settle in for a chat and even a good laugh. Friends always made one feel better, even when they did not know what was wrong.

Catrina had promised her grandparents to be home before evening chores and had slipped out with her wool cloak and a clean, fresh apron. She had decided to walk to the Miller cabin, and perhaps stop by Christina's on the way. Perhaps she would check on the sheep. She did have a vested interest in their welfare now, after all.

Really, it did not matter what she did. She had just wanted a distraction. So, when the footpath wound by Christina and Hilda's place, Catrina had picked her way down the sloped ground and into their dirt yard. Hilda kept the dirt neatly swept. Catrina certainly approved of the tidiness. She had lifted her skirts to avoid the damp dirt and a territorial hen, strode across the clearing, and knocked on the door. No one had answered. *Well, they might be around back, minding the livestock,* Catrina had thought.

She had wandered around the back of the house to the sheep pen. For the most part, settlers fenced in their kitchen gardens and fields and let their animals run free. They kept their animals *out*, rather than *in*. But sheep were different. Sheep were helpless, pitiful creatures that would skip right into a wolf's gaping jaws. So Christina and Hilda penned them in at night, then set them free to graze during the day.

Catrina had frowned when she scanned the backyard. Something felt wrong. The evening felt too still, too silent. As if something waited, just out of sight. The sheep seemed to feel it too. They were restless and afraid. They bleated and pushed against one another in anxious, nervous motions. Where were Christina and Hilda? And where was their old sheepdog?

Catrina heard a rustle at the tree line. She froze and squinted into the shadows. The evening sun had dropped beyond the ridge and darkness filled the spaces between trees like a heavy fog. That darkness was creeping closer. Soon, the entire clearing would be plunged into the black of night. She glanced upward. The sky had bruised to a soft purple. It was later than she had realized.

The undergrowth at the edge of the woods rustled again. Catrina took a step back. She should not have come. She swallowed. Her mouth felt dry. She took another slow step backward. She did not want to make any noise. She did not know what stood in the shadows beyond the tree line and she did not want to know. The sheep's fear was evidence enough that no good could come of it, whatever it was.

A low, wet growl erupted from the shadows. Catrina's hands clenched. Her knuckles whitened as her fingernails dug into her palms. She knew what that was.

The undergrowth rustled again and a wolf burst

into the clearing. Catrina saw the whites of its eyes gleam beneath the rising moon. She heard the hot, hungry whiffle of its breath and sensed the desperation, the hunger in its movements. She screamed.

Eli did not stop running. He jumped over a fallen log and stumbled over a ditch. A branch whipped across his forehead. He wiped his face and felt blood on his fingertips. He did not slow down. The woman screamed again. Eli's feet pumped faster. His breath came in shallow, ragged gasps. His shoulder slammed into a tree. He flinched as his body spun around. He righted himself and kept running.

The forest was growing darker. Tree branches reached for him with bony, shadowed fingers. He could not see where he was going. He pushed himself to run faster. His chest would burst. He wiped the blood from his forehead again. And then, thankfully, the spaces between the dark trunks began to lighten. He could make out an opening ahead. And then he was out of the forest, stumbling into a clearing and the faint remnants of daylight.

A woman stood in front of a sheep pen. She stood with a straight, indignant spine and a stick in her raised hand. Her eyes flashed with fury. Eli gasped. *Der Herr*, it was Catrina. His Catrina. Yes, he thought as a protective wave washed over him. *His* Catrina. He watched, powerless, as a wolf raced around her and lunged through a broken railing. It growled and snapped its jaws at the sheep inside. Eli could hear the clang of its teeth. He did not stop running.

Catrina stumbled to the wolf and swung the stick

down with all her might. The wolf yelped and twisted its body out of the way as the stick crashed down beside it. Mud splashed upward, splattering the wolf's matted gray fur and Catrina's crisp white apron. Catrina shouted. But this shout did not sound like the ones before. It did not sound afraid. It sounded positively *furious.*

The wolf spun around and darted away from Catrina's stick as she heaved it down again. The wolf was gone before it hit the ground. Mud splashed up once more, this time splattering Catrina's bodice and white neckcloth. She stood, trembling, with the stick raised over her head, as the wolf raced across the clearing and disappeared into the woods. She screamed again—it sounded like deep, guttural rage—and threw the stick with all her might. It landed halfway across the clearing with a dull thud.

Eli did not hesitate when he finally reached her. He threw his arms around her and pulled her against him. He would never let her go again. Never. He felt her body soften. A great shudder passed through her and she went limp against him. He held her close with one hand and stroked the back of her head with the other. Her prayer *kappe* had come loose and her raven-black hair tumbled out in glorious disarray. Her hair felt like silk beneath his fingers. "Shhhh. It's all right. It's all right now." He breathed in the scent of her. She smelled like lavender and sky. "The wolf's gone now. You don't have to be afraid."

She stiffened and pushed back from him. "I am not afraid. I am furious."

"Oh." Eli frowned. Had he done something wrong? Was it because he had not reached her in time? He had left her to fend off a wolf, all by herself. A wolf! And she had done it! "I am so sorry I was not here."

Catrina shook her head. "How could you possibly know to be here? What a silly thought."

"But you said that you are furious."

"Not at you, Eli. At *this*!" She picked up the corners of her apron and held it up to him. "I am filthy. Filthy!"

"Oh." Eli smiled. He tried not to. But his lips curled up on their own accord. "Oh."

"Do not laugh at me, Eli Webber! Don't you know how much I hate mud?"

"*Ja.*" He forced his lips into a frown, but his eyes still twinkled.

"My apron is ruined. Absolutely ruined."

Eli cleared his throat. "You really should wipe your face." He motioned to her cheek. She rubbed her skin with her hand, looked at her fingers, and groaned. "This is just too much. For heaven's sakes."

"Catrina, I think that you are forgetting something."

She frowned and patted at her face with the hem of her apron. "What?"

"You fought off a wolf." He gave her an incredulous look and threw up his hands. "That was . . . remarkable."

"Oh. That. Well, it was nothing, really. It was the getting dirty that proved problematic."

"Proved problematic? Catrina! You went after a wolf with a stick!"

"Hmmm. Yes. One does what one must. And now, I really must find some clean water." She looked around, distracted and irritated.

"You act as if the only part that bothered you was getting dirty."

Catrina shrugged. She licked a finger and rubbed at a spot of mud on her white linen neck cloth. "It was only a wolf."

"How very strange you are, Catrina Witmer."

Her eyes jerked up to his. "I can assure you that no one has called me strange before. Prissy, yes. Persnickety. Difficult, even. But never strange. I find myself to be perfectly normal, thank you very much."

"It is definitely not normal for a young woman to chase a wolf with a stick."

She shrugged again. "I don't see why it shouldn't be."

Eli shook his head and stared at her. Here was a side that he had never seen. Had anyone? "Trust me, it is quite out of the ordinary."

"People have such strange priorities." She went back to rubbing her neck cloth with a wet finger.

Eli shook his head again. "Why did you do it? You could have run, or jumped behind the fence, or done any manner of things besides going after that wolf with a stick."

Catrina stopped rubbing her neck cloth. She furrowed her brow and looked into his eyes. "You don't know?"

"No. I have no idea what could have possessed you."

"I did it for you."

Eli's mouth fell open. A few beats passed before he remembered to close it again. "For me?"

"Of course. For who else would I ruin my best apron and neck cloth?"

"But . . ." He felt so many things at once that he was not sure he could feel anything at all. For *him*?

She had fought a wolf for *him*? Correction. She had ruined her clothing for him. Apparently, that was the greater sacrifice.

"Oh, Eli. Surely you would not expect me to let a wolf carry off your wool? All I could think was that you needed that wool." She shrugged. "What else was I to do?"

What else was I to do? Eli could think of about a hundred things she could have done besides going after a hungry wolf with a stick.

"Catrina, you are a wonder. An absolute wonder. I don't . . . I don't know what to say."

"How about thank you?" She flashed a dazzling smile.

"Thank you! Thank you so very much."

"And, you could say that you will weave me a fine bolt of linen straight away to replace this." She shook her apron at him.

"Straight away."

She nodded. That lovely smile stayed on her lips. She could have gotten anything with that smile. Eli swallowed. If he did not maintain control he would go down on one knee, right there in the mud, and ask for her hand in marriage. She was a wonder. Truly.

"Now, I must away."

"Wait until I can escort you. I need to make sure the sheep are secure. Until Christina and Hilda return with their sheepdog, that wolf is likely to return. Wait until they come back and I will walk you home."

"You cannot expect me to wait here to be received looking like this." She shook her apron again for emphasis. "I will see myself home, thank you very much."

Eli frowned. "I'm afraid that the wolves are still about."

Catrina raised an eyebrow. "Then I shall carry a stick."

Eli could not argue with that. "You are not going to let me dissuade you, are you?"

"No. Of course not." And with that, she turned on her heels and marched away.

Well.

Eli watched her until she left the clearing and disappeared behind the trees that lined the wooded footpath. At least there was still some daylight left. Eli started to worry, then told himself not to be foolish. She had managed just fine, hadn't she? What an extraordinary woman.

Perhaps it was best that she had run home to clean up. If she had stayed another moment he might not have resisted the urge to declare his love for her. He had a vague memory that he had decided to push her away.

What a silly decision that had been.

Chapter Twelve

Christina and Hilda returned home soon after Catrina left. Jacob Miller walked beside them with a hatchet in one hand and a mallet in the other. Eli remembered meeting Jacob at the worship service earlier in the week. He was a pleasant enough man, if a bit rough around the edges. Jacob was the type of man who would build a cabin with nothing but his own two hands and his will. Indeed, he most likely had. If Eli had been less secure he might not have been fond of him. Particularly when he had heard that Catrina and Jacob had had a brief, albeit failed, courtship. Eli cleared his throat. Perhaps it had been a bad idea to stay behind.

Hilda frowned. "What a surprise, Eli. What are you doing here?"

"Saving your sheep." He took off his black beaver-felt hat and rubbed his fingers through his hair. "Actually, Catrina saved your sheep." He looked away when Jacob narrowed his eyes and stared at him. Eli did not feel particularly manly in that moment. "I came along a moment too late, but . . ." He cleared his throat again. "Anyway, I thought I ought to stay and make sure the wolf didn't return." He jerked his chin toward the fence. "There's a loose slat. The wolf nearly got in."

"A wolf!" The color drained from Christina's face. She looked behind them, then slid closer to her sister.

Hilda's frown deepened. "We had just noticed the broken slat and fetched Jacob to fix it. He's a fine carpenter." Her eyes swept over the sheep. "No losses?"

"No. Thanks to Catrina."

"Hold on." Jacob waved his mallet over the sheep. "You mean to tell me that Catrina saved those sheep?"

"*Ja.*"

"Catrina Witmer?"

"*Ja.*"

"The Catrina Witmer that lives here, in this settlement."

"*Ja, ja.* That is what I said."

Jacob's eyebrows went up. He gave Eli a sidelong glance. "You're sure?"

"Of course I am sure! I saw it with my own eyes. I heard her scream and I had just made it into the clearing when I saw her fight off a wolf with a stick. She saved the sheep all right."

"Hard to believe." Jacob looked perplexed. He wiped his forehead with his arm. "She let a fox get my hen, you know." He laughed. "Or nearly did. Greta saved it."

Hilda smiled. "That sounds like our Catrina."

"If I remember correctly, there was mud between her and the fox. So that was that." Jacob's mouth curled into a half smile. He looked like he was enjoying the memory. "You should have seen Greta that day."

Christina laughed. Her cheeks had regained some

color, but her eyes darted back to the tree line. "Is it gone, do you suppose?"

"*Ja,*" Eli said. "Catrina gave it a good scare."

"Hard to believe," Jacob repeated. He looked perplexed as he walked toward the loose section of fence. He stopped and turned back to Eli. "Why do you suppose she did such a thing? What could have gotten into her?"

Eli felt warm satisfaction spread through him. He knew why. But he was not going to tell, of course. Catrina had fought a wolf—had ruined her clothing—for him. She had not done the same for Jacob Miller. Eli tried not to grin. He really shouldn't gloat. But Catrina had chosen him over a man who could mend fences and plant fields and build a cabin with only the sweat of his brow and his own biceps.

It had been a good day. A very, very good day.

The next morning, as Eli, Gertrud, and Catrina worked together, Abram Ziegler bounded through the open door. "There she is!" he boomed. "The hero of New Canaan."

"Abram. Really." Catrina's porcelain cheeks reddened. She kept her eyes on her spinning wheel. "It was nothing."

"Nothing! It's the talk of the settlement, my dear. No one can quite believe it."

"No?"

Abram laughed. "It is not exactly like you to do such a thing, if you don't mind my saying so."

The wheel shuddered to a stop and Catrina spun around on her stool. "Why ever not, Abram Ziegler?"

Abram put up his hands, palms facing Catrina.

"No harm meant, little lass. Don't come after me with a stick, now. I am not sure I could hold you off."

"Abram, you do vex me."

"That is why you like me."

Catrina gave an exaggerated sigh and turned back to the spinning wheel.

Abram grabbed the three-legged stool by the hearth, walked to Catrina's side, and set it down with a thud. "Now," he said as he lowered his oversized frame onto the small seat, "tell me everything."

Frena breezed into the cabin. "I saw you come in, Abram. Tea? We've some redroot." She untied her scoop and hung it on a peg.

"Thank you. That sounds perfect. Especially if there's something to go with it."

Frena laughed. "We've some cold apple pudding from last night."

"Ah. I knew I came to the right place."

"Go on and tell the story, Catrina," Frena said as she rummaged around the hearth. "I want to hear it again." She glanced over at Abram. "That is why you're here, isn't it?"

"*Ja*. And for the apple pudding, of course."

"Of course."

Everyone stared at Catrina. Except for Gertrud. She was the only one whose attention did not wander from her work. Even the loom stopped clattering. Eli wanted to hear the story from Catrina's perspective.

Catrina thought that it would seem rather anticlimactic, but after she finished her tale, Abram shook his head and let out a long, low whistle. "*Der Herr* had his hand on you. What were you thinking?"

Catrina shrugged.

"You should have seen her when she stormed into

the cabin afterward," Frena said. "She was livid. Her apron will never come clean. She had mud splattered everywhere—even her face. Oh, you have never seen such a sight!"

Abram chuckled. "Our darling Catrina, covered in mud. I would have thought that you would let the wolf take whatever it wanted before you allowed such a tragedy to occur."

"Mud is not tragic," Catrina said with a defensive bite to her voice.

"It is to you," Frena said.

Catrina frowned. Why shouldn't she mind dirt? Dirt was, well, *dirty*. She couldn't help that it bothered her so. Then again, why didn't it bother everyone else? Perhaps *they* were the ones with the problem.

"Why did you do it?" Frena asked. "You never did say. And it is so unlike you . . . Not that you aren't brave. But you just hate anything . . . unpleasant."

Catrina had had enough. After all, wasn't she supposed to be the hero of the hour? And yet, all anyone could do was remind her that she preferred staying clean to staying dirty. As if good hygiene were a crime. She raised her chin a fraction. "If you must know, I did it for Eli. He is a fine weaver and a fine man. And I would not see his wool taken." She nodded. "I did it for Eli." There, she had said it. Perhaps that would change the subject.

Instead, it made Gertrud's breath catch in her throat. Her hands trembled as the wool passed between them. Catrina refused to look at her. She turned back to her spinning wheel, raised her chin a fraction higher, and began to pump the treadle.

Abram slapped his knee. He leaned forward and

winked at Catrina. "Ah. Have you found a young man for yourself, then?"

Eli startled in his seat and knocked his elbow against the loom's crossbeam. He cleared his throat and then rubbed his elbow. He looked like he wanted to sink into the floor and die. Gertrud shot him a look that could melt stone.

Catrina just laughed. "You are too much, Abram."

Eli swallowed. He cleared his throat again. Catrina considered putting him out of his misery—it was a terribly awkward moment, after all—but she decided against it. A roomful of witnesses was no place to declare one's affection. He would have to suffer through it. Besides, Catrina had no desire to hear whatever Gertrud might say. No, best to stay on her good side. After Gertrud's disapproving looks and veiled references to the past, Catrina feared that Gertrud knew what Catrina had done in Philadelphia two years ago. And, based on the expression on Gertrud's face, she might use that ammunition if she thought that Catrina had plans to ensnare her darling brother.

Ah, well. There was time enough to entice Eli into a courtship. And, by then, surely Gertrud would come around. Surely.

Catrina had not clarified the nature of their relationship. Eli had nearly jumped out of his skin when Abram put it so bluntly. *Found a young man for herself,* indeed. Eli did not know whether to be beside himself with embarrassment, or beside himself with gratitude that Abram had brought the situation out into the open. After all, he was tired of dancing around the subject.

Eli stopped himself. *No, you are not. You decided to give up Catrina, remember? Whether she returns your affection or not is irrelevant. Better for you if she doesn't return it.*

And yet, he found himself obsessively replaying Catrina's retort in his head. *You are too much, Abram.* What did that mean? Abram is too much because he makes silly, untrue declarations—or because he made a declaration that *is* true. Dash it all! What was a man to think?

Eli pumped the foot treadle. He wanted to run out of the cabin after so much attention had been drawn to him. He could still feel eyes on the back of his neck. But, leaving would send a clear signal that he was uncomfortable with the teasing. And Gertrud would know how much he wanted to break his promise to her.

Then again, maybe by staying he was showing that he wasn't uncomfortable with the implied relationship. Maybe he *should* run out . . .

Hang it all!

Eli let out a sigh of relief when Abram began to talk again. Anything to get everyone's attention away from his supposed relationship with Catrina.

"It is too bad that Gertrud was not there," Abram said as he polished off the last bite of the apple pudding. He wiped his long, bushy beard and patted his generous midsection.

"And why is that?" Gertrud glanced at him with a haughty, cautious expression.

"Ah. Since you asked." He shrugged and gave her an innocent look. "You are enough of a wildcat that you could have fought a wolf without a stick. Just that glare of yours would have been enough."

Gertrud shot him an icy stare.

"*Ja.* That one."

Gertrud made a noise in the back of her throat and turned back to her spinning wheel. Abram grinned and watched her for a few beats. Then he looked over to Eli. "So, my friend, when shall we have dinner together? I always have dinner with newcomers to welcome them. It's the neighborly thing to do." He shrugged and put on that innocent expression again. "And, since I don't cook, it is up to you to invite me to your place."

"Oh." Eli swallowed. Gertrud would not like this at all.

Frena laughed. "Don't look so surprised, Eli. You'll get used to Abram. Eventually."

"Tonight?" Abram asked.

"Uh, well . . ."

Abram stood up and slapped Eli on the back with a massive hand. Eli's body jolted forward. "Wonderful good," Abram said. "See you tonight." He began to whistle as he strolled out the door. He stopped in the threshold and signaled to Gertrud. "Meat pies are my favorite. Since you asked."

"I did not ask."

"No? I could have sworn I heard you . . . Ah, well. At least now you know."

Gertrud made that sound in the back of her throat again. It almost sounded like a growl and Eli smiled. Wildcat indeed.

Eli wanted to talk to Catrina. He felt almost desperate to tell her how proud he was of her, how much it meant to him that she had saved the sheep for him.

But, Gertrud hovered beside them all day, and she insisted that he go with her when she left to prepare the evening meal. "If that man shows up, I won't entertain him alone," she had said. "It's your duty to chaperone me. You'll have to suffer through his company alongside me."

And that was that.

Eli was not sure that Abram really would show up. Why would he want to spend any time with Gertrud that he did not have to? Eli cringed when he realized what he was thinking. He did not mean to criticize Gertie. She was his sister and he loved her. It was just that sometimes, she could be so . . . difficult. But wasn't that the way of love? Loving difficult people was not easy. But it was always worth it.

And, of course, Gertie had her reasons for being difficult. Eli, of all people, was duty bound to understand that.

"I smell something in the spider!" Abram's deep voice boomed across the campsite. Eli jumped. Gertrud looked up from the fire and scowled.

"There's my wildcat."

"Your wildcat? Really, Abram. I am not your wildcat."

"Ah. My apologies. You are your own wildcat. You belong to no one."

Gertrud sucked in her breath. "That is not what I meant."

"And yet, it is what you said."

"Abram Ziegler, I . . . I . . ." Gertrud opened her mouth and then snapped it shut again. Her head shook back and forth.

"It's all right, little lass. I know that I have this effect on the fairer sex sometimes. Can't even form words in my presence, eh?"

Gertrud began to shake. Actually shake! Oh, she was frustrated now. Eli tried not to smile. But he did. Worse, his shoulders began to rattle with suppressed laughter. Gertrud had been bested. Oh, how she had been bested! Eli leaned forward. He could hardly wait to see what Abram would say to her next.

Abram settled onto the log beside Eli and rubbed his hands together. The log shifted under his weight. "Now that we've gotten the pleasantries out of the way, let's eat. Whatever you've got there smells heavenly."

"It is only salt pork and corn cakes," Gertrud said as she slid the iron spider off the coals.

"Well, it is the best-smelling salt pork and corn cakes I've ever smelled."

Gertrud did not respond, but her expression softened a fraction. "I hope you brought a trencher. We've only the two."

"Don't worry about that. Serve yourselves and I'll eat from the spider. Whatever's left. *All* that's left."

Gertrud shook her head. But Eli thought he caught the faintest trace of a smile on her thin lips. "Suit yourself."

"Don't worry, my dear. I will."

All in all, it was a very strange dinner.

Catrina had had enough waiting. She needed to tell Eli exactly how she felt and get things moving along. She had been hesitant long enough. Eli had passed more than enough tests. Catrina nodded as she pulled another egg from the chicken coop. It was time to take matters into her own hands. Eli Webber did not stand a chance.

She heard footsteps behind her and backed out of the coop. Her heart jolted in her chest until she realized that the footsteps were too heavy to be Eli's.

"Collecting eggs to make me a nice cake, are you?"

Catrina shook her head. "You've beaten the sun to our doorstep." The eastern sky was streaked the color of fresh cream. Darkness still clung to the western sky where a few brave stars twinkled in the growing light.

Abram patted his musket. "The deer rise early, little lass."

"You will bring us some venison?"

Abram shrugged. "Perhaps."

Catrina brushed a chicken feather from her sleeve, then looked up at Abram and cocked her head. "What has gotten into you, Abram? You look so serious. Are you ill?"

Abram raised an eyebrow. "You could say that." He set the end of his musket against the ground and leaned against it. "Tell me about the Webbers. Have they no game?"

"What?"

"The Webbers. Why haven't they any fresh meat? Why are they still living off salt pork?"

"Oh." It was not a question that Catrina had expected to hear. "I doubt that Eli is much of a hunter."

"Hmmmm." Abram shifted his feet, picked up the musket, and slung it over his shoulder. "As I suspected."

"He really is not like any man I've met before."

Abram winked at her. "That, little lass, is why he is perfect for you." And with that he turned on his heels and strolled away. Catrina stared at him as he left and tried to think of what to say. But he was already at shouting distance. And it would be ridiculously undignified to shout a protest across the clearing. Especially when they both knew that the protest was utterly untrue.

Catrina watched the sun rise through the open window as she waited for Eli. The fresh, wet, morning air billowed into the cabin. Her eyes kept drifting to the field between her front yard and Eli's campsite. He should have appeared by now. Finally, she rose from her spinning wheel, stepped to the window, and leaned out of it in a most undignified way. She looked far too eager to clap eyes on a young man and scolded herself for her lack of propriety. But, alas, she could not think of propriety at the moment. She could only think of *him*.

"Where is Eli this morning, Grandmother?" She leaned out the window a bit farther. Any more and her toes would be off the ground and she might tumble out the other side.

"Do you not know? He is not coming today."

Catrina's attention snapped to her grandmother. She raised her head so quickly that it hit the top of the windowsill as she drew it back inside. Catrina rubbed her scalp as she spun around to face Frena. Her skirts swished. "Why ever not?"

"Where on earth have you been, Catrina? In your own world, daydreaming, I imagine."

"*Ach*, just tell me where he is going today."

"He is not going anywhere. Everyone is going to him. Today is the day the menfolk build the Webber cabin."

"Oh." Catrina's heart sank into her stomach. She swallowed. "Oh." Once the Webber cabin was built,

Eli would move the loom there. They would not work side by side anymore.

"You ought to start baking. The men will need to be fed."

"*Ja.* Of course." She slid between the spinning wheels and bumped her hip against the loom as she made her way to the hearth.

"It will be a godsend to have space to breathe again, *ja*?" Frena smiled, then let her face drop to a frown when she saw Catrina's expression. "You can still see him, you know. He doesn't have to work here every day for you two to have a courtship."

"We should cook a chicken. The men deserve to be well fed for their efforts."

"Catrina, you ignored what I said."

Catrina sighed. "Gertrud does not want him to court me. That is obvious, is it not? If he is not working here, I do not know that I will see him at all anymore."

"*Ach.* Gertrud cannot keep him from courting you."

"Can't she?"

Frena hesitated. "Maybe. She has a powerful influence over Eli. He is devoted to her." She frowned. "It is almost as if she's got some sort of hold over him."

Catrina's brows snapped together. "What do you mean?"

"*Ach.* I should not have said that. Forgive me."

"But what did you mean?"

Frena shook her head. "I have already said too much. I will not allow myself to speak ill of a neighbor."

"No. Of course not." But Catrina could not help wishing that Frena had said more. Catrina had also been wondering if Gertrud had some hold over Eli. Perhaps he was just a devoted brother with infinite patience for his poor, widowed sister. The furrow in Catrina's brow deepened. No one could have *that* much patience. There was more to this story than was being told.

Catrina brought a rabbit stew and griddle cakes to the Webber worksite at noon. She did not have time to bake bread—an all-day affair—and had decided she could not spare a chicken. Fortunately, Georg had taken a fat rabbit the previous evening. A pinch of salt, flour to thicken the broth, a few root vegetables— Catrina was able to stretch the meat to fill a worksite full of hungry bellies. Getting the stew across the clearing was the greatest challenge. Dash it all! Why hadn't she thought of that before?

After some deliberation, Catrina filled the wooden water buckets with stew, balanced the yoke over her shoulders, and trekked back and forth between the Webber place and hers, until she had transferred all the stew from her cauldron to Gertrud's. All she had to do was reheat it over their campfire, and the men would have a good, hot meal.

Next time, she would make something easier to transfer. Meat pies, perhaps. But stew stretched the meat so much further. This wilderness business really was not her style. It could be so very vexing. There was a butcher shop near her father's place in Philadelphia. It had been a lovely, sensible shop. And it never carried rabbit.

Ah, well. Some things can't be helped.

The worksite echoed with shouts and thuds. Smoke billowed into the sky—after passing through Catrina's nose and lungs—from the fires used to burn brush.

The settlement's children scampered around the roaring bonfires. They kept watch over stray sparks and dragged fresh branches into the flames as the men cleared a space large enough for a cabin.

The men had already felled the trees and had stripped the bark from the logs. They had chosen carefully—the trunks had to be tall, sturdy, and relatively similar in diameter. Catrina stirred the stew and thanked *der Herr* that she did not have *that* job. Chopping trees seemed altogether dreadful. It was exhausting work. And dangerous. Those monstrous trees crashed down with the force of an avalanche. A man had to make sure he worked the tree just so, or he could be crushed. She was glad that she had not been present for that. It would have worried her to see Eli beneath the bulk of a towering, unstable tree, chopping away until the entire thing collapsed beside him in a dreadful, roaring crash.

Jacob Miller had the most building experience, so he led the work. The other men fell into their jobs with enthusiasm and collective grit. Catrina appreciated the effort—especially since she did not have to participate. The men swarmed the clearing like busy ants, carrying this and that, hauling debris, shouting orders, and slapping one another's backs when something went well.

Catrina coughed. The wind had changed direction and swept the smoke into her face. Her eyes burned. She pulled out her white linen handkerchief and breathed through it until the wind shifted again.

As the smoke whipped away in another direction, she saw Eli standing beside Jacob. Jacob rubbed his chin as he pointed to one log, then another. They looked to be the widest and straightest logs. Then,

Jacob nodded and picked up his ax. Poor Eli looked terribly out of place as he picked up his own ax. He watched Jacob and imitated his movements. Catrina smiled. What a dear man, trying his best to fit in where he clearly did not belong.

They were two peas in a pod, Eli and her. Her smile widened. How could she have ever doubted that they were right for each other? Oh, sure, a woman like her might choose a man who welcomed heavy labor and dirty chores, but those men would never understand her outlook. They would wonder why she couldn't just settle down to the farm life and ignore the dirt and deprivations. But Eli, he understood. He was as out of his element as she was. They would make a perfect team. She was sure of it.

Catrina watched as the men hacked a U-shaped chunk from both ends of the log. Jacob motioned toward a square of bare, level ground and Eli nodded.

"They'll have the walls up by nightfall."

Catrina looked up from her seat by the campfire and saw Greta Miller standing beside her. "I don't like to watch," Catrina said. "It looks so complicated. And dangerous. How will they ever stack the logs high enough?"

"After they stack the first few, they will use some logs to build skids—ramps—and roll the logs up."

"What if they roll down again? And crush the men rolling them?"

Greta waved away the smoke that billowed toward her face. "It happens."

"*Ach.*" Catrina leaned forward and stirred the rabbit stew. "I've had enough."

Greta laughed. "Jacob knows what he's doing. They'll be fine."

"It is not Jacob that I'm worried about." Catrina nodded her chin toward Eli. "It's Eli. He isn't cut out for this. It is a miracle he hasn't cut off his foot yet."

Greta laughed again. "He isn't even holding the ax right."

"Let's feed them so we can go. I can't take it anymore. Eli is an accident waiting to happen."

"At least they have Abram," Greta said. "He knows what he's doing, same as Jacob."

"He could probably build a cabin alone. He's big enough anyway. He must be six feet five, if he's an inch."

"Taller, I'd say. You know, some men do."

"Do what?"

"Build a cabin by themselves. Not everyone gets to settle in a community like ours. Those men, the ones who strike out alone, or with just their wives and children, they take a week or two to do it, but they manage. Somehow."

Catrina shook her head. "How remarkable."

"*Ja.*"

"Working together, our men will have it done in a day or two."

"I'll be glad when it is over. It makes me nervous. Silly, isn't it?" Catrina felt a moment of embarrassment. She and Greta had become fast friends, despite their rocky start, but Greta still seemed so much more capable than Catrina. Catrina was not jealous exactly, she just could not understand how anyone could manage the hardships of the backcountry and not be driven to exasperation. Greta did not seem to mind dirty aprons or muddy hosen or fingers that turned red from scrubbing the linens with home-made lye soap.

"No." Greta put a hand on Catrina's shoulder. "That's not silly at all. It's dangerous work. Anything could happen." Then, she smiled and squeezed Catrina's shoulder. "But nothing *will* happen. You'll see."

Catrina nodded. She did not want to think about it anymore. "I wonder if Abram managed to get a deer this morning."

Greta settled onto the log beside her. "*Ja.* Abram was made for the backcountry." Greta's eyes followed Jacob's movements as she spoke. Catrina noticed and smiled to herself. She was glad that those two found each other. It was a good marriage—a love match—not a hasty relationship pushed upon them out of necessity. It was not uncommon for men and women to marry in the backcountry out of convenience. Although labor division was not as strict in the wilderness as in proper society, men and women did different work and they needed one another. It was not easy to make a go of it alone.

Yes, it was a good thing that Catrina had not gotten more entangled with Jacob. She would never have loved him as Greta did. That intangible spark was missing. He was handsome and tall and brooding—but she had had enough of handsome and brooding. She wanted a best friend. She wanted someone who understood her and cherished her. She wanted Eli Webber.

"He gave it to the Webbers," Greta said.

"Gave what?" Catrina had been staring at Eli in a

most undignified manner. She had forgotten what she and Greta were talking about.

"The deer. It seems that the Webbers are still living off salt pork."

"Ah." Catrina smiled. "*Ja.* I imagine so."

"It is true, then. Eli does not know how to hunt?"

Catrina laughed. "No. I should think not."

Greta's face became serious as she watched Eli struggle to ease a log into place. "Do you think that he will make it out here? There is plenty of work for him back east. He could make a good living."

Catrina stared at Eli's unsure movements. He grimaced as he held the log steady while Abram and Jacob wedged the notched end into place atop another notched log. Eli's beaver-felt hat was missing and his red hair stood straight up. Mud covered his black boots and the knee of one woolen hose had torn. He had removed his waistcoat and sweat dampened his white shirt. He looked altogether exhausted. "He will make it," Catrina said.

"How do you know?" Greta asked.

"I just do." She could not explain it any better than that. But deep down, she knew. He would not be defeated and neither would she. They would survive the backcountry. Together. Even if he did not know it yet.

Chapter Thirteen

Everything was happening too fast. Before the next Sabbath, the Webbers' campsite had transformed into a clearing large enough for a kitchen garden with a stout cabin in the middle. It was time to move the loom. Eli did not feel at all ready. He wanted to stay in the warm, familiar sanctuary where he could hear the clack of Catrina's wheel beside him and smell her cooking wafting from the hearth. Dash it all, he did not want to take his loom home and set up his own place. He wanted to remain a part of Catrina's life.

There was something he could do about it. It would be so easy. All he had to do was tell her that he loved her. He had doubted for a long time that a woman like Catrina could love a man like him. But after the wolf . . . well, a woman like Catrina did not fight a wolf bare-handed unless she had a very, very good reason. Saving the wool was not enough. She liked to spin and weave, but no one liked to spin and weave *that* much. No, she had done it for him. She had to have feelings for him. She *had* to.

All right, so maybe he was not one hundred percent convinced. But he had his suspicions. And oh, how he wanted to act on them! Only Gertrud stood in his way. Eli sighed as he whacked the loom's cross-beam with a wooden mallet to loosen the joints. He felt himself coming apart with the loom. This would never do.

But, he had promised Gertrud that he would not leave her and that he would not pursue Catrina. He was a man of his word. So that was that. Catrina flitted around the room, offering to reach for this or hold that. Gertrud's face looked unusually placid as she hauled the dismantled treadle to their handcart. *Of course it does. She is getting her way.*

No, that wasn't fair. *She is only trying to protect me.* Eli did not doubt that Gertrud's intentions were honorable. His sister truly believed that there was something lurking beneath Catrina's grace and beauty. What on earth it could be, Eli did not know. Catrina was perfect as far as he was concerned. Oh sure, she might prove difficult from time to time, but who didn't? *We all have our foibles. And if Catrina's is tidiness and primness, so be it. Actually, scratch that. That is one of the reasons that I love her. Her faults and foibles make her who she is. As a matter of fact, I am not sure they are faults at all. They are simply her. Wonderful, perfect her.*

Eli inhaled and released a long, wistful breath. The loom lay in pieces at his feet, like the misplaced skeleton of a beloved companion. He had worked as slowly as he could. There was no way to drag it out any further. He had to leave. When would he see Catrina again? Would they have any interaction beyond the worship services? Would their relation-ship be more than long, stolen glances as they sat in their separate sections and wondered what could have been?

Eli heaved a heavy crossbeam from the floor, stumbled, and dropped it on his foot. Dash it all! He yelped and hopped in place, then gritted his teeth and picked up the beam again. He had to keep his mind on his work—not on Catrina.

Catrina gasped and ran to his side. "Are you all right?"

Eli managed a crooked grin. "It isn't the first time I've dropped something on my foot."

Catrina smiled. Eli could see she wanted to say something. He watched her eyes follow his sister as Gertrud strode out the door with the warp roller in her arms. Catrina's eyes slid back to him. "I am going to miss you, Eli Webber."

Eli's stomach dropped. It would not hurt to tell the truth. Nothing more, nothing less. He would not lie and he would not lead her on. "I am going to miss you too, Catrina Witmer." And then he scooped up the crossbeam, settled it on his muscled shoulder, and strode out the door without looking back. If he did, Eli knew that he would say far more than he should.

Eli's cabin felt far too quiet. It was a good cabin, sturdy and watertight—Jacob Miller had made sure of that. But, it was not Catrina's cabin. It did not have the warmth of her hearth or her smile. It did not have the smell of her meat pies and apple puddings or the sound of her skirts swishing as she swept past his loom.

"The quiet is good," Gertrud said. The only sounds

were the clack of her spinning wheel, the thump and swoosh of his loom, and the snap of the sparks that occasionally jumped from the fire. It had been quiet at Catrina's cabin—neither she nor her grandparents were loud or boisterous people. But that had been a different sort of quiet. There had been a familiar, understood camaraderie in it. And the occasional joke or word of encouragement to remind each other that they were not alone.

Had he ever felt so alone as he did now? Had he ever felt that Gertrud's stern, silent presence was enough for him? No matter. He had put himself in this situation and he would do his duty. "*Ja*," Eli answered. "The quiet is good."

Gertrud nodded. The strand of wool whispered through her calloused fingers.

Eli sighed. He felt very small inside.

The spinning wheel clattered to a stop. Eli heard Gertrud rummaging through the burlap sack beside her. "We've barely any wool left." She stood and stretched her back. "I am going to call on Hilda and Christina to ask about the shearing. Surely it is nearly time."

Eli nodded as he slid the shuttle between the threads of yarn. He pulled the beater back and forth with a dull thud.

"Come with me." Gertrud reached for the scoop hanging from a peg by the door. Eli let go of the beater, cracked his knuckles, and started to rise from the bench. Gertrud smiled. "Christina will welcome a visit from you, I am sure."

Right. Eli rubbed his lower back and settled back onto the bench. "I was just stretching. You go on without me. Our dear Christina will have to muddle on without me."

"*Ach.*"

Eli did not turn around.

"You are a young man. But you won't be young forever. Grab life while you can. You cannot stay with your old, widowed sister forever."

Was she hearing herself? Did she realize what she was saying?

"*Ja.*" Eli clenched his jaw to keep from saying what he really wanted to say. "You make a fine point."

"So you will come?"

"Absolutely not."

"Eli, you can be so tiresome sometimes."

Eli grinned and craned his neck to face her. "That is precisely why you love me."

"I will be back in time to cook your dinner," Gertrud said as she marched out the door. She was not smiling.

Eli shook his head and settled back into his weaving. He tried to focus on anything, *anything* but Catrina Witmer. Nothing worked, of course. *If only I could fall for Christina.* But of course, he could not choose whom he loved. If he could, life would be so much simpler. And so much less rewarding.

The sound of footsteps in the yard pulled Eli from his thoughts.

"Hello?" Catrina's voice!

Eli jumped up so fast that he whacked his head on a ceiling beam. Dash it all, these cabins had a low clearance. Eli rubbed his head and barreled outside. He skidded to a stop in front of Catrina. "Hello." He grinned sheepishly and cleared his throat. Had his excitement been too obvious? Of course it had. Hang it all, he was no good at wooing a lady.

Catrina laughed and her eyes sparkled. A genuine smile. "I am glad to see you too, Eli."

He stared at her for a few beats and she stared back. "Oh. Sorry. I should invite you in."

Catrina nodded and started for the door.

"But I can't. Gertie's gone. We would be unchaperoned and it would not be proper." He frowned and rubbed the back of his neck. "Not that I have improper intentions." Oh, for heaven's sake. Why had he said *that* of all things? "What I mean to say is . . ." He tried to remove his hat, realized it was not there, and raked his fingers through his hair. "It is good to see you, Catrina."

She laughed again. "*Ja.* To be sure."

He stared at her. She did not say anything else. "Why are you here?" he asked. "Wait. That is not what I meant . . . I just wonder why . . ." He cleared his throat. "Lovely weather today, *ja?*"

"*Ja.* Lovely." Catrina smiled at him like a cat that had cornered a canary. Eli had the distinct feeling that she was enjoying this.

"I hear that Abram's flax harvest is coming along nicely," Eli said. "And, uh, the Widow Yoder has had good fortune with her herb garden. The barley in the Grubers' south field is already planted." Eli ran his fingers through his hair again. "You did not come to discuss the flax harvest or the barley harvest or the weather, did you?"

Catrina smiled that sly cat smile. "I came to bring you this." She lifted her hands and Eli saw that she held something wrapped in an old cloth.

"Oh. I didn't notice." He had been too busy staring at her impossibly blue eyes and thinking about how they sparkled. And talking about the weather and his proper intentions. Had he *really* said that?

"To thank you for the gift of sugar."

"Ah. Then I shall have to give you sugar more often."

She smiled and passed the package to him. He lifted a corner of the cloth and grinned. "Pie?"

"*Ja.*"

He let out a contented sigh. "You make me happy, Catrina." He swallowed. Had that been too bold? She was staring at him with a strange expression of amusement on her face. It made him feel distinctly uncomfortable and giddy at the same time. A beautiful woman had never stared at him like *that* before. "Stay and have a slice with me?"

She shook her head.

No, of course not. It would not be proper for him to entertain her alone. "Not that I meant for you to come in. Dash it all, would you like to take a slice home with you to eat?"

She shook her head again. That sly cat grin widened. "You are a dear, Eli Webber."

"Oh. Am I?"

"You know that you are."

He certainly did not.

She smoothed the front of her apron and adjusted her prayer *kappe.* "Walk me home, won't you?"

Eli's stomach jolted into his chest and dropped back down again. Escorting Catrina home sounded like a splendid idea. "*Ja.* Let's just put the pie on the table." The excitement was short-lived. His conscience hit him as the pewter pie plate thudded against the rough, hand-hewn table. He had made a promise to Gertrud. He should not lead Catrina on by walking her home or lingering to chat, or staring at her with adoration as he had been doing. He hoped that last one had not been too obvious.

He walked out of the cabin with a slumped spine and tight jaw. "I am sorry, Catrina. But I cannot spare the time just now. I have to stay here and—"

"But Eli, you cannot possibly expect me to walk home all alone today."

"No?" She had just walked from home all alone.

"No." She shook her head hard. A tiny furrow appeared between her eyes. All Eli could think about was how adorable that tiny furrow looked. "Abram tracked a bobcat this morning. It's wandering somewhere near the settlement. I couldn't possibly face such a thing alone."

"You only face down wolves, then?"

"Oh. That." She waved her small, delicate hand. "An aberration, to be sure."

"Ah. To be sure." Eli's lip curled into a half smile. "You know that bobcats are rather small. Not much bigger than a housecat."

"Oh." Catrina straightened her posture. She looked away. "Then perhaps it was a cougar. One cannot be expected to keep the names of all these wild beasts straight."

"No. One cannot."

Catrina turned back to face him. She stared squarely into his eyes. Eli felt his stomach quiver again. "So you will accompany me home?"

"I cannot allow you to succumb to wild beasts."

"Indeed not." She placed her hand on the crook of his elbow. "Lead on."

Eli swallowed. Her hand felt warm and soft against

his arm. He could feel the gentle pressure through the sleeve of his black coat. Only women swooned. Eli would never swoon. He only *felt* like he would swoon. He cleared his throat and tried to stand a bit taller. Her hand felt very, very nice against his elbow.

"Our cabin is terribly quiet now," Catrina said as they began to stroll across the field that separated their homesteads.

"Is it?"

"I miss the sound of the loom." He thought that her hand tightened against his arm, although the movement had been almost imperceptible. "I miss *you* at the loom."

"Oh." *Oh!* Eli swallowed. "I miss you too."

Catrina sighed softly. Eli thought her breath sounded like the wings of a butterfly. When had he become so embarrassingly romantic in his thinking? Catrina Witmer would drive any man to ridiculous thoughts of butterfly wings, he supposed.

"You know, we did speak about my using the loom." She turned and looked up at him. Her eyelids fluttered. He could feel himself falling into those big blue pools.

"*Ja.*" However did her eyes get to be so blue? How was it even possible?

She sighed again. "But I had so much spinning to do for you that I barely used the loom while it was in my cabin." Those wide blue eyes blinked. "Perhaps I could visit from time to time. Just to use the loom, of course."

Eli nodded. His mouth felt like it had filled with sand. He could not possibly form words. Not when she was staring into his eyes like that.

She let her gaze drop. "Oh, I do hope that I have

not been too forward! But you don't mind, do you, Eli?" Her gaze jerked back to his face. "You don't think me forward, do you? You understand?"

"*Ja.*" He nodded and patted her hand that still rested lightly on his arm. "I understand." But he did not understand. He did not understand at all. In the time it took to walk across the field, he had broken his promise to Gertrud. He did not know how it had happened. All he knew was that he wanted to continue to fall into those sparkling blue eyes. He wanted to jump and shout with happiness. Catrina would call on him—or on the loom, rather. Regardless, she would be near him again. He could hardly wait.

Until he thought about what Gertrud would say. It would be all right, surely. After all he had not *really* broken his promise to Gertrud. He was not courting Catrina. He was merely being a good neighbor. And could he help the fact that his neighbor happened to be the most beautiful woman he had ever seen?

Gertrud was vexed. No, *vexed* was not the word. She was beside herself with worry. She shook her head as she stared at her brother. "You said that you would not pursue her."

"And I did not."

Gertrud raised an eyebrow.

"She called on me—on us—and asked if she might weave on our loom from time to time." He spread out his hands. "It was the neighborly thing to do."

"And being neighborly was your only motivation?"

Eli hesitated. He rubbed the back of his neck. "Dash it all, you know it was not."

Gertrud gave him a sharp *I-told-you-so* look.

"But I kept my word. I did not pursue her."

"She pursued you?" Gertrud's expression sharpened. "As I predicted."

"Please don't."

"You are young and naïve, brother mine." She shook her head. "Why can't you trust me to keep you safe?"

"*Ach*, Gertie. I am not a boy anymore. Why can't you trust me to be a man?"

Gertrud swallowed and turned away so that her back was to him. They were at a stalemate, then. Her shoulders began to shake, ever so slightly. Had he made her cry again? When Gertrud spoke again, she said the words so softly that Eli almost could not hear. "Because I love you too much," she whispered. He had no answer to that. "Life is difficult, Eli. I would not see you make it more difficult by attaching yourself to a woman who will bring you sorrow all your days."

Eli tried to think before he spoke. This conversation had become delicate. He was not fond of delicate conversations. He shifted his weight from one foot to another. His elbow moved a little too far to the left when he did so and knocked Gertrud's mending basket off their table. The cabin was barely large enough to fit a table, a spinning wheel, and a loom, even when the straw sleeping pallets were folded in the corner for the day. He sighed, righted the basket, and began tossing the fabric scraps back inside. "I believe that she will do the opposite, Gertrud."

Gertrud did not answer for a long, heavy moment. She swallowed and smoothed down her prayer *kappe*.

"Perhaps you should trust that I know more about her than you do."

"I appreciate your concern. I appreciate your love for me. But, I believe that you are wrong."

"Oh, Eli." Gertrud looked like something terrible had happened. Eli felt as though he would do almost anything to save his sister from whatever she was feeling that would make her so distraught. He had tried his best, after all. He had not pursued Catrina. *She* had come to *him*, stared at him with those impossibly blue eyes, and invited herself back into his life. It had happened so quickly he had not been able to think what had been happening. He had only been able to think about those dazzling blue eyes. Eyes that blue could hardly be believed. How could they possibly be real?

"You are not even listening to me." Gertrud's expression had shifted to sadness. As if she had lost something and could not get it back.

"I am listening. I told you that I will not pursue her and I will not. I have not."

"But that is precisely the problem. She is the type of woman who pursues a man. Don't you see? She has set her sights on you!"

Eli tried very hard not to let the corners of his mouth curl into a smile of wonder and amazement. Gertrud was right. Catrina was pursing *him*. Catrina! Beautiful, perfect Catrina. She had stared into his eyes, asked to call on him, baked him a pie, put her hand on his arm in a perfectly proper fashion—and he had felt such electrifying emotion through that light, proper touch! Eli swallowed. Nothing like this had ever happened to him before. It was glorious.

Chapter Fourteen

Catrina was surprised when Gertrud pulled her aside after the worship service. It was a lovely spring day, mild and full of sunshine. Catrina had hoped that Eli would pull her aside during luncheon and eat with her, but he had remained preoccupied with every other settler. Did he really have so much to say to everyone else? Catrina had contented herself with making friendly conversation with the Widow Yoder—who actually did have interesting tips on the best ways to dye wool—and with Greta Miller.

Had Eli not picked up on the myriad of hints that Catrina had dropped the last time they spoke? Her eyelashes might have fallen off if she had batted them any harder. She had gone so far as to invite herself to call on him. Yes, the loom was an ideal excuse, but it had certainly been forward of her. Well. Desperate times call for desperate measures. And she had begun to feel rather desperate to prod Eli along.

How on earth had he *still* not gotten the hint?

The wooden trenchers and pewter plates had barely been scraped clean before Gertrud had pulled alongside Catrina and taken her arm. Catrina had almost gasped. Gertrud was the very last person she expected to take her arm in such a friendly fashion. "I thought we might walk home together," Gertrud said without smiling. "We are neighbors, after all, and can hardly pretend that we will not be walking in the same direction."

Ah. Gertrud would not act as if she and Catrina were on friendly terms. "No, we cannot."

"I would like to speak with you," Gertrud said as she began to steer Catrina toward the path.

No, she did not seem friendly, after all.

Catrina glanced around to see if someone might come and rescue her from a conversation she did not want to have. No one came. Most notably Eli did not come.

Catrina waved to Greta and the Widow Yoder, who had both become entangled in a conversation with Barbara Gruber about cures for the croup. They waved back and did not move forward to rescue her. Oh well. Her grandparents had already returned home, so she had no excuse to stay behind. Georg had an unfortunate case of gout, so he and Frena had returned home early so that he could elevate his ailing foot.

And so Gertrud and Catrina set out together in a most uncomfortable manner. *Perhaps she means to apologize. After all, her brother has almost declared his intentions. She may have realized that it is better to support us than to push us apart.* Catrina frowned as they made their way up a hillock and onto the footpath. Her breath began to come more quickly. She hoped that Gertrud assumed she was out of breath from the walk and not from nerves. She tried to convince herself that all was well. *Perhaps Gertrud's hostility was purely in your own mind. After what you did in Philadelphia it is easy to believe that everyone knows and that everyone has judged you.*

Gertrud did not speak until they were well clear of the other settlers. The silence of the woodlands settled around them. They heard only the crunch of their shoes on the dry leaves that littered the forest floor. Gertrud inhaled and let her breath out slowly. She shook her head. "I have thought long and hard about what to say to you."

"Oh?" Catrina gave the woman a sidelong glance. What exactly was she about to say? The tightness in Catrina's stomach, and on Gertrud's face, told Catrina that it could not be good.

"One has to be careful about such . . . delicate matters. After all, you are one of us now, even though you were not in the past."

Catrina felt her chest constrict. She tried to swallow and could not. Gertrud knew. Oh, she knew. There would be no escape. Not even at the far edge of the colonies, amongst the wolves and wilderness. Catrina raised her chin a fraction. She had repented. She would not be ashamed. No matter how humiliating this moment was about to be. She would not run and hide. She would face Gertrud and the terrible, terrible truth.

Gertrud seemed to have trouble forming words. She ran her stout, calloused fingers down her apron in a nervous gesture. She picked at an invisible spot on the white linen. "I used to frequent your father's shop in Philadelphia." She sighed and looked straight ahead. She kept walking with steady, determined steps. "I have heard the stories. And I believe them to be true." She paused and lowered her voice to a tone that sounded so calm and sure it made Catrina shudder. "I know them to be true."

Catrina did not deny the stories. She did not deny anything at all. They walked for a while in silence. The wind whispered through the trees and rippled their skirts. "So you understand why I do not believe you to be a suitable match for my brother," Gertrud said at last.

Still, Catrina did not respond. She would not make this any easier for Gertrud. She would not lie, she would not deny, she would not beg anyone to understand. But she would not make it easy for anyone to remind her of what she had done. She would not rush to condemn herself. She had put it behind her. And behind her it should stay.

Gertrud's brown leather shoes continued to beat a steady rhythm against the forest floor. Yellow sunlight poured through the canopy and cast bright patterns across a sea of waving ferns. "I do not want to tell my brother, Catrina. I do not want to tell anyone."

Catrina's breath sharpened. Was that a threat? Would Gertrud tell if Catrina stepped over an unspoken boundary line that separated her from Eli? Catrina felt her hands clench into fists. Her nails dug into the soft flesh of her palms until it hurt. She would not escape her past. She would not outrun it. How foolish she had been to think that she could try.

Her only comfort was that Gertrud had not told Eli yet. He did not know. Thanks be to *der Herr*, Eli did not know. Yet. Would Gertrud tell him? Did Gertrud mean it when she said she did not *want* to tell? The ground felt unstable beneath Catrina's feet. She could not believe it had come to this. The only way to be sure her secret stayed safe was to stay away from Eli. Forever.

Gertrud turned and smiled at Catrina. "I am glad that we had this talk. I am sure that all will fall into its rightful place now."

Catrina looked away. She was sure that her rightful place was with Eli. Even a woman who had made a terrible mistake deserved to be with the man she loved. Didn't she? Catrina felt a hardness settle inside her stomach, as if she had swallowed a stone. The world moved past them in slow motion. Her head swirled. She wanted to run away and lie down and clamp her eyes shut. She wanted everything to go away. No, not everything. Only the past. But now she knew the past would never go away. And if Eli found out . . . Would he still love her? Catrina was not willing to find out.

Eli woke up the next morning full of joy. He hummed his favorite song from the *Ausbund* as he chopped the day's firewood. His fingers fumbled over the yarn as he threaded the loom. Catrina would call on him today! Strictly speaking, she would call on the loom. But he suspected that her interest lay in more than weaving. He had not failed to notice her coy smiles, her light touch on his arm, the beating of her thick black eyelashes. Oh, she could not have been any clearer. Catrina Witmer wanted to spend more time with him. With him! It was almost too good to be true.

Eli rubbed his hands together and let out a happy sigh. Today would be a wonderful day.

"You are in a fine mood today, brother mine."

"Indeed I am, Gertie."

"Why?"

Eli grinned. "I suppose you already know."

"Mmmmm." Gertrud's lips narrowed into a thin line. If Eli didn't know better he would think that her expression held a trace of guilt. She made that face whenever she knew she had gone a step too far to protect him from whatever danger her mind had imagined. That expression reminded him of the time she had hidden his new sled when he was a child so that he couldn't race down a steep hill with his friends. He had stayed inside instead, listening to the whoops and shouts of his friends while Gertrud sat by the fire with tight, unspeaking lips. She had apologized later, when he found his sled beneath her sack of wool in the barn, and explained that she could not bear to see him hurt. He had said that no one had ever been hurt sledding. And she retorted that someone had, surely, even if he did not know them personally. She always had a way of making sense when her case shouldn't have made sense at all.

Eli considered asking her if she had done something to "protect" him. He watched her calloused fingers pick a burr from the soft bundle of wool piled on her lap. She worked hard for him. She had made sure that they stayed together, as a family. She had forgiven him for what he had done to her. Eli frowned and turned his attention to the loom. He would not confront her today. She only wanted what was best for him. There was no point in stirring up trouble by asking why her face looked guilty. He owed her a peaceful life and he would give that to her, no matter how much it ate away at him.

A knock on the door startled Eli to attention. His heart somersaulted into his throat. Catrina had come! He ran his palms over his unruly hair and brushed a crumb off his waistcoat. How long had that been there, he wondered. Gertrud frowned, rose from her spinning wheel, and walked to the door. She glanced back at Eli with a concerned expression, then turned back to the door, took a deep breath, and opened it.

"Don't look so happy to see me, Gertie," Abram's voice boomed through the threshold.

Eli let out the breath he had been holding. His body deflated and his shoulders slumped. He had been so excited for Catrina to call. Well, no matter. She was sure to come soon.

"Abram." Gertrud's clipped voice was all business. "What a surprise."

"What a *pleasant* surprise, you mean."

Gertrud stared back at him. Eli had never seen her tongue-tied before she met Abram. She always had a retort on hand.

"Ah, Gertie. I see that you are unable to speak in my presence. That disarming, am I? Well, good looks can be a curse."

Eli laughed. "Come in, Abram. Before my sister slams the door in your face."

"She would not dare. Not to such a handsome face."

Gertrud stepped aside as Abram rumbled past her. She stared at him with a look somewhere between exasperation and confusion. Oh, thought Eli, this should be fun. Abram flashed a mischievous grin as he sauntered past Gertrud and slumped onto the hand-hewn bench beside the table. "Sorry to disappoint

you, my girl, but I have not come to call on you."
Abram shrugged. "Came to discuss the flax harvest."
He raised his eyebrows. "Although, if the disappointment cuts too deep, I could arrange a social visit on
the morrow. . . ."

Gertrud's face turned an interesting shade of red.
"I would like no such thing, Abram Ziegler." She
spoke in a clear, calm voice, but her jaw trembled.

Abram responded with a nonchalant shrug. "Ah,
well." He turned to Eli and began to talk details
about the upcoming flax harvest. Gertrud continued
to stare at him with that expression of exasperation
and confusion. Eli tried to focus on Abram's predic-
tions regarding how many bushels his crop should
yield, but all he could think was that his sister had
finally met her match. It took all his strength to sup-
press a chuckle. He could not imagine how a good-
natured, giant of a frontiersman with bright eyes, rosy
cheeks, a bushy beard, and a gap between his front
teeth had managed to best Gertrud. But he had. Oh,
had he ever!

"Now, little lass," Abram said once the talk of the
upcoming harvest was completed. He turned to Gertrud
and leaned forward on the bench. His large, meaty
wrists rested on his knees and his hands dangled.
"I wonder what you've done with that venison. A nice
stew perhaps?"

"Oh." Gertrud cleared her throat. "*Ja.* Thank you
for the deer. You did not have to—"

"*Ach.*" Abram cut her off with a wave of his hand.
"Anything for you." He winked at her and she clamped
her mouth shut. Abram shrugged. "But, if you wanted
to thank me, I suppose I could stay and sample some
of that venison. I'm a busy man, but I reckon I could

take the time. Since you seem so eager to thank me. I would not want to disappoint you."

"I did not mean . . . that is to say, thank you for the venison, but—"

"You are very welcome, little lass," Abram interrupted before Gertrud could explain her position. "Can't have you eating salt pork now that you've settled. Eli's got his qualities, but hunting is not one of them, eh?"

Eli shrugged and grinned sheepishly.

"My brother is perfectly capable of providing for us."

Abram nodded thoughtfully. "That he is. To be sure." He stared at Gertrud until she looked up and met his eyes. "But venison sure is good, *ja*?"

Gertrud gave a small smile. It curled her lips as if she could not quite help herself. "*Ja*. It is."

Abram nodded. "How kind of you to have me for dinner."

Gertrud's brows snapped together. "Dinner?"

Abram's expression looked a little too innocent. "You just invited me."

Gertrud narrowed her eyes. "You have a way of twisting words, Abram Ziegler."

"Do I? Hmmm. I will have to look into that." He smiled. "After dinner. I believe you said we were having venison?"

Gertrud sighed and shook her head, but that smile returned to her lips. "*Ja, ja*. Venison it is." She shook her head again, but the smile remained. Eli had forgotten how her face softened when she smiled. She smiled so rarely. He was glad that Abram had dropped by. Now, if Catrina would just follow suit . . .

* * *

Catrina never appeared that day. Eli sighed as he pulled the curtain closed that separated his sleeping pallet from his sister's. He would have to build them each a bedstead, now that they were settled. But his thoughts did not stay on such practicalities long. As he kicked off his leather shoes and shrugged out of his black coat, all he could think of was Catrina. Why had she stayed away today? He had been sure that she would call on him.

A dark thought came to him as he unfastened the hooks and eyes on his waistcoat. Had Gertrud interfered somehow? Had she said something to Catrina? Eli dismissed the thought immediately. What could Gertrud possibly say to scare Catrina away—especially after Catrina had been so eager to call on him? Surely, she could not hold anything over the poor girl. Oh, Gertie had been full of veiled warnings, but Eli did not take them too seriously.

There could not be anything wrong with Catrina Witmer. She was perfect in every way.

Chapter Fifteen

Eli woke up the next morning wrestling over his feelings for Catrina and his promise to Gertrud. He wondered if he should call on Catrina. Perhaps she had taken ill. That would explain why she had not come to use the loom as agreed. Or maybe she simply had too much to do that day. It was spring, after all, and the settlement had come awake after a long, quiet winter to plow and sow and take advantage of all the bounty nature bestowed after the last snows receded. Spring was a busy time for them all. Only Eli and Gertrud lived by a different rhythm. They were not servants to the seasons, but rather to the demand for clothing, which stayed steady year round.

What had he promised Gertrud, exactly? Eli frowned as he pulled up his woolen hosen and used a ribbon to tie them into place above his knees. How could he keep that promise and stay true to his heart? How could he make up for his past wrongs? Could any sacrifice make up for what he had done to her?

Eli listened to the sounds of the cabin awakening. He heard Gertrud stack kindling on the hearth. Metal scraped against metal. Water poured and splashed.

He sighed. He did not want to open the curtain that separated the room. When the curtain opened he would have to face the day. More importantly, he would have to face his sister. He would have to choose whether to stay loyal to her or pursue the woman he loved. If only Catrina would call on him today! The answer seemed so clear when she stood before him, gazing at him with those impossibly blue eyes.

But when it was just he and Gertrud, Eli's nerve faltered. The guilt came flooding back and that terrible day in the forest came back to him in gut-wrenching flashes. He could still smell the acrid, woodsy scent of the brush fire, hear the dull thud of the ax against oak, and see the flash of sunlight against the metal blade. Most vivid was the sound of the crack as the stout trunk gave way. Gertrud had forgiven him. But he had not forgiven himself. He did not know if he ever could. Worse, he did not know if he should.

"Eli, are you still abed?" Gertrud asked through the curtain.

"No." He slung the curtain aside and stalked to the hearth. "I'm up."

Gertrud's face fell. "You look unwell."

Eli shrugged and looked away. "I'm fine."

Gertrud looked at him for a moment too long before she turned her attention back to the fire. She did not look convinced. A guilty look rippled across her features before she clamped her face into a hard mask.

Eli sighed. It was going to be a long day. Unless Catrina showed up. That would make everything all right, at least for the time they were together, regard-less of what the future might bring.

Catrina did not show that day, or the next, or the next. By midweek, Eli slogged through his chores with heavy steps and a slow, sinking feeling in his stomach. The steady, friendly rhythm of the loom could not soothe him. His thoughts kept turning to the cabin on the other side of the Witmer field. Sometimes he saw Georg and Frena bent over the dirt, their hands pushing and prodding the earth in quick, practiced motions. But Catrina never appeared.

Eli kept the shutters open after nightfall and stared across the field, hoping to catch a glimpse of that graceful, self-assured silhouette. The outline of a woman's body appeared against the pink sky and Eli jolted to attention. His heart leapt into his mouth at the thought of seeing her. But he quickly realized that was not Catrina. That was Frena scattering feed to the chickens. Eli exhaled and closed the shutters. The room darkened and Gertrud called for him to light a candle.

"Do you suppose that Catrina has taken ill?" Eli asked as he carried the lit candle to the table and set it in the pewter holder.

"Ill?" Gertrud shook her head. The spinning wheel clattered as she pumped her foot on the treadle. "No. Why would you think that?"

"She has not come to use the loom as we had agreed."

"Ah." Gertrud's face took on a look of concentration.

She seemed to be choosing her words carefully. "I saw her yesterday."

"Did you?"

"*Ja.* She was carrying a basket in the direction of the bake oven."

Eli nodded. "She bakes on Wednesday."

"Does she? What a strange thing to notice."

Was that strange? Wouldn't it be stranger *not* to notice the comings and goings of the woman he loved? "Perhaps. But I have noticed, nonetheless."

"Then she is well enough."

"*Ja.*" Eli hesitated. He cleared his throat. "I thought I might call on her to make sure that she is well."

"But now there is no need. She was baking only yesterday."

Eli paused. He rubbed the back of his neck. His sister's logic was sound. "*Ja.* That's true enough."

"Good. She is well. We are well. All is well." She lifted her foot from the treadle and the spinning wheel creaked to a stop. "I'll get your supper now. That will set you to rights."

Eli sighed. Not even a good meal was enough to set him to rights. And for that to be true, the situation had gotten very bad indeed.

As the week rolled on each day blended into the rest. There was firewood to chop, breakfast to eat, and the morning's weaving to do. They ate a cold lunch and he continued weaving until dark. They ate a warm supper, went to bed, and started over again the next day. He felt that he might go mad from the repetition, which was quite odd. After all, this had been his life for years and he had never questioned it before. He had been reasonably content, in fact.

Until Catrina Witmer appeared in his life. And

now, he felt that he could not go another day without seeing her. Each hour dragged into an eternity as he waited to hear her clear, girlish voice outside the threshold, see her shining face as she strode into the cabin, or feel the light touch of her hand against his arm as he escorted her home again.

This would not do. And yet, it would have to do, for he had no other choice.

Catrina stood at the window and gazed across the field toward Eli's cabin. Smoke rose above the trees and curled into the sky to join the clouds. She sighed and turned back to her grandparents. They lingered over breakfast as they chatted pleasantly about the spring planting. The morning sun streamed into the cabin and painted the dirt floor yellow. Frena stoked the fire and stirred the porridge. Everything felt normal and ordinary. Except for Catrina's heart. She looked back out the window. The clearing between her and Eli felt as empty and distant as she did. Had she done the right thing to stay away from him? Of course she had. She had no other choice.

Catrina rested her elbows on the windowsill and leaned her chin on her hands as she stared at Eli's cabin. Gertrud emerged from the door with a wooden yoke on her shoulders. She steadied the two buckets that hung from the yoke as she swept across the clearing and plunged into the woods. Catrina sighed. She knew why Gertrud wanted her to stay away. That was the worst part of it all. Catrina believed that Gertrud was right. Or, if not *right*, she was afraid that Gertrud was at least justified. She was only trying to protect her brother.

That was what made it so painful. Catrina could
not even blame Gertrud. Catrina wondered if she
would do the same thing if she were in Gertrud's
place. She felt the shame of her past whispering over
her shoulders and settling against her back like a
dark cloak. How she wanted to tear it off, fling it
away, and be free of it all!

No, she realized, she would not do the same thing
as Gertrud. For the black mark she wore only clung
to women and she would not stand for that. *He* had
done worse than she, for he had convinced her to go
with him. *He* had instigated it all. But only she suffered the penalty. *He* had suffered no penalty at all.
Worse, he had been congratulated in some social
circles—unsavory circles mind you, but still.

She would not blame herself more than others
blamed *him*. But she also would not grow bitter over
what she could not change. It was unjust that she
bore the blame alone, but life was unjust.

Instead of dwelling on that she would think of the
good. She would think of the future.

She would believe in redemption, for redemption
was real. Catrina knew because she had experienced
it. She was not the same person that she had been in
the fall, when she first arrived in New Canaan and
tried to snare Jacob Miller. And she most *certainly* was
not the same person as when she made that terrible
decision in Philadelphia with *him*.

The problem with redemption was that it occurred
in the heart, in secret places where no one else could
see. Catrina let out a low, ironic laugh. If only redemption showed on the skin! If only it left a physical
mark to show the world that one had been remade.

The thought occurred to her that because *he* had

not taken any blame, *he* had not realized his need for redemption. He would go on living the meaningless, riotous life of a rake. Perhaps, all things considered, life was more unjust to him. For he would never know he needed to change and would miss out on all the peace and fulfillment that she had found because of her fall.

"What is it?" Frena asked from across the cabin.

"What is what?"

"You laughed."

"Oh." Catrina had not meant to laugh out loud. She bit her lip and pushed away from the windowsill. "Do you mind if I go ahead and leave for the worship service? I feel too restless to wait this morning."

Georg swallowed a mouthful of porridge and wiped his mouth on his sleeve. "What she means is that she has not seen Eli in a week and does not want to wait any longer."

Frena smiled. "Go on. We'll see you there."

Catrina did not respond to her grandfather's good-natured comment about Eli. She wanted to spill out her feelings and tell her grandparents everything that Gertrud had said to her. But that would mean bringing up her past. And that would just make her feel even more ashamed. Some things were best left unsaid, even if she had to navigate the situation on her own. Days like this she felt like a ghost ship on a vast and endless sea, sailing alone, into nothingness. How could she do the right thing when she could not even ask for advice?

Well, it could not be helped. She had shut the door on her past and that door must stay shut. She would not remind her family of what she had done by telling them about Gertrud's demands. And so Catrina kept her mouth closed as she tied the ribbon of her scoop under her chin and fastened her leather shoes. She pulled at one of her woolen hose to straighten the wrinkles and marched out the door without saying another word.

Her heart thudded into her shoes and shot back to her chest when she passed through the threshold and looked beyond the field. There was Eli, walking away from his cabin. He seemed small and alone against the backdrop of towering pines and vast, empty sky. Catrina smoothed her apron and scanned the Webber yard. She did not see Gertrud. Everything in her shouted to run toward Eli and tell him how she felt. But she warned herself to be cautious. She could not afford to throw her reputation away after she had finally regained it.

Eli had been looking at the ground as he walked and his face rose to meet her gaze. Catrina watched him from across the field that separated them. She did not lower her eyes. She stared back at him with all the intensity and longing that she felt digging into her heart.

Eli stopped walking and they stared at each other without moving for a moment, both waiting for the other to come forward. Neither did. Catrina wondered what he was thinking. He had not come to her. An entire week had passed since she saw him last and he did not come to her door and ask why. He had let her stay away from him.

She sensed he wanted to speak to her. She could see it in the way his eyes met hers, in the way his body had jerked to a halt when he saw her. Her heart warmed as they continued to stare at each other.

A child's voice drifted from the wooded footpath

and through the field. The noise broke the spell and Catrina knew that she could not bear it any longer. If Gertrud told Eli the truth, then so be it. Love was worth the risk. Love was worth everything. What good was redemption if she did not use it for love? Catrina gathered her skirts and began to walk toward Eli. Her feet picked up speed as she strode across the field, until she was running toward the man she loved. She felt as if the earth pushed her forward every time her shoes hit the ground.

A look of amazement and joy spread across Eli's face. And then he was running too. Catrina could feel her heart pounding against her breastbone. Her breath came in ragged gasps. And then he was there. His body shuddered to a stop and they stood, face-to-face, in the middle of the field. She started to throw her arms around his neck and pull him close, but she stopped herself.

The moment turned awkward. Why had she run to him like that? Why had she made such a forward display of her feelings? Catrina swallowed. Her gaze fell to his feet. His leather shoes had been polished to a shine. She wanted to say a thousand things. She said nothing.

"Catrina?"

She raised her eyes to his.

"Catrina." He said the words with reverence. He was not asking her to speak. He simply wanted to say her name. She understood. In that strange moment, it almost felt that neither of them were real.

"I did not want to stay away." There, she had said it. She would tell him. She would tell him everything. Let the consequences rest with *der Herr*.

His Adam's apple bobbed. His hand moved across

the back of his neck in an anxious, restless motion. "I did not want you to."

"You aren't like other men."

Eli looked confused. He started to smile, then shrugged. "No."

Catrina shook her head. "It is a good thing."

"Ah."

Catrina smiled and Eli's face brightened. "I would tell you that you are not like other women, but that would make me like other men, wouldn't it? I am sure they say those things to you often."

Catrina eased closer to Eli. She could sense the steady rhythm of his chest, rising and falling. He smelled like wood smoke and pine. "But when you say it I know that you mean it."

Eli gave her a wonderful, shining smile. He looked completely happy. "In that case, you are not like other women."

"I have played games with other men. I've been coy and flirtatious, and hinted that they should pursue me. I tried to do that with you last week. I tried to signal to you."

Eli swallowed again.

"But I don't want to play games anymore. I want to tell you plainly. I care for you, Eli Webber. There, I've said it. I've never come out and said such a thing before." She laughed. "But I don't think you will believe me if I don't say it plainly."

Eli's hand found hers. His skin felt warm and rough and wonderfully familiar. "I might not have." His grin looked boyish and surprised, as if he could not quite believe it still. Could life really be so generous? "Not when you are so beautiful and I am so, well . . . the way I am."

Catrina laughed again. "I love you because you are the way you are." She sucked her breath in through her teeth and clamped her free hand over her mouth. She had not meant to go that far! She had not meant to say the word *love*!

Eli's eyes sparked. He tightened his grip on her hand. "You do?"

Catrina swallowed. She stared into his blue eyes and nodded. "*Ja.*"

Eli's face took on an intense expression. "And I love you." He looked more serious than she had ever seen him.

Catrina felt as if she might float away. Everything within her wanted to dance and shout and sing. She had found him! She had found the man who would love her for who she was. Only one thought kept her grounded to the earth. She had to tell him the truth about her past. If he truly loved her, he would understand. And if he didn't . . .

Eli stood and stared at her as if he still could not quite believe what had happened. He shook his head and broke into the brightest grin Catrina had ever seen. He took off his hat, ran his fingers through his hair, and replaced his hat. Then he took a deep breath and let it out slowly. He nodded. "There is only one thing to do."

"What?" A small, impossible hope crept into Catrina's heart. Would he? Would he really?

"Marry me."

He really would.

Chapter Sixteen

Marry me? Why in heavens had he asked that? What kind of fool of a man proposes to a woman he barely knows when his sister had warned him to stay away?

A fool of a man who knows it is the right thing to do, that's who. Eli stared into Catrina's blue eyes. They were wide and deep as water. He knew that she was the one. He could sense it in his bones. He could see it in the way she looked at him. He felt it in the connection they shared when she said he was not like other men. He had done the right thing—the only thing he could do. Dash it all, he would let the consequences rest with *der Herr*. Eli had found the woman of his dreams—beyond his dreams really, for he had never dared to dream that a woman like Catrina Witmer could be his. And he would not let her go.

She gazed up at him. Her cheeks had flushed a bright pink and her chest rose and fell in a quick rhythm. The moment felt as if it would drag into eternity. He needed an answer!

But what if she said yes? Eli felt his Adam's apple bob in his throat. His mouth felt dry as sandpaper. What had he done? Had he broken his promise to

Gertrud? No. No, he had not. He had promised not to pursue Catrina and he had not. *She* had pursued *him.* She had declared her love for him first.

And if Gertrud thought he had promised to deny Catrina after she declared her love, well, that was going too far. No man in heaven or earth could stop himself from proposing to Catrina in a situation like this. She loved him, for goodness' sakes! She loved *him*!

Peace settled into Eli's heart. He had kept his promise to his sister. He could not help the fact that Catrina loved him and that she told him so boldly. The circumstances had gone beyond the scope of any promise. They had nearly gone beyond the scope of reality!

And yet . . .

Catrina opened her mouth to speak. Her breath caught in her throat as tears rose into her eyes. Eli's chest constricted. What had he done? "Catrina, I am so sorry. I didn't mean—"

Catrina shook her head, raised her finger, and pressed it to his lips. "Eli, you silly, wonderful man. I am not crying because I am upset. I am crying because I am happy. Don't you know anything about women?"

Eli shook his head in a quick, nervous motion. "No." He most certainly did not.

Catrina smiled. She dabbed her eyes with her sleeve. "Yes. Of course."

"Yes, you will marry me?"

Catrina laughed. "What else could I mean?"

"We've only known each other for a few weeks."

"Are you trying to convince me to say no?"

"No!" Eli cleared his throat and shifted his weight from one foot to another. "I just . . . Will your grandparents mind?"

"They have waited a long time for a man like you to find me. They won't care that the courtship was quick. All that matters to them is that I marry the right man." She looked away and a strange expression flickered across her features. Something was troubling her. "I should tell you something."

"*Ja.* All right." He offered her his elbow and she slid her arm around his. "But tell me on the way. We can't miss the service. We've a wedding to attend!" He gave her a sly, sidelong glance.

"Today?"

Eli shrugged. Suddenly, he felt very confident. That was not a feeling to which he was accustomed. He knew that he should see this through while that confidence lasted. He feared the spell would end and Catrina would see him for who he was—awkward and sensitive and utterly unable to woo a beautiful woman. "Why wait?" He put his free hand over hers and pressed her soft, warm flesh against the crook of his arm. "I love you. I don't want to spend another moment without you." Something like this had never happened to a man like him before. He would not let anything take this happiness from him. He would marry her today and they would be man and wife until death did them part. No power in heaven or earth would be able to separate them.

Catrina laughed. "All right, Eli. Today it is. I have been waiting my whole life to find you and I don't see any reason to wait any longer either."

Eli pulled her to him. She smelled like lavender and rain. He wanted to hold her against him forever.

She was perfect. Perfect in every way. Her soft, warm hand fit perfectly in his. They were meant to be together. Eli felt no doubt. He drank in her touch for a long, wonderful moment, then stepped back. He slid his hands up her arms, rested them on her shoulders, and peered down into her eyes. "Let's do this right. We need to speak to your grandparents."

"All right." She snuggled against him as they turned and walked to her cabin. He let his arm fall around her narrow shoulders. The motion felt so right, so familiar. He could not believe this day was real. He almost thought that he was in a dream. But the brightness of the sun against his eyes and the soft earth beneath his feet seemed real enough. Catrina's living, breathing body seemed real enough. Eli's heart thudded against his rib cage. It was real. All of it. Never had there been a happier man on all the earth.

Except for one nagging thought. Eli craned his head backward as they walked and scanned the clearing around his cabin. No sign of Gertrud. She had gone to the creek for water and planned to meet him at the service. He should speak to her. But he would have to wait for her to return if he did. And, if he spoke to her now, Catrina would see how much Gertrud was against the match. He couldn't do that to Catrina.

No, his mind was made up. His conscience was clear. He had not pursued Catrina. She had pursued him. And then everything had fallen into place so perfectly that it was like a dream. He would not break that dream. He *could* not break that dream. He owed it to Catrina. And maybe, just maybe, he owed it to himself. Gertrud would understand when she saw them together. She would recognize Catrina's purity and innocence and realize that there was no need for concern. Whatever Gertrud thought Catrina had done, it could not be true. Gertrud would see that soon enough.

"What is it?" Catrina asked.

Eli stooped and kissed the top of her head. Her freshly starched prayer *kappe* smelled like sunshine and lye. "Nothing." He let out a long, thoughtful breath. "Nothing at all."

Georg and Frena could see the news on Catrina's face as soon as she and Eli bustled into the cabin. Her eyes shone with joy. Frena grinned and leapt up from the table. Catrina nodded.

Frena's hand flew to her mouth. She glanced at Georg.

Eli grinned foolishly and tightened his grip on Catrina's hand. She looked at him and waited with her contented cat smile. He cleared his throat. "I, uh, I have . . . what I meant to say is . . . Would you . . . Is it all right . . . I plan to . . ."

This was not going well. Catrina patted his arm. "What Eli is trying to say is that he wants to marry me."

"Ah." Georg smiled knowingly and looked at Frena. She returned the smile. "It's about time, my boy."

"Oh. I was afraid . . ." Eli rubbed the back of his neck. "That is to say, we have not known each other very long."

Georg shrugged. "You are good for her. Time won't change that fact."

Eli swallowed and nodded. Catrina's eyes danced.

Poor, darling Eli. For a moment, he had looked so pale she thought he might pass out. Did he really think that her grandfather would turn him away? Didn't he know that they had waited years for a good man like him to make an offer?

No. Eli did not know that. He did not know anything about her past. He did not know that she had always attracted the wrong sort of man. She had never met anyone like Eli Webber before. Thanks to *der Herr* the wait was over. She had found him and she would never let him go. "We are going to marry today." There, she had said it.

Eli flinched. His Adam's apple bobbed as he swallowed. She squeezed his hand to reassure him.

Georg stroked his gray beard. He nodded. "As I said, I'd rather see you settled than wait any longer. We've waited long enough."

Please, please don't say anything else. Not now, when everything is so bright and beautiful and perfect. Would Eli wonder what her grandfather meant? Could he imagine that she and her grandparents had spent years worrying that no one would have her after what she had done? Or worse, that the only man who would have her would be like the one who had ruined her.

But that fear was over now. She had found a good man. And she would marry him today. She would not let him go. She would not risk losing the only man who ever loved her for who she was on the inside, rather than what she looked like on the outside.

Frena looked serious and thoughtful. "I agree with your grandfather. You deserve a good man. And I believe that Eli is a good man." She let out a long breath of air. "I have never been so relieved in all my life, truth be told. I did not think this day would ever come." A strange laugh escaped her lips. "Indeed, if you had not insisted on such a short engagement, I might have insisted on it myself!"

Oh, please do not say anything more. Do not hint at your relief! What will Eli think? There was only one reason that a beautiful, young woman would be deemed un-marriageable. Catrina cut off the thought. She would tell him, but not now. Not in front of her grand-parents! She had suffered enough humiliation. She could not bear to relive *that* with them again. This was a moment for celebration, not shame.

She turned her head toward Eli and gazed up at his face. They would have a few moments of privacy before the ceremony, surely. She would tell him as soon as they did. She would not allow him to marry her without knowing the truth. No marriage should begin with secrets. Her stomach constricted at the thought of telling him. The brightness of the moment dimmed. What if he did not understand? What if he decided that he could not love her any-more?

Catrina dropped her eyes. Eli stood beside her, happy and trusting. He had no idea who she was. He had no idea that she had to tell him something that might destroy everything they had. He pulled her closer and she forced a smile. She wanted to trust him enough to believe that he would still love her.

No other man had.

The Gruber farm looked like any other farm as they veered off the footpath and into a spacious clear-ing. A handful of chickens pecked at the bare earth until a dog loped across their path and scattered the birds in an explosion of feathers and squawks. A horse whinnied from somewhere behind the cabin. Settlers gathered near the open door. The men chatted in low voices and tipped their hats when the Witmers appeared. The women held infants and chased toddlers as they stole a few minutes of conversation with neighbors who had been too busy with the planting to visit. Everything looked so ordinary and familiar.

But nothing was ordinary today. Everything had changed and nothing would ever be the same again. Catrina smiled when Eli steadied her as she picked her way down an embankment and into the yard. Everything was brighter and more beautiful now that she was his. His neighbors' smiles were wider, the blue of the sky more brilliant, the color of the leaves more vibrant.

Gertrud's frown was more intense as well. She had been standing beside Abram Ziegler with a slight hint of amusement on her face when Catrina emerged from the woods with her grandparents and Eli. That slight hint of amusement disappeared instantly. Gertrud's mouth twisted into the sourest expression imaginable—and that was saying quite a lot, since Catrina suspected that Gertrud had a lifelong habit of sour expressions.

Well, there was nothing to be done. Catrina would have to tell Eli about her past, and Eli would stand up to Gertrud and say what must be said. Gertrud took a step toward him. She looked as if she could not quite believe her eyes. Eli continued to walk toward his sister, but before he reached her, she shook her head, spun around, and stalked into the Gruber cabin.

"Your sister is not pleased," Catrina whispered. Eli stopped and looked at Catrina. She wondered if her fear showed on her face.

"It's all right."

"Is it?" Catrina knew that it wasn't. Her last conversation with Gertrud echoed in her ears. It *had* been a threat, hadn't it? She would have to tell Eli before Gertrud did. But would that be enough? A slow, sinking feeling began to creep up from her toes and spread through her stomach. Marrying Eli would not be the end of it. Gertrud would not allow it to end.

Eli continued walking across the clearing. He paused after a few steps and twisted around. "You're not coming?"

"What?" Catrina had not realized that she was still riveted in place. She felt as if her feet could not move. "Oh." She picked up her skirts and hurried to catch him. But every step felt like a stab against her chest. Every step brought her closer to the truth that she had tried to hide. Gertrud knew. Catrina swallowed. Her neck cloth felt too tight. Would Gertrud make sure that everyone else knew too? Would she stop at Eli? Or would she destroy Catrina's reputation throughout the entire community to keep her brother safe from a fallen woman?

The worst thing was that Catrina was tempted to believe that she deserved it. Didn't Gertrud have a right to protect her brother? For, it was true. Catrina was a fallen woman. No, she reminded herself. She would not carry that label—even in her own mind. For everyone fell, just in different ways, and it was not right that her type of fall received so much more blame than other types of falls.

Eli smiled his warm, loving smile. "It's all right. Everyone gets cold feet. But don't worry. You've made the right decision." He adjusted his black beaver-felt hat and looked away. "If I may be so bold as to say so."

Catrina smiled despite the churning within her heart. She could not resist his innocent, boyish expression. "You may."

Eli laughed. "Really, it will be all right. Once we are married, everything will fall into place. You'll see."

She wanted to believe that he was correct. But she knew that life had a way of punishing women who made mistakes. "Eli, your sister looks so upset to see us together. What will happen when she finds out that we are to be married?"

Eli cleared his throat. He took off his hat and ran his fingers through his hair. "Ah, well. Let me worry about that. It will be all right. She'll come around when she sees how happy we are." He stared into her eyes. "And how perfect you are."

Catrina dropped her gaze and studied the ground. A chicken stalked past her leather shoe. "Do you know why she is against the match?"

Eli frowned. He cleared his throat again. Catrina could sense his hesitation. "Not really."

It was an evasive answer and Catrina wondered how much Gertrud had told him. "Eli." Catrina raised her eyes back to his and took his hand. "I have to tell you something."

"What is it?" His face looked so trusting and honest. He had no idea what was coming.

Catrina took a deep breath. She would tell Eli now,

before she could lose her nerve—or Gertrud told him first.

"Hold on." Eli's attention jerked to the two elders, Amos Knepp and Abraham Riehl, as they walked past. "I need to tell Amos to marry us today. He's just been made bishop for New Canaan, *ja?*"

Catrina nodded. "A few days before you arrived."

"I'm sorry, but can you wait for just a moment? I need to catch him before he starts the service."

Catrina sighed. She really needed to tell Eli before the service began. But not now, when he was distracted. This was a conversation that deserved his full attention. "All right. But please hurry. I need to talk to you."

"*Ja.* Just give me a moment."

Catrina caught Eli's sleeve as he turned away. "When will you tell Gertrud? It would not be right to surprise her during the service with unwelcome news."

"*Ja.* I have been thinking the same. Don't worry." He put his hand over Catrina's. She had not realized how tightly she held his sleeve. "I'll do the right thing."

Catrina nodded. She knew that she could trust him. But would he ever trust her if he discovered her secret from someone else's lips? Or if he discovered it *after* they were married? Catrina watched Eli make his way to Bishop Amos. The crowd parted to let him into a circle of men. They bellowed their hellos. Someone asked when the linsey-woolsey cloth he had ordered would be ready. Catrina could not make out the rest of the conversation. Until she heard a whoop and a shout and all of the men began to slap Eli on the back. Eli glanced back at Catrina with a goofy, sheepish grin. She laughed. Everything would be all right. It had to be.

Catrina hoped that she would be able to catch a moment alone with Eli now that the announcement had been made, but the cluster of men hurried to her side and shouted their congratulations. Eli looked at her and raised his eyebrows. "That went well," he whispered.

"It's about time Catrina was settled," Amos said. "You've done well for yourself, Eli."

"I never saw it coming," Abraham said. "An unexpected match, to be sure."

"That's the best kind," Amos said.

Abram Ziegler pushed his way between Amos and Abraham. "What's all this commotion?" he boomed.

"Eli and Catrina are getting married today," Amos said.

"Ah. Of course." Abram's eyes twinkled. "It's a good thing the distance between Catrina's old home and her new one is short. I would hate to have to venture far to sample her cooking."

Catrina laughed. "Abram, will you ever stop?"

"No." Abram slapped Eli's back so hard with his oversized, meaty hand that Eli jerked forward. "And I suppose with both you and Gertrud under one roof I can save some time."

"What?" Catrina's brow creased. "Gertrud?"

Abram shrugged. "What's a man to do? She's got it bad for me, I tell you. I almost feel sorry for her."

Catrina laughed again. "Abram, you are incorrigible. You and Gertrud. The very idea!"

Abram shrugged again, then scooped Catrina into

a bear hug. "Congratulations. It's about time Eli asked you."

She looked up at Abram as her feet slid back to the ground. "Everyone keeps saying that, but we've only known each other for a few weeks. I feared that everyone would find it too sudden."

Abram shook his head. "It makes sense."

"Does it?" Catrina glanced around, but did not see Gertrud. "To everyone?"

"All I know is that I've seen the way old Eli looks at you. He'll treat you like a princess."

"Oh, Abram. You always say too much." Catrina's porcelain cheeks flushed pink.

"You do act like a princess, you know . . ." He held up his hand and pushed down a finger for every point that he listed. ". . . Can't get your clothes dirty, can't butcher the hogs, can't walk barefoot in the dirt, can't—"

"That is quite enough."

Abram's eyes twinkled. "Good." He turned to Eli. "Now, Eli, you make sure to treat her like a princess. I would hate to have to teach you a lesson."

"Abram! Stop threatening my husband-to-be!" Catrina tried to give him a serious look, but she could not stop herself from grinning. Abram had a way of pushing everyone to laughter.

Abram returned the grin. "Because if you don't treat her right, she might grow melancholy and forget to bake me the apple puddings I love so much."

Catrina shook her head and laughed. "And I thought you were concerned for my welfare."

Abram winked. "All right. Enough jokes. I am happy for you both. It's a good match."

The rest of the men nodded thoughtfully. Catrina felt a happy glow. If everyone supported the marriage, then surely Gertrud would come around. Eli must have been thinking the same thing because he turned to Catrina and whispered, "I'll find Gertrud."

Catrina nodded and watched him slip away. Her smile faded to a frown as she watched him wander past the Gruber cabin. How would she find the privacy to tell him her secret before they said their vows?

Chapter Seventeen

Eli found Gertrud behind the Gruber cabin. She stood alone, staring past the clearing, into the forest.

"Gertrud." Eli said her name softly and carefully. She did not turn her attention to him.

"Do you remember the forest in Germany?" She kept her eyes on the towering pines and the dark, secret spaces that formed between their massive trunks.

"*Ja.* Of course." Eli walked to her side and they stood, shoulder to shoulder, staring into the distance.

"The forest was different there."

"*Ja.* I suppose."

Gertrud sighed. "It was. That forest was tame. The wolves and bears had been driven away. The biggest trees had all been felled. It was familiar, safe. You knew what to expect. There were no predators left."

Eli turned his head so that he could see Gertrud's face. Her expression was distant and sad. It hurt him to see that look and he turned his gaze back to the tree line. "I never thought about it."

"There were fairy tales, of course. Legends of

witches and monsters and the like, but they weren't real. Everyone knew they weren't real."

"All right."

"It isn't like that here." Gertrud's fingers ran across her apron in a nervous gesture. "There are still predators in these woods. And they aren't fairy tales. They're real." Gertrud turned her face to his. "Do you know the most dangerous kind of predator?"

Eli shifted his weight from one foot to the other. He didn't like the direction of the conversation. "No."

Her eyes bore into his with a dark intensity. "The ones that you don't recognize as predators."

"I don't understand."

"I think you do."

Eli let out a long, slow breath and dropped his eyes from hers. "I'm going to marry her, Gertrud."

"Oh, Eli." Her words came out in a slow, soft whisper.

"I didn't break my promise to you. I didn't pursue her."

"No?"

"No."

"You arrived with her and her grandparents, everyone grinning like one big happy family. I knew when I saw the expression on your faces that it was over."

"It isn't over, Gertrud. It's just beginning! My life, my happiness—can't you be happy with me?"

"How did it come to this?"

Eli tore his hat from his head and ran his fingers through his hair so hard it hurt. "Come to what? Marriage? Happiness? I told you, I did not pursue her!"

"She proposed to you, then?" Gertrud looked suspicious.

"Not exactly."

"Then what happened exactly?"

"She told me that she loved me."

"Ah."

Eli ran his fingers through his hair again, then slammed his hat back on his head. "She pursued me. She said it first. And once it was said, well . . . I did not break my promise when I responded in kind."

"*Ach*, Eli. Just listen to yourself."

"I kept my word. I said I would not pursue her and I did not."

Gertrud paused. She closed her eyes. "It only shows her true character, I suppose. If only you were able to see."

"What do you mean?"

"What do you expect from a woman who is bold enough to declare her love to a man? It isn't proper."

"She got carried away. She didn't even mean to say it." Eli shook his head. "But none of that matters. Can't you just be happy for me? Can't you trust me?"

Gertrud inhaled deeply and released the air in a long, slow breath. "No."

"Gertie."

"It's because I love you, Eli. And not with the kind of shallow, self-serving love that your Catrina Witmer gives. I love you with the deep, dependable love of a sister."

"Her love is real, Gertrud."

"Oh, Eli. Nothing about Catrina is real."

Eli did not respond. He thought carefully about his words. There were a great many things that he wanted to say to Gertrud, but he knew that every one of them would sound angry and harsh. He held back. He counted to ten. He reminded himself that Gertrud's disillusionment was his fault. He had destroyed her life. The least he could do was accommodate her feelings. "I am sorry that it hurts you, Gertie, but I'm marrying the woman I love today."

"It doesn't hurt me, Eli." The words came out in a sharp staccato. "It hurts you. Can't you see that all I want is to protect you?"

"Gertie. Please." Eli shifted his feet. He glanced behind them. "I need to go."

"Wait." Gertrud swallowed. Her face looked pinched and worried. "I need to tell you something. I didn't want it to come to this, but you've left me with no choice. If she won't come clean, then I will have to do it for her. It's the only way to protect you."

Eli rubbed his eyes. His head hurt. This was not what his wedding day was supposed to be like. "All right. Tell me. And then I will tell you that it doesn't matter."

Gertrud snorted. "Oh, it matters."

"I'll decide. Go ahead."

But Gertrud hesitated. Eli could sense the struggle within her conscience. The strain was written across her face. Gertrud swallowed. She licked her lips, opened her mouth, then closed it again. She sighed and looked out at the forest.

Abram's voice boomed across the backyard. "Where is the bridegroom? Run away, has he?"

Eli's attention shifted. He had left Catrina waiting. Did she feel neglected? Abram barreled around the corner of the cabin. "There he is!" He winked at Gertrud. "And his lovely sister."

The moment had passed. Whatever Gertrud had wanted to say, she had waited too long to say it. She would not have a chance, now.

Abram frowned when he took in Gertrud's pained expression. "What's the matter, old girl?"

Gertrud shook her head. Her mouth stayed in a tight line.

"Everyone's waiting," Abram said.

"All right," Eli said. "We were just . . ." He sighed and let the words die away as he flicked a speck of dirt from the knee of his breeches.

"Ah, I see."

"What?" Eli's chest constricted. Did Abram know that Gertrud opposed the match?

"Poor Gertie is feeling sore."

Gertrud's face jerked up to look at him. "What?"

"Don't you two know any words but 'what'?"

Gertrud glared at him. "Don't you know not to talk about a woman's feelings?"

Abram shrugged. He scratched the side of his face. His thick fingers tangled in his black beard. "All I was going to say was that I know what's wrong."

Gertrud's face tightened. Eli felt his stomach sink. This was a private, family matter. He didn't want anyone else to know that Gertrud held Catrina in such low regard.

"You most certainly do not," Gertrud said in a voice that was calmer than her expression.

"Ah, but I do." A slow, sly smile crept across Abram's face. "You are sore that Eli's getting hitched and you're not."

Gertrud sucked a sharp breath of air in through her teeth. Her eyes looked as though they could shoot fire.

Abram put up his hands. "Now, now. Don't take it

out on me, sweet thing." He winked at her. "Because I could remedy the problem, you know."

Gertrud looked as if she had swallowed a goose egg and it lodged in her throat. She tried to speak but choked on the words.

Abram shrugged. "Too taken by the offer to reply, I reckon. Well, I do have that effect on women." He turned to Eli and nodded his chin toward the front yard. "Come on. They're waiting for you."

Gertrud stood riveted in place as she watched Abram saunter away. "What in heavens was that about?" she asked after the flames had retreated from her eyes.

Eli smiled. Then he began to laugh. "I think it was a marriage proposal, sister mine."

The flames returned to Gertrud's eyes. She could set something on fire with the force of that look. "It most certainly was not." Neither of them spoke as she watched Abram disappear around the corner of the cabin. Her expression shifted to an emotion that Eli could not read. Her hand moved to her forehead. She patted a bead of sweat from her hairline. She swallowed again. "Was it?"

Jacob and Greta Miller strode into view. Greta waved for Eli to come. "We can hardly wait, Eli! I am so happy for Catrina. And you, too, but I don't really know you—you aren't a friend of mine. I don't mean . . ." She shook her head and her smile widened. "I always say the wrong thing."

"What she means is that she's happy for both of you and we're waiting, so hurry up." Jacob Miller was not one to sugarcoat his words with social niceties. Greta laughed. "*Ja*. Something like that."

Eli returned Greta's smile. They had only met a few times, but he had thought she was nice. Perhaps it was because she had a tendency to say too much. He knew all about that.

Gertrud frowned and straightened her prayer *kappe*. She would not get a chance to tell Eli whatever it was she wanted to tell him about Catrina. She sighed and followed the rest of the group into the front yard. Eli could sense her unhappiness, but he knew that there was nothing he could do to help her now. He would worry about it tomorrow. He refused to worry today. Today was the best day of his life.

Catrina had waited impatiently for Eli while he spoke to Gertrud in private. A stream of women had hurried to Catrina's side as the news spread across the clearing. Everyone wanted to congratulate her and announce that they had known all along. "Really?" she asked. "Because it seems a very unlikely match, does it not?"

Then, everyone had to admit that it did. Although the Widow Yoder insisted that she had seen Catrina and Eli together at the last service and knew that opposites attract. "This was meant to be."

"*Ja!*" the crowd agreed.

"We are nothing alike," Catrina reminded them, and laughed.

"That is why I said opposites attract, dear," the Widow Yoder retorted as she wagged a thin, knobby finger.

Catrina smiled. "I thought you might think that we are marrying too soon."

"No," Barbara Gruber said. "Not in the backcountry. Marriages happen fast here. A woman cannot manage alone."

"Nor a man," Berta Riehl added. "They don't last long without a woman. A man doesn't know the first thing about cooking or sewing or washing or mending. They are helpless out here in the wilderness without us."

"Well said!" Barbara agreed.

"You know, Greta and Jacob did not know each other very long before they married."

Catrina nodded. "True." She remembered that situation all too well. She expected to feel that familiar pang of embarrassment at the memory of her failed courtship with Jacob, but it did not come. She realized that the embarrassment had lifted entirely. She had a new life to live now. Someone loved her and she loved him. Whatever had happened in the past did not matter. She had made her mistakes—and she had moved on.

The realization jolted her. Could she put away her mistake from two years ago, in Philadelphia? Perhaps knowing that she was loved and accepted would be enough. Catrina wanted that to be true. But it could not be. Not yet. First she had to come clean. She had to tell Eli about the mistake she made. Then she could truly be free.

A stab of worry shot up her spine. What if he did not want to marry her after she told him? Well, that can't be helped. Either way, she would be free—either free to go on with him, or without him. Either way, she would not be hiding behind a secret anymore.

"Catrina, you really do look distracted." Christina

tugged Catrina's arm. "Are you that nervous about the wedding? I should think a woman who fought off a wolf would not be afraid to make a little vow."

"A little vow?" Hilda shook her head. "Christina, stop teasing the poor girl. She is clearly about to faint from nerves."

Catrina did not want them to guess what was really troubling her. And besides, it did seem perfectly reasonable to be nervous about committing to a man for the rest of her life. "*Ja.*" She put a hand over her chest. "I am a little faint. I really would like to speak to Eli." She had to get a moment alone with him. She had to tell him her secret.

"Absolutely not!" the Widow Yoder said. "That is the last thing that poor man needs. We all know that his nerves are far worse than yours. Why, he should consider himself fortunate that he hasn't fainted dead away by now. The poor dear."

"Really, that is too much," Barbara Gruber said.

"*Ach,* if you know Eli, you know I am right."

Christina laughed. "She is right. I wonder if Eli will survive the service. If we hear a thud coming from the men's section, we know what happened."

"I am not sure Catrina appreciates your comments," Barbara said. "This is her husband-to-be that you are talking about! Men don't faint!"

Catrina smiled. "If any man did, it would be Eli. And I love him for it."

The Widow Yoder patted her hand.

"He doesn't try to be what he is not, you know," Catrina said. "He is kind and gentle and loving. He doesn't go ransacking the forest, hunting and shooting and proving how manly he can be. He doesn't chop down trees and skin game like some big, burly frontiersman. He is very talented at his work and he works hard and cares about people and loves me for who I am."

Goodness! Had she just said all of those things to a crowd of women? She had not meant to. It just came pouring out. There were so many good things to say about Eli that she did not know how to stop. How could other women not see it? How could they all not be madly, head over heels in love with him? Of course, it was a good thing that they were not. That would be terribly awkward.

"Ah, here he is now." Everyone's attention turned to Eli, Jacob, and Greta as they filed into the front yard. Gertrud followed a few steps behind, her face a tight mask. Catrina felt a rush of relief as the women hurried to take their places on the benches that the men had set out in the front yard. She was glad that no one had time to respond to her emotional comments about Eli's qualities. But the relief only lasted an instant. The men surrounded Eli and swept him to the men's section of benches. She would not be able to speak to him.

Catrina felt her stomach drop. She barely noticed as Greta motioned for her to sit beside her. She slid into place and stared at Eli as he settled onto the bench across the aisle. Her stomach continued to sink. She had a terrible choice to make. She could go on with the wedding without disclosing her secret to Eli, or stop the wedding in front of the entire congregation. It was an impossible situation. No matter what she did, she would hurt Eli. How had it come to this? Why hadn't she said something earlier? If only she had faced the truth head on, instead of avoiding him out of fear and shame. She had wanted her past to go away, but avoiding Eli had not made it go away. It had only made her burden greater. She had missed her chance to tell him. And now it was too late.

Catrina leaned forward on her bench. Her heart thumped against her teeth. She swallowed and tried to push the tension out of her throat. She had to stop the wedding. She could not start a marriage with a lie.

Chapter Eighteen

Catrina waited for her moment. She told herself there would be time. Amish weddings came at the end of a church service. She would wait until the right moment. The congregation sang hymns from the *Ausbund*, listened to a sermon, and sang again. The three-hour service crept by with agonizing slowness. During every pause, every quiet moment, Catrina told herself that now was the moment. She must tell them to delay the wedding. But each time, she hesitated too long and missed her opportunity. The sun slunk higher in the sky. The dew dried on the wild grass and the air warmed until her hair felt damp with sweat beneath her white linen prayer *kappe*. The service would be over soon. Catrina shifted on her seat. She kept glancing across the aisle to Eli. He looked so happy and determined. Once, his eyes cut to her as she stared at him. He nodded and grinned. The innocent wonder inside his blue eyes made her chest constrict. He loved her. He loved her for who she was and he wanted to marry her. Today.

Then, before she knew it, Catrina was standing in front of the congregation, arm in arm with Eli. His hand felt warm and strong on hers. She looked up at him and their eyes met. The congregation sat behind them, watching. She felt all attention on her. Someone coughed. A child whispered and a woman said, "Shhhh." Boots shuffled against the bare earth. Everyone focused on them and the vows they would make.

Catrina did not want to extinguish the spark that danced in Eli's eyes as he stared down at her. If she told him they could not marry, the light would go out of those eyes. She did not stop the wedding. She wanted to. She should have. But she could not humiliate Eli. What would everyone think if she declared that the wedding could not go on? They would think that he was not good enough for her. And they would be wrong. So, so wrong.

If anyone wasn't good enough for someone else, it was that she was not good enough for him.

Bishop Amos read from the Bible and said the words that are said at weddings. Catrina tried to listen, but she could not pay attention. The moment was coming when she would have to say "I do." Those two, tiny words had such great meaning. They would bind her to Eli forever. He would be trapped in the arrangement, even if he wanted out once he learned the truth. Would he want out? Would he regret marrying her? Would he feel betrayed?

Eli nudged her side. Nervous laughter rippled through the congregation. Her eyes shot to Eli, then to Amos. "Oh." More laughter, louder this time. Amos nodded at her. His expression looked urgent and concerned. "Go on, then," he whispered.

"Oh." Catrina realized this was it. This was the moment she had been dreading throughout the entire service. She was out of time. She could not stop the wedding now, in front of all these people!

The ground felt unstable. It rolled beneath her feet as dark spots began to dance before her eyes. She felt a strange, nauseous sensation as her stomach sank into her feet. Her body drifted away, into nothingness. . . .

Catrina awoke on the ground. She felt warm and safe. Strong arms cradled her head and she could smell the familiar, comforting scent of wool and pine. Lean muscles tensed beneath her soft flesh. She opened her eyes. The world swam and bubbled and she could not remember where she was.

And then Eli's face came into focus. She had never seen an expression of concern like the one he wore. The color had drained from his face and his jaw tensed in a sharp, hard line. His eyes were wild. They roved across her in quick, panicked movements, searching for broken bones, for whatever might be wrong. He must look worse than she did, and he was not the one who had passed out at his own wedding!

Voices murmured from behind Eli. "The wrong one fainted!" someone shouted. Laughter and more murmuring. "She's not fit for the backcountry, poor girl." Catrina tried to raise her head. They did not understand. She was not given to fits of the vapors! She just could not bear to begin her marriage on a lie and she could not bear to humiliate Eli by stopping the wedding. Fine! Let them think she was too delicate to handle her own wedding! She would protect Eli. She would make sure they all knew how much she loved him.

"Catrina. Catrina, are you all right?" He whispered her name and ran his warm, calloused hand along her cheekbone. He was so fixated on her that he didn't seem to notice the concerned whispers behind him. All he could see was how much he loved her. Catrina knew that she loved him just as fiercely.

"I do," she said. The words came out in a slow croak. She sounded more like a frog than a beautiful bride. *Oh well, no one is perfect.*

The entire congregation roared with laughter. She had done it. She had married him. Not even unconsciousness had been able to stop her.

Eli felt that he was drifting through a dream. Everything had happened so quickly that nothing felt real. He hovered by Catrina's side throughout the meal that the settlers always shared after services. He refused to leave her for an instant and every so often he asked if she felt all right. His hands hovered near her waist and shoulders, ready to catch her if she should faint again. Catrina smiled and shook her head and insisted that she was fine. Eli refused to take any chances. This was his wife. His *wife*!

Amos and Abraham both stopped to pat Catrina's hand and murmur over her delicate nature. Catrina thanked them politely, but she frowned when they drifted away. "Everyone thinks that I'm so prim and proper." She raised her chin a fraction and smiled. "I prefer the term *conscientious*. And there is nothing wrong with that."

Eli grinned. "Nothing at all."

"You know that I didn't faint because I . . ." That adorable little wrinkle formed between her eyebrows. She closed her mouth and the frown returned.

"I know."

Catrina smiled. "How can you? You don't know what I was going to say."

Eli shrugged. "Oh, I know enough about you by now. You fought a wolf single-handedly. You manage to create the most wonderful delicacies from an un-derstocked backcountry kitchen. And, on top of it all, you manage to stay perfectly presentable, without a wrinkle or stain anywhere. That is not a drawback. That is an absolute talent!

"You don't see my . . . *conscientiousness* as a weak-ness?"

Eli shook his head. "I see it as a strength. It is part of who you are. And I love all of you—even the idio-syncrasies." He cleared his throat. "If they were idiosyncrasies. I am not saying that they are." Couldn't he manage to be debonair on his wedding day? He was not saying what he meant to say. But she looked pleased, anyway. Her lips began to curl into an indulgent smile. "I think you are perfect," Eli said. "No, you *are* perfect."

Catrina's face changed and she looked away. She continued to smile, but the expression looked wistful, as if she could not quite believe him. He watched her for a moment, but she did not look back up at him. What was she thinking? Was he wrong to tell her she was perfect? Wasn't that what husbands who are head over heels in love with their wives should say? Espe-cially if they believed it. And he did.

Someone asked if there was cake. The question rumbled through the small crowd of families holding wooden trenchers and pewter plates.

"Catrina is the one who bakes cakes," the Widow Yoder said.

Eli had not thought of cake. Catrina, whose love of sugar was infamous, would not have cake to celebrate her wedding. How remarkable. This had truly been a day like none before.

"It isn't a celebration without one of Catrina's cakes," Greta said. She turned to Catrina. "I am so sorry. I should have baked something for you."

Catrina laughed. Her troubled expression disappeared. "How could you? You didn't know there would be a wedding until right before the service began!"

"I guess I just want you to know that I'm happy for you and that I'm glad we're friends."

Catrina put her hand on Greta's arm and squeezed. "I don't need you to bake a cake for me to know that." Catrina's lips slid into a sly half smile. "Besides, we all know what happens when you try to bake a cake."

Greta put her hand over her eyes and shook her head. Jacob slung his arm around his wife's shoulders and looked down at her with a smug expression. "Yes, we do."

Greta elbowed him playfully. Jacob raised an eyebrow. A few people chuckled. They all remembered when Greta tried to impress Jacob by baking a cake with honey. Greta had been sure that she had found an ideal solution to the backcountry's sugar shortage. Until she broke into the hive and discovered that the "honeybees" were wasps. The situation had gone downhill from there. Eli had heard the story already. The settlers were quite fond of telling it.

So many people sifted past the newlyweds to offer congratulations and slap Eli on the back that Eli did not have a chance to look for Gertrud. But the knowledge that she was there somewhere, quietly disappointed with the match, nibbled at the edge of his happiness. He wished this could be a day of pure joy, but that was impossible. This was real life and real life could never be that simple. He would have to deal with Gertrud *and* hold on to his happiness. Somehow everything would fall into place. It had to.

But the small, nagging feeling told him that it would not all fall into place. He had made a promise to his sister and broken it. No, that was not true. Strictly speaking, he had kept his promise. But the hurt it caused his sister was the same, nonetheless. If it were anyone else, he would expect them to step aside and understand. He would expect them to be reasonable.

But it was not anyone else. It was Gertrud. After he destroyed her life, the only reasonable thing was to commit the rest of his life to her happiness. He owed her. But he had gone against her and broken her heart. Again.

Eli looked down at Catrina. She maintained her soft, lovely smile, but he could see the strain behind it. The expression looked practiced, faked even. He felt a catch in his chest at the thought. It could not be as Gertrud said; Catrina could not be hiding something. Not from him.

But there was something behind that smile. Something careful and afraid. Something secret. *Could* she be hiding something? Could Gertrud be right? He looked away and caught a flicker of movement across the clearing. Gertrud stood alone beneath a pine tree with a wooden trencher balanced in her hands. Her venison was untouched. Her face looked hollow with disappointment and worry. Their eyes met and Eli felt a shudder shoot through his spine. Der Herr, *don't let her be right. Not now, after it is too late.*

He dropped his eyes. Catrina leaned closer to him. It felt so good and so right to have her by his side. He breathed in the scent of lavender and rain that lingered on her freshly washed prayer *kappe.* How could he even *think* that she was hiding something? Her eyes flicked up to his and her hand tightened around his arm. He felt guilty and contrite. He owed Gertrud a lot, but that didn't mean she was right.

He would not let his thoughts run away like that again. Catrina had nothing to hide and he would not betray her by thinking that she did. Everything would be all right. He had married the perfect woman. Nothing could possibly go wrong now.

Catrina could not believe her good fortune. Life with Eli was better than she could have imagined. He was thoughtful and considerate. He never raised his voice. He wanted nothing more than her happiness.

He was perfect.

Life with Gertrud, on the other hand, was not perfect. She watched Catrina with narrowed eyes from the far side of the cabin. They barely spoke. Catrina expected a quarrel when they first arrived home after the wedding. But Gertrud only sighed and sank onto the stool in front of her spinning wheel. Her shoulders slumped in resignation. It was that look of defeat and sadness that bothered Catrina the most. She thought it would be easier if Gertrud shouted and threatened. But instead, Gertrud refused to confront her. She did not rail against her or accuse Eli of making a bad match. She simply sat at the spinning wheel and stared at the wool wrapped around the wheel. Gertrud did not break the Sabbath by pumping the foot pedal or feeding the wool. She only sat and stared. Occasionally her stout, calloused fingers ran over a length of white wool, as if seeking comfort. But the wheel did not turn.

Catrina wanted it to be a day of celebration. Even Gertrud could not steal her joy. She had married the man of her dreams! Catrina wanted to sit by his side in perfect contentment. But she needed to tell Eli about that terrible decision she made two years ago in Philadelphia. It would not be easy. She could not speak freely inside the one-room cabin, where Gertrud could hear every word. "Let's sit outside," Catrina said, and took Eli's hand. "Fresh air would do us good, *ja*?" She swallowed and glanced at Gertrud. "And we could talk . . ."

"Oh. That sounds lovely. But it's raining."

"It is?" Catrina tensed. She had not noticed. She had been too focused on the need to come clean to Eli. Her stomach sank. She would not be able to tell him until the weather cleared. Of course, she could force the issue and insist they go out in the rain. But no, she would not drag Eli outside to hear difficult news and get soaking wet on their wedding day. Better to wait. She felt thankful for the excuse the rain gave her. She could not help feeling relieved.

A small, nagging feeling told Catrina she should

not put it off, that the longer she waited, the harder it would be to go through with it. But she told herself it would not make a difference. Surely they deserved one day of happiness together. What did another few hours or another day matter? She would tell him as soon as the weather cleared. And then . . . well, who knows what would happen then?

The rain did not stop and the new family spent the day together in a strange mix of joy and tension. Eli's good-natured conversation filled the strained silences and hid the awkward looks that passed between the women, but his exuberance could not cover up the truth: Catrina shared a small cabin with someone who did not want her there. Thanks be to *der Herr*, Eli's joy strengthened her. She managed to ignore Gertrud's sidelong glances and disapproving expressions. She suspected that Eli suffered in silence as well, but he said nothing that might mar her happiness or make her feel uncomfortable in her new home.

Catrina saw that Eli watched his sister with hurt eyes. But whenever Catrina turned to him he forced a smile. Perhaps *forced* was not the right word. He was elated to have her for his wife. She knew that to be true. It was written all over his face and in his quick, excited movements. He ran his hands through his hair more often than usual. He bumped into things and sent pewter plates and mending baskets flying onto the dirt floor. And always, that big, goofy grin lit up his face like a child who had been given the best, shiniest present he could have imagined.

Eli and Catrina fetched her belongings early the next morning, as soon as the rain stopped. She still had not found the right time to speak to him about her past. She wanted to get the words out on the way to her grandparents' homestead, but the walk was too short. She told herself she would do it on the way back.

Georg and Frena met the couple in the doorway, hugged Catrina, and helped gather her things and carry them to Eli's handcart. The morning felt full of promise as they headed back to the Webber homestead. The sun hovered above the tree line and pointed bright, happy fingers toward her new home. Everything felt right and good. She strolled by Eli's side as he fought to steer the handcart across the muddy field. Every few steps the wheels caught on a stone or a ditch and they had to stop, work the cart free, and give it a good shove to get it started again.

Catrina knew this was her chance. She did not know when they would be alone again. She hesitated, but she knew the longer she waited, the harder it would be to tell him. She gathered her courage and opened her mouth to speak. At the same moment, a quilt slipped off the cart and Eli dove for it. He thumped his elbow against the side of the cart and splattered muddy water on his waistcoat as his knee crashed into a puddle, but managed to catch the quilt before it hit the wet earth. He straightened, adjusted his black beaver-felt hat, and held the unsoiled cloth toward Catrina like a prize. She laughed as she took it from him, refolded it, and tucked it deeper into the cart. She winked at him. "I think you and I will get along just fine, Eli Webber."

He grinned. "I usually drop things instead of catch them."

Catrina laughed again. "You're perfect, you know."

"*Ach.*" Eli smiled sheepishly and looked away. Catrina recognized the boyish expression, but she caught something else in it too. There was a flicker of emotion that looked like shame. She recognized it because she knew it so well. But what on earth would Eli have to be ashamed of?

The thought of shame reminded her that she had to tell him now, before she lost her chance—or her nerve. She swallowed and looked down. How would she explain it all? How to form the words? She cleared her throat. "Eli, I have to tell you something."

"Catrina!" Frena shouted from across the field.

They would not have their moment, after all. Catrina did not know whether to be relieved or disappointed. No matter how hard she tried, she had not had a chance to come clean to Eli since the wedding yesterday. She would have to try harder. She hoped she was not finding excuses to put it off. It was easy to think that she'd get to it in the next hour, or the next day—anything to put off what she feared would happen when she told him.

Eli struggled to stop the handcart as Frena hurried to catch up. She was out of breath when she reached them, but her eyes were shining. She held up a small burlap sack. "I forgot to give you this."

Catrina gasped. "The sugar!"

"For you, my sweet."

"I already took my share. This is yours."

"We want you to have it all."

Catrina took the bag and pressed it to her chest. "It's the best wedding present you could have given me."

Frena grinned. "I know."

Catrina waited for her grandmother to head back home, but she lingered beside them as they finished the walk back to the Webber cabin. Frena chatted about the weather, the lovely wedding service, and how happy the couple looked. "And your grandfather and I are happy too," she added. "So very happy for you both! We didn't think you'd ever find a good match."

"How could she lack for a good match?" Eli laughed. "I'm sure she had suitors lined up, beautiful as she is."

Frena's expression fell. Catrina knew that her grandmother had not meant to say too much. Frena was so happy, she had gotten carried away in the moment. Catrina knew all about that. She had gotten so carried away in the moment that she had married a man without telling him the full truth about herself!

Catrina did not know what to say. She wanted to tell Eli the truth. She had tried to tell Eli the truth. But now the moment was gone—her grandmother was there and they were almost to the cabin. Gertrud stood in the threshold, watching them. Catrina closed her eyes against the glare of the sun. She could see an orange glow from behind her closed lids. Birds twittered from the edge of the forest and a calm breeze whipped at her skirts. She would do the only thing she knew to do to make her feel better about the situation. "Let's celebrate with a cake tonight. We didn't have any sweets after our wedding."

Eli put his arm around her and squeezed. "You and I think alike. Frena is right, you know."

"About what?"

"That we are a perfect match."

"Yes." She stood without moving for a long, warm moment. The sun shone across her skin as Eli's strong, firm arm held her. She was almost completely happy. When she opened her eyes again she would not think about her worries. She would think about cake. Cake made everything better.

Chapter Nineteen

Monday was Catrina's baking day, and she started on the dough as soon as she unpacked her belongings and Frena left for the fields. She took care of breakfast as the dough rose, then punched it down to rise again. "Can we go for a walk?" she asked as she folded a white cloth over the wooden mixing bowl.

"Sure. As soon as I finish this," Eli said from his place at the loom. He patted the stool in front of her spinning wheel. "Until then, let's work together." He loved to weave with her by his side. A look of relief passed over Catrina's face as she settled into place by the spinning wheel.

Eli watched her from the loom with a soft smile on his face. She was his wife. His *wife*! He hoped she didn't mind that he kept watching her. But he could not help that he loved to watch her. She looked so beautiful and pure and peaceful. She was perfect.

He wished that he could be perfect for her. But he was not. And that knowledge bore into him every time she looked up at him with big, trusting eyes. Sometimes he could not meet her gaze when he thought about how horribly he had failed someone he loved in the past. And now he was responsible for another human being. What if he failed Catrina like he failed Gertrud four years ago?

Catrina's spinning wheel clattered to a stop. "I have to go now." She put the risen dough in her basket to take to the community bake-oven, then lingered beside the loom on her way outside. She lowered her voice to a whisper. "Can we talk after I return? I would like to speak to you as soon as possible. I wish I could stay, but if I don't get the baking done, you'll have no bread for dinner."

"Of course." Eli felt a warm glow inside. His wife wanted to talk to him. Maybe they could stroll through the woods and hold hands while they chatted. How nice that would be. He would be sure to tell her how much he loved her.

Catrina slipped outside, the cabin door banged shut, and Eli was alone with Gertrud for the first time since the wedding. He sighed and shifted on the hard wooden bench. His hands kept flying over the loom. Maybe she would not interrupt him if he made a show of how busy he was.

But she did interrupt him. Of course she did.

"I don't believe that she will last long," Gertrud said.

Eli thought it was a strange thing to say. He expected her to criticize the match or tell him how much he had hurt her. "What do you mean?" He had learned that asking a question was often the best diplomacy.

Gertrud sighed. She rubbed her eyes. "She hasn't the backbone for the backcountry. Do you think she has ever gotten those perfect hands dirty?"

Eli would not fall into the trap. "No, and I love her for it. She does not need to get her hands dirty. She's not a farmer's wife."

"So you will wash your own clothes and plant your own kitchen garden and slaughter and pluck your own chickens?"

"*Ach.* Can't you see I'm busy? And can't you see that she does what needs to be done? She just does it in her way and on her terms. There's nothing wrong with that—there's nothing wrong with a woman who knows her own mind."

Gertrud frowned as she stood over Eli's shoulder. "You're blocking the light, sister mine."

"Am I?" She murmured the words in a way that told Eli her mind was focused elsewhere. She did not move. "Truth be told, she is more pleasant than I expected."

The loom shuddered to a stop. Eli smiled and swiveled on the bench. "Do my ears deceive me, or did you just compliment my wife?"

"*Ach.*" Gertrud waved her hand. "That does not mean that she is a good match. But that's over and done. You can't take it back now."

"I don't want to take it back."

"No, you wouldn't. Not yet, anyway." Gertrud's gaze turned to the window, as if she were watching for Catrina's return, even though they both knew she would be gone for a while. It would take time to build a fire in the community bake-oven, let it heat the oven until the flames burned down, then scrape away the ashes and put the bread in to bake. "I want to tell you the truth, Eli. It disturbs me that she is so pleasant. Nothing ever gets to her. She is so peaceful and placid that it frightens me. It is as if she is biding her time. . . ."

"For heaven's sake, Gertie! Biding her time for what?" Eli stopped. He closed his eyes and let out a

long breath of air. Had he just raised his voice at
Gertie? He had not meant to do that. "I'm sorry." He
shook his head. His eyes stayed closed. If he opened
them and saw the concern on Gertrud's face he
thought he might break. "But please stop with your
ridiculous accusations. Catrina is not biding her time.
She is not going to ever hurt me or let me down or
do whatever it is you fear she will do."

"Maybe it is not fear of what she will do, but of
what she already has done." Gertrud's face looked
still and resigned. A vein in her throat pulsed. "And
when someone has done something in the past, they
are likely to do it again."

Eli opened his eyes. He set his jaw in a hard line
and stared at his sister. "All right, Gertrud. Enough.
What is it that she did? Go ahead." He waved his
hands with exaggerated enthusiasm. "Tell me."

The color drained from Gertrud's face. She opened
her mouth, then closed it again. "I don't like the way
you are looking at me."

"I am looking at you like a man who is tired of hearing his wife slandered."

"The truth is not slander."

"All right, then tell me the truth and I'll decide
what to make of it. You don't need to protect me. I
am sure that when you tell me it will be nothing and
then we can move past this obsession of yours."

"You don't know what you are asking. If I tell you,
it will hurt you."

"And you think this doesn't hurt me? You think I
like wondering what in heavens you believe my
Catrina has done!"

"No."

"All right then."

"I am sorry, Eli. All I wanted was to protect you. And now, I don't think that I can anymore."

Eli shook his head. This would drive him mad. He needed to put an end to it. But before he could demand answers, he heard a low whistle in the front yard. The happy tune drifted in through the open door and broke the tension in the small, one-room cabin.

"Hallo!" Abram's deep voice boomed across the threshold.

Gertrud tried to push her distraught expression aside as she smoothed her apron and pushed a stray lock of hair beneath her prayer *kappe*.

"Come on in," Eli shouted. *Thanks be to* der Herr *for timely interruptions.*

"Ah, I was hoping to see a lovely young face," Abram said as he appeared in the doorway. His large frame shut out the sunlight and he had to duck to clear the threshold.

Gertrud's face tightened. "Catrina is not here."

"Catrina?" Abram grinned and tossed his beaver-felt hat onto the table. "Who said anything about Catrina?"

A small smile turned up the corner of Gertrud's mouth, but she immediately forced her lips back into a frown. "You ought not tease like that, Abram. It isn't nice." She turned her back to him and found something to do at the hearth. A metal pot scraped against the coals. "The very idea."

"You know I never tease, Gertie." Abram stared at her with a remarkably serious expression.

Gertrud jammed the poker into the fire harder than necessary. Sparks exploded and escaped into the mud-and-stick chimney. Eli knew that he would have to replace it with stone when he could. But these things took time. They had to get settled first, then improve the cabin.

"What can we do for you, Abram?" Gertrud asked finally. She never turned around.

Abram watched her bustle around the hearth for a moment before he dropped onto a bench and rested his elbow on the hand-hewn table. The wood creaked under his weight. "Getting ready to harvest the flax."

"Ah." Eli slid his legs over his backless bench and turned around to face Abram instead of the loom. "That is welcome news."

Abram scratched the side of his face. His fingers caught in his bushy black beard. "Tomorrow. If the weather holds."

Catrina's voice floated into the cabin. "We'll have a work party!" She clapped her hands as she waltzed through the open door. Eli felt as though the sun had come with her. The entire room felt brighter, cleaner, more alive. She smelled of flour and wild grass. He smiled. "I missed you."

"I missed you, too. I came back early so we could go for that walk." Their eyes locked until Abram guffawed. "Newlyweds are incorrigible, aren't they, Gertie? How do you stand it?"

Gertrud pretended not to hear.

"Do be nice, Abram," Catrina said. "One day the tables will be turned and you will be the newlywed."

Abram leaned back against the table. He smiled. "Let us hope so, my dear." Abram's eyes cut to Gertrud, then back to Catrina. Catrina cocked her head and raised an eyebrow at Abram. He looked up at her and shrugged.

Catrina shook her head and shot him a confused look.

"You were saying something about a work party?" Abram asked as Catrina settled onto Eli's bench.

"Yes. I will bake something. There may be some wild strawberries to be had. A strawberry pie, perhaps? I might faint from happiness."

Abram nodded. "Well, I won't deny you, little lass. If you want to bake me something, who am I to argue?"

Catrina laughed.

"And, if you want to come and help me with the harvest, I won't argue that, either."

"You have such a talent for turning things around to your advantage," Catrina said, and laughed again.

"It is a mighty fine talent, to be sure."

"Did you know that is my favorite thing about New Canaan? No, it is my favorite thing about being Amish."

"What is?"

"That everyone helps one another. When I lived in Philadelphia, people surrounded me. But they were mostly strangers. They came and went as they pleased, and rarely stopped to help one another. Here, we are on our own in the middle of the wilderness, but we are not really *alone*, are we? I have seen this handful of families give more to one another than the entire population of Philadelphia ever could."

Abram looked at Catrina thoughtfully. He rubbed his beard and nodded. "*Ja.* I lived in Philadelphia for a few months. That was when I first came to America from Germany, before I set out on my own." He looked at Eli. "Catrina knows this, but did you know I lived for nearly a decade as a trapper before I settled here? I came over earlier than the rest of them, you see. But when I lived alone in the woods, I never felt as alone as when I lived in a city. There's nothing as lonely as living near hundreds of people who don't know who you are." He nodded toward Catrina, but continued to address Eli. "She's right, you know. Anyone here will help you. Oh, they don't always get along, but when push comes to shove they'll be there for you."

Eli nodded. His eyes cut to Gertrud, who was still fussing around the hearth with her back turned to them. She would be there for him if push came to shove. He just had to win her over to Catrina's side. That sounded simple, but with a strong-willed woman like Gertrud, it was not simple at all.

Catrina thought about what she had said to Abram long after the conversation drifted to the flax harvest and the price of linen. Did she mean what she had said to him about never feeling alone? Yes, she did. A happy warmth spread through her at the realization. She had felt alone in New Canaan just a few weeks ago. Something had happened since then to make her see that she was not alone, that her neighbors cared about her.

Eli had happened.

Everything would be perfect if she had not brought herself to ruin two years ago. That one mistake hung around her neck like a chain, even though Catrina had promised that she would not look back or blame herself any longer. Only Gertrud held on to that blame. But that was enough. It only took one person to turn a secret into common knowledge.

Working side by side with Eli as his wife—his *wife*!—had almost been enough to distract Catrina from her stress. She had never been so happy as when her fingers flew over the loom while Eli stood behind her with his warm, calloused hands resting on her shoulders. Her hands knew where to go and her mind focused *and* relaxed at the same time as the *clackety clack whoosh* filled the small, cozy room. Those were her favorite moments of her new marriage—the smell of wood smoke rising from the fire, Eli's warm, solid presence standing near, the light from the sun falling across the dirt floor to cast a warm glow over her face.

But Catrina could not pretend everything was all right. She could feel the cloud of confusion and frustration around her new sister-in-law. Catrina had hoped Gertrud's disapproval would seep out and disappear, like snow melting into the ground to leave fresh, new earth ready for the planting. And Catrina was ready to sow a new relationship with Gertrud. She would start fresh, if only given the chance. She would make this work, both for Eli and for her new sister-in-law.

But that was not to be. After Abram left, Gertrud's looks sharpened, as if she had made a decision. Catrina could sense that it was not a good decision. She held her breath as she swept past Gertrud's spinning wheel, as if the woman might stand up and shout the truth at any moment. The weight of the secret became an aching tightness in her chest. She had to speak to Eli before Gertrud did. She had to do the right thing. She had tried for two days—and for two days she had not managed to do it. She would not let another moment slip past. She would not allow anything to intervene.

"Let's eat before we take that walk, *ja?*" Eli said as he closed the door behind Abram. "A day of sitting at the loom works up an appetite."

"All right." Catrina tried not to show her frustration. She would take Eli outside to talk after dinner, no matter what.

The food stuck in her throat during dinner and would not go down. Catrina could not swallow when she saw Gertrud's cold, hard stare from across the table. Eli did not seem to notice. Or if he did, he never addressed his sister's brooding silence. Instead, he smiled more, held Catrina closer, and complimented her work with greater enthusiasm than ever before. Catrina wondered if that was his way of telling her that everything would be all right, that he supported her. Or perhaps he was only doing what came naturally to him. Perhaps he was oblivious to Gertrud's icy reception. She was his sister, after all, and it is easy to be blinded by love of family.

Eli pushed his plate aside and patted his lean stomach. "Wonderful good meal, Catrina."

Catrina smiled. "Now, how about that walk?" Her stomach dropped at the thought of what she would say to him. But she had to press forward.

"I'd love to. There's nothing I'd rather do than steal a few minutes with you. Just let me chop some wood first. The woodpile's nearly gone and the fire will go out if I don't take care of it now."

"Oh." Catrina frowned. She did not want to have to wait another moment to come clean to Eli. But she would have to. She did not want to alarm him by making it sound too urgent. Besides, what could another hour hurt? Two days had already flown by. "All right. As soon as you chop the wood, then."

"*Ja.*" His eyes sparkled. "Looking forward to it."

Catrina's chest constricted. He did not know what was in store. He thought they would have a lovely, happy stroll. Instead, she would break his heart. Would he understand? Would he blame her? Would he wish they had not married?

Eli hummed as he put on his beaver-felt hat and strolled outside. The women settled back into their spinning. It was the first time Catrina and Gertrud had been alone since the wedding. Catrina did not know what Gertrud would say. She hoped she would say nothing. She hoped they could spin side by side and pretend everything was all right.

They could not.

Gertrud let out a long, frustrated sigh. Her foot slid off the treadle and rested flat on the dirt floor. The spinning wheel clicked to a slow stop. Gertrud continued to stare at the smooth, worn wood. "I need to talk to you."

Catrina felt her stomach slip away and drop into her feet. She swallowed and took her foot off the treadle of her spinning wheel. The mechanism whined to a stop. "All right."

Gertrud did not turn to face her. She kept her eyes on her spinning wheel. "I have debated and debated about what to do."

Catrina did not answer. She would not make this easier on her new sister-in-law.

"I have not told Eli." Gertrud ran a fingertip along the smooth arc of the spinning wheel. "I almost did. But then I thought better of it. What's done is done. I don't want to hurt him now that—" She paused and cleared her throat. "Now that he's married. It cannot be undone."

"No. It cannot."

"And I do not think that you should tell him either."

Catrina stiffened. "That is not for you to decide."

"I know what's best for my brother. I won't see him hurt. Anyway, you can't tell him now. How would he feel when he realizes that he married you under . . . false pretenses."

"I do not believe that he would regret it."

"Then why haven't you told him?"

Catrina's stomach dropped again. "I've tried. But I haven't had the chance." The first two days of her marriage had flown by as if she were in a dream. She could not believe how the hours had slipped past. "As soon as he finishes chopping wood I plan to tell him everything."

"No." Gertrud shook her head. "Think of how it would hurt him if he learns that you have lied to him from the day you met."

Catrina spun around on the bench to face her. "I never lied to him."

"An omission of truth is a lie." Her voice sounded steady, calm, and strangely sad.

"No. It isn't like that. I was just about to tell him." Catrina stood up. She could not listen any longer. If only she had taken that walk with Eli before he went to chop wood! If only she had tried harder. How had she let two days slip past?

Gertrud looked at her for the first time during the conversation. "I cannot bear to think what it will do to him if he learns you are not who he thinks you are.

And if you ever leave him . . ." Gertrud shook her head. Her eyes gleamed with moisture.

Catrina forced a calm expression on her face so that Gertrud could not see her hurt and confusion. She smoothed her apron and adjusted her prayer *kappe*. "I would never leave Eli. What a strange thing to say."

Gertrud flinched. "Strange? We both know why you would."

"No. You're wrong. You aren't making any sense."

"Please, Catrina." Gertrud's eyes took on a pleading expression. "Don't hurt my brother."

The room was very, very quiet. Catrina could hear the wind rustle the pine needles across the clearing. She could hear her heart thump inside her chest and the quick, sharp hiss of her breath through her teeth.

"He has been through far more than you know," Gertrud said.

Catrina's face burned. She sat back down and met Gertrud's gaze. "I must tell him the truth. There can be no secrets between us."

Gertrud gave a hard, steady stare. "It is too late for that," she said quietly.

"No. It's never too late. We only married yesterday. I was just about to tell him."

"I cannot allow it."

"You cannot stop me."

Gertrud sighed and looked away. In the distance they could hear the steady thump of an ax. "No. But I can plead with you to do the right thing."

"The right thing is to tell the truth."

"No, that would only hurt him. Don't put him through it now. He's head over heels in love with you. It will crush him to learn the truth. The right thing to do is to spare him." Gertrud's fingers tightened in her lap. "And never leave him."

Catrina shook her head. She did not know what to say.

"I love my brother. Can't you understand that?"

"Is it love to keep the truth from him?"

"It is when the truth serves no purpose but to hurt him. What's done is done. You cannot change it now. Better to move on and try your best to love him."

"I do love him."

Gertrud made an expression that Catrina could not read. It looked like resignation. "Do you?"

"Of course I do."

"I wish I could believe you. I wish more than anything that I could believe you."

Catrina shook her head again. It was too unjust. How could anyone think she did not love Eli?

"I could go to the bishop," Gertrud said.

"Why would you do such a thing?"

"Only to protect my brother."

Catrina could not answer. She did not know what to say. She could not defend herself. Gertrud was right—Catrina had not told Eli before they married, and she had not told him in the two days since they'd been married. She had tried to tell him, but it did not matter. All that mattered was that she had failed.

"But it won't come to that, will it?" Gertrud's expression looked desperate. "You'll do what's best for Eli, won't you?"

Maybe Gertrud was right. Maybe it would be selfish to hurt Eli just to clear her conscience. Maybe it was best for him to never know. Catrina closed her eyes. She could not think straight. When she opened them again, Gertrud was still staring at her. "Please,

Catrina. Please. For me. For Eli. Just spare him the hurt. He's been through enough."

"All right."

Gertrud clapped a hand over her own chest and exhaled. "Thank you, Catrina." The words came out in a whisper. "Thank you."

Catrina did not know how to feel. She did not know if she had done the right thing. She only knew she loved Eli and wanted what was best for him. She would do anything for Eli, even if it meant keeping a secret that burned a hole inside her.

Chapter Twenty

Catrina tried not to agonize over whether or not it was right to protect Eli from her past. She had not told him anything on their walk yesterday. Instead, she had listened to him tell her how much he loved her. It had felt wonderful and terrible. She did not know if she was helping him or hurting him by staying silent. But she had kept her agreement with Gertrud and said nothing. Now it felt too late to change her mind.

Catrina tried to put aside all thoughts of the past. Today was the flax harvest and she felt grateful for the distraction. She would pretend everything was all right. Just for one day, at least. Tomorrow would be another day and she would deal with it when it came.

Sunlight shone from a crisp blue sky and warmed the fields that surrounded Abram's cabin. The flax smelled of fresh laundry and ripe grass. Their bright yellow stalks waved happily in the breeze. Catrina took a deep, long breath and closed her eyes. Spring was a wonderful time. The sun, the warmth, and the promise of new linen shifts, aprons, and prayer *kappes* from a good flax harvest. She was not so keen on the actual harvest part, but that could not be helped.

Abram, Eli, Gertrud, and Catrina stooped in the sun to pull up the narrow stalks by the roots. A sickle would cut the stalks too short. It took a good, hard pull to free the plant from the earth, and sometimes she ripped the stalk from the roots. Catrina felt more than a little satisfied when she brought up the entire root cluster intact. Then she shook the bundle of stalks to free the dirt. She tried to keep the dirt from sifting onto her skirt and bodice, but soon gave up. When she couldn't hold any more stalks in her hand, she tied a stalk of flax around the bundle and stacked it alongside the other bundles.

They could harvest the field in half a day, working together. But Catrina felt that was far too long. Her back began to ache from the constant stooping. Her fingers ached from gripping the stalks. The sun's rays no longer felt warm and kind. They became sweltering and harsh. She worried that her skin would burn and kept adjusting her neck cloth to cover the sliver of pale skin beneath her upswept hair.

After a while—she thought it must have been hours, but judging by the sun's position, it was not nearly so long—Catrina stopped and stretched her back. "I think we need some water, *ja*? I'll fetch it."

Gertrud cut her a look, but Eli and Abram each gave her a grateful nod. Catrina watched their hands fly over the stalks, pull them, shake them, tie them, toss them aside, then repeat the process. *I am simply not cut out for this. Really, I am no good to anybody. I move twice as slowly no matter how hard I try. Everyone is much better served if I do something that I am good at to help. Surely there is more that I can do than fetch water and fumble over the harvest.*

She thought about her role as she picked up Abram's

yoke and balanced it over her narrow shoulders. The wooden buckets felt heavy even without water. *Truth be told, I am not cut out for this, either. I wish that I could be tougher and stronger.* At home, Eli or Gertrud fetched the water. Catrina kept to the indoor chores: baking, cleaning, mending, and of course, spinning and weaving.

The buckets were far heavier on the return trip from the creek. Catrina stumbled over a log and sloshed water across her bodice. She managed to catch herself before she fell to the ground, but the buckets swung from the yoke and knocked against her ribs as she straightened back up. Catrina flinched and sucked in her breath. There would be bruises across her rib cage by the morrow. Ah well, that was life in New Canaan. Catrina thought about what her fate might have been without New Canaan and she felt grateful, even as the damp wool of her bodice began to make her skin itch.

What if things had turned out differently with the man in Philadelphia? She would not have lived with the shame that came after his desertion. But she would not have found Eli, either. She would have lived in a nice house along cobblestone streets with a servant to draw the water, scrub out the fireplace, and beat the linens.

And she would have felt empty. Her life would have had no meaning.

Catrina smiled as she rolled her shoulders to adjust the yoke. Everything had worked together for the good. If she had stayed with *him* she would have lived a life without love or adventure or challenge. Bruised ribs were a small price to pay for freedom. And freedom, she realized, was what she had earned. She had found a sanctuary in the wilderness where she was free to make her own choices, forge her own path, marry the man she wanted to marry.

And she had married the right man. He would always see her as an equal. He would always encourage her to be herself. So what if she wasn't as stoic as the other women in the settlement? So what if she couldn't bear to spend her days mucking out manure or scrubbing laundry until the lye stripped the skin from her fingers? She did not have to. She had forged the perfect path. She had found love *and* a career. Marrying a weaver meant she would always be needed at the spinning wheel or loom, not the fields or barnyard. Today was the exception, and it reminded her to be grateful.

After her realization, Catrina picked the flax with a bit more enthusiasm. Just a bit, mind you, but every bit helps. The men had been grateful for a cup of cold, clear stream water, although Gertrud had seemed more irritated than thankful. She still drank, however, even if she did so with a face that looked as if the water were flavored with lemons.

"Something is eating away at our dear Gertrud," Abram said as he tossed another bundle of flax on the pile.

Gertrud stiffened as she finished swallowing the ladleful of water. Abram winked at Eli. "Then again, something is always eating away at poor Gertie. Best learn how to make the best of things. Life is hard. That cannot be changed, but how we react to it can be."

"*Ach.*" Gertrud dropped the ladle back into the bucket and waved her hand. "What do you know of it, Abram?"

"Enough." He sighed as his meaty hands tied a

bundle of flax with a quick, deft movement. "More than enough."

Catrina knew a little of Abram's past. Ten years ago, the girl he was to marry had broken the engagement at the last moment. She was not willing to venture to America and take her chances in the backcountry. She stayed in Germany, married another, and settled into a predictable life of the hardship she knew, rather than the hardship she did not know. Abram had spoken of her a few times during the year they had known him. He still wondered what had become of her. But the last time he spoke of her it was to tell Georg that he was glad she had chosen to stay behind. "Some people are made for adventure and some are not," he had said. "She would have been unhappy all her days. And I would have been unhappy all my days if I had stayed. I had to see what was beyond the sea, beyond the tree line, beyond the next mountain."

Catrina thought about that conversation as she watched Abram's interaction with Gertrud. Gertrud would not have stayed behind. She *did not* stay behind. She had come to America and taken on the risk and challenge of the backcountry. Gertrud was not afraid to work hard. She knew how to do what must be done. Catrina felt sure that her sister-in-law could find shelter in a blizzard, patch a waistcoat when there was no needle to be had, or forage food from the wilderness. She was a survivor.

This realization did not make Catrina fond of her sister-in-law, but it did give her a grudging admiration for her. That was a start, anyway.

More importantly, Catrina realized why Abram could not stop teasing Gertrud. He admired her too. He had almost married a woman who could not share his life or vision. Did he think that Gertrud would? She was certainly capable of making it in the back-country. But what about that sour nature of hers? Catrina shook her head. Sometimes she did not understand men. *Ach, well. Perhaps I am putting the cart before the horse. Abram teases everyone. That does not mean he wants to marry everyone!*

Catrina was determined to do her share of the harvest. But as she watched Abram's hands fly over the flax bundles, she felt that she was barely contributing to the effort. She managed to put together a few more bundles before she stretched her back again, wiped her forehead with her sleeve, and announced that she would see to lunch. Now that was something that she could do right.

Eli grinned. "I was just thinking how hungry this makes a man."

Abram nodded. "See what you can do. I've a little of this and a little of that in the larder. But I know you can work wonders in the kitchen."

Catrina smiled and wiped her hands on her linen apron. She had found something to contribute.

Catrina felt satisfied with her endeavors when she returned to the field to call the others to the noon meal. Abram had been right when he said he had "a little bit of this and a little bit of that"—there was not enough of any one ingredient to make a proper recipe, and yet she had managed. She always did when it came to cooking. That was where she shined. Especially baking. Yesterday, she had baked a cake to celebrate her wedding, and a pie for the work party. Eli had helped polish off most of the cake. Now, the pie sat on the table beneath a cloth, looking delightfully tempting. Perhaps she would have two slices instead of one. That would make the day almost enjoyable.

Eli and Abram bounded into the cabin with grins and grimy hands. She ordered them to wash in the bucket by the hearth as she ladled venison stew into wooden trenchers and pulled the iron spider from atop the coals. Lard sizzled against the cast iron. It had fried the corn cakes a lovely golden brown.

The men jostled to reach for the nearest trencher. Abram nearly knocked over a pewter cup.

"Careful, now," Catrina said, and laughed. She wiped her hands on her apron, closed her eyes as Abram said the blessing, and then watched the men devour the meal. They shoveled the food into their mouths as if they hadn't eaten in days. Broth ran into Abram's beard and he dabbed his whiskers with his sleeve, then poured another spoonful of stew down his throat.

Catrina broke off a piece of warm, greasy corn cake and crumbled it into her stew. It was a good day, after all.

"We found the work much slowed in your absence," Gertrud said when she walked into the cabin, took off her scoop, and hung it on a peg.

"Oh?" Catrina's gaze jerked up from her trencher to Gertrud. Her sister-in-law took a place at the table and sampled the stew. "The food's good. But a good day's work in the field is better." She slurped the spoonful of broth and swallowed. "You've done little today."

"Done little today?" Catrina had spent most of the morning crouched over a hot fire, sweating, choking on the wood smoke, burning her fingers, and trying to coax a meal from a handful of ingredients.

Gertrud stared at Catrina from across the table and raised her eyebrows. Gertrud looked as if she believed every word she had said.

Catrina turned her face toward Eli. He would say something, wouldn't he? Gertrud was his sister, but *she* was his wife. Catrina waited. She felt her face burn and knew her pale skin had flushed red. Why did her complexion give her away so easily? How she wished she could pretend not to care!

Catrina continued to wait. She heard the sound of chewing, of a pewter spoon clinking against wood. The room was very quiet. And still, Eli did not speak. Abram sighed and set down his spoon. He wiped his mouth. "Catrina worked in the way that she works best."

Gertrud's eyes cut from Catrina's to Abram's. They narrowed along with her lips.

"Everyone has different talents. Hers are in the home, at the hearth. Yours might be in the fields, but that does not make your contribution any more valuable. A body's got to eat, doesn't it?"

Catrina was torn between satisfaction at Abram's defense and disappointment that Eli had not defended her himself. But, the conflicting emotions were forgotten when she watched Gertrud's reaction. Shock made her forget anything else.

Gertrud stared at Abram for a moment, then looked down at her wooden trencher. The room was even more silent than before. Catrina felt the tension swell like a soap bubble, until something had to burst. Gertrud picked up her spoon and dredged it through the stew. Steam curled upward and carried the scent of roasted meat. She shrugged and her face softened. "*Ja.* It is very good food."

Catrina nearly gasped. Had Gertrud just compli-mented her? Had Abram made Gertrud see things in a different light? The thought was shocking. Too shocking. Gertrud was not the type to take someone else's opinion to heart. And yet . . .

Eli looked as shocked as Catrina. Their eyes met across the table and he shrugged, then grinned. Catrina could not return the grin. Her stomach felt heavy. How could he act so nonchalant? Perhaps he did not realize how much Gertrud's accusation had hurt.

Ah well, Gertrud had almost acknowledged her wrongdoing, even if she had not gone so far as to apologize. It was a good start. Catrina watched the relief on Eli's face as the conversation turned to other things and they all resumed eating. Perhaps she would find a time to tell him that she wanted him to defend her. A marriage should be built on honest communica-tion, after all. Catrina stopped chewing. The food stuck to her throat. What a foolish bind she had created. Her marriage was not built on honest communication. But what could she do about that now?

Eli felt satisfied as he watched the flax field trans-form into neat clusters of bundled stalks that stood upright to dry beneath the spring sun. His back ached from the constant tugging and his arms burned, but they had accomplished the job. Perhaps everything would be all right. Catrina seemed happy and they had a good harvest of flax to support them. Along with the wool from Hilda and Christina's sheep, their weaving business should prosper. It was a good, simple life and it was almost perfect. Almost.

Every time he caught Gertrud watching Catrina, Eli felt the weight of *almost*. After Abram defended Catrina at lunch, Catrina had seemed distant. She still smiled when he looked at her, but he could sense a wistfulness in her eyes. And could he blame her? Of course not. He had failed her. What kind of husband lets his sister criticize his wife—especially in front of another person? Eli jerked the flax with sharp, frustrated movements. Why hadn't he said something? He had had the perfect defense in his mind. His mouth had almost opened to say it. Instead, he had remained silent and let Abram stand up for Catrina. Abram had said almost exactly what Eli had wanted to say. But that just made him feel worse.

Eli wanted to explain to Catrina why he could not stand up to his sister. Would she understand? Was that a risk he could take? He had lived with the shame and regret for so long that he could not fathom speaking it to another person—much less the woman he loved. What would she think of him if she knew what he had done? He already felt as if he did not deserve her. Eli frowned as he tied a stalk of flax around the bundle with a quick, overhand knot. He tossed the bundle beside the others and stole a glance at Catrina. She looked beautiful in the afternoon sun. The rays bathed her skin in a soft orange glow. He did not deserve her.

But Eli would think about that later. This evening, on the walk home, he would apologize and explain, no matter how ashamed he felt. For now, he would distract himself with other thoughts. Like the way Gertrud had stopped her criticism and agreed with

Abram. Now that was an interesting development! Could the rough-and-tumble frontiersman be getting to his sister?

After the last of the flax had been bundled and stood upright to dry, Eli took off his straw scoop and freed his hair. His scalp felt itchy and damp from the heat. It would feel good to collapse onto the straw pallet tonight. Later, after the flax dried, he would have to help Abram ripple the flax to deseed it, ret it by soaking it in water to rot away the outer husk, and then beat it into soft, silky threads. But tonight, he would sleep like the dead.

Chapter Twenty-One

Catrina could not sleep that night. She was exhausted from the harvest, but her mind would not rest. She kept agonizing over her decision to protect Eli from the truth. Catrina wondered for the thousandth time if she had done the right thing to give Gertrud her way. Gertrud knew her brother well, so perhaps she did know what was best.

And yet, Catrina could not ignore the churning inside her heart. She could not bear to withhold the truth from the man she loved. She did not know what to do. She did not know what was best for him.

By morning, she decided she could bear it no longer. She would tell him everything. Even if it hurt him. She wanted to feel good about her decision, but she did not. She felt more conflicted than ever.

At sunrise, Eli surprised Catrina by suggesting a walk in the woods. Her stomach jumped. Perhaps it was meant to be—perhaps she *was* supposed to tell him everything. His suggestion felt providential. Yes, she would tell him everything. There, she had decided. Relief spread through her. "I was going to suggest a walk if you did not," Catrina said as they set off through a grove of hemlock. "I would like to speak with you about . . . something." Eli nodded but did not reply. His expression changed and he looked distracted as they wandered through the woods and along the creek. His foot slipped in the mud and he slid down the bank as his arms windmilled. He splashed into the water, but managed to stay upright. Catrina laughed as he brushed his woolen hose and grinned at her. "You can't wipe water away."

"No." His grin widened. "But I can try."

This was the Eli that Catrina had married. Not the strained, taciturn man who hid behind his loom when Gertrud's sharp tongue whipped through the cabin. Catrina's smile faded. She should say something. Eli bounded up the bank, slid on the wet earth for a moment, then regained traction and hurtled himself past the mud. He nodded and offered Catrina his arm. "All right, then. Back to our stroll."

Catrina laughed, then stopped. She had to tell him now. "Eli?"

"*Ja?*" A rabbit bounded over a fallen log, darted across their path, then disappeared behind an oak tree. Eli's head shifted to follow the movement.

"Eli?" Catrina tapped his arm with her free hand. "Are you listening?"

"*Ja.* Of course."

Catrina could tell that he was not. If she did not know better, Catrina would think he knew what she was going to say and was trying to avoid the subject. Perhaps she should avoid it too. Perhaps Gertrud was right. Was she about to hurt Eli unnecessarily? No, dash it all, she had decided to tell him. She *would* tell him. "I need to talk to you about something that you will not want to hear." She felt the muscles in his arm stiffen.

He cleared his throat. "Have you ever seen a sky so blue?"

Catrina leaned her head back and looked through the canopy. Pockets of blue peeked through the branches like a bright, shimmering tablecloth beneath dark lace. She frowned and looked back at the ground in front of her feet. She was likely to fall if she continued to look up while moving forward. "It is lovely, but that is not what I wanted to talk about."

Eli sighed. "No. Of course not." His shoulders slouched. "You wanted to talk about me." Catrina heard a small crack in his voice. He suddenly looked small, despite being so tall and gangly.

"No. I need to talk to you about what happened...." She did not know what to say. All of her courage drained out of her body and soaked into the forest floor. Her tongue stuck to the roof of her mouth. "I worry that ... You should know ..." What if Gertrud was right and this would only cause more pain? What if she went to the bishop? What if she twisted Catrina's story into something worse? Catrina hesitated. Was she being selfish to purge her conscience? Was it kinder to protect him from the truth and carry the pain alone, forever?

Eli nodded. His face turned grim. The muscles in his jaw worked even though his mouth stayed closed. "You deserve better," he said finally.

"What? No." Catrina felt shocked. How could he think that? He was the one who deserved better. She shook her head. "Oh, Eli."

"I've needed to tell you that I ..." He licked his lips and turned his face away. His mouth opened, then closed again.

Catrina thought that he must be referring to the

awkward moment at Abram's when he did not defend her to Gertrud. Catrina was hurt, but she could not bear to see Eli so broken up about it. He must have been feeling guilty about it since yesterday afternoon. "She's your sister, I understand that. But that's not what . . ." Catrina felt the conversation slipping away from her. She had not wanted to make it about Gertrud. She had wanted to address the root of her own problem, not make Eli feel bad because he fell short during one stressful conversation.

"No." He shook his head again, but more slowly this time. It was a sad, defeated movement. "You cannot understand."

"I could if you would tell me." Catrina meant it in a supportive way, but the words sounded flat when she said them, probably because she felt ashamed. He was trying to apologize to her at the very moment when she had failed to share her own shame with him. She felt like a bad person, a bad wife. She knew that she was being too hard on herself, but she did not know how to go easier on herself. After two years of regret, her opinion of herself was not high.

Eli flinched. He opened his mouth to speak but Catrina interrupted before he could talk. "I'm sorry. I did not mean it the way it sounded. You have your reasons, I'm sure." She wished that she had said nothing. It had been foolish to try and tell him the secret that Gertrud had begged her not to tell. She had upset Eli and she had not even gotten to the upsetting part of the conversation! She sighed and looked back up at the sky. "It is a very lovely blue."

Eli's face relaxed. His jaw stopped clenching. "Yes," he said. "It is."

* * *

Eli had been determined to speak to Catrina. He wanted to tell her why he could not stand up to Gertrud. He wanted to explain everything—every last detail of what he had done and why he owed his sister everything. Perhaps if he told her, the guilt would stop eating him alive. Or perhaps Catrina would realize that she had married someone who did not deserve her.

He had decided to start by apologizing for his lack of backbone at the flax harvest and go from there. But, that had not happened. He had become flustered and tongue-tied. He had acted like, well, like himself. Dash it all, he could not go on like this. He couldn't tell her and he couldn't *not* tell her. Eli took off his beaver-felt hat and ran his fingers through his hair. It was impossible.

He could hear the spinning wheels through the open window. He could not bear to follow Catrina back into the cabin. Not yet. He had failed to tell her anything. Worse, she had seemed distant and upset throughout their walk. He didn't blame her. What kind of man let his sister criticize his wife? If only he could have explained better.

But explaining meant telling her everything. And how could he do that? How could he look into those wide, innocent eyes and tell her what kind of man he really was?

And so he had talked of the sky and the weather. Eli shook his head. He had failed. Again. He could feel Catrina pull away from him emotionally. It was all his fault. He would have to try harder.

Chapter Twenty-Two

Catrina felt as if she were walking on the edge of a knife. She still had not been able to tell Eli what she wanted to tell him, not when she saw how much it would hurt him during their last conversation. Gertrud must be right—telling Eli about her past was the wrong thing to do. But she could not stop feeling guilty about it. No matter what Catrina did, she felt conflicted and miserable. What if Gertrud were right? Worse, what if Gertrud were wrong? What if Catrina had added to her shame and failure by withholding the truth? Was it wrong to withhold the truth for a good reason? Was any reason good enough? Dash it all, she would drive herself mad if she did not stop agonizing over those questions.

After Catrina agreed to keep her past a secret, she and Gertrud began to develop a wary truce. But Gertrud's eyes still followed Catrina everywhere she went. Everything Catrina did felt measured and judged. No matter how hard she tried, Catrina felt that it could never be good enough.

That afternoon, when the tension stretched long, anxious fingers across the cabin and closed around her throat, Catrina felt that she would jump up and shout if Gertrud said another word in judgment. No, that was not quite accurate. Gertrud had not actually said anything that day. It was her cold, steely silence that ground Catrina's nerves down. If only Gertrud would say something, then Catrina would be able to call her out for it. But she could not criticize *silence*. What would she say? *You don't talk enough?* That proved nothing!

Eli did not say anything either. He hunched over the loom with a clenched jaw and slumped shoulders. He had brooded since their failed conversation in the woods. Perhaps he felt the same disappointment and frustration that Catrina did. This was not how the marriage was supposed to be! She felt a growing distance between them. Maybe she had been wrong to keep the truth from Eli, even though she did it to protect him and to please Gertrud. Maybe she had built a wall between them. How could the marriage work if there were secrets between them? But Gertrud was sure that it was the only way. . . .

A loud knock shook Catrina from her thoughts. Abram strode through the open door before she could finish telling him to come in. He surveyed the silent cabin and took a seat on the bench beside the hand-hewn table. "Awful quiet today," Abram said as he leaned an elbow against the oak tabletop. He scratched his knee and straightened one of his woolen hose. "Cat got everybody's tongue?"

"Something like that," Catrina said. She did not stop her spinning wheel. Eli's loom clacked and swooshed as the women's spinning wheels clicked. Other than that, no one spoke.

"I came to the wrong place, I see. Thought an old lonely bachelor might get some friendly conversation."

He looked at Catrina and raised his eyebrows. "Or a bite to eat."

Catrina smiled. It was good to have Abram in the room. His warm energy neutralized the tension. "I can always count on you to appreciate my culinary talents."

"That you can, my dear."

Gertrud's spinning wheel slowed but did not stop. She cut a sidelong glance to Abram. "I would say that we can always count on you to appreciate gluttony."

Abram slapped his knee. "Do my ears deceive me? Did our Gertie just make a joke?"

Gertrud raised her chin a fraction. Her fingers continued to work a length of wool around the wheel. "*Ja.* I suppose I did."

"Hmmmm." Abram's hand ran through his thick black beard. "Sounds like our Gertie's in a better mood than I thought. She might even be good company."

"Don't push it, Abram."

Abram shrugged. His lips curled in a lazy half smile. "It's a nice day. Good for a walk. Would you be good company on a walk, or would you bite my head off for existing?"

"I would do no such thing." She pumped the treadle of the spinning wheel a little harder. "You persecute me for no cause, Abram Ziegler."

"Ah. Another joke. My, you are in fine form today."

"I do not bite heads off. I simply do not have time for nonsense."

"Mmmm. Nonsense." Abram grinned. "So you *would* accompany me on a walk and not bite my head off?"

"Of course. I just told you I do not bite heads off. I simply cannot abide tomfoolery."

"All right. If you insist." Abram stood up and headed for the door. He stood in the threshold and waited. His finger tapped the doorframe in a slow, steady rhythm until Gertrud looked up at him.

"What are you doing, Abram? I've told you I have no time for nonsense."

"You also told me that you would accompany me on a walk."

"I did no such thing."

"Oh, but you did. And I believe you to be a woman of your word. Let's see, your exact words were, 'Of course.' That was in response to my question, 'So you *would* accompany me on a walk and not bite my head off?'"

Gertrud frowned and returned her attention to the spinning wheel. "You are an incorrigible man, Abram Ziegler."

"Uh-oh." Abram shook his head. "You are not keeping your word. Remember, you said that you would accompany me on a walk *and* you would not bite my head off. The second clause is as important as the first." He smiled. "To me, anyway."

Gertrud let out a sharp exhalation. She pulled her foot from the treadle and shot up from her stool. "Fine. Have your way, Abram. You have worn me down and I will walk with you just so that you will stop twisting the meaning of my words!"

Abram raised an eyebrow and looked at Catrina. "She is so eager to walk with me that she raised her voice from the excitement."

"From the irritation, Abram!" Gertrud said as she pulled her straw scoop from the peg on the wall and shoved it over her prayer *kappe*. "Make no mistake about that!"

Abram winked at Catrina. "And yet, she is going with me. That is not the actions of a woman who is irritated, is it?" He shrugged. "Seems more like the actions of a woman who is smitten with a man."

Gertrud's breath shot out of her mouth in a sharp hiss. She tied the ribbons of her scoop around her throat in a hard, fast movement, then tugged at the knot to loosen it. Oh, she was mad now! Catrina expected Gertrud to pull off her scoop, slam it down, and sit back at her spinning wheel.

But she did not.

"It's all right. Women just can't help themselves around me." Abram laughed and his big, booming voice filled the cabin. Gertrud responded in a most unexpected way. She smiled. Her lips almost curled into a grin. And then she snorted.

"I'll take that snort as a laugh," Abram said. "Hurry up and let's go while I'm on your good side." He offered his arm and she took it. Eli's eyebrows shot up and he glanced at Catrina. They could not quite believe it. Abram paused in the doorway and looked back at them. "I'd like to see what being on her bad side is like."

Catrina wanted to laugh, but she could not. She knew exactly what that was like and there was nothing funny about it.

Eli noticed a difference after Gertrud and Abram left the cabin. Some of the tension swept out the door with his sister. Not all of it did, though. That concerned him. What had happened in the days since he had married Catrina? There had never been tension before. But he had never brought a bride home to a disapproving sister before.

He and Catrina chatted and even laughed a little as they waited for Gertrud to return. It felt awkward to speak freely, as if they still did not quite know each other yet. Eli felt shy and unsure, even though he knew this was the perfect time to tell Catrina why he could not defend her. It was the perfect time to explain everything. He swallowed and waited for the right moment.

"There's something I've wanted to tell you," Catrina said before he could speak. "But I don't know if . . ."

"No. I need to tell you first . . ."

Eli stopped midsentence and they both looked up from their work when they heard Gertrud's footsteps at the door. Eli frowned. He had failed to talk to her yet again. He wondered what Catrina had been about to say, but the question faded when he saw his sister sweep into the cabin.

"Well?" Eli asked as Gertrud untied the ribbons of her scoop. He grinned.

"Well, what?" Gertrud said. She wore the same serious expression she always did.

"How was your walk with Abram?"

"It was a walk. What is any walk like? You move your legs, you pass trees and hills and end up back home again."

"You know that's not what I meant! What did he say to you?"

"He said the flax is dried and ready to ret. We should go on the morrow. It's a good crop, dried white and not brown."

"*Ja*, that is welcome news. But what did he *say*?"

"Was that not saying something?"

"Gertie."

She shrugged and slid into place at her spinning wheel. "What did you want him to say?"

"Oh, I don't know. Maybe something about his intentions?"

Gertrud snorted. "Intentions? I think not."

"So Abram Ziegler asked you on a walk just to discuss the flax harvest?"

"Perhaps." She made a show of focusing on the wool in her hand.

Eli smiled. "And perhaps not." He glanced at Catrina. "I think our Gertie has gotten herself a suitor."

"Do not be ridiculous. I have done no such thing. And I most certainly have done no such thing with the likes of Abram Ziegler." She began to pump the treadle with her foot. "You know, sometimes a walk is just a walk."

Eli raised an eyebrow. "And sometimes, sister mine, it is not."

He noticed that Gertrud seemed particularly thoughtful for the rest of the day. It was almost as if she were mulling over his words and analyzing the walk. But that would be ridiculous.

Catrina's secret burned within her. She could feel the anxiety building and building, until she knew something in her would snap.

That snap came the very next morning. Catrina woke up scratching the skin beneath her thin linen shift. She sat up, pulled up her sleeve, and saw bright red welts covering her skin. Her stomach churned as it had ever since she agreed to withhold her past from Eli. Stress. The rash must be from stress.

Catrina pulled her wool skirt over her shift, slipped into her bodice and laced it closed, then pinned her oversleeves in place to cover the sleeves of her shift, which served as a nightgown by night and an undergarment by day.

"If Catrina's still abed at this hour I will have to go on to Abram's myself," Gertrud's voice said from the other side of the curtain.

Dash it all! She had not meant to oversleep. They were supposed to help Abram ret the flax today. That would be another mark against her. Would she ever be good enough? Catrina's neck began to itch. Dash it all again! She had to calm down.

"In a hurry to see Abram this morning?" Eli asked in a good-natured voice.

Gertrud grunted. Something banged and clanged in the fireplace.

"I'm coming!" Catrina shouted through the curtain as she stood on one leg and pulled a woolen hose up the other leg. She had to hop to keep her balance and she thumped into the wall.

"Are you all right?" Eli asked.

"Fine!" She yanked the hose above her knee, tied it in place, and began to pull the other hose up. This time, she hopped onto the sleeping pallet, lost her footing, and tumbled onto the straw mattress.

"What in heaven's name?" Gertrud muttered from the other side of the curtain.

Catrina was not herself at all. She was not the type to fall down or wallow about on a straw mattress, with one hose on, one halfway off, as she tried to regain her balance. *It is only stress,* she reminded herself.

Eli was not convinced. He noticed the red welt on her throat as soon as she pushed the curtain aside. He stared at her as she tucked the curtain behind the hook on the wall to create one open room. Gertrud looked past her and frowned. "You've left your pallet out." She rubbed her temples. "Really, we've got to go."

Catrina cringed. Another thing that she had failed to do. They had to fold and stack the pallets during the day to make room.

"She's unwell!" Eli said. He shouted it, really.

Gertrud looked up toward the sky with the expression of a long-suffering saint on her face. "I'll meet you there."

"No! I'll have to fetch help. You stay here. We can't leave her alone."

Gertrud let out a long breath. She sank onto the bench beside the table and began to tap the wooden surface with a slow, impatient *tap, tap, tap.*

Catrina wished that she had remembered to cover her throat. She had been in such a hurry to get ready that she had forgotten to wrap her neck cloth around her collarbone and tuck it into her bodice. Dash it all! She doubled back to her trunk of clothing, pulled out her neck cloth, and threw it into place.

"Hold on, now." Eli hurried to Catrina's side and pushed the cloth aside. He looked stricken as he studied the rash. His worry made *her* worry and a new welt appeared on the soft white skin of her throat. *Yes,* she thought, *this must be stress. How else could a new welt appear so fast?*

Eli did not stop to listen to theories. Catrina feared that the poor man might pass out from concern. He looked convinced that death was imminent. He ran to fetch Ruth Yoder before Catrina could stop him. The elderly widow had some knowledge of herbs and remedies and would not mind calling on Catrina, but Catrina hated to be a bother. Everyone thought she was delicate and unfit for the backcountry. She hated to reinforce that opinion.

She did not hate seeing Eli fall over himself to get help for her. He dropped his hat, knocked over a basket of raw wool, and stumbled over a wooden bench on his way out the door. His antics made her feel loved. Only a man who cared about her would become so flustered over a rash. His last words before he ran through the door were something to the effect of "measles or the pox."

Gertrud sighed and shook her head. "He'll work himself into a state of illness over nothing. And then we'll be fetching the Widow Yoder on *his* account."

Catrina just smiled to herself and scratched her elbow through her sleeve. Dash it all, but everything itched. At least she felt loved. That almost made the itching worth it.

Gertrud and Catrina waited in silence until Eli returned with Ruth Yoder at his heels. It had been a long, uncomfortable waiting period, as neither woman wanted to speak to the other. Indeed, the worst thing about this whole debacle of a morning was that Catrina knew she had done one more thing to frustrate her sister-in-law. The sun was nearly above the tree line by now. What must Abram think? She hated that he would have to ret the flax by himself because of her.

"Ah!" Ruth said as she strode through the door and untied her scoop. She tossed it on the table and headed straight for Catrina. "Let's unpin your sleeve."

"All right." They worked together to unfasten the detachable sleeve from the bodice, then rolled up the sleeve of the thin linen shift she wore underneath.

"Wonderful good."

"What?" Eli's face jerked. He had been hovering over them the entire time. He had raked his fingers through his hair so many times that it looked as though a wild animal had nested on his head. A very red wild animal. "What can be good about this?" His hands made big, excited circles in the air.

"*Ach.*" Ruth rolled the sleeve of Catrina's shift down and began to pin her outer sleeve back onto her bodice. "It is only hives."

"Hives?"

"*Ja.*" Ruth nodded and fastened the last pin. "Mix a spoonful of warm water with a spoonful of vinegar to stop the itching."

"That's it?" Eli looked confused. "I thought hives came from excessive worry."

"*Ja.*" Ruth nodded again. "I have often found that to be the case."

"But . . ." Eli's face crumpled.

Catrina forced a smile. "It is nothing, Eli. Sometimes hives come from other things."

"Such as?"

"Oh, I don't know." Catrina scratched her neck. "No one does. They just appear sometimes."

"When someone has excessive worry," Ruth said.

"But . . ." Eli stared at Catrina. He shook his head.

"Take something for your troubles, Ruth." Catrina did not want to broach the subject of stress. What would she say to explain her worries to Eli? "I made dried apple pie today. The children would like it, *ja*?" Ruth lived with Jacob, Greta, and their two adopted children—all of whom enjoyed a good apple pie.

"They would. Growing like weeds. You can't feed them enough." Catrina smiled and gathered the left-over slices. At least she could give something back.

As soon as Ruth left, Eli insisted that she stay in bed. Catrina refused. "I've already caused us to miss the first of the retting. I won't lie abed while you two make up for the loss I caused. I will come and help."

Eli frowned. He rubbed the back of his neck. "I cannot go along with that." He looked miserable. "But you know I can never say no to you."

"You are a darling, wonderful good man. Now move aside and we will be on our way."

"Oh, I don't know. I don't think it's such a good idea. . . ."

But Catrina had already stridden to the door and pulled her scoop from its peg. "Remember what Ruth said. If this is caused by excessive worry, then I must go. Staying here will only make me worry more because I will feel guilty that I can't help."

Eli sighed. He rubbed the back of his neck again. After a pause he nodded. "All right. But don't tax yourself. Promise me that."

"I promise." Catrina stood on her tiptoes and kissed the tip of his nose. "I hope you don't mind that your wife looks like a red-spotted calf."

Eli grinned. "You are still the most beautiful woman

in the world. Those hives will have to work harder if they want to change that."

Catrina felt warm inside. She realized that she felt a good bit less itchy. Feeling loved certainly is good medicine.

Chapter Twenty-Three

Abram was knee-deep in a stagnant pond when they reached his land. The flax had to soak in water until the outer layer rotted away. Retting was really just a fancy word for rotting and Eli wondered why it wasn't called rotting instead. The fouler and scummier the water, the better, because it rotted the flax quicker than clean, running water. That was one reason Abram had chosen this plot of land; it had a nice (if you could call it that) stagnant pool of yellow-green slop.

"Hallo there," Abram shouted to them as he sloshed out of the shallow water to greet them.

"I'm sorry," Catrina said. "It's my fault we're late."

Abram saw her expression and frowned. "Sun's not halfway up the sky yet. Plenty of time to get the work finished. Don't fret yourself about it, little lass." He started to pick up a bundle of flax and hesitated. His attention slid back to Catrina. "What's ailing you?"

"I'm fine," she said, and readjusted her neck cloth. Eli could tell that she did not want to draw any more attention to herself.

"You look ready to faint," Abram said to Catrina, then jerked his chin toward Gertrud. "That pretty face of yours looks almost as sour as Gertie's this morning." He grinned. "Notice I said *almost.*"

Gertrud pursed her lips as she cut past him to the bundles of flax that lay beside the pond.

Abram watched Gertrud march by him and smiled. Then he turned back to Catrina. "Got some spots, eh?"

"*Ja.* I suppose you could say that."

"You look like Greta's old milk cow, Rose. The one with the red spots."

Catrina turned to Eli and they both laughed. "That's just what I was saying," she said.

Abram raised his eyebrows. "Because it is true."

"Abram, mind your tongue. I do not find that a favorable comparison."

Abram scratched his chin. "No? Rose is a very friendly and reliable cow."

"Abram, you really are incorrigible."

"I left some of the rippling for you to do so you don't have to get your pretty little feet wet. So maybe I'm not so bad after all."

"Did you?" Catrina clapped her hands together. "You are a dear!"

Eli realized what a sacrifice Catrina had been willing to make. She thought that she would have to slog through that foul green water. Well, he would not have allowed that anyway. He would do everything he could for Catrina. Especially since he couldn't control Gertrud's attitude toward her. His frustration over that made him try to make it up in other ways. But, he felt himself falling short no matter what he did. And now, Catrina had broken out in hives! His poor, perfect wife suffered from excessive worry. That was his fault. He had failed her.

Eli watched as Catrina picked up a bundle of flax

and took it to the rippling board that Abram had set atop a table. Long, thick nails stood in a row across the board, rather like a large, metal comb. Catrina pulled the bundle of flax through the nails and the seeds popped off and bounced onto an old length of cloth laid on the ground below. Afterward, Abram would collect the seeds from the cloth and use them for next year's planting or for animal feed.

Eli waited until Catrina had pulled the flax through the ripple board a few times before he nodded and turned away. She seemed all right. But he would keep a close eye on her. It would not do for her to work too hard. He wished she had stayed abed. But she had wanted to come and he was not the type to order his wife about. Some men did that, but he thought it ungentlemanly. It was downright unacceptable, to be honest, despite what the law had to say on the matter. He much preferred an equal partnership built on friendship and trust.

There he went again, rattling on about trust when he still had not told his wife about the terrible thing that he had done to Gertrud four years ago.

"Too scared to get your feet wet?" Abram called from the water.

"*Ach.* I'm coming."

"Slowly." Abram grinned and swept his palm across the surface of the pond. An arc of slimy liquid shot through the air and splattered Eli's breeches. He leapt back and Abram laughed. "They're going to get wet anyway."

Eli shrugged. "I can't argue that logic."

"Best plunge right in. And don't think about it."

Abram jerked his chin toward Gertrud. "Like your sister here. She's put you to shame."

Gertrud stood thigh deep in the stagnant water as she pushed an armful of flax stalks beneath the surface. Her face looked calm and vacant as she focused on her work. If the foulness of the pond disturbed her, she did not show it. "A woman like that is worth her weight in gold in the backcountry, I tell you." Abram shook his head. "Not even a grimace."

If Gertrud enjoyed the compliment, she did not show it. Eli sighed as he unfastened and removed his leather shoes, rolled down his woolen hosen, and peeled them off. He tossed the hosen behind him and debated whether or not to roll up his breeches. He decided that would be pointless.

Gertrud slogged out of the water to retrieve another bundle of flax. The stench of algae and rot wafted from Gertrud's wet skin. Eli sighed. He really wasn't cut out for this any more than Catrina was, but one must do what one must do. Tomorrow he would be all the more grateful to be back at his loom. He heard Catrina humming as she stood at the rippling board. *At least she doesn't have to go in.* That thought gave him the strength to plunge into the water with an armful of flax.

Eli had expected it to be cold, but the water felt warm as a hot stone that sat in the sun all day. The heat felt as wrong as the smell. Oh well, there was nothing for it. He pushed through the oily, stagnant water until it lapped past his knees. Then Eli separated the stalks and pushed them beneath the water. He did not think the job could get any worse, until he stooped down and his nose was just above the surface. That was definitely worse.

"Here," Abram said, and handed him a stone. Eli had not expected it to be quite so heavy and his knees buckled. He tried to lock them back in place before Abram noticed. Eli lowered the rock onto the stalks to weigh them down, then waded back to shore for the next load. The process went on long enough that he forgot to care about the smell or the heat of the water. After a while, he was ready to eat and hoped that Catrina had left to prepare something for them all.

But when he looked up, he saw something he never expected to see. Catrina stood in the stagnant water. The warm green liquid lapped around her calves as she waded toward him. Each step looked like an act of will. Her face had become a mask of concentration and suppressed disgust.

"Catrina! What in heaven's name are you doing?"

"My part."

"This is ridiculous!"

Gertrud straightened up and stared. She shrugged and stooped again to push the flax beneath the water. "It's only right that she does her part. Especially after she caused us to tarry this morning."

Catrina swallowed. She said nothing as she took another slow, painful step.

Eli did not know what to do. He could see her misery deepen as the water did. But worse than seeing her in the sludge was hearing Gertrud's words. They were true, but there was more than one way to do one's part. And truly, he would rather have a hot lunch waiting for him right now than to have Catrina help with the retting. What kind of madness was this? Catrina could not bear a spot of mud, much less bathing in pond scum! She had proven herself with the wolf. This was asking too much. Sure, it was an unpleasant job for him, but for Catrina it must be downright unbearable.

He would say something. He had to. But he felt frozen in place as the water sloshed around Gertrud's arms and her face took on a stony, unreachable expression. How could he appease two people he loved without hurting either one? Eli opened his mouth to say something, anything.

"Gertie, what's the matter with you?" Abram asked. Eli closed his mouth. He waited to hear Gertrud's reaction. Her face shot up. She looked surprised. She was not used to being challenged. Eli realized that he had let her get away with far too much over the last four years, but what else could he do? Abram was right to challenge her. Eli only wished that he had said something first.

"You don't want to eat?" Abram's voice boomed across the water.

Gertrud's mouth tightened. "What kind of question is that?"

"One that deserves an answer."

"*Ach.*" Gertrud shook her head and dropped a stone atop a bundle of flax. The water splashed upward and splattered her face. She frowned and wiped her lips with her sleeve.

"Dinner isn't going to cook itself," Abram said. "And I for one would like to eat today."

"Eating is all you want to do any day."

Abram smiled. "I have my priorities straight."

Gertrud shook her head.

"I suppose you will take care of it, then?"

"Take care of what?" Gertrud pushed a strand of hair beneath her prayer *kappe*. Her fingers left a wet streak across the white linen.

"Dinner."

"I most certainly will not."

Abram shrugged. "Then you will not eat."

"*Ach.*" Gertrud shook her head again.

"Well, go on then." Abram made a shooing motion with his hand.

"I have no intention of wasting the day breathing in wood smoke and stirring a pot when I can be working outside in the sunshine, getting something accomplished."

"Funny, I thought that getting dinner was an accomplishment. Can't eat otherwise."

"You know what I mean."

Abram raised his eyebrows.

"Accomplishing something worthwhile," Gertrud said.

"Ah, yes. Because eating is not worthwhile."

"Abram Ziegler, that is enough."

Eli cleared his throat. He needed to say something now, before Abram said it all for him. He was torn between loyalties, but dash it all, his wife came first. He plunged ahead. No one spoke to his wife that way, not even Gertie. "It will be enough when . . ." Eli lost his grip on the stone in his hand. It slid into the pond and water splashed his face. He sputtered and spit. He felt sick and spit again. He wiped his face with his sleeve. "I was saying—"

But Abram did not give him a chance to finish. He and Gertrud were staring at each other without any thought of Eli. "It will be enough when you apologize to Catrina," Abram said. Abram's voice softened as he spoke, but the words cut off Eli, nonetheless. Eli groaned inside. Now he had done it. He had missed the chance to defend his wife!

"*Ja.*" Eli nodded as he wiped his face again. "I was just about to say . . ." But no one was listening to him.

They had not even noticed he had tried to speak at all. "Abram's right." He raised his voice so that everyone would hear. "I was just about to say that." Abram and Gertrud still did not notice him. Their eyes stayed locked on one another.

Catrina's eyes cut to Eli, but the look of hurt on her face clamped his mouth shut. Eli ran his fingers through his hair. It did not matter what he had been about to say. He had not said it first. That was all Catrina saw. She did not see that his heart had leapt to defend her. That he had been about to defend her, despite his duty toward Gertrud. If only he had not hesitated. If only he had not been so rattled that he let the rock slip from his fingers. He was a clumsy oaf. A failure. He wanted to tell Catrina all that he was thinking. He did not. How could he possibly explain?

Gertrud's mouth opened, then closed again. She was still staring at Abram.

"You know I'm right, Gertie." Abram's voice remained soft, but his eyes held a seriousness that could not be ignored.

"Humph."

"Catrina's sick with worry over something—that's why she tarried this morning. I wonder if you know what that worry could be?" Abram rubbed his hand across his mouth. "Surely it could not be your lack of approval?"

Gertrud's eyes snapped to his. "You go too far."

"Do I?" Abram shrugged. "A little appreciation seems perfectly reasonable to me."

"Why should I appreciate you?"

Abram smiled. "You know I'm talking about Catrina."

Gertrud raised her chin. She swallowed and smoothed her prayer *kappe*. "All right. Fine. You win. I acquiesce that you have a point. Perhaps it isn't a reasonable or valid point, but it is a point, nonetheless."

"Gertrud."

"Oh, fine." Gertrud spun around and stared at Catrina. "I apologize. Would you please go get dinner?"

"And?" Abram gave a half smile. He looked as if he were enjoying this.

"And I appreciate your cooking."

"Bravo!" Abram grinned. "Now, was that so hard?"

Judging by Gertrud's expression, it had been very hard indeed.

Catrina did not want to talk to Eli on the way home. It was becoming more and more difficult to understand why he refused to defend her. She appreciated that Abram did, but it almost made the situation more painful. Abram's concern highlighted Eli's lack thereof.

She stole a glance at Eli as they cut across a field of barley. The setting sun highlighted his red hair. A warm breeze rippled through the barley stalks to transform the field into a river of golden waves. The scene could have been idyllic. But Eli's face looked pinched and he refused to meet her gaze. What was the matter with him? Was he upset with her? Was he disappointed that he had married her? Was that why he always looked at his sister with that resigned expression? Had he come to agree with Gertrud?

Catrina's heart caught in her chest when she realized that Eli's expression was one of regret. Did Eli regret marrying her? She felt a cold, hard shiver run up her spine. She knew what would make him regret marrying her. Had he learned the truth? Was that the cause of his long, painful silences and downcast eyes?

She would have to ask him. No, she could not do that. Too much time had passed. How could she explain why she had kept her secret for days after they had married? That was the problem with secrets. The longer they stood between two people the more powerful they became.

Catrina glanced behind her. Gertrud was just out of earshot. Catrina turned back to Eli. This was her chance. She would test the waters. "Truth is never easy, is it?" Catrina said to him in a low voice.

Eli swallowed. "No."

"But it is the only way."

Eli nodded but did not meet her eyes. Catrina waited for him to respond. Perhaps he would take the hint and tell her what he knew. She did not want to have to say it first. "There is something that I have not spoken to you about . . . something that should have been told before we married," Eli said after a long pause. His face twitched. "It has created a barrier between us."

He did know. She was surprised at his calm. But then again, sometimes a hard calm was the most difficult response to bear. Catrina's father had been terribly calm before he banished her from his home forever. People were often at their cruelest when they were calm. Catrina would rather see an outburst of emotions, which burned out as quickly as a flash fire, than a decisive calm.

But Eli was not cruel. It was not in his nature. That was one reason why she loved him. Then how could he be so calm right now? Perhaps it was resignation. She glanced behind them again. Gertrud was still out of earshot. Catrina put a hand on Eli's elbow. She took a deep, unsteady breath and chose to trust him. "It does not have to create a barrier."

Eli laughed. Something in that laugh made Catrina's stomach turn. She recognized the anger, regret, and pain inside the bitter chuckle. It was a sound that she never thought she'd hear from Eli's mouth. "Then you do not understand," he said.

Catrina's hand fell from Eli's arm. Her body felt cold. Could this really be happening? After all that she had overcome? Could Eli—her loving, thoughtful Eli—condemn her? "I understand more than you know," she said softly. "I understand that a single mistake can cost a lifetime of regret."

Eli's face hardened. It was not an expression that suited him. His eyes were made to sparkle. His lips were made to smile. Catrina wished that she had not started the conversation. But it was too late now. She had to see it through, for better or worse. Eli's gaze stayed on the distant tree line. His jaw clenched and unclenched in a tight rhythm. Catrina could not bear to wait for what he was going to say. She could not bear to hear what he would say, either. She waited with her heart in her throat. "You should not have married me," he said at last.

Catrina felt as if she had been punched in the gut. That one, simple sentence was the most painful thing that she had ever experienced. Her Eli was not her Eli. He did not want her after all. He did not defend her because she was not worth defending. All of her fears had come true. All of her bravado, her belief in redemption, her hope that she could start anew—all of it evaporated. She would have to continue to pay the price for her fall. And oh, what a heavy price it was. Catrina swallowed. She smoothed the front of her bodice and straightened her sleeve. "No," she said in a very quiet voice. "I should not have. I am sorry that I did." There, she had said it. She had admitted how wrong she had been to marry him while keeping a secret from him. And now, she would have to pay.

Chapter Twenty-Four

Catrina could not stay. She would not stay. They were married now and that could not be undone. But how could she live in a house where she was unwanted? Where every movement was watched with cold, calculating eyes that condemned her for a foolish mistake she had made when she was only a girl? Perhaps she could go to the bishop and tell him what she had done. Perhaps he could grant an annulment and free Eli from her. That was what he wanted. He had as good as said it. She loved him enough to set him free.

They did not speak again as they walked home. When they entered the cabin, the fire had burned down and the room felt cold and desolate. Catrina shivered and rubbed her arms. Eli did not move toward her. A few days ago he would have put an arm around her and held her close until she warmed. Now, he stalked to the hearth and began to stack fresh kindling. Still, he did not speak. Catrina watched Eli's back as he dropped another stick of kindling into place. He did not turn around. She felt invisible, forgotten. Perhaps, in his heart, she was already gone.

Her mind swirled with plans. None of them made sense. None of them would work. But she could not think straight. All she could think was that she could not stay here any longer. Each minute inside the cabin stabbed her with condemnation. She did not belong there. She never had.

She would leave as soon as Eli fell asleep. He would awaken alone and feel relieved. He would not have to live with the regret that he admitted he felt.

Moonlight slipped through the shuttered windows and painted white streaks across the cabin walls. Catrina slid into her skirt and bodice without lighting a candle. She moved with the stealthy silence that comes with heartbreak. Each footstep sounded empty and meaningless. She felt as if she were already gone, as if she were already a ghost in the house.

Catrina glanced back before slipping out the door. The cabin looked neat and orderly in the thin moonlight. The loom and the spinning wheels stood empty and still. How she wished for the days of their courtship again, when the loom clattered and the spinning wheel turned and anything seemed possible. Nothing felt possible anymore.

The door shuddered as she closed it. She stared at the rough-hewn wood as she hovered just outside the threshold. The man she loved slept on the other side of that door. But he wished they had not married. She loved him enough to leave. It was what he wanted. And she would not humiliate or delude herself any longer by staying.

Catrina closed her eyes and ran her fingers down the door. The wood snagged her soft skin. She could see Eli's face when he had been so in love with her. His big, goofy grin was imprinted inside her mind. He had been head over heels with adoration. He wanted her more than anything.

And now he did not want her at all.

Catrina opened her eyes. She sighed and stepped backward. The night would fade into morning soon. She could not wait any longer. It was time to go. But where? Back to her grandparents? No. She could not face disappointing them. She walked without thinking, until she could no longer see the cozy, familiar clearing. She walked until trees blocked the moonlight and she felt more alone than she ever had before. Catrina wished that she could walk forever and never stop. When she stopped she would have to face her problems. And she could not bear to face something that had no solution.

Eli woke up cold. He slung his arm across the straw pallet and felt cool, empty bedcovers. His eyes shot open. Where was his wife? He struggled into his woolen hosen and fumbled through the curtain. A terrible, terrible thought crept up his spine.

No. No, it could not be true.

He stared at the hearth. Empty. His eyes darted across the still, silent room. Empty. He told himself that Catrina was outside. Everything was all right. She went to fetch water or . . . or . . . something. There was an explanation. There had to be.

But that cold, unrelenting shiver up his spine told him otherwise. She had left him. She had realized who he was. No, she had realized who he wasn't. He was not man enough for her. He could not stand up for her. He could not take care of her or protect her as she deserved. He had failed.

Eli's words echoed inside his head. *You should not have married me.* He could still hear them ringing in his ears. Catrina's face had looked startled, then calm after he had said it. He had had a wild, distant hope that she would disagree. She might have told him that she was glad to have married him or that she loved him enough to overcome his failures.

But that was not to be. Catrina had run her long, slim fingers over her bodice to smooth a wrinkle, then adjusted her sleeve, before answering him. She looked perfect. She *was* perfect. Nothing was out of place. Her gaze had turned distant, then. "No," she had said in a very quiet voice. "I should not have. I am sorry that I did."

Nothing could have been more devastating than that statement. His wife had become cold and un-feeling. And he had driven her to that point. He had kept his past secret. He had chosen Gertrud over Catrina and allowed his sister to push and push and push until Catrina snapped and could take it no more. She had become physically ill. And now, she had had enough. She was sorry that she had mar-ried him.

Eli threw open the door. His pulse thudded against his throat with a fierce hope that he would see her standing alone, silhouetted against the sunrise. But she was not there. The first streaks of light ran gray fingers across the clearing and illuminated the empti-ness. There was only dirt and the wild grass that tried to overtake New Canaan's fields. Catrina was gone.

* * *

Catrina walked until she could not walk anymore and then she kept walking. She almost wanted to get lost. That way she could disappear. But, that was childish foolishness. When she stopped to pull a stone from her shoe, Catrina realized that she did not recognize her surroundings and felt a stab of panic. So much for the bravado she had felt just moments before. The wilderness could swallow a settler forever. If she kept going westward she might walk and walk forever and never find her way again. The New World stretched into endless forests and unknown mountains. Suddenly, Catrina regretted her rashness. What had she been thinking? No one can run away from his or her problems. Problems always follow, until they are solved. Hadn't she learned that when Gertrud appeared in New Canaan with knowledge of Catrina's past?

She stopped, leaned against a sturdy oak, and closed her eyes. After a moment she realized that she could hear running water in the background. She knew to follow the river. It ran through the settlement, so if she walked alongside the bank, it would eventually take her home again.

Catrina stumbled through the underbrush, pausing every now and then to listen. The sound of water grew louder. How could she have been so foolish? She was not afraid of wolves or bobcats. Bears were a different matter, of course, but she had wandered the woods many times without meeting one. No, what scared her was the thought of walking forever and never reaching home again.

Home. The word made her think of the snug cabin she shared with Eli and Gertrud. She did not think of her grandparents' place anymore. But how could home be a place where she was unwanted? She wondered what Eli was doing now. The sun was above the tree line. He would know that she had left by now. He would wonder where she had gone. *She* wondered where she had gone as well, but that was another matter.

Did he let out a long sigh of relief when he discovered her absence? Was he thankful to be free of her and her secrets? Lies, Gertrud had called them. Lies. Had she told him? She must have. There was no other explanation.

The water rose to a low roar. Catrina pushed a pine branch aside and saw white water rolling and skipping across the clear, rushing river. She would make it home again if she followed the water. But where would home be? Catrina could not bear to face it. She would have to move back in with her grandparents and endure the shame. Her husband did not want her. There was no place else to hide. She had already hidden in the farthest outpost possible. And she had been found.

Catrina sank onto a large, smooth rock. The surface felt warm and reassuring beneath her palms. She would stay awhile. She could not face going back just yet. She drew her knees under her chin and listened to the hum of the river. A school of minnows darted around the rock. Sunlight flashed off their silver scales and dappled the surface of the water with gold. It could have been beautiful and peaceful. It was not.

Eli woke Gertrud. "Have you seen Catrina?" Gertrud jumped up when she saw his expression. She put a hand on his shoulder. Her voice sounded softer than Eli expected. "Has she left you?" Her face looked full of pain and sympathy.

Eli's Adam's apple bobbed in his throat. He did not look up. "I don't know. I think so."

Gertrud sighed and followed Eli outside. He swept his hand across the empty clearing. "She's gone." He had expected it. Catrina had made her feelings clear the night before. But still, his world crumbled. He had to catch his breath. He had to understand how it had come to this. He leaned against the cabin and let his knees buckle. He slid down the wall, sat down hard in the dirt, and put his head in his hands. Gertrud settled onto the ground beside him.

"You'll ruin your skirt," Eli said. "You're sitting in mud."

"You know I don't care about that."

"No."

Gertrud leaned her head against Eli's shoulder. She did not speak, but Eli could feel something warm and reassuring in her silence. They stared at nothing until Eli finally spoke. "I suppose you're happy now."

"Oh, Eli." Gertrud pressed a hand to her forehead. She squeezed her eyes shut. "This does not make me happy."

"You wanted her gone the entire time she was here."

"No." Gertrud lifted her head from Eli's shoulder. She put a warm, calloused hand on his arm. "I wanted her to be better than she was. I knew it would end like this. I wanted to protect you from this."

"Gertrud." He shook his head in a slow, resigned movement. Something welled up from his stomach. He could feel it building. The hurt and frustration could not be tapped down. He blamed himself. But Gertrud had played a part in it as well. "Don't you see that you helped cause this?" His voice was stronger and louder than he meant it to be. But he could not stop. His Catrina was gone. "Don't you see that you helped drive her away? If you had accepted her from the beginning she might still be here."

Gertrud sucked in her breath. She sat still and silent for a long, difficult moment. "I pray that you are wrong. Surely I did not . . ."

Eli shifted away from his sister to look at her. Her face looked pale and drawn. Her brows crunched together in an expression that seemed caught between confusion and regret. Gertrud rubbed her hand across her mouth in a slow, anxious movement. She stared at her leather shoes. "I have seen you hurt for so many years. I could not bear to see more hurt come into your life."

"You have seen *me* hurt? I don't understand."

She let out a shaky breath of air. "There are things that we should have spoken of, but have not because of the pain it would cause us both."

Eli clenched his jaw. He could not talk about *that*. He could only bear so much at one time. "I can't—"

"I understand. We won't speak of that today. Not now." Gertrud turned her face to his. Her eyes were wet, but she held back the tears. Her lip trembled from the effort. "Just know that I wanted you to be free from it all. I wanted you to be happy. And I knew that Catrina would not bring you that happiness. She would only bring you more pain."

"How? I love her."

Gertrud nodded. "I know. That is why I have been so concerned for you." Gertrud put her hand on

WHEN LOVE FINDS YOU

Eli's elbow. Her fingers tightened around his arm. "I wanted to protect you from it all."

Eli shook his head. "You cannot protect me from life. We both know that."

Gertrud nodded. "No. But I thought I could protect you from her." She stared at him for a moment as she planned her words. "Catrina left a man in Philadelphia."

Eli's expression changed. His jaw flexed. "Go on."

"They were not married. She was ruined, of course. But that is not my concern." Gertrud swept her hand through the air. "That was in the past, before she came to be one of us."

Eli's face looked very, very serious. He did not respond.

"The problem is that *she* left *him*. People said that she was the type of woman who chooses a man and leaves him when she tires of him. She had no shame, no remorse. It was all a game to her."

Eli let the words sink in. He shifted his legs and stared into the distance. "That does not sound like Catrina."

"No. But all of Philadelphia society agreed. I have it on very good authority. You never went to the shops. I was the one who heard it all."

Eli's eyes stayed on the tree line. Memories of Catrina spun across his mind. Had it all been an act? Had it all been a game? He was not the type of man to attract a woman as beautiful as Catrina. Was it all some sort of sick, calculated joke to her?

He could not believe it. He would not believe it. Gertrud was wrong. They were all wrong. He would find her and she would tell him it was not true. None of it was true.

"Are you all right?" Gertrud asked in a voice so soft that he could barely hear it.

Eli nodded. "I will be. When she tells me none of it is true. She never would have kept it from me."

Gertrud closed her eyes. The tears that she had held back began to slip through her clenched lids. "Oh, Eli. How I wish you were right."

Eli managed to force a little smile. "Bear up, Gertie. We'll both find out soon enough."

Gertrud's eyes flew open. "What are you going to do?"

"I'm going to find my wife."

Chapter Twenty-Five

Catrina sat on the rock until her legs fell asleep. She stood, readjusted herself, and sat back down. She did not know what else to do. Her stomach rumbled. She had not eaten. A wiser person would have brought food. A wiser person would have made a plan.

A wiser person would not have run away with Jack Steward. There, she had allowed herself to say his name in her mind. What did it matter now? She could not pretend that he did not exist. He did exist and he would go on existing, no matter how far into the wilderness she traveled. Even after he died, he would still exist inside her memories. She would never be free.

"Catrina?"

Catrina flinched and spun her head around. Someone had found her.

"Greta?"

Greta Miller waved and skidded down the embankment with a yoke balanced on her shoulders.

"What are you doing here?"

Greta looked surprised. "I could ask you the same thing. I come here every day to draw water."

Catrina's body tensed. She glanced around the woods. "You cannot mean that I am behind your homestead?"

Greta nodded. "Where else would you be?"

"Well, not here."

"Where then?" Greta continued to smile as she shrugged out of the yoke and dropped a bucket into the river.

"I walked for hours."

Greta laughed. "You walked in circles, then."

"Oh, for heaven's sake." Catrina put her face in her hands. Could she do nothing right? She couldn't even get lost in the woods properly. Who couldn't get lost in the wilderness?

Greta stopped laughing. She pulled the bucket from the river and set it down with a thump. Water splashed over the lip and sloshed over her leather shoes. "Something's wrong."

"*Ja.*"

Greta sighed. She stared at Catrina for a moment, then walked to her and sat down on the rock. "Move over."

Catrina scooted to the edge of the rock to make room. "I'll fall off."

"You might." Greta pushed her gently, then pulled her back by the sleeve before she toppled off the rock.

Catrina gasped.

"That got your mind off it for a moment."

Catrina tried not to laugh. She could not help but smile. "You are as incorrigible as Abram Ziegler."

"*Ja.*" Greta leaned back onto her hands, stretched out her legs, and crossed her ankles. "Now tell me what's wrong. Why are you here and why did you walk for hours?"

"*Ach.*"

"It's all right. You can talk to me."

"No, I can't."

Greta looked hurt. "Of course you can."

"No. You are too good. I can't tell you."

"Too good? Tell Jacob that, please!"

"He adores you."

"*Ja.* But nobody's perfect. We have our conflicts, our ups and downs, just like anyone else. And then we make up and everything is better than it was before." She put her hand on Catrina's shoulder. "It will be the same for you and Eli."

Catrina stiffened. "How do you know this is about Eli?"

Greta smiled. "Because you've only been married a few days. No one learns how to get along right away. It takes time."

Catrina shook her head. "No. It's more than that."

Greta continued to stare at her. Catrina felt as if the entire world were staring at her and judging her in that moment. Her face felt hot. She pressed the heels of her hands into her eyes. She was tired of running from herself. The words came out before she could stop them. "I ran away with a man."

"Oh." Greta sounded surprised. She twisted around on the rock. "Where is he?"

"What? No." Catrina shook her head. "He's not here. I don't know where he is. Still living in Philadelphia, I suppose."

"Oh." Greta let out a little noise that sounded

almost like a laugh. "I thought you meant that you were running away with him *now*."

"Now?" Catrina shook her head so hard that a strand of hair slipped from her prayer *kappe* and fell across her face. "No. Of course not."

Greta smiled. "Ah."

Catrina pinched the bridge of her nose. "I meant I ran away with a man two years ago." The smile faded. Greta would not be her friend anymore. It had been nice while it lasted.

"And?"

"And what?"

"Well, what's the problem?"

Catrina spun around to face Greta. "I just told you!"

"No, you told me you had a problem two years ago. You are here now, married to Eli, so obviously you solved it."

"Oh." Catrina's expression changed. She looked as if she'd never had that thought before.

"You should go home now."

Catrina shook her head. "Eli doesn't want to be married to me anymore."

"He said that?"

"Yes. Well, no. Not exactly. He said that I shouldn't have married him."

"Hmmm." Greta narrowed her eyes. Her fingertip tapped against the rock. "I know a little something about misunderstandings. It's a wonder that Jacob and I ever managed to marry. But all our difficulties could have been avoided if we had simply told each other the truth—the whole truth."

"Yes, I'm sure." Catrina watched the river bubble and jump as it swirled past the rock. She thought how nice it would be to escape as easily as water does. "But you had nothing to hide. All you had to do was admit your feelings. I have to admit what I've done."

Greta readjusted her legs. She waited a while before speaking. "Do you trust Eli?"

"Yes. Of course."

"If you trust someone, you will trust them no matter what you have to tell them."

Catrina sighed. "I cannot argue that." She gave Greta a sidelong glance. "I wish I could."

"And besides, what harm is there in telling him? You're leaving anyway. You may as well tell him before you go."

"How did you know that I'm leaving?"

"You said you've been walking for hours."

"Oh, right."

"Thankfully, you are no better with directions than you are with mucking out a pigpen."

"I am not laughing at that. I am entirely too upset."

"You thought it was funny."

"No, I did not."

Greta raised her eyebrows.

"All right. It was a little bit funny." Catrina slid off the rock. Her knees buckled and she had to hop to catch her balance. She had been sitting too long. "Thank you."

"For my wit?"

Catrina laughed softly. "For your advice."

"I hope you take it. I've seen the way Eli looks at you. He has to love you."

Catrina brushed off the back of her skirt. "But is love enough?"

Greta looked surprised. "Of course it is."

"You make it sound so simple."

Greta smiled. "Not everything has to be as complicated as we make it."

Catrina felt foolish. She never should have snuck away in the night. She should have confronted Eli and asked what he meant when he announced that she shouldn't have married him. The worst thing he could say could not be worse than the worst thing she could imagine him saying.

She rushed into the cabin, breathless and damp with sweat. She had run most of the way home. Her hair must be a mess. She pushed the loose strands beneath her prayer *kappe* as she glanced around the room for Eli. "Where is he?"

Gertrud sat at the spinning wheel, but she was not spinning. She stared out the open window with a blank expression. Her face came alive when she saw Catrina. She spun around on her stool. "You came back."

"*Ja.*"

"I thought you'd left us." *Us.* The word caught Catrina's attention, but she did not have time to dwell on it.

"No. Well, sort of. I mean, I thought he wanted me to leave." Catrina shook her head. How could she explain? "I mean . . . I'm here now. I'm not leaving him. I love him."

Gertrud jumped up from the stool. "You mean you're not leaving us?"

"No." She shook her head. "I didn't mean for it

to get this far out of hand. I didn't mean to hurt anyone."

"No?" Gertrud searched Catrina's expression with hurt eyes. "How else were we to feel?"

Catrina stared at Gertrud with a blank expression. She could not believe what she was hearing. Gertrud was hurt that she had disappeared in the night? Gertrud wanted her to come back?

"I know that you left Jack Steward. That was his name, wasn't it?"

"*I* left *him*?"

Gertrud nodded. "That is what they say."

Catrina could not think or speak. It was all too unjust. So bitterly unjust. "Where is Eli? I must speak to him."

"I don't know. I've been sick with worry. He's beside himself. Neither of us knew where you were."

"You were worried for me?"

"Of course I was." She glanced out the window. "And for Eli. I have no idea where he is. And after what I said . . ."

Catrina felt weak. She put her hand against the wall for support. "What did you say?"

Gertrud's face crumpled. "I told him what I had heard."

"What exactly did you hear?"

"That you left Jack Steward after you tired of him. You played a game with him and didn't care about the consequences."

Catrina swallowed. The dirt floor felt unstable beneath her feet. They all believed him over her. Her word meant nothing because she was a fallen woman. Jack Steward had done the same as her, but his word was still good. Society greeted him with a pat on the back and knowing smiles, even as they banished her to the ends of the earth. "I have to find Eli. I have to tell him the truth."

"I don't know where he is." Gertrud wrung her hands and stared out the window.

"I'll find him. And when I do, I'll tell him everything."

"I didn't think that you were coming back. When we woke up and you were gone, I thought . . ."

Catrina saw a deep, broken regret in Gertrud's eyes.

"I never meant to leave," Catrina said in a soft, reassuring voice. "I was afraid that Eli didn't want me."

"I thought you weren't coming back."

"It's all right. I did come back. And I'm not leaving again."

"No, you don't understand." Gertrud continued to wring her hands in sharp, anxious movements. "I went to the bishop."

Catrina felt the room swirl around her. Her hand clutched a rough, round edge of the log wall. She forced herself to stay on her feet. "Why? Why would you do such a thing?"

"Because I was afraid. Eli was gone and you were gone. Everyone left me. I was alone and I didn't know what to do. I just wanted someone to fix the problem. I just wanted it to be all right."

"So you told the bishop everything."

Gertrud looked down and nodded. "*Ja.* I thought it was for the best. I was afraid that you were lost in the woods and that Eli would be lost looking for you."

Catrina did not answer. She stood clutching the wall, her face pale.

"I thought the situation had spun out of control. I thought we needed help."

"Now the situation truly is out of our control."

Gertrud nodded. "I'm sorry. This is not what I meant to happen."

Neither woman said what they were both thinking—Catrina might not be able to stay now, even though she wanted to. If the community rejected Catrina, there was nothing they could do to keep her in New Canaan.

Eli came home long after the sun had set and the moon had risen. "I could not find her." He looked as though he had aged ten years. "I went everywhere. I didn't tell anyone what has happened though. I didn't want to embarrass her. No one knows that she has left and no one has seen her except for Greta Miller. She said not to worry and that I should check to see if she's come home yet."

Gertrud was still sitting by the spinning wheel, staring out the open window. "She was here. She has not left you."

"Thanks be to *der Herr*." Eli looked as if the weight of the world had lifted from his shoulders. "Where is she?" His eyes darted across the empty hearth, the bare dirt floors, and the silent table.

"She went back out to find you. To make things right." Gertrud could not shake the expression of surprise that was still on her face. "I was wrong about her, Eli. She came back. I was so sure that she would leave you and never come back."

"Everything will work out now. I'll find her."

Gertrud shook her head. Tears eased from her eyes.

She did not bother to wipe them. "I've made a terrible mistake."

Eli froze. "What have you done?"

"I told the bishop everything that I had heard."

Eli ran his fingers through his hair. He did not know what to say.

"What will happen now?" Gertrud asked in a trembling voice.

Eli swallowed. "I don't know."

"What will you do?"

"We will face tomorrow when it comes." He hurried to the door. "Stay here in case she comes back. If she does, tell her to wait here for me. I won't rest until we make this right."

It was close to midnight, judging by the moon. Eli did not know where to go. Was Catrina wandering the woods alone, searching for him? Surely not. She was too sensible for that. Where would she go? He rubbed the back of his neck and swept his eyes across the clearing. A light flickered through the slats in the shutters on the Witmer cabin. He saw a movement in the darkness. The slivers of yellow light disappeared, then reappeared. Eli broke into a run.

He watched the slim shadow move across the field toward him as he ran. The dark form slowly took shape in the moonlight. He could see pale skin and flowing skirts. His feet beat across the field faster.

And then she was there, standing face-to-face with him, her long black hair tumbling down her back, her blue eyes wide. They both stopped and stared at each other. Eli was not sure what to say or do. What would happen now? He rubbed the back of his neck and looked down. Her feet were bare.

"You aren't wearing shoes."

"No. When I saw you coming, I didn't take the time to put on shoes. I had called on my grand-parents to find out if they had seen you and I took off my shoes because my feet hurt from walking all day."

Catrina looked away. "There is so much that I should have told you. I'm sorry, Eli. I've made everything worse by keeping it from you."

He stared down at her. She did not meet his eyes. "What happens now?" The words sounded thin and shaky.

He lunged for her and picked her up in a quick, strong motion. She gasped, then laughed.

"I know how you hate to get your feet dirty."

She relaxed in his arms and laid her face against his chest. "Does this mean that you still love me?"

"Of course I still love you."

She buried her face in his shoulder. "I wasn't sure. After what I did."

"What did you do?"

Her hands tightened around his shirt. He could feel her breath catch in her chest. "Don't you know?"

"No. I don't know because you haven't told me."

"But, Gertrud told you."

"Gertrud told me what she has heard. That doesn't mean it is the truth."

Catrina shifted her weight and turned up her face to look at him. He readjusted his arms around her body so that she could meet his eyes.

"You don't believe what you heard?" she asked. Her face looked pale and desperate in the moon-light. Eli could see how much she wanted to be loved.

"I don't know what to believe. Not until I hear it from you."

Catrina could hear Eli's heartbeat beneath his homespun shirt. He smelled of wool and soap. She was not sure what to do. It would take all of her courage to say it all out loud. But she would do it because she had to. For Eli's sake and for hers.

"I'm taking you home," Eli said. "Then you can tell me everything. *Ja?*"

"*Ja.*" She whispered the word into his shirt.

He lowered her to the ground and set her gently on her feet. "Wait." He put a hand on her shoulder for balance, then lifted one foot and tugged at his leather shoe. "Here," he said as he pulled it off and handed it to her.

Catrina took it and laughed. "It's much too big."

"Wear it anyway. Can't let you walk home barefoot."

Catrina slid her small, soft foot inside and wiggled her toes. "Thank you."

Eli smiled and handed her his other shoe. He waited until she fastened the leather straps as tightly as she could, then took her hand and walked slowly toward home. They didn't speak. Catrina tripped over Eli's shoes a few times, but he steadied her. They kept walking, hand in hand beneath the moonlight, until they reached their own front yard. The thin white light gave the clearing a soft, unearthly glow.

"Let's not go in yet," Eli said. He motioned to a stump beside them. "I'd like to hear what you have to say first. Just you and me."

Catrina nodded and sat down on the stump. She looked down at her feet. They stuck out from beneath her long wool skirt and looked comically large in Eli's big leather shoes. She would have laughed if it had been any other time. But she could not laugh now. She took a deep breath and closed her eyes. She could not look at him while she said it. "I met a man two years ago."

Eli flinched. "So at least some of it *is* true."

Catrina swallowed again. She did not want to remember. "He was charming, dashing, handsome. He was everything a girl is supposed to want and I fell for him with all I had. He made me feel loved. He made me feel alive." She opened her eyes, but refused to meet Eli's gaze. She looked down, but could still feel Eli's eyes on her. "He convinced me to run away with him. He promised we'd be married, but we weren't. When he learned that I was with child he abandoned me."

Eli did not respond. Catrina did not look up. She kept staring at his big leather shoes. "He told everyone that *I* abandoned *him.* He made himself out to be the innocent. He made me out to be a temptress. The truth was bad enough. I *did* run away with him. That alone was enough to ruin me. But he made it so much worse!"

"Why would he lie about you?"

Catrina tried to interpret Eli's tone of voice. She still could not bear to look at his face. "Because he went on to ruin other girls. It was much easier for him to seduce them if he kept a reputation as an innocent."

"Ah."

"He came from a prominent family. Everyone heard the story. It became the scandal *du jour.*"

"And everyone believed him?"

"Yes. Of course. As I said, he came from a prominent family."

"So do you."

Catrina shook her head. "A woman's reputation is far more fragile than a man's."

"It isn't right," Eli said in a hard voice. There was a trace of anger there, and Catrina wondered if it were directed at her or at society.

"No. But that's what happened."

"Yes."

"I went home to my parents and they would not have me again." Catrina looked up. She could not read his expression. Was the hurt in his eyes for her or for himself?

"You said that you were with child?" he asked gently. His hand moved and she thought he might touch her. She wanted to feel the warm comfort of his hand on her shoulder. But he ran his fingers through his hair instead. He did not touch her.

"I miscarried. Early on. My mother said it was the stress that did it."

Eli breathed in and out. He did not say anything. Catrina waited. Still, he did not speak.

"My mother said that I should pretend it never happened. My grandparents had just converted and were leaving for New Canaan. They thought I could have a second chance at life if I went with them. I had no choice, really. There was nowhere else that I could go. No one else would have me." She wished he would say something. Anything. She wished he would reach out and put his hand on her arm. He did neither. "It was terrible, at first. I didn't fit in. I couldn't farm. I wanted to go home so badly I could not bear it. But, I had no home to go back to. My father will never speak to me again, you see. But then, I met you. And I felt loved again. I felt that I belonged again." Catrina's eyes flicked up to meet his. They stared back into hers, warm and steady. "That is all of it, I suppose."

Eli nodded. He closed his eyes and let out a slow, shaky breath. "Why didn't you tell me this before?"

"You loved me." Catrina put her face in her hands. "And I didn't want you to stop loving me." Eli didn't respond. He opened his eyes and stared at her. Catrina had to know what he was thinking. She could not bear it. She kept her hands over her face. "Are you angry that I kept it from you?" The second question was harder to ask. She did not know if she could bear the answer. "Are you angry that there was another before you, when I was still unmarried? Can you still love me?"

Eli felt his world spin away from him. His wife, his *perfect* wife, had hidden the truth from him. She was not so perfect, after all. He did not speak for a long time. He did not want to hurt her. He did not want to be unfair to her. But why, *why* had she kept it from him?

He stood up and backed away from her. He thought she would tell him none of it had happened, that Gertrud and all of Philadelphia had been wrong. But Gertrud had been right. Oh sure, Gertrud had been wrong about some of the details—but enough of it was true. Catrina had not been honest. She was not trustworthy. She was not innocent. She was not perfect.

"Eli?" Catrina watched him back away. "Please. Say something."

Eli did not trust himself to speak.

"Eli?" Catrina's breath caught in her throat. She looked away and pressed her palm to her mouth.

Eli wanted to make her pain go away. He wanted to touch her face and tell her he understood. But he didn't understand. Why didn't she trust him? Why had she kept the truth from him? Eli ran his fingers through his hair. "I don't know why . . ." He walked away before he said more than he should.

He stood at the edge of the woods, his back to Catrina, as thoughts swirled inside his mind. Why was he upset? Was it because his wife wasn't perfect? Eli's jaw clenched. He shook his head. No. Only a fool would believe someone could be perfect. What mattered was that she was perfect *to him*. And she was. Heaven help him, she was.

She still was.

He frowned and rubbed the back of his neck. He didn't care about Jack Steward. He didn't care that she had run away with him. She was still the same woman he had married. She had not changed. She had done all those things before he met her. He just didn't know about it until now.

And that was the problem. He *did* care that she had kept it from him. Hadn't they believed in each other? Hadn't they trusted each other? Why had she shut him out of her heart? He would never do that to her.

Eli stopped short. He could hear the sound of his breath in the silent woods. His heart thudded in his ears. He couldn't believe himself. He *had* done that to

her. He had not trusted her enough either. He had
not told her what *he* had done.

Eli turned around.

Catrina had not moved from the stump. She
watched him with wide, anxious eyes as he strode
toward her. He did not stop to think before he spoke.
He needed to know why she did not trust him. He
did not blame her for keeping her past a secret—he
had withheld his past from her too. But he had to
understand why. So he plunged right back into the
conversation he had run away from.

"No, I'm not angry," he said. "I'm hurt. Why would
you keep it from me? How could you think that I
could ever stop loving you?"

"Because Jack Steward stopped loving me. Everyone stopped loving me. My own family disowned me."

Eli lifted her chin with his hand until her eyes
stared into his. "I am not any of those people. I will
never stop loving you."

Catrina could not breathe. She could not speak.
He still loved her. Thanks be to *der Herr*, he still loved
her. She stared into his eyes. She expected his face to
be hard and condemning, but instead his eyes looked
soft and his expression thoughtful. No one had ever
looked at her like that after they knew. Catrina could
not quite believe it. Would everything be all right?
"When you wouldn't speak to me . . . when you walked
away, I thought . . ."

"I needed some time. I didn't want to say anything
I might regret. I didn't understand why you didn't
tell me."

Catrina's stomach churned. She should have told

him. She knew she should have told him. She had been wrong to believe any good could come from hiding the truth. "I'm sorry. I should have trusted you enough to tell you. I knew that you were not like anyone else. That's why I fell in love with you." Her lips trembled. He put a hand on her shoulder. His touch felt warm and comforting. It made her feel brave enough to go on. "But now that you know, do you see me . . . differently?"

"No." He ran his fingers through his hair. "I was shocked at first, I guess. I didn't believe it when Gertrud told me. But the worst of it isn't true anyway. And I don't hold the part that is true against you. I don't care that you were with another man before me. As long as you chose me, that's what matters."

"I did choose you."

"*Ja.*" Eli gave a faint, hesitant smile. "You did."

"You're not angry, truly?"

"Oh, I could be." He rubbed his eyes with a thumb and forefinger. "Maybe I was, for a moment. But not at you." He looked away. "I could be very angry at Jack Steward, and your father, and everyone else who spoke ill of you." Eli's jaw flexed. He paused and stared into the dark, silent woods. The moonlight painted the leaves silver. "But if it had never happened, I would not have you now." He looked back at her and smiled. "It's funny where life can take you. And if we can let go of the past, we can enjoy where we go. I can be angry that they hurt you, or I can be thankful that it brought you to me. I think I'll choose the latter."

"Thank you, Eli."

"For what?"

"For believing me. For believing *in* me."

"I wouldn't be worthy of you if I didn't."

Catrina did not know what to say. No one had spoken of her with such reverence before. No one had thought she was worthy of anything after what she had done. Catrina grabbed Eli's sleeve and tightened her hand into a fist. "I'm so sorry I left in the night. It's just that, after what you said yesterday . . . I was so afraid that you didn't want me anymore. You said you wished you had not married me."

Eli looked confused. Then he clamped his eyes shut. "No. Oh no." He slid his arms around Catrina and pulled her against him. Her cheek pressed against the hollow in his throat. "I meant that you shouldn't have married me because of what *I* had done. Not because of what *you* had done."

"But you have not done anything."

Catrina felt Eli's Adam's apple bob against her cheek. "I kept a secret from you too." He hesitated. "And mine is far worse than yours." Eli pulled away from Catrina and looked at her. She had never seen his face so serious.

"I cannot believe that."

"I killed Gertrud's husband and son."

Catrina's mouth fell open. She could not find words. Eli's hand raked through his hair, then ran across his brow. His jaw clenched. "It was an accident, but it was my fault."

"Tell me." She reached for his hands. "I will understand, I promise. Just as you understood what I have done."

Eli nodded. "We had just come to Pennsylvania and we had to build a cabin. I didn't know what I was doing. Neither of us did. But what else could we do? I was pulling the logs up to make the wall and I lost my grip on one. He was standing beneath it and couldn't get away in time. It struck him on the head." Eli exhaled. His hand trembled. "He died the next day. And so did their son. Gertrud was expecting and she went into labor from the shock. It wasn't time yet and the baby was too small to live. All of that happened because I was too weak to hold onto the log. Gertrud lost everything because of me."

"Oh, Eli." Catrina threw her arms around him and drew him to her. "It wasn't your fault."

"It was. Nothing you say can convince me otherwise. That's why I have to be good to Gertie, no matter what she does. Don't you see? I owe her everything. If it weren't for me, she would be happy right now. She would have her husband and son."

"Accidents happen, Eli. They cannot be helped."

Eli shook his head. "This one could have been."

"But you have forgiven me for something that I did intentionally. Can't you forgive yourself for something that you did by accident?"

He took her hand in his and tightened his fingers around it. "Please understand. Nothing can free me from this guilt."

Catrina did understand. But she knew that he was wrong. She also knew that she could never convince him of that. Thanks be to *der Herr*, he loved her. He still wanted her. But their problems were not over. No, they were not close to over.

Chapter Twenty-Six

Eli, Gertrud, and Catrina listened for the knock to come. The bishop would come calling today, surely. And he would bring the rest of the elders. Eli's greatest fear was that they would tell him and Catrina to leave the settlement. He squared his shoulders and set his jaw. If they had to leave, they had to leave. He would stand by Catrina no matter what came.

Gertrud slumped over the spinning wheel, distractedly feeding the wool. She was not at all herself. Well, none of them were. And it was Gertrud's fault. She should feel bad. He hoped she felt bad. He frowned and ran his fingers through his hair. Dash it all. That wasn't the right way to feel. If he kept that up nothing would ever get better. They would just keep going in circles of resentment until their family fell apart.

Catrina dropped a pewter cup on the hearth and the sound rang out against the silence. Everyone jumped. Catrina glanced at Eli and he tried to give her a reassuring smile. She looked much paler than usual. She was not herself at all. Catrina did not drop things. She did not fumble and stumble as he did. She was perfect.

No, he remembered. Catrina wasn't perfect. Eli understood that now. She was a person, like anyone else. She had a complicated, regrettable past. But that made him love her all the more. She was better than perfect—she was human, with all the flaws that came with that. She wasn't a caricature of a woman. She was real. And she had overcome her past to become a better person. Didn't that show more character and strength than someone who had never had to overcome anything at all?

Someone pounded on the door. Eli straightened in his seat. Catrina flinched. A look of panic flashed across Gertrud's face. The bishop was here. The knock came again, louder this time. Well, there was nothing to be done but stand up and face the situation. "I'm coming." Eli glanced at Catrina and tried to give a reassuring nod. It came out more like the stiff bow of a man headed for the executioner's block. Oh well, nobody's perfect. Not even his lovely Catrina.

Eli took a deep breath and opened the door. He did not see the serious face of the bishop on the other side. Instead, he saw the smiling face of Abram Ziegler. Eli had never been so happy to see anyone. "Come in, man! Come in!"

Abram's smile dropped into a serious expression. He glanced over Eli's shoulder, looked at the women in the room, then turned his focus back to Eli. "I need to speak to you. In private."

"Oh." *Oh.* Abram knew. Perhaps the elders had sent him to let them down gently. How long until the entire settlement descended on them, shouting and waving pitchforks? Eli ran his fingers through his hair. His imagination was getting out of control. But could anyone blame him? They were in a mighty uncomfortable situation. A weaker man might have just walked away or, at the very least, blamed his wife for the stress that had descended upon them. A realization jolted through his bones. He swallowed and stood up a little taller.

He was not a weak man. He might not shoot or hunt or skin game or lift heavy objects. But he stood by his wife and knew right from wrong. *That* made him a strong man. Suddenly, unexpectedly, he felt pretty good about himself. He felt satisfied with who he was. Catrina loved him for who he was, after all. Not for who he was not.

Eli stepped outside and pulled the door shut behind him. He was ready to hear whatever Abram said. And it could not be good. Abram looked too nervous for it to be good. Abram took off his beaver-felt hat and turned it around in his hands. He shifted his weight from one leg to the other. "I don't know how to say this so I'll just go right out and say it."

Eli swallowed. He braced himself for the condemnation that was coming.

"I'd like to marry your Gertie."

Eli's face jerked. "You'd like to *what?*"

Abram shrugged, then gave a sheepish grin. "She's not getting any younger and neither am I. It's almost too late for us. So I can't see waiting any longer." He kept turning his hat around in his thick, meaty hands. The hat looked small when held in those large hands. "So, what do you say? Do you give us your permission?"

"My permission?" Eli cleared his throat. He closed

his eyes and slumped against the back of the door. He had never felt so relieved. This was not about Catrina, after all. He opened his eyes and shook his head. "You want to marry *Gertie*?" He lowered his voice and leaned closer. "Are you sure?"

Abram laughed. His eyes sparkled. "I'm sure all right."

Eli cleared his throat again. He glanced toward the window to make sure no one could hear. "But why?"

Abram slapped him on the back so hard that he stumbled forward. "Why ever not?"

"Oh well . . ." Eli could think of a few reasons, but he did not think it would be nice to name them.

"She's tough, Eli. She's a survivor. I like that. And, she's got a heart of gold beneath that no-nonsense exterior, you know. I see how she cares for you. Everything she does is to protect you."

Eli nodded. This was true, but it did not make it easy to live with.

Abram shrugged. "I like a woman who keeps me on my toes. I've met my match with her. And I think she's met her match with me. It's a good fit."

Eli nodded again. He knew that Abram enjoyed teasing his sister. He knew that Abram seemed to enjoy her company. Eli suspected he had begun to court her. But *marriage*!

Abram sighed. He kept turning his hat in his hands. "All right, Eli. Don't make me say any more. I'm not the type of man to sweet-talk about a woman. Can you just take my word for it that I love her and let's be done with it?"

"Done with what?" Eli felt lightheaded. He had been so worried that it was hard to calm his nerves.

Was Abram not going to talk about Catrina at all? If not, where was the bishop?

Abram frowned. "This conversation. Give us your permission and be done with it."

Eli laughed. "You don't need my permission. Go ask Gertie for yourself. She's her own woman."

Abram nodded, but his expression remained serious. "That she is. I would not try to tell her what to do any more than I would tell a wildcat what to do." He put his hat on his head and tapped it with a relieved, carefree gesture. "I suspected you would agree with me on that matter. You aren't like other men, Eli."

"And Gertrud isn't like other women. She might turn you down flat. I've no idea what's in that mind of hers. It's her decision to make. Not mine."

"Challenge accepted." Abram winked, cut around Eli, and marched into the cabin.

Gertrud straightened in her seat when she saw Abram. Her hands flew to her hairline and she worked to tuck loose strands beneath her white linen prayer *kappe.* "Abram, what a surprise."

"A pleasant one, I hope."

"That is yet to be seen."

Abram smiled. The twinkle returned to his blue eyes. "I've a proposition for you, little lass."

Catrina glanced at Eli, who stood by the door with a look of surprise still on his face. He was not quite sure what would happen. Would Gertrud storm out of the cabin? Would she tell Abram to never speak to her again? Oh, this was going to be good. He raised his eyebrows at Catrina in a *just wait* expression.

"A proposition?" Gertrud frowned. "I cannot imagine."

"No?" Abram cracked his knuckles. "I think you can. I think you've been imagining this for some time."

"Humph."

Abram smiled. "We both know that you are madly in love with me."

"Abram Ziegler, I ought to throw you out of my cabin for your insolence."

"And yet, you do not deny it." He glanced at Eli. "She does not deny it." Eli did not reply. He had no intention of getting in the middle of *this*.

"If you have something to say, you best go on and say it. I'll count to ten and then I'll throw you right out of my cabin."

"It's high time we married, little lass."

"Well, I never."

Abram grinned. "You've been thinking the same. Admit it, old girl."

"I most certainly have not."

Abram's expression weakened. A flicker of concern danced across his features, then disappeared. He sighed. "Ah, well. Can't win them all."

"No."

"I'll go before you kick me out." He headed to the door.

"Now wait right there, Abram Ziegler. I said that I had not been thinking the same. I did not say that I would not accept."

"Ah." Abram froze. He turned around slowly. "And?"

"And nothing. I would like to, but I cannot." She turned away, straightened her lips into a tight line, and stared out the window.

Abram glanced at Eli, then back to Gertrud. Eli frowned. He was not sure what was happening.

Abram looked thoughtful. He pulled the bench from beneath the table and sat down. "Why can't you?" Abram rested his elbows on his knees and leaned toward Gertrud. Eli had never seen him look so serious.

Catrina stood up. "Eli and I will go for a walk. You two will want to be alone."

"No," Gertrud said. "Stay. It involves you. I cannot marry Abram because of *you.*"

Catrina could not believe what she was hearing. "Because of me?"

"*Ja.*"

Everyone stared at Gertrud. She maintained a tight expression that gave nothing away. Her eyes stayed on the woods beyond the window. She cleared her throat. "I took away your chance for happiness—yours and Eli's. I do not deserve to find happiness myself."

"Oh." *Oh!* Catrina had never been so surprised. She suspected that Gertrud felt contrite. But this!

"What happened?" Abram asked.

"I thought that I was protecting Eli. You must understand that. After everything that I had heard about you . . ." Gertrud swallowed and swiveled in her seat until she faced Catrina. "I should not have believed such spiteful gossip. I should have given you a chance."

"I have no idea what's going on," Abram said.

Gertrud sighed. "I can't tell you everything. It isn't my place. Just know that I hurt Catrina because I believed something about Catrina. And I . . . I told that *something* to the bishop."

"Ah. A very indelicate *something* about Catrina?"

Gertrud cleared her throat. "*Ja.*"

"That involves a scoundrel by the name of Jack Steward?"

Everyone in the room but Abram gasped.

"How did you . . ."

"*Ach.* I was a trapper before I settled here—you know that. Trappers trade their furs. And when you trade you hear things."

"You mean . . ." Catrina's face lost its color. "You knew? All this time, you knew what I had done?"

"*Ja.*"

"And you never held it against me."

"Why would I? The only one I would hold it against is that Steward fellow."

"Abram, I don't know what to say."

Abram shrugged. "I've made my own mistakes. And I wouldn't want them to follow me for the rest of my life. Doesn't seem right that your mistakes should follow you."

Catrina felt a warm, happy glow build inside her chest. She had not realized how loved she was until now. Eli, her grandparents, and now Abram. All of them treated her as if she was worthy of their love. It made her feel that she *was* worthy of it.

"I wish that I had treated you as Abram has," Gertrud said. "Can you forgive me, Catrina? And can you, Eli?"

Eli nodded. "I know why you did it. I understand."

Catrina did not know what to say. Gertrud was asking for forgiveness? From *her*? Then she realized that there was only one thing to say and she must say it quickly. "*Ja.* I forgive you."

"You're sure?"

"*Ja.*"

Gertrud nodded. "Very well." She turned to Abram. Her eyes glinted with something that looked like joy. Catrina had never seen the expression on Gertrud's face before. "I accept."

"Do you?" Abram cocked his head to the side. "Do you really?"

"I just said it, didn't I?"

"Yes. You sure did."

"And you have pointed out that I am a woman of my word."

"That I have."

"Then there we are."

"*Ja.* There we are."

Abram hesitated. It was the first time that Eli had ever seen him at a loss. The poor man looked as if he did not know what to say or do. "I thought it would take a while to wear you down."

"I am entirely too sensible for that type of nonsense. You should know that."

"*Ja.*" Abram shrugged as a goofy grin lit up his face. "So here we are."

"*Ja.* Here we are." They continued to stare at each other. "What happens now?" Abram asked finally.

"I have no idea," Gertrud answered.

Eli smiled. It would be a very unusual marriage. And a very good one.

The mood changed in the cabin right away. A great weight had lifted from Gertrud. She actually smiled—*smiled!*—as she sat on the bench beside

Abram and murmured about their wedding plans. They sat with their heads together like two schoolchildren conspiring at their desks. Catrina even thought she heard Gertrud humming a cheerful song. How very outrageous.

Catrina knew that she should be spinning, but she could not. She was too restless and distracted. The comforting, familiar feeling of wool between her fingers could not keep her mind off her situation. It felt so strange to sit in a room where everyone knew her past, and no one cared. She almost felt free. She *could* have been free. Gertrud had apologized and would no longer hold Catrina's past against her. If only the story had not gotten out first!

When the knock came, Catrina was prepared. She straightened in her seat and nodded to Eli. He nodded back and mouthed, "I love you." Catrina smiled and looked down. The humiliation was bad enough to endure alone, but having to put Eli through it was even worse.

When Eli opened the door, Amos Knepp and Abraham Riehl stood with their hats in their hands. Both men looked acutely uncomfortable. Eli turned back to Catrina. "The bishop's here," he said. His face turned red and Catrina knew that he was embarrassed. Oh, how awkward this would be!

Catrina stood. She remembered to keep her posture straight and maintain her poise. She would not show the humiliation that she felt. She would believe in redemption, even if they did not. She knew that the rest of the people in the room believed in her redemption too, and that knowledge increased her strength. Eli, Gertrud, and Abram were on her side.

But would that be enough if the rest of the settlement condemned her? "I'll get some redroot tea."

The men nodded.

"Come, sit down," Eli said, and motioned to the bench beside the table. The two men shuffled to their seats in silence. The room felt very tense. Amos's finger tapped against the table. The sound echoed against the stillness. Abraham readjusted his feet. "I suppose you know why we are here," Amos said at last.

Eli nodded. "*Ja.*"

Catrina did not look up as she ladled water from the cauldron into two pewter cups. She tried to put all her focus on the tea.

"We do not like to have to call on you over such a matter." Abraham's hand ran over his beard. He frowned. Catrina dropped a handful of redroot leaves in the pewter cups and carried them across the room. Her footsteps sounded too loud against the soft dirt floor. Catrina set the pewter cups on the table and glanced at Gertrud. Her sister-in-law's face looked as white as her linen prayer *kappe.*

Amos picked up a pewter cup, blew across the top, and set it down again without taking a sip. He opened his mouth, then closed it again. This was going to be painful. No one wanted to start the conversation.

"We may as well go on and say it," Abraham said. Catrina's muscles tensed. She waited for everyone to turn and stare at her. But instead, Abraham and Amos turned toward Gertrud.

She shot up from her seat. "I was wrong. None of it is true!" Gertrud shook her head. "No, it is true— most of it anyway. What I mean is that I was wrong.

It was in the past and does not matter now. I never should have told you."

Abram put his arm around Gertrud's shoulders. "She's right. I've known all along and I say it matters not."

Amos and Abraham looked at each other. Their faces looked strained and serious. Amos ran his fingers through his beard. Catrina's heart thudded against her breastbone. She sat down on the stool in front of her spinning wheel. She did not think that her legs would hold her if she stood. And then a very strange thing happened. Amos smiled and Abraham returned the smile. "Then our visit has been in vain."

"What?" Gertrud looked confused.

Amos spread out his hands. "Catrina cannot be held responsible for what she did before she converted to our ways."

"No?" Gertrud sat up straighter. "No." A faint smile tugged at her lips.

Catrina felt a great weight lift from her shoulders. Her entire body seemed lighter. Eli looked as if he had just heard the happiest news he could ever hear. His face was alight with joy. Abram nodded thoughtfully.

Abraham cleared his throat and shifted in his seat. "So, you see, we did not come to reprimand Catrina. We came to ask Gertrud to stop sowing division within the settlement."

Gertrud flinched.

"But," Amos cut in. "It seems that it is unnecessary for us to bring up such an unpleasant topic, since Gertrud has already brought it up herself. And has admitted her wrong in it."

"Indeed," Abraham said.

No one spoke for a moment. No one quite knew what to say. The visit had gone far, far differently than anyone had expected.

Amos and Abraham waited a few moments, then nodded and stood. "Looks like the barley crop is doing well," Abraham said.

"And I hear the flax harvest brought in a good store," Amos added. Eli and Catrina nodded, then looked at each other. Was that all? Was it really over?

"We've got the evening chores to see to," Abraham said as he put on his hat. "Best be getting on."

"Wait." Catrina jumped up from her seat. "Did you . . . I mean . . ." She bit her lip. "Did you tell anyone?"

Both men shook their heads. "No," Amos said. "Of course not."

They had not told! She was not ruined! She could go on living as she had been!

Although that was not strictly true, was it? She would not go on living as she had before because she would no longer be running from herself. She would not live in fear that someone would discover the truth. The worst had already happened and she was still accepted. She was still loved. Suddenly, she did not care if anyone else in the settlement found out. It did not matter anymore. She was free.

Chapter Twenty-Seven

Catrina was free, but Eli was not. The upcoming wedding kept him distracted, but his thoughts kept turning back to Gertrud's first marriage. Today's happiness would not undo the pain she had experienced in the past. There would always be a black hole in her life from that loss. And it would always be his fault.

No one seemed to notice his concern. The cabin was a whirl of activity. The women ran about doing a baffling array of chores to set up house for Gertrud. They made lye soap from ashes, laundered clothes, aired linens, sewed bedcovers, and goodness only knew what else. It was all a man could do to focus on his weaving.

Best of all, Catrina and Gertrud did all of it together. Sometimes Eli had to listen very carefully to believe what he was hearing. They often laughed together—laughed! Once he even heard Gertrud giggle. It was enough to give him the vapors from the shock of it, if men could have such a thing.

Seeing Gertrud's joy was almost enough to draw Eli from his guilt. Almost, but not quite. For that dark, unspoken fear continued to whisper against the back of his mind. *Happiness like this cannot last.*

What if another tragedy strikes? And what if it is your *fault again?*

He tried to push the thoughts away, but every time he closed his eyes, he heard the crack of the log as it crashed down on his brother-in-law. He felt the panic tear through him again. At night, he often shot up in bed, the image as fresh as if it had happened that day.

Worst of all, Eli knew that a wedding meant that there would be a work party. They would have to enlarge Abram's cramped cabin to make room for Gertrud. Eli lived in fear of work parties. He dreaded marriages and births because it meant he would have to help build a new addition or a new cabin. He usually managed to take the least risky job—after all, no one looked at him and thought he was fit to haul logs. But, this would be the work party for his sister's marriage. He could not get out of that. The thought gripped him like a vice. How would he manage? What if he hurt someone again?

Finally, the dreaded day arrived. Catrina was nearly as nervous as Eli. She knew how he feared that he would make a mistake. But he would not hear of backing down. He would do his part for his sister. There was nothing else to be done. How could he refuse to do his job when the entire community was watching?

Abram greeted Eli with a slap on the back that was much too hard. It was going to be a difficult day. Catrina frowned and took Gertrud by the sleeve. "I'm afraid," she whispered.

"So am I."

"What do you say we get started?" Abram asked in his loud, booming voice.

Eli swallowed. "I say . . . great?" He looked around. "But where is everyone?" The clearing was empty except for Jacob Miller, who stood with one leather boot on a felled log and an ax in his hand. He looked like the very picture of manliness. Eli felt like the exact opposite.

Abram laughed and slapped him on the back again. "Too busy with the planting. Jacob and I felled the trees a few days ago. We've already stripped and notched them. All we have to do is put them in place. That's easy for just three men to do. Couldn't spare anyone else."

Eli nodded, but the color drained from his face. Catrina and Gertrud looked at each other. This was much worse than they thought it would be. With only three men, Eli would be integral to the work. He would have to do the same job he had done when he had the accident.

Gertrud shook her head and spoke to Catrina in a low voice. "Everyone came out to build your cabin. Eli managed to do the small jobs. He can't get away with that now. There's no one else to do the work."

"But he can't do it," Catrina whispered.

"At least the felling is done. He only needs to help stack the logs to make the walls." Neither of the women said what they both knew. That was the job that scared Eli the most. It was what had killed Gertrud's first husband.

They watched Eli walk across the clearing to where Jacob stood beside the felled logs. Eli's hands clenched open and shut. Catrina wanted to cry. She knew how scared he must feel.

"How high are we building?" Eli asked.

Abram jogged to Eli and held up his hand so that it was higher than his head. "High enough so that I can stand upright inside the addition." Abram grinned. Eli did not. He swallowed and adjusted his hat. "That's pretty high."

"*Ja*. That it is. But it's just a lean-to. The construction is fairly simple." Abram rubbed his hands together. "Let's get started!"

Catrina could not watch. She sat down on a stump and faced the other direction. Gertrud sighed and dropped onto the ground beside Catrina. "We ought to find something to do. I cannot bear to hear them work, even if we can't see them."

"We shouldn't have come." Catrina scratched a patch of skin beneath her neck cloth. "I think I'm breaking out in hives again." They could hear the sound of logs being dragged across dirt and grass. Eli grunted. Wood thudded against wood. This could not be over soon enough. "How much longer will it take?"

Gertrud twisted her head to see behind them. "They've only laid the foundation for the lean-to. They've barely even begun."

Catrina rubbed her eyes with the heels of her hands. "Let's go put lunch on. I can't take this anymore."

Gertrud nodded. "Neither can I."

Eli was having a very bad morning. The logs were so heavy he could barely roll them into place. His hands were already damp with sweat and the smooth wood slid off his palms. And the worst was yet to come. His stomach felt queasy and his mouth was dry. Everything in him warned him to walk away. He could not be trusted with this.

When Abram and Jacob put the skids up, Eli knew that the real trouble had begun. They would have to roll the logs up the skids to get them into place. Eli stared at the log wall and wiped his mouth. It was only chest high. They would have to stack at least three more logs. He was not sure that he was strong enough. And if his strength gave out . . .

But he would not back down. He would do his part. And he would make Gertrud happy. It was the least he could do.

"Keep your attention on the log, Eli!"

"What? Oh!" Eli shifted to get a better grip on the log as he, Abram, and Jacob rolled it up the skids. "Mind your work or there'll be trouble for the both of us."

Eli nodded. He knew that all too well. His shoulders burned as he pushed the log upward. Every muscle in his body strained. He gritted his teeth and pushed harder.

"Almost there!" Abram shouted as the log cleared the top of the skids and slid into position. "Steady, now! Hold it!"

Eli used all of his strength to hold the log steady as Abram and Jacob fitted the notches carved in each side into the notches carved in the log beneath it. The log locked into place with a satisfying thud. Abram sighed and wiped the sweat from his forehead.

"It's getting too high," Jacob said as he studied the wall. "I'll work from above. You two work from below."

Eli nodded and let out a long exhale. Thanks be to

der Herr they didn't ask him to hold the log from above. That was the worst thing they could ever ask him to do.

Catrina could not stand it anymore. She had hidden in the kitchen long enough. All morning, she had heard thumps and thuds and shouts. Each time she cringed and prayed to *der Herr* for Eli's safety. Catrina wiped her hands on her apron and straightened herself. She had been leaning over the hearth longer than she realized and her back ached. "I'm going to see the progress."

Gertrud set down the bowl in her hand and nodded. "Surely it is almost over."

Catrina walked around to the back of the cabin and shook her head. Eli and Abram stood at the bottom of the skids, their arms bracing a log, while Jacob worked from above with a length of rope. The rope whirred as the log bounced and scraped up the skids. "I can't look," she whispered, and turned away. "It's bad enough that Jacob is leaning over far enough to lose his balance and fall on his head. But poor Eli! He looks about to faint. He's like as not to be crushed!"

Gertrud put her hand on Catrina's shoulder and held it there. "Bear up, Catrina. There's nothing we can do. And best to keep your voice down. Eli's liable to hear if you keep hollering like that. It will only make him more nervous."

"I don't holler."

"All right."

Catrina sighed.

Gertrud shielded her eyes from the sun with the

blade of her hand. "This was a bad idea. Let's go back inside." But she stayed riveted to the ground. "I don't like how far Jacob is leaning over."

"He knows what he's doing. He's done it for years, remember? He's the best builder in the settlement."

Gertrud nodded, but did not answer. Her mouth was too tight.

That was when it happened. Afterward, Catrina could not remember exactly how it had happened, only that it had. Abram looked over at them and grinned at his fiancée. Gertrud smiled back. That one small moment was all it took to distract him. It was a moment that could change everything forever.

Jacob leaned forward another fraction to help ease the heavy log over the top of the skids. The log was almost in place when Jacob lost his balance. Catrina watched in slow motion as his mouth opened and a low, surprised shout roared from his lungs. He teetered on the edge of the highest log for a long, terrible moment, and then plunged off the wall. The rope flew from his hand and whirred through the pulley.

Abram's attention shot from Gertrud's smile to where Jacob had just been. But Jacob wasn't there anymore. Abram's face flickered with surprise. He didn't know what had happened. Both he and Eli stood in the log's path. There was not time for them to jump out of the way. The skids blocked their escape on either side. Catrina heard a high-pitched shriek and realized that it came from her throat. She wanted to look away, but her eyes could not close in time.

* * *

Eli could not jump to either side; the skids blocked his path. He could not step backward in time; the log would catch his legs and crush them. Some instinct told him to duck and take Abram down with him. Or perhaps his knees buckled from fear. He preferred to believe the former. Either way, he collapsed in a crumpled heap with Abram beneath him as the log roared past his head and thudded onto the ground. It kept rolling for several yards. He stayed crouched on the ground for a long, agonizing moment. Had he survived? Yes, he realized after a few heartbeats. He had. He uncurled his body as Catrina bounded toward him. She knocked into him so hard that he hit the ground again. He held on to her and stumbled to his feet to see if he could stand. He could. He really was all right.

"You're alive! You're not hurt!" Catrina's eyes scanned him in a quick, panicked motion before she threw her arms around him again. "I thought it hit you."

"Abram?" Gertrud hovered over Abram, her face twisted with fear. She shook him and he groaned.

"I'm alive," Abram said. "But I won't be for long if you keep shaking me like that."

"Don't ever do that again!" Gertrud said. She was almost crying, and the words came out in a shout. Abram turned to face his fiancée. He was smiling. "If fear of the grave won't keep me in line, then you certainly will."

"You're not hurt, then?"

"No. I don't think so. Except for where Eli walloped me. I'll have a bruise in the shape of his fist, I wager." He stood up, stumbled a little, and managed to slap

Eli on the back. "Reckon you saved my life. Thanks for that."

"I did?"

"*Ja.* You did."

"Wait!" Catrina shouted. "What about Jacob?" Everyone froze. They had been so relieved that they had forgotten him for a moment.

"I'm all right," a weak, shaky voice said from around the corner of the half-built wall. "Just knocked the breath out of me." They heard his boots scrape the dirt and a groan as he straightened his back. When he rounded the corner of the cabin, his face looked drawn and pale. "I don't know what to say."

"What do you mean?" Eli asked.

Jacob looked beside himself, and Eli realized the man was overcome with fear and shame. He knew those emotions well. "I could have killed you both," Jacob said. He held his hand over his mouth for a moment, then dropped it. "I nearly did." He shook his head. "I know better than that." His voice sounded very low, as if it might break.

"Eli pushed me down in time," Abram said.

"But what if he hadn't?" The shame and fear showed in Jacob's expression. "I've never made a mistake like that."

Eli could not bear to see the look on Jacob's face. "It was an accident. Sometimes accidents can't be helped. They just happen."

Jacob looked thoughtful for a moment. Finally, he nodded, but his face stayed grim. "You forgive me, then?"

"There's nothing to forgive. It was an accident."

Jacob nodded again. He turned and studied the log wall, then looked back at Eli and Abram. "Do you mind if we quit for the day? The truth is, any one of us could have died today, and I'm pretty shaken up about it. I'd like to go home and tell my wife I love her. I ought to do that more often. I *will* do that more often."

"I don't mind at all."

Eli waited until Jacob had gathered his tools and left before he turned to Gertrud. "I'm sorry you had to see that. Are you all right?"

"*Ja.*" But her face still looked too pale. Eli knew that everything must have come rushing back to her in that terrible moment when the log crashed down on Abram.

"I'm all right because of you," Gertrud said. "You saved Abram."

Eli swallowed. "I did." The full weight of the moment began to hit him. He had saved another man. And not just any man—Gertie's man! But that would not bring her first husband, Johan, back. It could not be enough. Why couldn't he have done something like that before? Eli shook his head. "I'm so sorry, Gertie."

Gertrud's eyes narrowed. "Whatever for?"

"I should have saved Johan too. If I could save Abram, why couldn't I save Johan?"

Gertrud's mouth opened and closed again. Her expression shifted from surprise to sorrow. "That is where your thoughts are at this moment?"

"*Ja.*"

"Oh, Eli. I've seen you hold on to the guilt for so many years. I cannot bear it anymore. The reason I was so worried about Catrina's past was because

I knew how much you were hurting over Johan's death, and the baby I lost, and I didn't want anyone to ever make you hurt again. Don't you see? All I want is for you to be happy. I want you to be free of it. I've got Abram now. And you've got Catrina. It's time to let the past go and enjoy the future."

"You don't want me to feel guilty?"

"No. Of course not."

"But, after what I did . . ."

"Do you want Jacob to feel guilty about what he did today?"

"No. That would be ridiculous."

Catrina and Gertrud both smiled at him.

"Ah. I see."

"Yes," Gertrud said. "I hope that you do."

Eli thought about it for a moment, then he pulled Catrina to him. She felt so right in his arms. His life had not gone as he had planned in the past. Neither had hers. But that was the past. Now they were here, together, and everything was going to be all right. There would still be challenges—life could not exist without challenges. But they would face those challenges together, without guilt and without condemnation.

And, they would face life's challenges with family at their side. Georg, Frena, and Abram would always stand by Catrina. Even Gertrud would now. And soon, there would be more family, if *der Herr* blessed them with sons and daughters and nieces and nephews. It would be a good life, whatever it brought, because Catrina and he knew how to face it—together, without looking back.

Don't miss the first book

in the Amish New World series,

Where the Heart Takes You

Greta Scholtz braved a perilous journey—and the loss of her beloved father—to find religious freedom in America. With two orphan children she's taken under her wing, she's trying hard to survive this rugged new world. So she won't let settlement elders pressure her into marrying reserved widower Jacob Miller. She and Jacob simply can't agree on anything—even if the unexpected feeling between them is proving an irresistible force. . . .

Enjoy the following excerpt from
Where the Heart Takes You. . . .

Pennsylvania Backcountry, 1737

Greta Scholtz wandered past the stumps of freshly cut hemlocks. She raised the blade of her hand to her forehead and squinted into the sun. The old milk cow could be anywhere. Greta felt just as lost in the strange, new land. She frowned, hitched up her skirts, and slogged through the muddy clearing.

"Rose!" Greta cut her eyes toward the forest. "Rose, where are you!?" She hoped that the cow had not wandered beneath those dark, towering pines. Backcountry settlers fenced in their crops and let their livestock roam free to forage and fend for themselves. Cows and hogs grew fat and happy on the bounty of the forest—unless they met a hungry predator.

The otherworldly howls of a wolf pack had woken Greta during the night and she could not rest until she knew that Rose had escaped their hunger. The young woman scanned the shadowed underbrush that lay beyond the clearing and imagined the quiet, stealthy beasts that roamed the foothills of the Blue Mountain. Here, at the far edge of the colonies, the New World teemed with bears, mountain lions, and bobcats.

A soft bell rang. Greta whipped her head toward the sound and grinned. "Rose!" She marched to the other side of the clearing, then hesitated before plunging into the old growth forest that separated her from the other settlers. *How can I overcome all of the dangers of the backcountry? If only Father were here.* But Father was not there. *And I will never see him again.* He risked everything to bring them to a land where they were free to worship as Amish, but he never laid eyes on the green hills of Pennsylvania.

Memories of the voyage pushed into Greta's mind. The small group of Anabaptists felt so full of hope when they boarded the *Charming Nancy*. After decades of persecution in Europe, Greta's people knew they would be safe in Pennsylvania. "William Penn made a place where everyone is free to worship as they see fit," Greta's father, Johannes, had explained. She remembered his smile as they plodded up the ship's gangplank with everything they owned stuffed into one small chest.

But Johannes Scholtz had not survived the voyage to see the Promised Land. He was not alone. One in nine passengers died on the voyage. Overcrowding, disease, and deprivation spelled disaster for the old and young. After they sailed, Greta heard rumors that profit-hungry trading companies preyed on German immigrants by crowding them into the hold like herrings. Others claimed that dishonest middlemen pocketed money meant to buy food for the voyage, condemning passengers to weeks of malnourishment.

Greta trudged toward the wayward cow. With her father gone, there was no man of the house to stand between her and backcountry predators. *I will learn to shoot a musket myself.* The other families in the tight-knit community would be happy to help her, but Greta wanted to show the settlement that she could handle the challenges of her new life.

And yet, here she was, chasing after Rose again. "I have to stop fearing the wolves." There was no one to hear her words but a deer that paused beneath a gnarled hemlock. The animal froze and stared at Greta with soft brown eyes. Greta cupped her hands around her mouth. "Rose! Come back!" The deer flinched, leapt across a rotten log, and disappeared into the forest.

No wonder the elders are pressuring me to marry. How can I possibly manage on my own? I do not want to be a burden on the community. But how can I settle for a loveless marriage with a stranger who takes me in out of charity? She sighed and pushed a stray lock of chestnut-colored hair under her prayer *kappe*. *And who do they expect me to marry, anyway? A widower twice my age? There are not many eligible bachelors out here, in the middle of nowhere.*

Greta emerged into a clearing and spotted her cow in the middle of the neighbor's kitchen garden, surrounded by crushed vegetables. A section of the fence that protected the crops lay broken on the ground. "Rose! No!" The cow raised her head, stepped forward, and flattened a head of cabbage with her hoof. Greta clenched her eyes shut and pressed a palm to her forehead. "Oh, Rose! What have you done this time?" She rushed through the front yard and grabbed the cowbell around Rose's neck. "Come on, Rose. Out of the garden! Please!" She glanced toward the cabin door. Greta had just arrived in the Anabaptist settlement, and this was not the way she wanted to make a first impression on her new neighbor. Rose chewed her cud and watched Greta with a dull expression. Greta pulled harder. The cow stood stock-still, then bellowed and took another step forward without warning. Greta lost her balance, fell backward, and landed hard in the mud. She groaned and wiped a splatter of dirty water off her face. *At least no one saw that!*

"I've seen pigs wallow in the mud before, but never a young lady." The deep, masculine voice startled Greta and she flung her head around.

A tall, broad-shouldered man stood over her. Dark eyes locked onto hers and Greta felt her stomach leap. She stumbled over her thoughts, unable to respond to his words. "Oh! I . . ." Her gaze moved from the man's eyes to his strong jaw, hardened features, and muscular build. Greta felt her face turn red and she looked down. "I . . . I . . . it is just that . . ." Greta shook her head and wiped her muddy hands on her white apron. The stranger leaned forward, close enough for Greta to catch the twinkle of amusement in his brown eyes. She cleared her throat. "Rose, she . . ." The man took Greta's hands and pulled her to her feet without any effort. His tall frame blocked the sun and she stood in his shadow, still unsure how to respond. She adjusted her prayer *kappe* and straightened her neck cloth, which modestly covered her shoulders and chest.

"Well?"

Greta frowned.

"Well?" the man repeated, and raised his eyebrows. Greta couldn't tell if the expression showed playfulness or irritation.

"My cow. She broke in."

"*Ja*, I can see that." The man offered a small half smile. "What do you plan to do about it?"

Greta hoped the smile was meant to make her feel more comfortable. *No, he must be making fun of me. I must look ridiculous with my muddy dress and trespassing cow!* "I . . . I will take care of all of this." Greta bit her lip. "I promise. I am sorry—"

The man nodded and glanced at the sky. "The day is almost over. And there will be no work tomorrow."

"I will come back after the Sabbath." Greta stared into the man's eyes, trying to decipher his emotions. "First thing."

"That will be much appreciated." The man tipped his hat and turned away.

Greta let out a breath of air as the tension in her shoulders relaxed. The man's gaze had felt so intense as he studied her. She wished she knew what he had been thinking. *Most likely, he is exasperated with Rose and me and is struggling to be polite. I must try harder to fit in here.*

Greta tugged on Rose's collar. "Let's go." The cow did not move. Instead the animal lowered her head and bit into a tarragon leaf. *Just when I thought I couldn't be any more embarrassed!* "Rose, come on!"

The man turned back around and raised an eyebrow.

He strode over to Rose and grabbed her collar. The cow raised her head and stared at him. "Time to go, *ja*?" The animal lumbered forward. Greta's cheeks burned as she marched after Rose and the stranger.

"I don't understand . . . Rose usually—"

"*Ja*," the man cut her off, and shrugged. "I will see you first thing day after tomorrow."

Jacob Miller frowned as he watched Greta Scholtz lead her cow into the forest. The memory of her steady gaze burned inside his mind. He had fallen into those lively green eyes and could not find his way out again. What was it about her that drew him in and would not let him go? *It must be the outrageous way that we met. She looked so ridiculous, sprawled on the ground with that adorable expression of shock on her face.* Jacob winced. He didn't want to find her—or any woman—adorable. His heart was still too raw. He shook his head and tried to force his attention back to his work. But his gaze lingered on the young woman as she strode across the clearing.

She must have felt humiliated, but she kept her head held high and promised to fix the problem instead of shying away. Though young and unprepared, she seemed eager to overcome the challenges of the backcountry. A familiar sense of loss flooded him. *I remember another woman like that.* He cut off the train of thought before the memories overtook him.

Remember, the Lord taketh away. . . .

Jacob knew that there was more to that verse. But after months of grief, he struggled to believe that the Lord giveth. Life in the backcountry felt like it was all take, and no give. Less than a year had passed since he had buried Marta with his own hands. He remembered shoveling cold earth over the grave and promising never to open his heart again. Jacob pushed aside the unwelcome warmth that Greta Scholtz forced upon him.

He needed to finish splitting a log before sundown. *What is the matter with you? Focus on your work.* But thoughts of Greta pushed into his mind as he struck his ax into the wood. He remembered the delightful sprinkle of freckles across her nose and cheeks. He remembered how she tried to look dignified as she lay sprawled in the mud. And he remembered the endearing quiver in her voice as she fought to overcome her embarrassment. Yes, that Greta Scholtz knew how to make quite an impression.

Jacob shook his head and let his smile drop back into a frown. He set down the ax and wedged a fat wooden peg into the crack he had hacked into the log. He wiped his hands on his knee breeches and picked up a massive wooden mallet. His face hardened as he raised the heavy mallet far above his head and swung it down against the peg. The force of the blow ricocheted into his shoulder and jaw. After enough blows the peg would force the wood apart. Then he would have to repeat the process again and again, down the entire length of the log.

Jacob sighed and swung the mallet down again. *Be practical. Prepare for winter. And, whatever happens, don't fool yourself into thinking that a captivating young lady can make things right again.*

Greta felt completely and utterly humiliated. The cowbell clanged as Rose followed behind her and the constant noise made her feel even more vulnerable and exposed. Even though she walked alone through the forest, Greta imagined everyone in the settlement hearing the bell, looking up, and laughing at her. She told herself that she was overreacting, but all she could think about was that man, standing over her with that hard, humorless expression.

Why did he stare at me like that? What was he thinking? She pressed her hands over her face and squeezed her eyes shut. *He was thinking about what a ridiculous woman I am! How could everything have gone so wrong so quickly!* Closing her eyes made everything worse because his image blazed inside her mind. His chiseled features . . . the way his hands closed around hers and lifted her without effort . . . his dark, mesmerizing eyes. Greta opened her eyes. The fact that she could not stop thinking about him made her as confused as his attitude did. *Whatever is wrong with me?* Greta felt her forehead. *Mayhap I am coming down with a fever. I must be delusional. Why else would that man make such an impression on me?*

She heard a shout and looked up. The six-year-old Fisher twins ran along the footpath that wound through the settlement. The woolen hosen on Peter's legs sagged, showing a sliver of bare calf beneath his knee breeches.

"Peter, pull up your hosen before you catch cold!"

Peter grinned and waved, then darted past without straightening his stockings. Greta shook her head, but smiled. Peter and Eliza's parents took sick and died on the *Charming Nancy* during the crossing. She remembered how she held the twins close and shared their grief as they endured endless days together in the dark hold of the ship. *If only I could take them in. They are alone in this harsh new world just like me.*

Greta sighed and gave Rose's rump a gentle slap. "Go on now. But watch out for the wolves, *ja?*" *If I had a husband, the elders would let us adopt Peter and Eliza.* She felt a stab of longing, then forced the emotion away. *I will not fall for the first man I meet in the New World. And I certainly will not fall for* that *man, no matter how much the elders think I need a husband. He could never be interested in me after today.*

The thought of that tall, broad-shouldered man with the amused half smile reignited Greta's embarrassment. She slunk across the clearing and flung open the door of a small log cabin. *I hope I never see him again. Except, that would mean never staring into those dark eyes again. . . .* Greta cut off the thought.

"My goodness, Greta." Ruth Yoder looked up from her mending with a startled expression. "Whatever has come over you?"

Greta sighed. "I'm sorry, Ruth. I've only been here a few days and I'm already disturbing your quiet evenings." Greta had felt like a disruption ever since she came to live in the small cabin. After the *Charming Nancy* arrived in Philadelphia, Greta and her fellow Amish made their way to the base of the Blue Mountain, at the very edge of the Pennsylvania frontier. The land had just opened for European settlement the year before and the new group joined a handful of Amish families who had already cleared land and put down roots in the wilderness.

The new settlers scrambled to house everyone and Greta felt fortunate that the group found her a cozy home with an elderly widow—although the elders made it clear that the arrangement was temporary. They insisted that the backcountry was no place for a single young woman and an old widow.

Ruth patted the bench beside her. "You are not disrupting, dear. I cannot tell you how lonely I've been since my husband died."

Greta sighed and slumped onto the rough, back-less bench. No roads had been cut through the backcountry yet, so settlers had to leave their wagons— and furniture—behind. The benches, and almost everything else inside the cramped cabin, had been handmade from whatever materials could be found in the Pennsylvania wilderness.

Greta wiped her brow with the corner of her apron. "It is not an easy life here."

Ruth let out a long, deep breath. "No, it is not." She looked down. "I thought that, after so many years of hiding our faith, my husband and I would live out our old age in peace. But it was not *der Herr*'s will."

"And I thought my father would live out his years here too, free and happy."

A smile broke across Ruth's wrinkled face. "But I am grateful that you have come to me. It is wonderful that more Amish are finding their way to our little outpost."

"To think that this was all forest just a few months ago," Greta said.

"*Ja.* One year ago, when my husband and I arrived here, there was naught but trees and wolves."

"We will make a new life here. I know we will."

"*Ja.* You are so young, Greta. You have your whole life ahead of you. I can only imagine what *der Herr* has planned for you here, in the New World."

Greta looked away. *How can I manage without Father? I feel so alone in this strange, wild land.*

"What is troubling you, child?"

"I'm afraid that I have not gotten off to a very good start here."

"Oh?" Ruth raised an eyebrow. "What happened today? You certainly came into the house like a storm."

"I heard the wolves and went looking for Rose."

"Is she safe?"

"*Ja.*"

"No harm done, then."

"Well, not exactly." Greta sighed. "Rose got into the neighbor's kitchen garden."

"Oh dear. Which neighbor? Not Jacob Miller, I hope."

"If Jacob Miller lives beyond that stretch of forest." She motioned in the direction of his farm.

Ruth suppressed a smile. "He is a handful, that one."

"Well, that is one way to put it." Greta put her face in her hands. "I can never see him again. I just can't face him after . . ."

"After what? It can't be that bad . . . can it?"

"Oh, Ruth! I fell in the mud and there he was standing over me with this expression of . . . of . . . complete disapproval! It was the most embarrassing moment of my life!" Greta thought she caught a gleam in the old woman's eye.

"Most women would be eager to see such a handsome man again. Hmmm?"

Greta scowled. She hoped that Ruth did not think she felt an attraction to Jacob Miller. That would be preposterous after he caught her in such an embarrassing situation. Absolutely preposterous. Greta cleared her throat. "If he's handsome then I certainly did not notice."

"No?"

"No."

Ruth shrugged and turned her attention back to her mending. "Of course, dear."

Connect with Us

Visit us online at
KensingtonBooks.com
to read more from your favorite authors, see books
by series, view reading group guides, and more.

Join us on social media

for sneak peeks, chances to win books and prize packs,
and to share your thoughts with other readers.

facebook.com/kensingtonpublishing
twitter.com/kensingtonbooks

Tell us what you think!

To share your thoughts, submit a review,
or sign up for our eNewsletters, please visit:
KensingtonBooks.com/TellUs.

Books by Bestselling Author
Fern Michaels

More by Bestselling Author
Hannah Howell

More from Bestselling Author
JANET DAILEY